Other ImaJinn titles
by D.B. Reynolds

The Vampires in America Series

Raphael (Book One)

Jabril (Book Two)

Rajmund (Book Three)

Sophia (Book Four)

Duncan (Book Five)

Lucas (Book Six)

Aden (Book Seven)

The Cyn & Raphael Novellas

Betrayed

Hunted

Jabril

Book 2 of the
Vampires in America Series

by

D.B. Reynolds

ImaJinnBooks

This is a work of fiction. Names, characters, places and incidents are either the products of the author's imagination or are used fictitiously. Any resemblance to actual persons (living or dead), events or locations is entirely coincidental.

ImaJinnBooks, Inc.
PO BOX 300921
Memphis, TN 38130
Print ISBN: 978-1-933417-51-6

ImaJinnBooks is an Imprint of BelleBooks, Inc.

ImaJinn Books was founded by Linda Kichline.

We at ImaJinn Books enjoy hearing from readers. Visit our websites
ImaJinnBooks.com
BelleBooks.com
BellBridgeBooks.com.

10 9 8 7 6 5 4 3 2 1

Cover design: Debra Dixon
Cover Concept: Pat Lazarus
Interior design: Hank Smith
Photo/Art credits:
Couple (manipulated) © Gevorg Gevorgyan | Bigstock.com
City (manipulated) © Matyas Rehak | Dreamstime.com
Tattoo sign (manipulated) © Soleile | Dreamstime.com

:Ljki:01:

Dedication

In loving memory of my Mom and Dad,
who left us far too soon.

Prologue

CYNTHIA LEIGHTON sped down the dark highway, hands clenched on the steering wheel, the roar of the engine drowning out the sound of her frantic breathing. Her eyes flicked anxiously from the nearly empty road to her rearview mirror, where a pair of headlights had suddenly appeared, racing closer in the predawn blackness. Already pounding adrenaline spiked even higher as she floored the gas pedal, and the big SUV leapt forward in a gratifying burst of speed. She stared at the headlights, low to the ground, the cool blue of an expensive sedan, and coming on way too fast. It would be on her in seconds. Was it him? Had he discovered her deception and come after her?

SHE GRIPPED THE wheel tighter, hands spasming a painful protest, as the sedan came up hard on her tail, so close she could barely see the headlights any longer. She swerved suddenly, trying to throw him off, convinced he would ram her if that's what it took. The SUV threatened to roll, tilting on two wheels as she skidded into the next lane, the seat belt cutting into her neck as she struggled to keep him in view.

The big sedan zoomed past, the driver not even glancing her way as he sped on to his own destiny—one that had nothing to do with her. Cyn slumped in the driver's seat, swallowing the hard ball of her fear, feeling the chill of the air conditioner as sweat coated her body. Why had she ever thought it was a good idea to get involved with more vampires? Had she expected them all to be like Raphael—beautiful, lying bastard that he was? Sure, he'd broken her heart, but all those Boy Scout virtues, like honorable and trustworthy, applied to him too. Powerful as he was, he ruled his territory with the loyalty and respect of his people, rather than fear.

But that's not what she'd found in Texas. No, here she'd discovered the very face of evil—Jabril Karim, Vampire Lord of the Southern territory and as despicable and vile a creature as she'd ever met. A vampire who enslaved those he desired and destroyed anyone who got in his way. And right now, that included Cyn . . . and the vampire hiding in the cargo compartment behind her, a vampire whose very life depended on Cyn getting to the airport before Jabril discovered they were gone.

She pressed harder on the gas, treading a fine line between speed and caution. She dared a glance at the clock on the dash. It was nearly sunrise. If she could just make it until then, they'd be safe.

She drove faster.

Chapter One

Houston, Texas, four days earlier

JABRIL KARIM watched silently as his lieutenant, Asim, slipped through the study door, saw him jerk to a confused stop when he noticed his Sire studying him from his seat behind the desk. Asim's narrow chest swelled with an indrawn breath as he fought visibly to contain his fear and Jabril smiled, perversely pleased.

"Well?" he asked in a bored tone.

"No one has seen Elizabeth in two days, my lord," Asim said, cringing slightly as he delivered the unwanted news. "And the guards have no record of her coming or going through the gate in that time."

Jabril pushed away from his delicate Chippendale desk and crossed his legs. "So, the little one has escaped," he said thoughtfully, smoothing the fabric of his trousers over one knee. He glanced up at Asim. "She won't succeed, of course. She belongs to me and, fortunately, the American law is on my side in this instance. But . . ." He raised a cautionary finger. "How to retrieve my property before it's too late?"

"I shall arrange a search," Asim offered eagerly. "She cannot have gone far."

"Possibly. But human children have great freedom of action in this country and, besides, Elizabeth can look quite mature when she chooses. I am reluctant to do so, but I fear we may need to engage someone to undertake this search for us. One who understands the society better, perhaps someone who specializes in these runaway children?"

Asim frowned. "There are such people, of course, if you think it wise. I will contact your lawyers and find out who handles these things. Let them earn some of the money you pay them for doing nothing. A private investigator, perhaps—" He gave his master an alarmed look as Jabril barked out a laugh. "Sire?"

"A private investigator, Asim! This is too perfect. You recall that unfortunate business on the west coast recently? Rumor has it Raphael used a private investigator, a *very* private investigator from what I hear, but one who resisted even that arrogant bastard's charm."

"You would hire a woman?"

"Oh hardly, Asim," he said with a dismissive flip of his fingers. "Talk to the lawyers and find a proper man for the job. But call this woman of Raphael's anyway. I want to meet her, and that bastard's ego could use a good pricking. Do you think he would mind sharing?"

"I think he would rather share with a snake, my lord," Asim said with a sharp smile.

Jabril laughed again, an unpleasant sound. "Just so, Asim. Just so. Let me think . . . it was Cynthia something. Lawson or Layland, or some such. Do you recall?"

"Leighton. Cynthia Leighton. Her father is Harold Leighton of Leighton Investments."

"Really? Well, isn't that interesting? Raphael moves in higher circles than I thought. All the more reason to take a look. Can you locate her?"

"Of course, my lord."

"Excellent. Tell her nothing on the phone, Asim. Insist she come in person; stress the delicacy of the situation."

"And if she refuses?"

"Oh, she won't refuse. Humans love a secret. And we are so very good at keeping them."

Chapter Two

CYNTHIA LEIGHTON trudged up the boarding ramp, following the rather substantial hips of the lawyer who'd been her seatmate and self-appointed best friend for the better part of the morning. More than three hours of listening to him drone on about his latest fascinating (yawn) triumph in the world of tort law. Cyn wasn't the kind of girl to make friends easily, but she did try to be polite. The lawyer had strained even her best intentions. Fortunately for him, the screeners had made her leave her pepper spray at the security checkpoint in L.A. When the Houston terminal came into view, she hoisted the strap of her backpack higher on her shoulder and took a firm hold on the telescoping handle of her carry-on bag, intent on a clean getaway.

The lawyer made a final play, pausing near the Jetway door to suggest she join him for a celebratory drink at his hotel. Cyn gave her watch a pointed glance—it was barely past one in the afternoon. She smiled her regrets and rolled away, quickly losing him in the crowded airport. Had the guy really thought she'd be interested in a little afternoon romp? Did she look that desperate?

Huffing an exasperated breath, she focused on the overhead signs, looking for baggage claim. Not that she had any bags to claim, but that's where the limo driver had promised to meet her. Following the general flow of the crowd toward the down escalators, she was struck by how all airports looked alike. No matter the supposedly unique architectural details they touted, it was still the same endless, long corridors filled with hard floors and wide open spaces that bounced all that noise around until you could barely hear yourself think, much less make out the latest garbled boarding announcement. She blew out an exhausted breath as she finally stepped onto the escalator, her gaze falling on a sign that welcomed her to Bush International Airport. What was it with politicians anyway, always rushing to put their names on everything? She couldn't think of a single politician who deserved his name on a sewage treatment facility, much less a major airport where everyone had to look at it all the time.

Geez, what a grouch! You need a drink, Cyn. No, what she really needed was a good night's sleep, one untroubled by dreams of a certain vampire lord. So what was she doing in Texas, about to undertake a job for yet another of the so-called undead? When the call had come two days ago, all she could think of was getting out of L.A., at least for a while. Putting a state or two between her and Raphael had seemed like a good idea, since nothing else seemed to work. Besides, half of her work as a private investigator was for one vampire or another. Most of it was pretty tedious stuff, tracking down old bank accounts and young relatives, but this new case had possibilities. Maybe it would be interesting enough to wipe away the lingering memories of sparkling black eyes and a slow smile. She sighed. Probably not.

A man approached as she stepped off the escalator, his plain black suit, white shirt and black tie screaming "limo driver" as clear as day. "Ms. Leighton?" he asked.

Cynthia gave him a somber assessment, a little surprised that he recognized her. She'd expected a sign, not a personal greeting. "Yes," she admitted. "How did you know?"

He smiled, a fleeting flash of teeth that changed his face completely for a brief instant. "I didn't, not for sure. Mr. Asim gave me a description, but he was pretty vague." He shrugged. "You looked right."

"Who's Asim?"

That obviously surprised him. "He works for Lord Jabril Karim, I thought—"

"Oh. We spoke on the phone, I guess." Which didn't explain how he knew what she looked like, but then nothing about dealing with vampires was ever simple or straightforward. "Okay," she said. "So, how do we get out of here?"

"This way. Can I . . ." He reached to take her backpack.

She shifted so it was out of his reach. "No, I'll carry this. You can take the suitcase, thanks. How far to the hotel?"

The driver collapsed the handle on her small suitcase, picking it up instead. "About thirty minutes, but Mr. Asim directed me to take you right out to the estate."

"Did he? How nice for him." She smiled to the take the sting from her words. "Unfortunately—" She paused. "You never told me your name."

"Scott."

"I've always liked that name—my first crush was a Scott—so I'll tell you what, I don't want to cause problems for you, but I got up before dawn this morning to catch my flight, after which I spent nearly two hours getting through check-in and security only to find myself trapped in a narrow metal cylinder with a fucking lawyer who was bleating directly into my ear for over three hours. I'm tired and I'm cranky and I haven't had a decent night's sleep in a month. So I'm going to the hotel, but I'm perfectly willing to take a cab if that gets you off the hook." She didn't mention that she was also set on going to the hotel because a package would be waiting for her there. A package that included her weapon of choice, a 9mm Glock 17 handgun. Cyn had no intention of visiting a strange vampire unarmed.

She pushed through the door and sucked in a lungful of filthy airport air. "Perfect," she muttered and raised an inquisitive eyebrow at Scott. "So, do I need cab?"

He blinked at her for a moment, as if he hadn't yet caught up with her rapid fire diatribe. "The Four Seasons, right?" he said finally.

"Yes." She smiled.

"The car's right over here."

As they pulled away from the curb, Scott caught her reflection in the mirror. "You should try a sleeping pill," he said.

Cyn met his eyes. "I have. I've tried them all. My doctor won't give me anymore, which is saying something in L.A. You can get pretty much any pill you want out there; all you have to do is ask."

"Meditation, maybe," he suggested, his attention on the long line of cars passing them by.

"There's an idea," Cyn said absently. "Find myself a guru." She didn't need a pill and she didn't need meditation. She needed Raphael to get the hell out of her life. Not that he was exactly *in* her life. Not anymore. Oh, no. Lord Raphael had taken what he wanted and run as far and as fast as his considerable money and power could take him. She'd thought it was love. Turns out it was simply a roving buffet with her as the entree du jour. She closed her eyes against the too familiar pain of loss and knew it wasn't that simple. Raphael hadn't left her because he didn't want her. He'd left because he did. Hundreds of years old and he still hadn't evolved past the male fear of commitment to one woman.

Of course, the full truth was probably even more complicated, but that was the nub of it and there was nothing for her to do but get over it. Over a month had passed since she'd seen him, since he'd walked away without looking back. She'd never been in love before; how long did it take to heal a broken heart?

Cyn leaned her head back against the soft leather and closed her eyes. In the front seat, Scott took the hint, popped a mellow CD into the player, and let soft music fill the silence until they reached the hotel.

SHE ROLLED OVER in her sleep, the hotel's soft bed adjusting to her movements, cradling her in its warmth. A weight settled behind her and she smiled, catching the scent of his aftershave—a hint of spice, barely there. She felt the glide of his skin as he stretched out next to her, as he reached to pull her close and tuck her within the curve of his big body, making her feel safe, protected. He was the only man who had ever made her feel that way, like someone worth fighting for, someone to cherish. His cheek was rough against her face, his lips soft as they explored her jaw, nipping at her ear lobe before kissing a path downward to linger over the curve of her neck. She stirred, her body responding to his touch as strong fingers slid between her legs and began to stroke gently.

A small moan passed her lips as he bent her leg forward and slid his cock down the cleft of her ass into the wetness between her legs. With the first stroke of his shaft inside her, she gasped, arching her back to open herself further, welcoming his intrusion, beginning to move with him. His rhythm gained urgency and he seized her hips, holding her firm against him as he drove ever deeper within her slick folds. She reached down and covered his hand with hers, pressing hard, crushing her clit, feeling his thick sex sliding in and out, opening her wide, stretching her tight around him. He groaned with hunger, bending to the curve of her neck once more. For a split second the warmth of his breath brushed her neck and then his teeth slid into her vein. She cried out, her orgasm sudden and overwhelming, rising from a quiet pool of need to a tidal wave of ecstasy in the space of seconds. She screamed as it swept over her, carrying him in its wake, leaving his roar of completion to vibrate in her very bones.

She lay within the circle of his arms, flushed with the passion of their lovemaking, her muscles relaxed, her desire sated. For the moment.

As if he knew what she was thinking, he chuckled low and sensuously, his breath soft on her cheek. "Sweet, my Cyn," he murmured. "So sweet."

THE PHONE TRILLED, jarring Cynthia awake. She blinked in the darkened room, reaching automatically for the hard, male body that should have been behind her and finding nothing but empty space. She closed her eyes and willed away the tears, curling her body around the ache in her chest. The phone jangled its wake up call again, and she reached out irritably, knocking the receiver away, listening to the automated voice spilling out. She lay there for a moment more, feeling the arousal of her body, the fine sheen of sweat that covered her skin. It was so real. So very real. And it was all a lie.

Throwing aside the covers, she forced herself to stand and head for the shower. One day at a time, wasn't that what all those anonymous help groups said? One day at a time. She wondered what they'd think about her using their mantra against the memory of her vampire lover.

CYN SWORE AS the hotel lobby's automatic doors opened and she stepped outside. "It's fucking freezing out here," she said to no one. "I thought Texas was warm."

"Cynthia Leighton?"

She stiffened, swinging around to stare at the man standing next to a long, black limo parked in the porte-cochere. No, not a man. A vampire. Not that most people would have noticed. The small things gave him away—a bulge in his upper lip concealing fangs emerging in an instinctive show of aggression, the too still way he watched her over the bulk of the limo. Cyn knew vampires, knew that as much as they might resemble humans, they were definitely different—better, stronger, faster. The *Six Million Dollar Man,* but without the plane crash. This particular vampire was looking at her with distaste, as if he desperately hoped he was wrong about her identity. She grinned, happy to ruin his night. "That's me!"

The vampire didn't crack even the shadow of a smile. "Lord Jabril Karim is waiting."

Cyn made a point of checking her watch. "My appointment is at seven." It was six o'clock, and Jabril Karim's estate was about forty minutes outside the city. She knew because she'd checked.

The vamp merely looked at her. Cyn opened the limo door and slid across the soft leather seat. It was going to be a long forty minutes.

Chapter Three

MIRABELLE WOKE. It was not a slow wakening, not a gradual return of the senses, as if from sleep. It was the clarity of difference between black and white, life and death. She was Vampire and she was awake.

Remaining perfectly still, she listened to the small sounds around her—a car moving slowly away from the house, a bird singing outside the window, voices from the kitchens beneath her rooms. But nothing closer. Safe. For now.

She sat up in the near perfect dark of a walk-in closet, throwing off blankets she no longer needed but used anyway. They comforted her, perhaps a memory of better times. The darkness itself was no impediment; her eyes compensated for the absence of light, making do with the small amount leaking from beneath the door, showing her the outlines and shadows of shelves and hangers, clothes and shoes. She sighed and climbed to her feet, pulled open the closet door and hurried into the bedroom beyond.

It was a spacious room, elegantly furnished with a huge four poster bed and heavy satin and velvet furnishings. Elaborate brocade drapes covered the wide windows, dark burgundies and blues to match the bed coverings. It was all very beautiful and very expensive . . . and nothing she would have chosen for herself. But then she never slept here. It felt safer, somehow, to hide in the closet. It was foolish, and ultimately pointless. But she did it anyway.

A tug on the thick rope and the drapes drew away. Beyond the window, the night was driven back by the bright, almost garish, artificial lighting of the estate grounds. Mirabelle stared out without seeing and wondered why she was so unsettled tonight. It was a night like any other. Wasn't it?

A knock sounded on the door and she turned, heading across the room with a smile. It was probably her sister Elizabeth who was her only real friend and the one bright spot in her nights. Only seventeen and still human, Liz lived in a separate building on the edge of the estate, along with the housekeeper and other servants. It had been days since they'd seen each other. Liz couldn't come every night, but she did try, and—

Mirabelle stopped before she reached the door and scented the air carefully. Her visitor was definitely human, but . . .

She glanced down nervously at her silky nightgown. It was a secret indulgence to her femininity, the last one left to her. She rushed back to the closet and drew on a long, thick robe, tugging it closed around her neck and tying it securely before going over to pull open the door.

"My lady." The servant outside lowered his eyes, unwilling to look upon her, even in the all-encompassing robe. "Lord Jabril Karim requests your immediate presence." He glanced up at her night clothing and tightened his mouth in disapproval. "That is, my lord requests your presence as soon as you are decently clothed."

Mirabelle flushed, more from humiliation than anger. Even the servants presumed to judge her, though it was *her* money that fed and clothed this man and his entire family. And because she was feeling unhappy and unsettled tonight, she did something she rarely did. She threw courtesy to the wind and closed the door in his face, locking it with a loud click.

A petty defiance, she admitted as she hurried back to the closet, and one that would probably come back to haunt her in the form of small holes in her clothing and erratic visits to her room by the cleaning staff. Not that she cared either way. She hated the so-called modest clothing Jabril Karim insisted she wear, and the rooms were little more than a prison cell. What did she care if they were clean or not? Still, if the old bloodsucker had sent someone to fetch her, it was probably important—to him anyway. And he had ways of punishing her that were far worse than anything the cleaning staff could dream up.

She stripped off the robe and nightgown, went into the bathroom and turned on the shower, letting the room fill with steam while she brushed her teeth. Jabril might complain she'd taken too long, but she'd be damned if she'd go without a shower. He knew very well that she woke long after he did, long after the other vampires in the house did. She was very young, as such things were reckoned. She'd been barely eighteen when she was turned, and that was only five years ago, a century or more younger than any of the other vampires living here. The sun had to be well below the horizon before she began to stir, which meant everyone else had been awake a good hour by the time she drew her first full breath of the night.

She rinsed her mouth and stepped under the hot spray, letting it pound away the tension, forcing herself to put aside her many grievances, shoving them far into the back of her mind. It was how she had survived this long, how she would survive long enough to break away someday, to take Liz and make a life for the two of them far away from Texas and Lord Jabril fucking Karim.

Chapter Four

THE THICK FABRIC of her skirt hung heavily on her hips, and Mirabelle tugged at it, trying to settle it comfortably around her legs. Her clothes were unrelieved black—ankle length skirt, t-shirt and loose black sweater, even a scarf to hide her long blond hair. Her shoes were black Nikes, and she wore black old lady socks that rose above her knees, as if somehow the sight of even the tiniest bit of her flesh would prove an irresistible temptation to the male vampires of Jabril's court.

Mirabelle didn't feel irresistible or tempting. She felt old and ugly, and she looked resentfully at the richly dressed men who filled the room. The penile brigade clothed themselves in silks and soft wools in a rainbow of vibrant color.

Mirabelle was the only female vampire on the estate. For that matter, she'd never even met another female vampire, although she knew they existed. Jabril Karim rarely sired female vamps. Normally, he had no use for women beyond the nutritional value of their blood and the sex that came with it—and his basement stable of human blood slaves provided that. He'd made an exception in Mirabelle's case, because she had something else he wanted . . . a lot of money.

Fortunately for her, he had yet to figure out a way to get to the money without keeping her alive, assuming a vampire could be considered alive. She didn't know the science of the matter, but she certainly *felt* alive. Sometimes she thought it would be worth dying for good just to keep Jabril from getting his slimy hands on her part of the money. But then, he'd just go after Liz that much harder, plus she'd be well and truly dead and unable to enjoy his reaction, so that kind of took away from the satisfaction of the whole idea.

With an effort, she forced her thoughts away from Jabril and his followers and onto something more pleasant, what little there was to choose from. She wondered where Liz was. Not that her little sister *ever* ventured into this part of the house at night. There were only two types of beings in this room—vampires and food. If you weren't one, you were the other. And Liz was determined to be neither, an aspiration

Mirabelle had every intention of seeing realized. Bad enough Jabril had succeeded in turning *her;* she would not stand by and let him turn her little sister as well.

A ripple of movement shivered across the room, and Mirabelle glanced up through her lashes. It was a big room, a "great" room her parents' architect had called it, with broad pillars dotted throughout the empty space. The pillars were only for effect—Mirabelle knew from a childhood spent playing here that they were quite hollow and not at all the marble monoliths they appeared to be. But that had been before her parents had died, before Jabril had claimed their home for himself. There were no children playing in this room, not anymore. A familiar wave of sadness rolled over her as she remembered all those other times. The grand receptions and parties of Texas society—fund raisers hosted by her parents and others, charitable events where guests stood around sipping cocktails and eating dainty finger foods before writing big tax deductible checks.

She sighed. Jabril had changed the room to suit himself, of course. He'd had most of the furniture removed—there was no need for couches or chairs when no one was permitted to sit, except him. He'd left only a few narrow tables along the walls interspersed with huge verdigris urns whose pale green reflected off the near white of the marble floor. Far overhead, the ceiling arched into a round glass-paned dome whose copper framing bore the same green patina of age. She remembered sunlight shining through those enormous panes of glass, filling the big room with—

She jerked her attention back to the present as double doors burst open to one side, and a hulking, half-naked vampire stalked in, glaring around the room as if expecting someone to challenge him. No one did. In fact, no one so much as met his gaze. They'd all learned long ago that Calixto's idea of a challenge was unpredictably flexible, depending on his mood on a given evening. Vampires might heal injuries quickly, but the pain still hurt like hell. The bodyguard stepped out of the doorway, standing to one side and nodding respectfully into the unseen room beyond.

A moment later, Jabril entered with a regal nod of approval for his guard's diligence. In appearance, the vampire lord was a fit forty-year-old, with black, tightly curled hair worn short, and dark chocolate eyes that were large and round, almost bulbous, with a yellow sclera. To Mirabelle, they had always looked wet—big, wet, yellow eyes. Yuck.

She dropped her own gaze quickly as he approached her. Jabril Karim al Subaie was the scion of a very traditional and conservative Arab family who'd been allies of the Saud dynasty for centuries, longer than even Jabril had been alive. He demanded respectful and submissive behavior from his servants . . . and his women.

Mirabelle tensed as the elegant leather shoes beneath his perfectly tailored trousers stopped in front of her lowered gaze. She waited, not daring to look up.

"Mirabelle, my treasure," he said finally. She fought not to curl her lip at the endearment. There was nothing even approaching affection between them. If she was his treasure, it was only in the most literal sense.

"My lord," she all but whispered.

"I wonder, my dear, if you have heard from Elizabeth lately?"

She felt a jolt of fear at his words. Shocked into looking up, she met his eyes for brief seconds before her gaze fell once again to his feet. "Elizabeth, my lord?" she managed. "I have not seen her since . . ." She thought desperately, trying to place Liz's last visit. "I believe it was five days ago, my lord. Just before dawn."

Had something happened? She wanted to scream the question at him, but forced herself to stillness, clenching her fists tightly in the folds of the heavy skirt. If he knew she cared, he would delight in keeping the information from her.

She was aware of his silent scrutiny as he stared at her, sniffing the air like an animal, as if he could somehow smell the truth of her words. But then, she could not lie to him. He was her Sire, her creator, and she was too young and too weak to resist him. He knew her mind nearly as well as she did. She had managed to keep some secrets from him, hidden away in the most private part of her mind, behind walls of misdirection and inconsequential detail. He'd never think to look for the truths she hid, because he had no idea they existed. But he would know if she lied in answer to a direct question. And she was not lying about this. If Elizabeth was missing, Mirabelle had no idea where she was.

"I see," Jabril said. "Well, that is troubling. Has the woman arrived, Asim?" he asked the vampire standing at his elbow.

"She just cleared the gate, my lord."

Mirabelle listened, eyes downcast, her mind bombarded with questions. *Where was Elizabeth? And what woman was Jabril talking about? Did she know something about Liz?* She was so caught up in her own questions that she almost missed Jabril's next words, jerking in fear when he spoke right in front of her.

"You will remain here, Mirabelle."

"My lord," she squeaked breathlessly, folding into a deep bow and remaining there until she was certain Jabril had moved well away. When she straightened, she did so slowly, her eyes still searching. It wasn't beyond Jabril to linger, only to punish her for disrespect. The vampires closest to her observed her cautious behavior with little snickers of disdain, and she felt a pang of old hurt. Once upon a time, these same vampires had treated her with the fondness due a younger sister. Over the months following her turning, they'd seen Jabril discard her, seen him treat her with utter disrespect. Seeking to please their master, they'd followed his example one by one until she'd been completely isolated, alone in a room full of vampires. Stifling a sigh, she ignored their snickers for now, knowing they could do no more than smirk. Until her twenty-fifth birthday, until Jabril had absolute control over her money, no one was allowed to touch her. No one except Jabril.

Mirabelle shuffled backward until she stood against the wall, head bowed, hands fisted at her sides, wanting nothing more than to be invisible. She gazed cautiously around the room, trying to gauge the mood of the other vampires. They stood in bright clusters, talking and laughing too loudly, their voices echoing off the marble floors and high ceiling. Jabril had moved to a low dais at the front of the room, seating himself on an oversized wooden chair elaborately carved with gilded detailing. The back and seat were cushioned in deep bronze satin with gold embroidered trim. *A throne by any other name*, Mirabelle thought.

She didn't care. Let him have his throne, let him have his sycophantic followers filling the room and jostling for position, trying to get close enough to preen and fawn for his attention. Not Mirabelle. The last thing she wanted was Jabril's attention. She'd much rather be hiding in her closet, checking the message boards for some sign from Liz. Because if Jabril truly didn't know where Liz had gone, she might have run, might have escaped this hellhole that had once been their home. And if that was so, she'd try to send word to Mirabelle, to let her know she was safe. They both knew Liz had to be careful, that any information she gave to Mirabelle could be pried from her mind by Jabril. But she'd send something. She wouldn't let Mirabelle worry for nothing. And Mirabelle was very worried right now.

A door in the back of the room opened with a bare whisper of sound. Mirabelle looked up along with everyone else and saw one of the vampire lord's many bodyguards slip inside. They were enough alike that she rarely bothered to distinguish among them. Hulking men with dark hair and dead eyes, dressed all in black from shoes to shirt. This one paused, his back to the closed door, and looked to the front of the room, questioning. Mirabelle followed his gaze and saw Asim whisper briefly to Jabril who raised his eyes and nodded to the bodyguard.

Curious, Mirabelle turned back to the entrance in time to see an unfamiliar woman stroll through. She was tall and slender, her dark hair hanging in a ragged shoulder length cut, her green eyes sweeping the room with a seemingly idle gaze. Mirabelle barely stifled the gasp of longing that stabbed through her hard enough to hurt. The woman was everything Mirabelle knew she would never be—beautiful, confident . . . free. That green gaze fell on her briefly, and Mirabelle saw a flash of humor. She knew in that moment it was all a pose, a deliberate play for attention. And it was working. Every vampire in the room was staring at the visitor hungrily, wondering what it would be like to bury his teeth in that slender, soft neck. Jabril and his vampires might disdain women as something lesser, but that didn't keep them from lusting after them all the same. Mirabelle sighed, loud in the silence. The woman met her eyes again and winked.

Mirabelle felt a flush of pleased surprise. A simple exchange, the wink of an eye, that's all it was. But it said so much: *We're together here, you and me. Two women in a room of fools.* She returned a tentative smile, but quickly lowered her gaze, suddenly embarrassed at how she must appear to this elegant woman, with her ugly clothes and drab scarf, not even a brush of mascara to bring out the color of her eyes.

"Lord Jabril Karim?" The woman's voice carried across the silent room, breaking the frozen tableau.

Jabril gave her a predatory smile, one that bore much more than the simple lust of his minions. There was cunning in that smile, and an avid hunger. Mirabelle hoped to live the rest of her long life without ever having that smile turned on her. Jabril nodded in acknowledgment. "Ms. Leighton, join us please," he said.

The woman started forward, the high heels of her fashionable boots clicking loudly on the marble floor. Like Mirabelle, she was dressed all in black, but the similarity ended there. Black pants clung to trim thighs before flaring slightly below the knee to accommodate mid-calf boots. She wore a cashmere turtleneck against the cold, and a leather coat fell to her ankles. Though Mirabelle was stifling, the woman seemed cool and at ease as she strode through the crowded room and stopped only inches away from the dais where Jabril presided.

CYN KNEW AS soon as she stepped into the room that it had been a mistake to come to Texas. Pausing on the topmost of two short steps down to the main floor of a big, echoing room, she could feel the eyes crawling over her skin, the testosterone so thick it was difficult to breathe. An idle scan told her there were only males here, and vampires every one of them. No, wait, there was one lonely female, young and terrified, wearing the cast off clothing from someone's Italian grandmother.

She drew a deep breath, taking some comfort from the weight of her Glock in its shoulder holster beneath the long, leather coat. They hadn't searched her, hadn't so much as asked if she was armed. At first, she'd thought it was the usual vampire dismissal of a mere human, but then realized it was not her humanity that made her less. It was her gender. The realization made her both more confident . . . and more cautious. Confident because she knew she could handle herself far better than most men expected. Cautious because she couldn't count on the norms of courtesy when dealing with Neanderthals of that stripe, especially not when those Neanderthals were also Vampire.

And speaking of Neanderthals . . . Her gaze ran over a half-naked giant standing to one side of the vampire lord, eyeing her suspiciously. Cyn wondered if he was a eunuch. She smiled to herself and looked directly at Jabril.

"Lord Jabril Karim?" she asked, although really who else could he be?

He gave her a regal nod and invited her forward. She crossed the space with a deliberately casual sway, using her height and long legs to good purpose. She paused at the base of the dais and considered taking that final step up onto the dais itself, wondering what the eunuch bodyguard would do if she tried. Self-preservation made her pause and give a little bow from the waist instead. "My lord," she said.

Lord Jabril's large eyes raked her from head to toe. It was more, and somehow less, than the lusting appraisal she usually got from men. As if he wanted her, but not as a woman. Or not only as a woman. She assessed him silently, waiting for him to make the next move. *Typical,* she thought. There he sat, the vampire lord on his make-believe throne, a prince and his courtiers. Raphael might be a treacherous pig, but he never styled himself a prince, at least not that she'd ever seen.

She grew irritated as the minutes dragged on, feeling more and more like a specimen in a zoo, but past experience with vampires and their games kept the irritation from showing on her face. Did this jerk think she would wilt under the weight of his regard? Not likely. She pasted a look of mild curiosity on her face and waited him out.

He gave her a full smile of genuine delight. "My associate, Asim," he said, gesturing. "I believe you spoke with him on the phone."

Cyn looked. Asim was altogether unremarkable, tall and skinny, with a sunken chest, dark hair worn a little too long, and the sallow skin of someone whose swarthy complexion no longer saw the sun. He gave her body a sweeping look from narrow, brown eyes, not even pretending courtesy, his gaze finally coming to rest on her face. Lovely man. Cyn was so very glad she'd come all the way to Texas to work for these guys.

Jabril stood and took the single step down off the dais, which left him standing too close to Cyn. She held her place, just barely. He was shorter than she, especially with her high-heeled boots, but that did nothing to mitigate the sheer force of his personality. She should have been prepared for it, having dealt with Raphael. Jabril Karim was a vampire lord. Hundreds, possibly thousands, of vampires, each powerful in his or her own right, owed their very lives to this man. He was dangerous and deadly, and Cyn would do well to remember that if she hoped to get back to California with her body and mind intact.

"Perhaps we should take our discussion into my office," Jabril said, his gaze never having left Cynthia's face.

She inclined her head in agreement and he turned immediately. Asim ignored her to trail after his master and the half-naked bodyguard, but Cyn was so distracted by the dance of Jabril's progress across the room that she forgot to follow. The entire room sprang into motion at once, with every one of Jabril's vampires swaying into his path and away, balancing their desire to be acknowledged against the fear of impeding his movement. Asim turned abruptly to spear a sharp look in her direction, indicating with an imperious jerk of his head that she should come along. Cyn bit back a laugh, enjoying the irritation on his face as she strolled slowly toward him.

As she neared the door, she passed the young woman, the single oddity in this room full of men. This close, the girl didn't look much over twenty—no matter that her youthful body was hidden beneath those bulky clothes. Of course, it was hard to tell with vampires, but something about this one said "young" to Cynthia. *Human* years young, and female. Definitely out of place here.

"Mirabelle." Jabril Karim's voice broke into Cyn's thoughts. The girl jumped, her eyes going wide with fear. "Come," he ordered.

Cyn frowned as the girl followed automatically, leaning forward like a dog on a leash. A dog who was afraid of being beaten if she disobeyed.

Jabril led them all into a small office. Asim entered last, closing the door on the eunuch bodyguard who remained outside in the great room, presumably guarding his master's privacy. The inside of the office was filled with tidy and somewhat effeminate furniture—a lovely Chippendale desk that looked almost too fragile to hold the weight of the ornate lamp on its corner, a few glassed-in bookshelves, and two brocade upholstered chairs with spindly legs that sat before the desk. A beautiful, and no doubt priceless, rug covered most of the floor, its colors vibrant in spite of their subdued shades of maroon and blue. Jabril circled the desk and sat, indicating with a graceful hand that Cyn should take one of the two chairs. Asim didn't sit, but stood behind the desk next to his master.

Cyn glanced at the girl, Mirabelle, expecting her to take the other chair, but she remained standing in the back of the room, huddled close to a second set of doors as though ready to bolt at the slightest opportunity.

"I trust your flight was uneventful?" Jabril Karim said to Cyn. He had a melodic voice, measured and even. She didn't know why it surprised her; he wasn't a bad looking man, his features stamped with the harsh lines of his desert ancestors, with lips as full as a young woman's and eyes that were a tad too prominent. But Cyn realized in that moment that she didn't like this vampire lord very much and wondered what had turned her against him. There was the faux throne room, of course, but she found that mostly amusing and not really much of a surprise. He was probably more than a few hundred years old and from a time when princes had real power. And though he might be insufferably arrogant, the truth was that as a vampire lord his power was also very real, and so a certain amount of arrogance was almost expected.

No, she decided, it was the girl that had made her take an instant dislike to Jabril Karim. The young woman was treated like an ill-favored pet and made to dress as if her femininity was something shameful to be hidden. Cyn didn't care how old the vampire lord was or where he came from. That kid was young and scared, and those big, blue eyes had been born in America, or Cyn would eat her boots.

She realized Jabril was waiting for a response and leaned forward slightly, crossing her legs in a deliberately seductive move. "The flight was what one expects these days," she dismissed. "You mentioned a matter of some delicacy, my lord?" Jabril's eyes flicked from her crossed legs to her face, where he held her gaze for a heartbeat before saying coolly, "Indeed. A very troubling matter, but one that requires a certain . . . discretion, I'm afraid. A young girl in my care has gone missing—"

"A girl?" Cyn's surprise was evident. A missing girl was the last thing she would have expected from this assignment.

Jabril's cool cracked a little at the interruption, but he continued smoothly. "Elizabeth Hawthorn. Her parents were dear friends of mine, and when they died I thought the least I could do was care for their children in familiar surroundings. It's so important for children to have some . . . constancy in their lives, wouldn't you say? I was pleased to find the courts agreed with me."

Cyn privately found it appalling that any judge would turn a child over to this bloodsucker and wondered what the going price was these days for a child's life. "Might I ask how old the missing girl is?"

"Seventeen," Jabril answered with an obviously calculated sigh. "And troublesome as all children are at that age, I'm afraid—the small rebellions of childhood."

Good God! A seventeen year old girl living with this bunch. No wonder she ran away. "How long has she been missing?"

"A week, at least. You understand, Ms. Leighton, it has been difficult for her, living here." He gestured around him with another deep sigh. "We are Vampire. She, of course, is not, being too young yet to make such a commitment, although I have hopes she will choose to join us."

He stood then and walked around the desk. Cyn rose automatically, stepping back to avoid touching him, but it was almost as if he pursued her intentionally, coming close enough to run his fingers down her arm to trail over the skin of her hand.

There was an odd feeling as he moved away and his fingers left hers. A spider web kind of feeling, as though he'd left something clinging to her skin. She fought an instinctive shudder, but he seemed not to notice, his attention already fixed on the silent young woman in the back of the room. She cringed as the vampire lord wrapped an arm around her shoulders. It was a practiced and yet awkward gesture, made more so by the difference in their heights—something Cyn hadn't noticed before now because the girl's submissive posture made her seem so much smaller than she really was. Cyn watched uncomfortably as Jabril all but dragged the terrified girl forward.

"Mirabelle chose to stay with us, didn't you, my treasure?" The threat was so thinly veiled Cyn couldn't imagine he thought anyone was fooled by the fond words. The girl gave a jerky nod, her gaze fixed firmly on the floor.

"Ms. Leighton can't hear you if you don't speak, darling girl."

"Yes!" she squeaked quickly. "I mean, yes, my lord. I wanted to stay."

He beamed like a proud parent. "My darling Mirabelle is shy, Ms. Leighton. She is our youngest and I'm afraid we indulge her. Children are so rare among us."

And thank the gods for that. "How long have you been living here, Mirabelle?" The girl's head came up, her eyes meeting Cyn's directly for the first time. In that brief moment, Cyn saw the rage burning behind the fear, quickly shuttered to show nothing at all.

"I was born here, ma'am," Mirabelle said softly. "This was my home before—" She swallowed hard. "After the accident, my master was kind enough to move his household here so Elizabeth and I—"

"Nonsense," Jabril interrupted. "How could I do anything less, child? Such a terrible loss for one so young. But we do what we can—"

"Wait," Cyn interrupted. "Are you saying Mirabelle is the sister of the missing girl?" Which would mean she was not much more than seventeen herself.

Jabril was looking at her in surprise. "Yes, of course. Didn't I mention that?" He looked at Asim for clarification. "How odd. I suppose I think of Mirabelle as part of my own family now." He stroked the girl's covered hair and Cyn fought the urge to slap his hands away.

"Did your sister—" She started to ask Mirabelle directly whether she knew her sister's whereabouts, but stopped mid-sentence at the flash of panic in the girl's eyes. "Did your sister take anything with her?" she said instead. "Anything to indicate where she may have gone?" Mirabelle seemed relieved and Cyn felt her unease grow.

"I don't know. Elizabeth doesn't live in this house, and we—"

"Too dangerous," Jabril interjected quickly. "My men are well-trained and superbly disciplined, but they are still, after all, only human . . . in many ways," he amended with a little smirk at his own cleverness. "Elizabeth is a lovely girl on the brink of womanhood. I felt it better for her to stay in the servants' quarters with the housekeeper."

"May I speak with the housekeeper?"

Jabril beamed at her. "You'll take the job then? Wonderful. Oh." He paused, as if a thought had suddenly occurred to him. It was such an obvious artifice that Cyn knew what his next words would be before he even spoke them. "Raphael won't mind you working for me, will he? We vampires can be so . . . possessive. I wouldn't want to tread on any toes."

Cyn regarded him steadily before replying. "The only toes in my life are my own, my lord. Lord Raphael employed me for a short time for a specific task which I completed to his satisfaction. I'm sure he'll tell you the same."

"Ah, yes, we heard there was some ugly business out there. Something to do with Alexandra, wasn't it? Not that I can imagine anyone foolish enough to try to challenge Raphael, but still . . ."

Cyn laughed. "My lord, the key to success in my business is client confidentiality. I would no more share the details of Raphael's business with you, than I would your business with him. I'm sure you prefer it that way."

"Of course," he snapped. He drew a calming breath through his nose. "You can start with the housekeeper," he said brusquely. "I've already spoken to her, of course. To little avail, I'm afraid, but perhaps you'll get something useful out of her." Gone was the charming vampire. He was clearly finished with Cyn and eager to get back to his own evening. "Mirabelle, why don't you take Ms. Leighton out to the back house? I'm afraid this has caught me at a bad time and I have much to do. Asim?"

Cyn watched, bemused, as Jabril and his henchman marched out of the room without so much as a "see you later." Apparently, since his rather crude attempt to get gossip about Raphael had failed, he had nothing further to say to her. Her mouth quirked up in a half smile and she turned to Mirabelle to say something unflattering, but the words froze on her tongue. The girl was holding a hand close to her chest, palm out in warning. "This way, Ms. Leighton," she said loudly, then gestured for Cyn to precede her through the outer door. Cyn shook her head in disgust. Why had she ever thought taking this job would be a good thing? *Why not a vacation in Hawaii, Cyn? Vampires in Texas? What the hell were you thinking?*

Chapter Five

AS SOON AS they were outside, Mirabelle leaned her head back and sucked in the cold night air. Cyn watched her curiously. "Don't get out much?" she guessed.

Mirabelle jumped. "Forgive me," she said quickly. "The servants' quarters are this way." She took off, shoulders hunched forward.

Cyn caught up to her and spoke quietly as they walked. "I see things, Mirabelle; I watch and make connections. It's why I'm good at my job. I know, for example, that Jabril doesn't really like women. Oh, he's not gay, never that. But he doesn't think women are worth much, does he?"

She glanced around quickly. "Let me show you something." She opened her leather coat enough to reveal the Glock 17 nestled in its shoulder holster before covering it again. "They didn't even ask me if I was armed, much less pat me down. It never occurred to them a woman would be carrying, I imagine.

"I figure the only reason I'm here is because I did some work for Lord Raphael, out in California, and Jabril is hoping to piss Raphael off by calling me here to Texas. I wouldn't be surprised if he's actually hired someone else, someone with a penis, to do the real work." She chuckled and glanced over. Mirabelle was silent, but she did seem to be listening. "It doesn't bother me, particularly. I get paid either way, and I've never been to Texas before.

"Anyway, given Jabril's low opinion of women, I have to wonder what you're doing here. And since this estate is owned by something called the Hawthorn Trust, which has public assets in excess of five hundred million, I figure it's not you he wants—no offense—but your money. How am I doing so far?

"Hey," she said softly, seeing tears fill the girl's eyes. "I'm sorry. Sometimes I'm not fit for polite society."

"No." Mirabelle rubbed her cheeks roughly, like a child. "No, you're right about everything. I'm so embarrassed," she said miserably. "What must you think of me?"

"Don't you worry about it, honey. I know vampires and what they're capable of. So tell me, does old Jabril in there ever let you out of his sight?"

Mirabelle shook her head. "This is the first time I've been outside alone in . . . God, it must be six months. Not since before summer when one of the maids went into labor unexpectedly. She should never have been in the house at that time of night. I don't know—" She shivered. "You should have seen the look on Asim's face when he realized what was happening." A sad, bitter smile crossed her face. "You wouldn't *want* to see what almost happened after that. I didn't even wait for permission, I ran as fast as I could to get some help. Some human help. Someone to get that woman and her baby out of this place before—" She shuddered.

"Okay, maybe there are some things I *don't* know about vampires," Cyn said with a grimace. "So, tell me Mirabelle, how did *you* get to be a vampire? I can't believe you actually chose to spend your nights with that bunch."

"No, I—" Mirabelle's head whipped around seconds before Cyn heard a door close followed by footsteps.

"Mirabelle?" A middle-aged woman appeared around the corner of the two-story building they were approaching. "What are you doing out here?" She gave Cyn a suspicious look. "And who's this?"

"Lord Jabril Karim sent me," Mirabelle said stiffly. "This is Cynthia Leighton. She's a private investigator. She's going to find Liz."

The woman gave Cyn a skeptical look, peering over pale-framed glasses attached to a chain around her neck. She had graying brown hair pulled back into a bun so tight she'd never need a face lift, and her gray skirt and jacket looked more like a uniform than a suit. She took a step closer and held out a hand. "Mrs. Elaine Peach. I'm Lord Jabril's chief housekeeper. Mr. Asim said you'd be coming by tonight. I'll tell you the same thing I told him. I haven't seen the girl in a week. She doesn't exactly check in with me."

"What made you realize she was missing?" Cyn asked.

Mrs. Peach studied her, then gave a little sniff and headed back the way she'd come, with a little wave for them to follow. They walked around the corner and entered the servants' house through a glass-paned door that led into a large, open kitchen. Ignoring the two men having coffee at the cafeteria-style table, the housekeeper kept walking until she reached an unadorned entryway. A small desk stood near what must have been the front door, with a simple bouquet of flowers in a cut crystal vase. The housekeeper finally stopped there and turned back to Cyn. "I don't actually have that much to do with Elizabeth. She has a tutor who oversees her schooling. But the woman was away for a week, a personal vacation, some family thing. I assumed the girl was . . ." She shrugged. "In her room, I suppose."

"What about her Child Protective Services caseworker? Does she meet her somewhere?"

"No, that woman comes here once a month." Mrs. Peach's tone left no doubt about how she viewed those regular visits. "Pokes into everything, as if we'd mistreat the child."

"Do you have any idea where Elizabeth might have gone? And why? Did she mention anything that was troubling her?"

"Elizabeth barely spoke to me. She wasn't rude; she simply wasn't interested. You'd probably have better luck with the caseworker. I think they actually got on rather well, considering."

"Considering?"

"Well, they aren't exactly on a par socially, are they? I mean, with her share of the trust, Elizabeth's already worth more than that woman will see in a hundred lifetimes. And she's—" Mrs. Peach stopped abruptly and gave a nervous, little cough. "Well. I can give you her name and number, if you'd like."

"I'd appreciate that, thank you. And the tutor, if possible."

"Of course. I'll see to it. Now, if there's nothing else?" She gave Cyn an absent look, her mind obviously having already moved on to her next task.

"Could I see her room, please?"

"Certainly." Mrs. Peach turned to Mirabelle, clearly thought better of it, and called into an adjoining room. "Kelli!"

Cyn noticed Mirabelle's flush of embarrassment, although she was pretty sure the housekeeper didn't. Mrs. Peach might be a great housekeeper, but her people skills made Cyn look like Miss Congeniality.

A slight girl in a pink uniform dress came into view, her eyes wide with curiosity. Thick brown hair was pulled back into a long braid to reveal multiple piercings in each of her ears, in addition to the small loop above one eyebrow.

"Kelli, show Ms. Leighton here where Elizabeth's room is and don't dawdle. You need to finish that silver tonight or there'll be no day off for you tomorrow."

"Yes, ma'am," Kelli said obediently. She looked up at Cyn with a wicked smile and the revealing flash of a tongue stud. "This way, please, Miss."

Elizabeth's room was on the first floor, in a quiet corner all by itself. Hers was the only door opening onto the hallway, and the hallway itself led directly to the kitchen, which was the one place on an estate of this size where some servant or other would almost always be awake. For all that no one seemed to pay much attention to Liz, someone had been careful enough to restrict her movements and associations. Or at least try to. Kelli led them into the modest room, going immediately to a transom window on the far wall and cranking it open, letting in the fresh air.

"It gets so stuffy in here, closed up all the time. That's the way Liz liked it, though. She liked her privacy."

Cyn was doing a quick visual survey, noting the absence of a lock on the door and the plain, straight-backed chair sitting against the nearby wall. The top edge of the chair back was scratched and gouged. Liz had fashioned her own lock, it would seem. Good for her. Cyn looked over at Kelli. "You were friends?" she asked.

Kelli frowned, giving Mirabelle a sideways glance. Mirabelle caught the look, and Cyn saw a knowing flash of dismay cross her face.

"I'll wait outside," Mirabelle said softly. "I can use the fresh air." She paused on her way out and without looking back said, "I love my sister." She glanced up then, tears sparkling in her blue eyes. "And I don't want him to find her." Then she left the room, almost running down the hallway.

Kelli waited until Mirabelle's footsteps faded completely before giving Cyn an uncomfortable look. "I didn't mean to hurt her feelings, but . . ." She shrugged. "She's a vamp. Anything I say in front of her might go right back to Lord Jabril. It's not her fault, but it's the way it is." She gave Cyn a searching look. "I need to know. If you find Liz, what happens then? I mean are you going to make her come back here? She'll be eighteen soon, you know. You can't make her do anything after that."

Cyn returned Kelli's stare. "No," she said finally. "There's no way in hell I'm bringing a child back to this place. I don't care if she's eight or eighteen."

Kelli studied Cyn, clearly trying to decide whether to believe her or not. "How do I know I can trust you?" she said. "I mean, Liz is a friend and . . . how do I know?"

"You don't," Cyn said honestly.

"Yeah." Kelli laughed awkwardly. "It sucks." She blew out a long breath. "Okay. I guess . . . okay."

"So?" Cyn said.

"So maybe we talked sometimes, Liz and me."

"Do you know where she is?" Cyn asked directly.

Kelli stared down at her hands which were tugging nervously on the pink uniform skirt. Her gaze darted up for a quick look, then she nodded decisively and pushed the door closed before turning to Cyn. "She didn't say anything specific about going anywhere. Not exactly. But . . ." She pinched her mouth and took a deep breath. "Liz got out a lot more than anyone knew. She's smart, a lot smarter than me, and not scared of nothin'. Not even old Jabril."

"So why'd she stay? I mean, it sounds as if she pretty much came and went as she pleased. So why come back at all?"

"Well, he has her sister, right?" Kelli said, as if it were obvious. "I mean, Liz was afraid what he'd do to Mirabelle if she left."

"Why now then?"

Kelli shrugged, avoiding Cyn's gaze. Her eyes darted around the room, coming to rest on the small, battered desk. "Liz sweet-talked a couple of the daytime guards at the front gate, you know. So they wouldn't report her. She's pretty. Did they show you a picture?"

Cyn realized with chagrin that, in fact, no one had given her any physical description of the girl, and she'd been so distracted by Jabril's games that she'd never thought to ask. *Real professional, Cyn.* On the other hand, the omission lent credence to her belief that they'd hired someone else to do the actual looking. She should have been insulted that her only value was as an irritant to Raphael, but mostly she was amused. They had no idea how irritating she could be. "No, no picture. Does she look like Mirabelle?"

Kelli snorted. "Who knows? Maybe once upon a time, but who can tell now?" She walked over to the desk and pulled open a drawer, sliding her hand all the way to the back and emerging with a couple of bent photos. "This is Liz," she handed them to Cyn, pointing.

Kelli was right. Elizabeth Hawthorn was pretty. More than pretty. A little too thin for her height, she had long, honey-blond hair, big eyes and a Texas beauty queen smile. In the picture, she was wearing tattered blue jeans that rode well below the glitter of a gold ring in her belly button and a sleeveless tank that revealed far more skin than Jabril would have liked. A loose necklace of some sort completed the outfit, the kind of thing you'd buy from a street vendor of *genuine* native art. She was leaning against a tall, skinny kid with broad shoulders that were all bone and sinew, as if he hadn't grown into his body yet, or maybe he just didn't get enough regular meals. Given the state of his clothing and hair, Cyn tended toward the latter explanation. "Who's the guy?" she asked Kelli.

"That's Jamie. He and Liz are pretty tight."

"Tight as in . . ."

"Doin' it."

"Any chance she's with Jamie?"

Kelli thought about it. "Maybe. But I don't know." Voices echoed suddenly down the hall and she darted a guilty look at the door. "Look, I've got to go. Can you meet me tomorrow, during the day? The Children's Museum. You know where that is?"

"I'll find it."

"Make it afternoon, I work late here tonight, so like two o'clock. Now I gotta get back to that silver, or I'm not gonna have a day off at all." She started out of the room, but Cyn stopped her.

"Thanks, Kelli."

Kelli nodded. "Tomorrow at two. I'll be there."

Cyn spent a few more minutes in Liz's room, going through the desk, checking the closet, looking for some indication Liz had planned to be gone awhile. It seemed likely the girl had run, but Cyn didn't want to rule anything out. Not yet. She stood from looking under the bed, brushing dust and lint off the knees of her black pants. "So much for good housekeeping, Mrs. Peach."

With a final look around, she left, closing the door behind her.

Mirabelle was leaning against the wall right outside the kitchen door. There were few lights this far from the main house and Cyn could barely see the young woman.

"I'm pretty much done here," Cyn said.

Mirabelle straightened and held out a piece of folded, white paper. "Mrs. Peach left this for you. It's the numbers you wanted, for Liz's tutor and the caseworker."

"Do you know her?"

"Mrs. Peach?"

Cyn gave her a little smile. "No. I mean the caseworker."

"Oh! Oh, of course. What an idiot." She flipped open the paper and looked at the name. "Ramona Hewitt. Sure, I remember her. I'm surprised she's still around. I didn't think any of them lasted that long. It's an awful job." She was quiet for the space of two breaths. "Mrs.

Hewitt cared, though. I really think she did."

"I'll give her a call tomorrow. I'll tell her you said, 'hi,' okay?"

"Sure." Mirabelle nodded. "I'll walk you back to the house, if you're ready. Although the car's probably waiting for you by now, if you want to leave. I mean, if you don't need to see Lord Jabril before you go."

Jabril hadn't seemed too eager to spend anymore time with Cyn tonight. And she certainly had no burning desire to see him. Ever again. "I think I'll call it a night, so the car it is. Thanks."

As they rounded the front of the house, Cyn pulled her coat tight against a slap of wind. "Is it always this cold in Houston?"

Mirabelle smiled. "Not usually, no. We're having a cold spell."

"Just my luck."

As they drew closer to the drive, Cyn saw the same silent vampire who'd driven earlier leaning against the car and looking bored. He straightened when they appeared, glaring at them both, as though it was their fault he'd had to spend his night lurking about the driveway.

"Okay, Mirabelle," Cyn said for his benefit. "Thanks for your help. I'll get back to Jabril as soon as I know something."

"My master's name is Lord Jabril Karim," the bodyguard growled. "You will refer to him accordingly."

Mirabelle froze, but Cyn barely glanced at him before shaking her head and opening the car door. "See you later, Mirabelle. Take care."

The driver stood outside long enough that Cyn began to contemplate calling a cab, but eventually he slid into the driver's seat, favoring her with a forbidding glare before turning around and starting the car.

Cyn stared out the window as they glided down the long drive. Endless manicured lawns stretched out to either side, dotted with artfully placed clusters of trees and flowers. Looking back, she could see the house itself, bathed in the glow of what must be hundreds of lights. Mirabelle stood on the porch, looking small and dull against the gleaming white house. Cyn turned around as they passed through the artificially rustic gate, thinking Liz wasn't the only Hawthorn daughter who needed rescuing.

Chapter Six

MIRABELLE WATCHED the limo glide down the long driveway, cutting an elegant line through the manicured lawns and out through the gates. She thought she saw Cynthia Leighton turn at the last minute, but it was probably her imagination, or wishful thinking. Wishing she was the one in that limo, the one driving through those gates going . . . anywhere. Anywhere but here.

She sighed, touching her scarf, tugging her clothes back into place before opening the door and slipping into the house. She paused just inside, listening, but there was no one around. They were all in the throne room, or maybe by now Jabril had excused them and gone downstairs to his personal harem in the basement for his evening's repast.

She hurried toward the stairs as quickly as she could, careful to maintain the proper decorum just in case. Her steps were smooth and measured, her hands at her sides, and her eyes on her own feet, on the stairs and then the carpeted floor in front of them. Her room was on the second level, in the back of the house. Closing her door behind her, she went directly to the closet, shutting that door as well and clicking the flimsy lock. She turned on the dim light overhead and yanked off the dowdy scarf, sighing in relief as she ran the fingers of both hands through her waves of blond hair. Next to go were the hated clothes, though she hung them carefully on a hanger, ready to be worn. She'd made the mistake once, in a fit of anger, of throwing the repulsive things to the floor. Jabril had been very unhappy at her disheveled appearance the next night and had made painfully certain it would never happen again. There had been no bruises afterward, no visible signs of his displeasure. He hadn't needed to resort to anything as crude as that. He was a vampire lord and she belonged to him, body and soul. The tiniest exertion of his will could cause her unspeakable pain, pain that left her writhing on the floor, begging for mercy while he looked on with cold dispassion.

She shivered at the memory and donned a pair of old, comfortable denims and a sweatshirt, leaving her feet with their sinfully polished toenails bare, she sat cross-legged on the closet floor and closed her eyes, listening. A vampire's senses were much finer than those of a human. Mirabelle could see in virtual darkness with ease, could hear a servant's heartbeat down the hall in the quiet house, and while the scent of blood was intoxicatingly strong, her entire sense of smell was greatly enhanced. She always knew when the humans on staff had brought food over from their own quarters to eat in the main kitchen during the day. She knew when the garbage had been left sitting too long and when the fruit on the counter was growing soft.

Not that she was ever permitted to actually enter the kitchens. And it wasn't as if she needed the food anyway. At least not *that* sort of food. What she needed, what every vampire needed, was blood. Fresh, human blood. Jabril had his stable of blood slaves, which he shared with Asim and those among his minions who were in his particular favor at any given time. Mirabelle's nutrition came from a plastic bag of anonymous blood, left hanging on her door knob three times a week like a gruesome do not disturb sign. Taking blood directly from a human had the potential to be an intensely sexual act. It was said to be unrivaled in its ecstasy, for both human and vampire. Which was why so many humans volunteered for it. And why Jabril would never permit Mirabelle to indulge in it. She had originally thought this was out of some obscene possessiveness, because she belonged to him. But later, she'd come to realize it was just his prudish idea of the proper role for a woman of his household. She was certainly the lowest vampire on the totem pole, but she *was* Vampire, and that put her in an entirely different class from the humans on the estate. One which required a certain female decorum, in his view.

The other vampires of Jabril's household, those not privileged enough to use the blood slaves, were permitted to hunt in the nearby city of Houston. Discreetly, of course, and only for volunteers. He was very clear on that. Jabril Karim was one of eight vampire lords who ruled all of North America, a position earned not through political patronage, but by brute strength. The entire southern United States was his territory, but Houston was his home. And no vampire wanted to be the one who made a mess in Jabril's back yard.

As Mirabelle sat on the floor of her closet, she located every person, human or vampire, on the second floor. The vampires were the easiest, distinguished by their sluggish heartbeats and the reek of old blood that seemed to never go away. But the vampires rarely visited the second floor. Jabril and his minions had rooms on the sublevel beneath the house. It was one more indicator of her lowly status that she resided on the upper floor, that her room had not one window, but an entire wall of windows. Mirabelle didn't mind. It reminded her of better times and kept her far away from the rest of them. Which was perfect for what she had planned for tonight.

She remained still for a final moment, listening. Satisfied, she turned and quickly removed the false front from what appeared to be a set of ordinary built-in drawers to reveal a small refrigerator hidden behind them. This had been her grandfather's room when he was alive. He'd been fond of midnight snacks and had liked being near the back stairway that led directly down to the kitchen. Mirabelle had nothing but good memories of her grandfather. She'd been ten years old when he died, five years before her parents' fatal accident. One of the many secrets he'd shared with her before his death had been his treasure trove of contraband goodies, foods his doctor had forbidden him after his third heart attack. Mirabelle had spent many joyful afternoons on the floor of the closet while Grandpa produced all sorts of delicious treats. She didn't know what had fascinated her most, the idea of a grown-up hiding things from her mom, or the way everything tasted so much better when it came from Grandpa's secret stash.

But what she pulled from within the small refrigerator tonight was very different from Grandpa's rolls of greasy sausage and fatty cheese. It was a sleek, top-of-the-line laptop computer, with a wireless adapter that picked up a clear, strong signal from the modem downstairs, a modem used by virtually every one of the estate's inhabitants.

It had been Liz's idea. She was the one who secured the password for the network and smuggled in the laptop during the day while most everyone in the main house was sound asleep. It was a way to break through the isolation Jabril tried to impose on them, a way for the sisters to communicate privately, far from the prying ears and eyes that were everywhere in this house.

Mirabelle booted up and logged onto the huge teenage website she and Liz used. There were millions of messages posted daily on this board, most of them the mind-numbingly trite exchanges of young teens all over the world. She scanned several messages and dropped in on chat rooms at random, blurring her computer trail before zeroing in on a search for a message from Liz. She found it on one of the public message boards.

Number1Cow, I'm ok. Don't worry. I'll be in touch. It was signed

Number2Cow. The cow designation was an old joke between them, a play on the nicknames their parents had used for them as children. Mirabelle had been simply Belle. Elizabeth had been Elsie. Belle and Elsie. They used to joke that their parents were confused about whether they were raising daughters or cows. After all, this *was* Texas.

Mirabelle closed her eyes, letting relief wash away the worst of her fears. She was still worried about where Liz was and what she was doing, but at least now she knew this wasn't some scheme of Jabril's to hold Liz prisoner so he could control her better. God knew it wasn't beneath him to pull something like that. As their parents' *dear friend* and close business associate, he had managed to get himself appointed the legal guardian of both girls when their parents died. Vampires, for the most part, lived discreetly, passing through society without most people ever being aware they were there. But that didn't mean the vampires were equally unaware of human society. Politicians were courted, donations made. Quiet laws were passed, and ancient and long-term interests were protected.

Jabril was shrewd and perceptive, and always very generous with political donations in the right places. No one had opposed the guardianship. Not Child Protective Services, who'd done a cursory investigation and found nothing objectionable in giving a vampire custody of two young girls. And not the judge who'd held a private hearing—in his chambers at night—for his good friend Jabril Karim.

Jabril had been careful enough, and patient enough, to wait the three years until Mirabelle turned eighteen. Three years and a day. He'd turned her the day after her eighteenth birthday. It had been an ugly thing, her first and only sexual experience. Brutal and perfunctory, as coldly done as a thief who steals a priceless heirloom only for the money it will bring. She'd been sick for months. Jabril had been furious, fearing she wouldn't survive. Not that he cared about Mirabelle, but if she died before her twenty-fifth birthday, her money would be lost to him forever, passing not to Elizabeth, but to the Hawthorn charitable trust, the one part of the family money Jabril had no hope of getting his hands on.

In the end, it had been Liz who kept her alive. The prospect of leaving her baby sister alone with the monsters had been motivation enough to get her out of her sick bed and on her feet, determined to stay alive until she saw Liz far away from Lord Jabril Karim and anyone like him.

Tonight, when Jabril told her Liz was missing, her first desperate hope was that her sister had finally run. Liz's own eighteenth birthday was only a few weeks away, and it was no secret Jabril was eager for the day he could turn his old friends' youngest daughter and gain full control of their estate. He wasn't satisfied with Mirabelle's share; he wanted it all. And since he'd gotten away with raping Mirabelle, why not Liz too? But Liz was stronger than Mirabelle and apparently she'd managed to escape. Mirabelle felt a rush of fierce pride for her little sister.

Footsteps echoed down the hallway, and she lifted her head, listening. Someone was coming up the marble staircase near the front of the house. She caught the distinct scent of old blood and frowned. With the careful, concise moves of long practice, she turned off the computer and stashed it in its hiding place, closed the refrigerator door and slid the drawer facade across the front. Only seconds later, she was on her feet and pulling the heavy robe over her jeans and sweatshirt. By the time a perfunctory knock presaged the opening of her door, she was sitting by the window, reading a book.

Asim's careful gaze scanned the entire room before coming to rest on her. "Do you know where she is?" he asked gently. Asim had been with Jabril for hundreds of years, a generational family retainer whom Jabril had brought over as Vampire to serve his own evolving needs. Asim handled all the details the vampire lord thought too tedious to concern himself with and was the only one of Jabril's minions who still treated Mirabelle with any kindness. He'd intervened on her behalf on more than one occasion, saving her from punishment at Jabril's hands. There were times when she suspected Asim actually saw himself as her protector, almost a stern father figure, or perhaps an uncle.

She met his inquiry with a confused frown. "My lord?" He wasn't really a lord, only Jabril Karim himself deserved that title, but she knew it pleased him.

"I know this is difficult for you, Mirabelle. I know you don't understand his ways, but what he does is necessary. For you and for all of us. The woman from the government agency will be here next week for her monthly visit. Elizabeth wasn't here for the last visit; she *must* be here for this one. Jabril will be most furious if she is not, and I needn't tell you who will suffer the brunt of his anger."

Mirabelle studied his face, looking for any indication he was playing her. She wanted, she *needed*, to believe he cared about her, that he could be trusted, that she wasn't utterly alone. She dropped her eyes with a sigh. "I haven't seen her, Asim. Honestly. She didn't say anything to me about going anywhere."

"I see." He seemed almost disappointed, and Mirabelle felt a flush of shame, feeling as if she'd somehow let him down. Tears filled her eyes and he looked away, seemingly embarrassed by her weeping. "Best you stay in your rooms," he said finally, walking over to the door. "His temper is uncertain tonight, and I don't want him to see you this way." He gave her a final, sorrowful look and left, closing the door quietly behind him.

With the door closed, Mirabelle let the tears come, great hiccupping gulps of tears, crying for all she'd lost. Not only her grandfather and her parents, but the dreams of a teenage girl—her first boyfriend, her first kiss, a husband, children. All the life she'd never have.

Chapter Seven

JABRIL FISTED THE blond slave's hair, yanking her head back and stretching her throat taut, until the thick outline of her jugular could be seen beneath the delicate skin. He lowered his head and sniffed, enjoying the sweet scent of her blood and the even sweeter stench of her terror. He waited, savoring the moment as the dark-haired slave with her mouth on his cock brought him to the edge of climax, then sank his teeth into the blond's neck. Her scream of pain made him hard once again, and he drank deeply until she was limp beneath him. He let her fall to the pillows to shudder convulsively in the throes of an orgasm triggered by the euphorics in his saliva. Sometimes he didn't bother to make the feeding pleasurable for the slaves, but sometimes he did. The possibility made them so much more anxious to please.

He lay back on the bed, reveling in the rush of fresh blood through his system, letting the dark-haired slave finish her eager oral ministrations. The door opened and he looked up to see Asim enter the room, his nostrils flaring with hunger at the scent of so much blood. He walked to the foot of the bed and stopped, his narrow eyes taking in the sight of his master and the well-used slaves.

"Ms. Leighton has returned to her hotel," he said.

"Excellent. What did you think of her, Asim?" Jabril ran his hand along the blond's naked hip, watching his aide's eyes tighten in hunger as the woman rubbed herself against Jabril with a needy moan.

Asim brought his gaze back to the vampire lord with a guilty jerk. "Prideful, mannish. Typical American female."

"But beautiful all the same."

Asim shrugged with studied nonchalance. "Her blood will taste like any other's."

"Perhaps not," Jabril disagreed. "Raphael has marked her, you know."

"I did not—"

"No, of course you didn't. It was too subtle and old; they've been parted for some weeks, I would imagine. Arrogant of Raphael, to claim such a one and then leave her lying about. He may find it somewhat difficult to claim her again."

Asim's gaze grew vaguely alarmed. "Did you—"

"A small touch. Because she's Raphael's and even that will infuriate him." He paused and gave his aide a sidelong look. "Have you eaten yet?"

"No, Master."

Jabril feigned surprise. "Well, then. This one's untapped tonight." He pushed the dark-haired slave away from his now flaccid cock, ignoring her small sounds of protest. Asim's face tightened in poorly concealed resentment, but he gave Jabril a little bow from the waist before grabbing the girl's arm and dragging her out of the room. Jabril smiled slightly and looked down at the blond, running an absent hand over her smooth skin while he thought about Cynthia Leighton. He suspected Asim was wrong about that one. Ms. Leighton's blood would be sweet indeed.

Chapter Eight

SHE STOOD ON a balcony, a sliver of moon the only light visible on the black sweep of velvet sky. On the beach below, the ocean moved restlessly, unseen in the darkness. Strong arms came around her, pulling her against a solid, thick chest, enveloping her in a hard embrace. She leaned back, closing her eyes in the sweet relief of his presence, the comfort of his arms. His lips brushed her hair and lingered to whisper in her ear.

"Where are you, my Cyn? Where did you go?"

"I'm here. With you."

"No. Say my name, sweet Cyn."

"Raphael," she whispered.

"So far away, *lubimaya*. Where are you?"

She frowned at his insistent questioning. What kind of a dream was this anyway? "Texas," she said, puzzled. "Is that what you want? I'm in Houston, Texas."

His arms tightened around her like steel bands and his breath ran out in a hiss of sound. "Why? Why Texas?"

"A job," she snapped, irritated now. She tried to push away his arms, but he held her fast.

"What job, Cyn? Who?"

"What do you mean 'who?' It's none of your business, but it's Jabril Karim. What does it matter?" She took advantage of the moment to push away from him. "What is this? If you must haunt my dreams, I like the sex ones a lot better."

His arms tugged her back again, his soft, sensuous laughter brushing along the entire length of her body. "Ah. Do you miss me, then, my Cyn?"

That was too cruel. She wasn't enjoying this dream at all anymore. It only made her sad. "Let me go," she whispered. "Just let me go."

The pillow was damp when the phone's wake-up call jerked her out of sleep, but she convinced herself it was no more than the sweat from a restless night in a strange hotel. She had no more tears to cry for

Raphael, no matter how many times he haunted her dreams. She ran her hands back through her hair, checking the time with a glance. It was a little before eight in the morning. A perfectly God-forsaken time to be awake, but she hoped to see Ramona Hewitt this morning at Child Protective Services. She had left a message the night before, but didn't plan on waiting for a call back that might never come. Instead, she would drop by and hope to speak with the woman for a few minutes. What she needed wouldn't take any longer than that.

An hour later, the elevator doors at Child Protective Services opened to the wail of a small child quickly shushed as his mother shoved something in his mouth with a guilty look around. Was the guilt because the child had cried? Or because the mother was using candy to quiet him at nine o'clock in the morning? The air of the dreary CPS waiting room was heavy with desperation, suffocating in its thickness. But there was nothing she could do for these people. She concentrated on her purpose in coming here and went directly to the reception desk, where a harassed-looking young woman sat answering phones.

Cyn waited until the receptionist had finished her call. "I'd like to see Ramona Hewitt," she said.

"Is she expecting you?" The young woman had a distinct Texas drawl, unfiltered by education or experience.

"No, but I only need—"

"You need an appointment. I can—"

"—a few minutes of her time. Tell her it's about Elizabeth Hawthorn."

The receptionist pursed her lips in irritation, then ran her eyes up and down, taking in Cyn's appearance—the pale blue jeans, artfully faded and worn, the soft leather coat, expensive haircut, clean, neat . . . money. The one thing government bureaucrats had learned to respect. "One moment." She picked up the phone, punched a few buttons and spoke into the receiver, turning away and doing her best to keep Cyn from hearing. When she turned back, her look of disapproval had only deepened, but she gave a little nod.

"Mrs. Hewitt will see you." She left unspoken her opinion on the matter and pointed to her left. "Down this hall, first left, second right, last office on the right." She spoke quickly, then glared at Cyn, daring her to ask for clarification. Cyn murmured her thanks, but she had already ceased to exist for the busy young woman as the phone resumed its insistent trilling.

Ramona Hewitt looked up when Cyn tapped lightly on the open

door. She was a fiftyish black woman, with smooth, perfect skin that would look exactly the same when she was eighty as it did today. Long, wiry hair had been gathered into a ruthless braid and wrapped tightly around her head to form a graying crown over a face that bore the lines of an easy smile. She wasn't smiling now. She gave Cyn the same once over as the receptionist and reached the same unflattering conclusion. "You can't be related, I know all her relations and there aren't many, none of 'em worth a spit, leaving those little girls the way they did."

"Mrs. Hewitt," Cynthia said in her most polite and professional voice. "My name is Cynthia Leighton. I'm a private investigator—"

"Investigator? You're about eight years too late, aren't you?"

Cyn stopped, confused. "I was hired by Jabril—"

"I've got nothing to say to you then." Hewitt was already turning away, paging through a fat folder on her desk.

"Did you know Elizabeth ran away?" Cyn interrupted. Hewitt closed the folder and stared at her. *Well, that caught her attention*, Cyn thought.

The caseworker frowned. "I can't believe that. Lizzie would have called me."

"That's why I'm here. I was told if she talked to anyone it was you. And I want to find her."

Hewitt huffed in disgust. "Why, so you can give her back to that God damned vampire?" It wasn't a curse the way Hewitt said it; it was a literal truth.

"No. Whether you believe it or not, I want to help her. Her *and* her sister, Mirabelle." Cyn pulled out a card from her backpack. It was the business card for Jessica's House, a teen shelter in L.A. run by Lucia Shinn, one of Cyn's few close friends. Cyn scribbled Luci's name and personal number, as well as her own cell number, on the back before handing it to the caseworker. "Before you decide I'm one of the bad guys, you might give this person a call. If, after talking to her, you decide that I might actually do some good, my cell's on the card and it's always on. I'll be in Houston until this case takes me somewhere else." She turned to walk out, but Hewitt's voice stopped her.

"How is Mirabelle?"

Cyn paused, turning back. "Not good. But I'm going to get *her* out of there too." She didn't wait for a response. She didn't need one. There was no doubt in her mind about what needed to be done. It would be easier with Hewitt's help, but she'd do it without her if she had to.

Chapter Nine

THE CHILDREN'S Museum of Houston was pretty easy to find. After all, how many buildings could there be with giant yellow pillars and a pagoda looking sign with huge pink letters spelling out "museum" across the front? Not to mention the roving gangs of screaming children who had clearly subdued their chaperones and were now planning a coup of some sort. Cyn leaned against an adjacent building, well back from the crowds, and used the vantage of her six foot height to scan the area for Kelli. She could see why the girl would want to meet here. There were so many people milling around, and so many of them were children, that a petite girl like Kelli could easily be mistaken for one of the older kids. Cyn caught sight of her around back of a fat pillar, her many earrings glinting in the sun as she peered out to search the courtyard for Cyn. Steeling herself against the onslaught, Cyn headed across the plaza, wading through the potential revolutionaries to reach Kelli's side.

"Hey!"

Kelli's face brightened, though her eyes scanned the area around them as if making sure Cyn was alone. "Hi," she returned. "Let's go inside. We'll pretend you're my mom." She gave Cyn that wicked grin again.

"Nice. What're you nineteen?"

"Twenty next month."

"Yeah, well I'm not old enough to be your mom. Why're we here?"

Kelli shrugged. "It's noisy and there's always lots of people. Plus Montrose is close by and a lot of the street kids hang around here, especially on Thursday nights. Families get in free and it's pretty easy to slip inside. Anyway, no one will look twice at a single mom and her kid."

Cyn bought tickets and nudged Kelli toward the door. "I don't want to be a single mom. Why can't I have a rich husband instead?"

"I don't know. You look like a single mom to me, like you're out there, you know? Looking for someone."

Great. "So how long've you worked for Jabril?" Cyn asked, changing the subject.

"Almost two years. Since I turned eighteen. A friend of my mom's got me the job. It's kind of creepy with all those dead guys sleeping all day, and the hours are weird, but it's okay."

"I don't think they're actually dead," Cyn commented. "So what do you do out there?" She started to lift her sunglasses as they went inside, but dropped them back down when she saw the hot colors splashed across every surface in sight.

"Cleaning, you know. Dusting, vacuuming, polishing the silver," her eyes rolled in disgust. "Pays well, though."

"You work in the big house too, or only the servants' quarters?"

"Sometimes the big house. During the day. No one's allowed there after dark. Don't want to gross out the big bad vamps by forcing them to look at lowly humans. Not unless you're one of the bimbos, anyway."

"Bimbos?"

"That's what we call the blood slaves Jabril keeps in his basement lair. Not a whole brain cell between them, although what they lack in brain cells, they make up in silicone. Those boobs can't all be real."

Cyn choked back a laugh. That was pretty much what she would have expected from Jabril and his ilk. "So, is there somewhere we can at least sit down? I'm feeling like a giant among the Lilliputians here."

"There's a cafe. It's mostly kid food, but they do have Starbuck's coffee."

"There is a God! Lead the way, child."

Cyn managed to snag one of the few adult-sized tables in the café and made Kelli hold onto it while she went in search of coffee. It wasn't a real Starbuck's, but it would do.

"So." She slid onto the bench seat across the table and passed Kelli an icky sweet chocolate chip frappuccino. "What do you know?"

Kelli licked whipped cream from her upper lip before saying, "Like I said, Liz used to get out during the day. Her tutor was clueless and besides, she only came twice a week. There's this one guard who always looks the other way, and a couple of others who were so-so." She rotated her hand, palm down. "They kinda felt sorry for Liz, being a kid with all those old guys. And, ya' know, vampires and all."

"They didn't worry she wouldn't come back? I mean Jabril doesn't strike me as an understanding employer."

"Huh, you got that right. But they knew Liz would come back because her sister was there. Plus . . ." She shrugged. "Liz wouldn't do that to the guys, get them in trouble like that."

"So what'd she do when she was out?"

"Came down here, mostly."

"This museum?" Cyn looked around. If Liz was in the habit of hanging around here, she might be here now.

"Nah, not here here. Just, you know, here. The museum district and Montrose, with the other kids. Well, and Jamie."

"Ah, yes, Jamie. What can you tell me about him?"

"What's to tell? His mom's a druggie, his dad's gone, or dead, who knows? Who cares? Jamie bailed a couple of years ago when he turned sixteen, been on the streets ever since. He spends a night here, a night there. Different shelters, hang outs. You know, like the other kids do. Liz used to give him money for food, sometimes a motel. They were pretty tight."

"So you said. You think Liz is with Jamie?"

"Maybe," she said, evading Cyn's gaze.

Cyn sighed. "Look, Kelli, someone needs to find her before Jabril does. It would be good if that person was me because I want to help her."

"He's got someone else looking, you know."

Cyn looked at her curiously. "You mean Jabril?"

"Yeah. Some guy who came around asking questions the day before you did. Old guy, buzz cut, smelled like cigars." She made a face. "You pissed off?"

"Honestly? I figured as much. Jabril's got old business with someone I did some work for awhile back. I think he's trying to fuck with that guy's head a little bit. It won't work, but Jabril doesn't know that. He also doesn't know that when I find Liz—and I will—I'm not going to be hauling her ass back to Lord fucking Jabril. We're going to hunker down somewhere safe, maybe with a nice view and a gorgeous spa, and celebrate her eighteenth birthday in style. And then I'm going to make damn sure she has a say in her future."

"That'd be nice," Kelli whispered. "But he'll take it out on her sister, you know. Mirabelle."

Cyn gave a very unladylike snort. "Kid, you don't know your momma very well." She chugged the last of her coffee, swung her long legs around and stood. "So, where can I find Jamie?"

Kelli stood up. "She's not with Jamie."

Cyn gave Kelli a hard look. "Where is she?"

The girl bit her lip, then gave Cyn a lopsided smile. "She's in L.A."

Chapter Ten

"DAMN." CYN SAT back down, shaking her head.

"Yeah, pretty weird, huh?"

"Not the word that comes to mind, no. How?"

"She's been planning it for a while. You know, getting money together and shit. She's got a fake ID that puts her over eighteen so she can get on an airplane alone. Couple of weeks she won't even need that anymore."

"Why L.A.?"

Kelly shrugged. "Why not? It's kind of like Texas, right?"

"Not really."

"Well, but, I mean it's sunny and everything, and everyone knows people are pretty laid back out there, so she figured it'd be easier to, you know, get a job, get a place."

"Did Jamie go with her?"

"Nah, they had a big fight about it. He wanted her to stay here, but Liz was totally set on getting out of Texas. I mean this is the state that gave her to Jabril in the first place, so why would she trust 'em now?"

"Why didn't Jamie want to go with her?"

"His mom. He checks in on her once in awhile, and he's got a little sister who lives with his aunt. I think he feels responsible."

"So Liz is alone out there. Can you get in touch with her?"

"She checks this web site we use, but . . ." Her voice trailed off and her gaze skittered away uneasily.

"But?"

"I haven't heard from her. I mean it's only been a few days so far, but she left a message the first day and I haven't heard anything since then."

"Perfect. Good planning." Cyn rubbed tired eyes, trying not to snap at Kelli, trying not to imagine all the things that could happen to a seventeen-year-old girl on her own in L.A. "All right, listen—" She stopped as her phone rang, then frowned at the display. It was a local number, and not one she knew. On the other hand, it definitely wasn't the vampires calling. She flipped the phone open. "Leighton."

"Ms. Leighton, Ramona Hewitt here. Can we meet?"

Cyn's eyes widened in surprise. That didn't take long. "Sure," she said to Hewitt. "Name the time and place, preferably before dark."

Hewitt made a wordless sound of agreement. "Where are you staying?"

"Four Seasons."

"Well, well. Fine. They've got a lobby bar. You can buy a public servant a well-earned drink."

"What time?"

"Let's make it four-thirty. The sun sets early this time of year."

"I'll be there," Cyn agreed. Hewitt hung up without saying good-bye, so Cyn snapped the phone shut and turned back to Kelli. "Where was I?"

"You were about to compliment me and Liz on our incredible planning."

"Something like that, but done is done. If you hear from Liz, you call me right away, got it? I'll give you my cell number." She dug in the backpack and pulled out one of her own business cards, writing on the back before handing it over. "If anyone asks, you tell them I gave it to you when I was out at the estate. In case you thought of anything that could help me, right? You tell Liz to call me, or give me a number where I can call her. Will she believe you if you tell her it's okay, that she can trust me?"

"Probably. Yeah, I think so."

"All right, but if not, give her that address." She indicated the address of Jessica's House she'd written on the back. "The phone number's there, too. It's a shelter for teenagers on the west side of L.A., run by someone I trust, someone reliable. If Liz needs a ride to get there, they'll take care of it."

"What're you gonna do now?"

"That phone call was from Liz's caseworker. Everyone seems to agree that Liz trusted her, so I'm hoping she'll know something that can help me. After that, I need to figure out a way to get Mirabelle on a plane with me back to California, and then I'm going to find your friend Liz."

Kelli's eyes were big as saucers. "He'll never let her go. Not Mirabelle. Even if Liz gets away, he's already got Mirabelle and her money. You don't know what he's like, what he'll do to her."

"Actually, I have a pretty good idea, but I'll figure something out. I can't abandon her there."

Kelli was looking at her as if she'd grown another head. "Why'd he call you? I mean, you sure don't seem to like vampires much, so why you?"

Cyn stood again, her mind already working the problem of Mirabelle. "Like I said before," she said distractedly. "He thought he could use me to get back at someone else. Unfortunately, that someone doesn't give a shit, so it won't work out the way he hoped."

"A boyfriend, huh?"

"No!" Cyn focused on the girl, surprised. "Why would you say that?"

"Yeah, I can tell," she said smugly. "It's a boyfriend thing."

"Whatever. Listen, you've got a cell phone, right?"

"Sure."

"Give me your number." She pushed the pen over and dug out another card, watching as the girl wrote her name and number in a childish hand, then took it back and looked it over. "Good. I've got to go. You'll be okay?"

"No problem. I'm meeting some friends later."

"And you'll call me if you hear anything? Anything at all."

"Yep."

"Okay. I don't know how much longer I'll be in Houston, but you can reach me on my cell phone wherever I am." She slung the backpack over her shoulder and gave Kelli one last look. "Thanks for this, Kelli. It's a good thing."

Kelli blushed and ducked her head. "Yeah, well. Liz is all right."

"So are you. You make a mom proud." She grinned. "Talk to you later."

She hurried out of the museum, figuring she had just enough time to get back to the hotel and her meeting with Ramona Hewitt.

Chapter Eleven

RAMONA HEWITT was already at a table when Cyn arrived. It had taken her longer than she'd expected to get across town because, contrary to the wide open image most people had of Texas, Houston was a big city, with lots of traffic.

Hewitt looked worn out. Her neat-as-a-pin blue suit was wilted and the tidy hairdo had a halo of wisps that had escaped their rigid confinement. A glass of Scotch sat on the table in front of her.

"I hope you put that on a tab," Cyn said, pulling out a chair to sit.

"I did."

"Good." Cyn signaled to the waiter who hurried over after leaving a trayful of drinks at the next table.

"What can I get you ladies?"

Cyn usually didn't drink, but today she'd make an exception. "I'll have an Absolut on the rocks, with a couple of olives and . . ." She looked at Hewitt, but the caseworker shook her head. Cyn pointed at the Scotch. "Can you put that on my tab and keep it open. Oh, and something to eat, maybe . . ." She grabbed the bar menu and perused it quickly, making a little face at the choices. "Far Eastern Bites, I guess, whatever that is." The waiter nodded and took off, stopping at another table on the way.

"Busy in here," Cyn commented.

"It's Friday," Hewitt said. "People like to start their weekend early." She took a sip of her Scotch and Cyn noticed she was drinking it neat. A real Scotch drinker then, which Cyn hadn't expected. Hewitt seemed more like the sherry type to her.

"So why didn't you tell me you cofounded Jessica's House?" Hewitt said.

Cyn shrugged. "Because I didn't. That's Luci's baby, not mine. She does all the work. All I did was write a check."

"Quite a big check."

"No more than Luci's. She had this dream when we were in college to create a place where runaway kids could feel safe. More like an obsession, really. It was the only thing she ever talked about. I wasn't that dedicated, but I believed in Luci and in what she was doing. I'm not that much of a people person, so I took the easy way out and wrote a check."

"And became a private investigator."

"Well," Cyn smiled slightly. "I became a cop first. Luci probably told you. Mostly to irritate my father, but I enjoyed it for a while."

"But not forever."

"No. Not forever. Like I said, I'm not much of a people person. I work better alone."

The waiter arrived with her drink and the promise of food to come. Cyn waited until he'd left, then took a long sip of her vodka, feeling it smooth away the snarls of the day, a nice warm slide all the way down. "So. You called."

"I did," Hewitt said. "How much do you know about Jabril Karim and his outfit?"

"More than most, less than some, I suppose. I know about vampires and how they work in general, their hierarchy and such. Jabril's got real power within their society, both personal and political. I wouldn't underestimate him. But as far as the two sisters go, Mirabelle and Elizabeth? I only know what I've been told, which isn't much. I can tell you without question Mirabelle is a virtual prisoner out there, and Jabril wants her money and nothing else. As for the Hawthorn Trust, it's a matter of public record, and I assume there are private assets as well. What I don't know is how he got ahold of her in the first place. He claims to be Liz's legal guardian too, is that right?"

"Yes, it is." Hewitt's jaw tightened in anger. "You may not believe this, but I tried to stop that from happening. I was the original caseworker assigned to the CPS evaluation, and I recommended strongly against granting that ungodly creature custody over those two girls. Just babies, they were. Fifteen and ten years old. What kind of a system would turn those children over to a monster like that? I didn't understand it then, and I don't understand it now. Even after what he did to Mirabelle, plain as day, no one said a peep." She leaned across the table, one fingertip pressed into the lacquered wood for emphasis. "It's money, is what it is. The whole system's bought and paid for. A smart guy like Jabril—I may not like him, but he's wily as a snake—a man like that knows where to put his money to do the most good. Those girls never had a chance."

"They didn't have any other family? No one with a better claim?"

"A half-sister up in Maine somewhere, from their father's first marriage. There was a lot of bitterness in the divorce and she was quite a bit older than the girls. I contacted her, but she wasn't really interested. You would have thought the money alone would bring her, but no. She had enough of her own, I guess. Or maybe she's one of the ten people left on Earth who don't care about money, I don't know. I recommended foster care. For all its problems, it would have been better. But I don't think the judge even saw my report. My *former* supervisor took the case over and the hearing was held in private, to protect the children's privacy, they said." She snorted. "To keep the whole damn thing a secret, more likely. They handed those girls over and never looked back. Judge retired a year later, a nice fat pension and a vacation house in the Bahamas. My supervisor? She got a shiny new job over in the mayor's office. Bought and paid for, I say."

"What's the deal with the money? The parents must have had a separate minor trust of some sort, in addition to the Hawthorn Trust. You can't turn over that kind of cash to kids."

"No, indeed, the parents were smart. I don't think they figured on Jabril Karim sticking his nose in, but they did what they could. The trust takes care of each girl 'til she's eighteen; they get all of the income until then, but can't touch the principle. At eighteen, each inherits fifty percent straight out. In Mirabelle's case, that effectively puts all of her assets at Jabril's disposal since, as I understand it, those vampires are controlled by whoever creates them." Cyn nodded and Hewitt continued. "The parents put in a little twist, something to help the girls grow up a bit before they started making their own decisions. If either of them dies before she turns twenty-five, her share of the trust goes right to the family's charitable foundation. No other heir can be named, not even the surviving sister."

"Which is probably the only reason Mirabelle is still alive."

"If you call it living. The law does, so I guess that's all that matters, but it's a crime what he did to that girl. A plain crime."

"And Liz ran because Jabril intends to do the same thing to her once she turns eighteen?"

"That's right. Oh, he'll claim it was her choice, exactly like he did Mirabelle, but it won't be. If there's one thing I know for certain it's that Elizabeth Hawthorn wants nothing to do with Jabril Karim or any other vampire. She's a perfectly lovely young woman who wants to grow up, get married and have babies like every other good American girl."

Cyn had to smile, wondering what Hewitt would think of the

choices she'd made in her life. "This is—" She broke off as the waiter appeared again to slide a platter of Asian tapas onto their table, along with smaller plates, napkins and silverware.

"Another drink?" He nodded at Cyn's nearly empty glass.

"Not for me." She glanced again at Hewitt's glass. "Another Scotch? Or something else?"

"I've got to drive home," Hewitt said with real regret, shaking her head. "I'll stick with this one."

"Nothing more, then," Cyn said to the waiter. He dashed off again, weaving his way through crowds grown even thicker while they'd been sitting there. Popping what she hoped was an egg roll into her mouth, Cyn chewed thoughtfully, then said, "Okay, so what you've told me so far is pretty much what I expected. But what I'd really like to know is if you have any idea how I can get Mirabelle away from him for even a couple of hours. Long enough to get her on a plane and on her way out of Texas."

Hewitt looked even more shocked than Kelli had. "This is not a creature to take lightly, Ms. Leighton."

"Cynthia," Cyn suggested. "Or Cyn."

"Cynthia," Hewitt amended. "If you cross him, I imagine Jabril can be quite ruthless. Not a few of his competitors have suffered setbacks over the years. He's been in this area quite a while, and from what I understand, he's had to change his habits somewhat, but I wouldn't count on his civility, if I were you. Those fancy manners are only skin deep."

"I believe you, but I have resources of my own. If I can get her out of Jabril's territory, his options are limited. And once we hit the Rockies, his hands are pretty much tied. Vamps are viciously territorial, and the boss out west even more than most."

"I'm afraid I can't help you there, but what about Elizabeth? If you leave Texas—"

"Liz is in California."

"California? But how—"

"A friend of hers. Any chance Liz would stay in touch with Mirabelle?"

"I don't know how. You've seen what it's like on that estate. I've tried to see Mirabelle a couple of times myself and been turned down flat. They wouldn't even get a message to her, telling me she didn't want to see anyone. Not that I ever believed it, but once she was over eighteen, I had no jurisdiction."

The waiter dropped the check folio on their table with a murmured, "Whenever you're ready." Cyn looked it over quickly and charged it to her room.

"I'll think of something," she said. "Anything else you can tell me?"

"Other than to be careful?" Hewitt shook her head and began gathering her things to leave. "Those are good girls, both of them. And their parents were good God-fearing people. They deserve better than what life gave them."

"Don't we all?" Cyn grabbed a couple of the egg roll-looking things and stood. There was an immediate shift in the human flow of the room as people positioned themselves to grab her table. "I probably won't talk to you again until I reach L.A., but I'll try to keep you up-to-date after that. And if anything pops here, you'll call me?"

"I will." Hewitt stood and offered her hand in a firm but friendly handshake. "I wish you luck, Cynthia. I'll say a prayer for you and those girls."

Cyn watched Hewitt march through the lobby toward the front doors, watched her pull a puffy, brown winter coat on over her blue suit and take the time to stop and zip it closed before stepping out into the freezing wind. She waited until the valet brought the car around and Hewitt was on her way, and then she spun around and headed for the elevator. She had an idea for extracting Mirabelle from Jabril's clutches, but she'd need to be a lot sharper than she was right now. She was tired and even the one drink was slowing her down. A lot of coffee and a hot shower. That ought to do the trick. But she had to call a vampire first.

Chapter Twelve

IT WOULD BE A couple of hours before sunset would catch up to the West Coast. Cyn spent the time with the fat yellow pages book, making notes, trying to think ahead to everything she might need in the hours to come. When it was finally time to make the call, her hands shook as she punched in the number. But she needed answers and this was the only place she knew to get them. She was relieved when an impersonal female voice answered.

"Raphael Enterprises."

"Duncan, please."

"May I say who's calling?"

She thought about lying, but this was Duncan, Raphael's number one guy, his lieutenant and closest advisor. He probably wouldn't come to the phone for someone he didn't know, so she told the truth. "Cynthia Leighton."

"One moment." It was said a little too fast, as though the woman had expected her call. Cyn's stomach was bouncing with nerves as she waited, terrified of hearing a certain honeyed voice on the other end of the line. But it was the ever so polite, so proper Duncan who picked up the line.

"Ms. Leighton, a pleasure to hear from you."

There was a note of sincerity in his voice and Cyn actually believed he meant what he said. It brought the press of tears to her eyes, and she thrust the emotion away angrily. "Duncan. Thank you for speaking with me."

"But, of course. Why would I not?" Again, his puzzlement was genuine, but since that only confused Cyn, she ignored it and pressed on with her own reasons for calling.

"I have some questions. Questions you might not want to answer, but I really need the information. It's a matter of life and death, and I mean that literally."

"Are you in some danger?" he asked quickly.

"No, no. Well, no more than usual. You know me," she joked

lamely, then sobered. "If a young vampire, let's say five years reborn . . ." She used the vampire's own term for the transition. ". . . tries to leave her Sire's territory, will he sense it? Will he know?" She could almost hear Duncan's frown as he listened.

"How old is this young vampire? The actual age from birth."

"Twenty-three now, eighteen when turned, and barely that."

"Jabril Karim," he said grimly. "Where are you calling from, Ms. Leighton?"

"Why does everyone keep asking me that? I have a job, Duncan. People hire me and I go where the job takes me."

"Ms. Leighton—"

She could hear the hesitation in his voice, hear the wheels turning. "If Raphael comes to the phone, I'm hanging up, Duncan. I mean that."

"You put me in a difficult position." He sighed. "Why am I not surprised? Am I right? Are you in Texas? Tell me that much."

"Yes," she admitted.

"I don't know what possessed you to deal with that one, but it no longer matters. You need to leave as soon as possible. I don't believe you quite understand what's at stake."

"You know, Duncan, forget it. I'm sorry I called. What is it with you guys? Fine, I fucked Raphael a couple of times. But he's the one who walked away. Not me. That does not give him, or any of you, the right to dictate the rest of my life. I will go—"

"Ms. Leighton—"

"—wherever I want—"

"Cynthia!"

Cyn stopped, drawing a deep breath. "Will you answer the fucking question or not? There's more at stake here than Raphael's dick."

Duncan choked back a laugh. "I have missed you, Cynthia. Against all odds, I *have* missed you. Very well. Again, I urge you to leave Texas immediately, but . . ." He overrode her burgeoning protest. "But, the young woman in question—and don't insult me by denying it—has been under Jabril's influence a very long time, from a very young age, and Jabril's methods are not kind. If he knows she is leaving, he will exert every effort to stop her, regardless of the cost to her, physical or otherwise. Do not expect her help in this, Cynthia. She will not be able to give it, even if she wants to. She will fight you."

"What if I do it in the daytime?"

"That would be best. She is young and the sun affects her much more strongly. But Jabril will never release her to you."

"Leave that to me. Once we cross out of his territory, will his hold weaken?"

"Certainly it will weaken. But it will not disappear until replaced by a stronger power."

She could hear the satisfaction in his voice. "Shit."

"Indeed."

"Can I drug her? Will anything work?"

"No. The virus will clean anything from her system much too fast to do any good. You should—"

He stopped mid-sentence, and Cyn could hear a silky, deep voice in the background. Her heart jumped and it was suddenly difficult to breathe.

"My lord—" She heard Duncan begin. She didn't listen any further.

"Good-bye, Duncan." She hung up. Her cell phone rang almost immediately, but Cyn didn't answer. She was tempted to turn it off, but was afraid Kelli might call, or even Liz herself. So she switched it to vibrate and watched it dance around the table a few times, her eyes never leaving the display as it shunted every call to voice mail. Finally, it was silent. She deleted the messages unheard.

Chapter Thirteen

IT TOOK SEVERAL hours and too many phone calls, but Cyn finally found companies in the Houston area that had the equipment and services necessary for what she had planned. After that, she took a long overdue shower, standing beneath the needles of hot water until her skin was bright pink, in a vain attempt to convince her muscles to relax even a little bit. Finally giving up on that, she wrapped herself in one of the hotel's big fluffy towels and blew her hair dry, then pulled out the bag of makeup she always threw into her suitcase but rarely used. She didn't overdo it, applying only enough to bring out the green in her eyes, the sharp edge of her cheekbones. Her clothes were chosen with equal care, designed not for comfort, but for impact. A short, black leather skirt clung to her thighs and showed off the curve of her firm ass. She had worked hard to keep it that way and was not above using it to her own advantage. She added a dark turquoise silk blouse, with a draped neckline that showed a fair amount of cleavage. Not enough to look slutty, but enough to be casually provocative. Her shoulder rig was an awkward fit with the slick fabric, but she tugged it on anyway. She wasn't going anywhere near Jabril Karim without her gun.

Her leather boots worked well enough, their high heels accenting the long length of her legs beneath the short skirt. She pulled on the leather coat over everything, her fingers automatically finding the cool metal switchblade in the bottom of one pocket. Guns were great, but vampires were fast, and if she needed something in a hurry . . . Well, it was always good to have a backup. Everything else went into her small suitcase. She took a final look around the room, slung her backpack over one shoulder and rolled her suitcase into the hallway and to the elevator.

The rental vehicle she'd arranged was waiting for her outside the hotel, manned by an eager young man who took great pleasure in demonstrating the various features of the big SUV, including every imaginable luxury convenience and a dazzling array of cup holders. The only features Cyn really cared about were the in-dash navigation system and the darkly tinted windows all around. She'd chosen this company for its specialty in renting to high profile clients who desired anonymity.

After dropping the young man back at his office—he said it wasn't necessary, but Cyn insisted—she turned on the GPS and headed for the Hawthorn Estate, now Jabril's personal lair in all but name.

"THIS IS MOST irregular," the guard growled. "Lord Jabril Karim is not expecting you."

"I know," she said with an ingratiating smile. "And I am sorry, but I really need to speak with him and it can't wait until tomorrow."

He frowned at her, and then turned away with a gruff, "One moment."

While she waited, Cyn checked her watch and walked herself mentally through the next hour or so. It was a few minutes past five a.m. and, according to the local paper, the next sunrise would occur around seven-thirty. She was cutting it pretty close, but her greatest fear was giving Jabril enough time to come after her. By slipping out as close as possible to sunrise, she was counting on the vampire lord not discovering anything amiss until he woke tomorrow night. By then, everything would either have already gone to hell or, if luck was with her, she and Mirabelle would be enjoying the view from Cyn's condo on the beach.

She listened as the guard spoke to someone on the house phone, probably Asim. He struck her as the kind of flunky who would control access to the big guy as a way of ensuring his own power base. When the guard turned back, she was ready with a brilliant smile.

"My lord will see you."

Cyn fought against the urge to roll her eyes. "That's very kind, thank you so much." Her effort to be pleasant garnered nothing more than a grunt in response, but the gate opened, which was all she really cared about.

Cyn parked the big SUV on the outward curve of the driveway, which put it far away from the front door and closer to the path leading to the servants' quarters in the back. She hoped such things wouldn't matter when it came time to depart, but one never knew. The front door opened as she reached the porch and a middle-aged man appeared, heading toward a couple of cars parked to one side. The very definition of clean-cut, the skin of his face gleamed and his nearly white hair was cut short enough that his pink scalp was clearly visible. This must be the other private investigator Jabril had hired, the real one. She knew the type. Former military, he probably had a very docile and very young wife at home, someone he'd brought from an island far away, somewhere where women were still subservient to men. She chuckled privately. More than one of those guys had been unpleasantly surprised when the little mouse became a real American woman. He ignored her, brushing past without even a glance.

Cyn turned as he went by. "You're looking for Elizabeth Hawthorn, aren't you?" she called.

He stopped, turning his head sharply to stare at her.

"Any luck?" she asked.

He shot an angry look at someone over her shoulder, walked over to his car and climbed inside, departing without so much as a word.

"I see you make friends wherever you go."

Cyn's gut clenched, but she made sure nothing showed on her face as she turned to confront Asim, who was blocking the door. "Asim," she said. "How lovely to see you again."

The vampire's gaze traveled down her body, lingering on the length of bare thigh visible below the short skirt, before meeting her eyes. "Is this how you do business, Ms. Leighton?" His expression told her exactly what he thought her *business* must be.

"I dress the part, Asim. Whatever works. I'd like to speak to Mirabelle again, if possible."

"You were hardly expected and it is nearly dawn," he said primly, but Cyn just smiled pleasantly. If he was waiting for some sort of explanation from her, he'd be waiting a long time. "Come this way," he snapped.

JABRIL KARIM LEANED back behind his desk and studied the cowering young woman. There was no pleasure in punishing Mirabelle. She didn't give even a pretense of fighting back, surrendering almost before he'd struck the first blow. Not that he stooped to actually hitting her. That was far too crude, and the evidence far too visible. Besides, he had no need to resort to such brute measures; as her Sire, he could inflict pain with a thought. She did cower prettily, he'd give her that. She was curled up like a dog over there in the corner, trembling so hard he could see it from across the room. Very satisfying in its own way, he supposed, and it was the only satisfaction he'd enjoyed thus far tonight. He hadn't even fed before business had intruded, an urgent missive from the head of his family in Saudi Arabia that demanded immediate action.

And now this business with Elizabeth. That idiot private investigator Asim had hired had found nothing—absolutely nothing here. Less than two weeks remaining until her eighteenth birthday, and she seemed to have vanished into thin air. Jabril had waited years for this opportunity; he'd bribed and cajoled the necessary authorities, put up with their intrusive investigations and inspections. He'd earned the right to whatever fortune the girl inherited. More, he'd earned the right to the girl herself. Elizabeth showed much more spirit than her older sister, and Jabril had greatly anticipated the pleasure of breaking her, of seeing her crawl at his feet and beg for mercy.

He pushed away from his desk in anger, shoving back the chair and standing so quickly that in her corner little Mirabelle gasped in fear. And now Raphael's whore had shown up unexpectedly, no doubt to report a similar failure, not that he'd expected anything useful from her anyway.

A soft knock sounded and Asim slipped into the room, glancing at his Sire before opening the door fully to admit the Leighton woman. Jabril tensed instinctively as she entered and he scented the faint but unmistakable whiff of Raphael that still clung to her skin, to the blood that ran in her veins. His hunger surged as she sauntered into the room, her long legs sliding like silk beneath a short leather skirt, breasts brazenly displayed. He imagined what it would be like to have her under him, those legs wrapped around his hips, his cock pounding her mercilessly, his teeth sinking into that smooth neck until her hot blood gushed down his throat. He grew hard at the thought, even harder when he imagined Raphael's rage at the trespass. Of course, it was hardly his fault that Raphael left this one to wander about unprotected. The other vampire lord had to know how tempting she would be to his enemies. He stared at the woman through hooded eyes, feeling the press of fangs against the soft tissue of his gums as they responded to his body's hunger.

"Ms. Leighton." It came out as more of a growl than he'd intended and he saw her eyes widen slightly as she took in his obvious signs of arousal. Her scent changed, sweetened by the tinge of fear, and his arousal grew. He could be on her in the blink of an eye, long before she saw him coming, long before she drew the gun concealed next to her soft breast.

He took a half step forward, his mind filled with thoughts of Leighton's naked body stretched beneath him, trembling with need, her blood running down over those full breasts to be licked away as she cried for release.

Mirabelle whimpered and the Leighton woman dropped away from his outstretched hand to crouch next to the stupid girl. He snarled angrily, the words that would punish already forming in his head. He stopped and sucked in a deep breath, drawing on the tremendous will that made him one of the most powerful vampires alive.

"Ms. Leighton." There was the smallest of tremors in his voice, and he paused to swallow before continuing. "This is unexpected and it is late. Did you have something for me?"

CYN KNELT ON the floor near the whimpering Mirabelle, fighting to breathe in air grown suddenly thick with equal parts of lust and fear. Jabril growled her name and she stared up at him, seeing the dark thoughts slithering below the surface of his eyes, the obvious swell of an erection beneath his elegant slacks. He smiled, plump lips drawing back to expose fully distended fangs. It was a terrifying sight. She struggled not to show her fear as he took a step closer, thinking of her gun and how fast he could move, and knowing one thing clearly. She did not want him to touch her again. She didn't know why it was so important, but her stomach revolted at the very idea.

Jabril repeated her name, then paused. When he spoke next, the fangs were gone, his eyes almost normal.

Cyn glanced at Mirabelle and stood to face him. "Thank you for seeing me, my lord," she said, forcing herself to forget his arousal of only moments before, to ignore the whimpering girl at her feet. "I know time is short, but I wonder if I might have a few words with Mirabelle? And perhaps take another look at Elizabeth's things? I've spoken to some people who believe they've seen her and to Mrs. Hewitt—"

Jabril frowned. "The caseworker," Asim provided.

"—and I may have an idea as to where she's hiding. It occurred to me, the sisters being close, that Elizabeth might have said something inadvertent to Mirabelle or perhaps left something lying about in a pocket or a drawer that could help me narrow down the leads."

Cyn concentrated on breathing as Jabril studied her. "My own people have turned up nothing," he said. "I see no reason why you think you might—"

She smiled. "Let us say, my lord, that my sources are somewhat different than those of your other investigator. There are hundreds of children, teenagers, living on the streets of Houston; Elizabeth is most likely hiding among them. As experienced as your man no doubt is at this sort of thing, it is more likely these children would run from him than tell him anything useful."

"Are you suggesting they will speak to you?" Asim didn't even bother to deny they'd hired someone else.

"As I said, Asim," she said without taking her attention from Jabril. "I dress the part. My lord," she continued. "I am confident I can turn this case around within twenty-four hours if I can narrow my search. There is a chance that Mirabelle—"

"Very well." That was all he said, but he continued to stare at her unblinking, as Mirabelle gasped in seeming pain and scrambled to her feet to stand, head bowed, hands clenched tightly at her sides.

"Sire," the girl whispered, her gaze riveted to the floor between her feet.

"Mirabelle, Ms. Leighton seems not to have done a thorough job on her last visit. If you could escort her to Elizabeth's room once more, please." Cyn ignored the intentional slight, more troubled by the change in Mirabelle's demeanor than Jabril's opinion of her skills. If the young woman had been cowed before, she was positively terrified now.

"Yes, my lord." Mirabelle's voice was barely audible as she sidled over to the door without ever once turning her back or raising her eyes from the floor.

"Do come right back, my treasure. The sun is near." Mirabelle flinched as if struck.

"Yes, my lord," she whispered again.

Cyn turned back to Jabril, her face schooled to show nothing. "Thank you, my lord." She probably should have said more, kissed his ass a little, but the only thing she wanted right then was to get the hell out of his sight. She followed Mirabelle through the door, turning her back on the vampire lord with an act of will, refusing to scuttle backwards like some sort of slave. Fuck him.

"WHAT DOES SHE want?" Jabril snapped when the two women were gone.

"She asked to speak to Mirabelle, my lord. She claims it is relevant to Elizabeth's disappearance, and the guard reports she was most insistent."

"Is it possible she's found something?" Jabril gestured for Asim to follow as he strode toward the elevator and his private harem, hunger goading him to hurry.

"Unlikely. The investigator remains confident he'll find the girl before it's too late. I hardly think Ms. Leighton can do better. She is the spoiled daughter of a wealthy man who plays at being a detective. No doubt she has tired of the local nightlife and wishes to find some excuse for dropping the case so she can go home."

"Perhaps," Jabril said absently as the elevator doors closed. He glanced at his watch, thinking only of the time left to partake of a slave or two before the dawn took him.

AS BEFORE, MIRABELLE halted right outside the door, breathing deeply. Unlike before, however, there was no sense of release in the action. She stood hunched over, her hands clenched, her breath gasping in and out. Cyn realized the girl was crying and reached out to touch her shoulder. Mirabelle flinched at the gentle contact, taking a step away.

"I'm sorry," Mirabelle said in a dead voice. "This way, please."

Cynthia frowned, but walked along quietly for a few paces. "Tell me, Mirabelle," she said conversationally. "If there was a fire and you had ten seconds to grab everything that meant anything to you, what would you take?"

Mirabelle gave her a startled glance before looking away quickly. Cyn thought at first she wouldn't answer, but then she said, "Nothing."

"Nothing?"

"He's already taken everything away. There's nothing here I want."

"That's what I thought. What about Elizabeth?"

"Elizabeth is gone. And I hope she stays that way. No offense, Ms. Leighton, but I hope you never find her."

"Oh, I've already found her."

Mirabelle stopped dead in her tracks, then spun toward Cyn with a frantic look around. "You can't give her to him! Don't you know what he'll do?"

Cyn gave her a little smile. "Think, Mirabelle. I know you have a mind, even if he never lets you use it. Why would I be here, searching Elizabeth's things, when I've already found her? Why not simply tell Jabril where she is and collect my money?"

Mirabelle scrunched up her face in weary confusion. "I don't know," she cried. "Please don't . . ." She gulped back a sob. "Please don't play games with me. That's all they ever do, all he ever does. And he hurts me. Oh God, he hurts me so much." She covered her face with her hands, and then suddenly raised her head, staring directly at Cyn, her eyes hot with hatred. "You want to know what I'd do if there was a fire in this damn house? I'd slit my own throat and hope to God they all burned to ash along with me. There's nothing here worth saving, not even me."

"Mirabelle." Cyn spoke sharply, alarmed by the girl's extreme emotional state. She needed her thinking clearly if this plan was going to work. "What happens when I leave here this morning? Will Jabril expect to see you again, or are you on your own until night falls?"

"What?" she asked, clearly thrown by the turn the conversation had taken. "Why?"

"Answer the question," Cyn demanded.

"No! I mean, no, he won't want to see me. He had some big deal earlier. I don't know what it was, but he didn't get a chance to eat much. So he's hungry. That's why he freaked out so badly when you walked in. You're human and female, and his control was slipping. This close to sunrise, he'll go right to his quarters and have a little blood orgy before he goes to sleep."

"So you'll be expected to go back to your room alone? And no one else will be there?"

"No. There's no one, but why—"

"What if I said I could get you out of Texas tonight?"

Mirabelle's eyes popped wide with fear before she all but collapsed to the ground at Cyn's feet. "No, no. You mustn't. You mustn't talk about such things. He'll know and he'll hurt me. He can't touch you. He's afraid of you or something, but he'll hurt me so bad." She was sobbing openly, sitting on the ground and hugging herself tightly.

Cyn crouched next to her, speaking directly into her ear. "Listen to me, Mirabelle. This is your chance. Do you understand? I can't give back what he took from you. I can't give you a husband and children and a white picket fence, but I can give you a chance for a real life. Something better than huddling in fear and waiting for Jabril to decide he doesn't need you alive anymore. There are better lords than Jabril, better places for you than Texas. This is your chance, Mirabelle. Take it."

"He'll know," she whispered miserably. "He won't let me go."

"That's right," Cyn agreed. "He'll know. But sunrise is in . . ." She checked her watch. "Less than an hour. I figure by now old Jabril is too busy seeing to his own comforts to worry about yours. You walk away with me and climb into my truck, and I'll do the rest."

"But where will I . . . the sun . . . I've never . . ."

"Trust me. Two minutes ago you told me you'd rather burn to ash than live this way. So, what've you got to lose? Besides, think of the mess if I let that happen. How in hell would I explain it to the rental car company?"

Mirabelle gave a strangled sort of laugh. "Do you really think I can?"

"I know you can." Cyn stood and held out her hand. "Now, let's get the hell out of here before the sun comes up."

Mirabelle stared first at her face, then at the proffered hand. Trembling all over, she reached out and placed her fingers in Cyn's, finally grasping firmly. Cyn tugged her to her feet and gave her a quick hug. "Let's make tracks, babe. The night is old."

Chapter Fourteen

IN THE SHADOW of the big house, Cyn helped Mirabelle climb into the cargo area of the SUV and drew the retractable cover over her. The young vampire was already growing weak as the sun nibbled at the horizon, and Cyn only hoped she hadn't miscalculated. Mirabelle needed to be at least semiconscious when they reached the small, private airport. There was no way in hell Cyn could get her out of the SUV and into the airplane by herself. With a final, careful look around, she turned the ignition key.

Human guards had already joined their vampire counterparts at the gate and Cyn remembered Raphael telling her—it seemed like a hundred years ago—that the closer it got to dawn, the more distracted and less reliable the vampire guards would be. She was counting on that distraction now and was relieved when the same vamp guard who'd admitted her before stepped out to block her way. She gave him a friendly smile, which he ignored, but he gave her only a cursory glance before stepping back to wave her through impatiently.

Cyn didn't draw a full breath until she hit the beltway. She'd taken time earlier to map her escape route, using the SUV's in-dash navigation system. She'd considered avoiding the highways altogether, sticking to the side roads, but in this case the most direct route was also the safest. Besides, being a California girl, she was most comfortable on a freeway and it was too early for the morning rush, so the route should be wide open. She checked her position and hit the gas, racing toward Ellington Field.

"You still with me, Mirabelle?" Cyn called back, glancing at the rear view mirror automatically, although there was nothing to be seen except the black cargo cover. She got a muffled groan in response, which worried her, but there was nothing she could do about it now. She had to make that plane, had to get them off the ground and heading for California. But what if she didn't? What if she was too late? Jesus, what then? She thought hard. If she missed the plane, she'd have to keep going on the ground. Between the tinted windows and the cargo cover,

Mirabelle would be safe enough from the sun. But how long it would take to reach the Arizona border and Raphael's territory? And how fast could Jabril find her in the meantime? He'd know where she was. Even if her only logical destination hadn't been Arizona, he had a blood link to Mirabelle and could track them better than any GPS device made. And in the meantime, Cyn would be trapped in a gas guzzling SUV with what was probably going to be a crazed vampire once dark descended.

A pair of headlights appeared in her rearview mirror out of nowhere, coming up fast. *Oh God,* she thought. *Was it him, had he gone looking for Mirabelle and found her gone?* She drove frantically, her gaze dancing between the road and her mirror, watching doom approach in the form of a low-slung sedan. He rode right up on her tail, so close she couldn't see his headlights, so close she was convinced he meant to ram her, to drive her off the road. She jerked the SUV into the next lane, swerving dangerously, and watched in stunned disbelief as the other car raced past, its driver not even glancing her way.

She sucked in a deep breath and kept going, shivering with chill as the adrenaline drained out of her body.

When the airport came into view, she used her cell phone to call a prearranged number and the pilot of her chartered jet guided her to the hangar. This particular airline offered certain amenities to the vampire community; their ads were subtle but obvious if you knew what to look for. As Cyn pulled into the relative safety of the private hangar, the sunrise was already a promise—or a threat—on the horizon. By the time the doors began to close behind her, the thinnest ribbon of light was visible. Remembering what Duncan had said about Mirabelle's greater susceptibility to the sun's influence, Cyn skidded to a halt as close to the small jet as she could get, then threw herself from the truck and around the back. The airplane cabin was open, interior lights beaming a welcome above the short stairway. It was only a few stairs, but Cyn gave it an almost despairing glance as she ran by. The airline might invite vampires, but they'd made it clear that passengers had to board the aircraft under their own power.

"Please let Mirabelle be awake enough to walk." She whispered the prayer to whatever gods protected vampires and their foolish human friends.

"Mirabelle," she called as the hatch swung up silently. "You still awake in there?" She checked the area before releasing the cargo cover.

MIRABELLE CURLED herself into a tight ball, eyes closed. The sun was nearly up, her brain knew it; it was like hot lava lapping against her skull. She was nearly crazed with fear, bombarded by sensations she'd never felt before. She should be home in her closet by now, hidden beneath her comforting blankets, shielded by walls, curtains and doors. When the heavy back hatch suddenly flew upward, she screamed incoherently and stared terrified at the woman who stood framed in the artificial light of an unfamiliar building.

"Mirabelle?" the woman said. Mirabelle blinked, trying to concentrate on something besides the steadily diminishing beat of her own heart. "Mirabelle, you've got to move, hon. There's not much time."

"Move?" Mirabelle rasped. She stared at the strange woman, struggling to see, to distinguish details against the thick fog that had rolled in from somewhere, hiding everything behind a veil of gray. She remembered fog. Her parents had taken them to a beach once in winter, her and Elizabeth. The puffy, gray clouds had been sitting on the sand like a wall of dirty cotton balls. It had been strange to walk through them, to feel the clinging, damp fingers of mist on her skin and hair.

". . . hurry . . . find us . . . I can't . . . Elizabeth . . ."

Mirabelle's attention sharpened. The woman was still talking. Elizabeth? What about Elizabeth? The woman wanted her to go with her somewhere. To see Elizabeth? Did Liz need her, was she hurt? Had Jabril taken her already? Mirabelle pushed herself up, awkward in the confined space. The woman gripped her hand to help. She was strong. Much stronger than Mirabelle. No, that couldn't be right. Mirabelle was Vampire. She should be stronger. She let the woman pull her to her feet, let her shuffle them along toward some stairs. Not too many stairs, only a few. Then they were inside. That was good. The sun was up; she had to get inside. It was dark here, safe. She tumbled into the darkness, felt something soft beneath her, and then nothing at all.

CYN STAGGERED under the abruptly dead weight of the vampire, barely making it to the narrow bed chamber in the back of the plane before letting her fall. She did her best to straighten out Mirabelle's limbs, then covered her with a light blanket, checked the temperature controls and slipped back into the main cabin. She closed the door behind her and ran down the short aisle, taking the stairs two at a time as she raced back to the SUV and grabbed her backpack and suitcase. She left the keys on the seat. The rental company would pick it up tomorrow, and the hotel would show her still in residence for two more days if anyone checked. It was a faint deception, but it was all she had.

The pilot was waiting in the doorway. He had that almost stereotypical look that all pilots seemed to have—average height, slender, middle aged, casually good-looking, but nothing to turn heads. He greeted her by name, taking her suitcase and stowing it with an impersonal smile before pulling up the stairs and securing the hatch. Cyn collapsed into the nearest seat and buckled in, her hands gripping the armrests as she waited for the plane to begin its journey onto the runway.

Minutes later, they were lifting into the sky and Houston was dropping away behind them. Cyn sighed in relief as every muscle in her neck seemed to relax at once. Their flying time to Santa Monica was about three hours, every minute of it through blessedly bright sunshine. She yanked off her high-heeled boots and stood to retrieve her suitcase, marveling at the thick carpeting beneath her bare feet. The leather skirt and boots went into the suitcase, replaced by her faded denims and a pair of socks.

She helped herself to a glass of wine from the complimentary stock and sank into the soft, comfortable chair, pressing buttons until it was fully reclined. There were times, Cyn thought, when it was good to be her father's daughter. He might not have been around much when she was growing up, and God knew they had little in the way of a father-daughter relationship even now. But at times like this, when she needed a last minute charter on a private jet, she was very grateful for the Leighton name and the generous trust fund that came with it. She was already half asleep when the intercom buzzed.

"We're at our cruising altitude, Ms. Leighton. It looks like a smooth ride all the way to L.A."

She pressed the reply button. "Thank you. I'm probably going to sleep until we land, so don't worry about me."

"Yes, ma'am. I'll let you know before we begin our final approach."

"Sounds perfect. Thanks again." She pulled up the blanket and fell asleep before she had time to wonder if she would dream.

Chapter Fifteen

SOMEONE WAS screaming. Cyn shot to her feet, stumbled and reached out, unable to see even her own hand. It was pitch black, blacker than a moonless night on the beach, with not even the faint gleam of starlight. She blinked rapidly, hands raised to touch her own face, her open eyes. The screams grew louder, filled with pain. Her heart beat wildly as she fumbled in the direction of the sound, flailing hands finding nothing to hold onto—no walls, no furniture, nothing.

The screams stopped, chopped off in mid-breath, and Cyn froze, struggling to breathe, to slow her pounding heart, to hear. The space around her was vast, echoing in its emptiness. A delicate sound broke the silence, a woman's soft voice, pleading in words she couldn't understand. A man's cruel laughter hissed out and with a wail of terror, the woman's torment resumed, filling the thick darkness with the sound of fear. Cyn crouched close to the ground, arms wrapped around her head in a vain attempt to block the terrible noise, lips clenched against a whimper of her own.

Something touched her in the darkness. It was the faintest brush against her bare arm, but it clung. Cold. Evil. Jabril Karim.

She ran. His laughter followed, delighting in her fear, reaching out to stroke her face, her back, random touches of greasy menace. She knew somehow he was toying with her; that he could pluck her from the dark and suck her under, drowning her in his oily miasma until her voice rose to join the chorus of hopelessness.

Arms came around her, holding her to a broad chest. She fought silently, refusing to give sound to her terror, kicking and punching.

"Softly, my Cyn." She froze at the familiar voice, honey sweet and velvet soft, wrapping her in safety, shutting out the screams, shutting out everything but his touch. The arms tightened, his cool strength washing away her terror, his sensuous lips soaking up the tears she didn't know she'd shed. She sagged against him, her arms sliding around his slim waist, clinging to his strength. "Sleep for now, sweet Cyn."

Los Angeles, California

CYN JOLTED AWAKE, her heart still hammering with terror. She fumbled with the unfamiliar seat controls, finally jerking the window shade open and letting daylight stream into the dark cabin. She closed her eyes in relief, feeling the nightmare fade away in the strength of that single beam of light.

The pilot's voice came over the intercom, soothingly normal as he announced their imminent arrival in the L.A. area. Cyn clicked on the small overhead light and finally found the right combination of buttons to bring the seat mostly upright. In deference to Mirabelle, she pulled the window shade back down, and then stood, stretching her arms to touch first the ceiling, then the floor. Someday soon she'd have to get a real night's sleep in a bed.

She made her way down the aisle to the small, dark room where Mirabelle slept. The young vampire was undisturbed, her blond hair a pale jumble in the faint light from the cabin. Cyn pulled the door closed again and stepped into the bathroom across the hall.

The seatbelt sign was flashing madly when she returned to the seating area. For variety's sake, she chose a different chair. Not that it mattered, they were all identical—big and comfortable and upholstered in soft, cream-colored leather. Designed to accommodate well-fed businessmen and women, she supposed. With a glance at the closed door in the back of the aircraft, she pulled up the window shade once again and watched the familiar sights of the L. A. basin rise up to meet her.

Cyn had landed at airports all over the world—some beautiful, some ugly, some green, some in the middle of the biggest cities on Earth—but there was a special feeling to landing at your home airport. It was knowing you would soon get in your own car and open your own front door, eat from your own refrigerator and take a shower in your own bathroom. And most blessedly of all, it was knowing you'd soon be sleeping in your own bed, beneath your own sheets. It was like no other feeling in the world. The plane came down with a gentle thump and she was home.

PART OF HER deal with the charter company was use of the aircraft in the private hangar until after sunset. It was one of those vampire-friendly amenities, along with the windowless sleeping quarters now occupied by Mirabelle. It had sounded great at the time, precisely what she needed. But once on the ground, Cyn was faced with the reality of waiting several hours for Mirabelle to wake up. And it was not even noon.

Too wound up to sleep or even sit still, Cyn prowled down the aisle and checked once more on the sleeping vampire. She left the door to the bedroom open a crack, so if Mirabelle woke, she'd have at least a little light to see by. She'd seemed pretty out of it in Houston, and Cyn didn't want her to freak out when she woke up in a strange place.

Out in the hangar, Cyn could hear the steady buzz of small aircraft taking off and landing on the nearby runway, mixed with the occasional whine of a private jet. This airport handled only general aviation, so there was probably nothing bigger on the runways than her own chartered jet. The hangar itself was big enough for two, but the company had assured her the building would be empty except for her.

Cyn preferred to be certain, so she did a quick walk-around of her own. There was a windowed office against one wall, with a couple of desks and the usual office paraphernalia, but the door was locked and the lights were off. A pair of restrooms and a maintenance room of some sort completed the grand tour. Once she'd checked the locks on all the exterior doors, she went back to the plane and sat on the stairs to rummage in her backpack for her cell phone.

There were several messages from Raphael's number, which she deleted without listening. It could have been Duncan calling, but she didn't want to chance it. Raphael was altogether too good at convincing her that whatever he wanted was reasonable. And besides, Cyn had her pride. He'd walked away from her weeks ago and now suddenly he was all hot to get a hold of her. Was it coincidence that she'd recently been in Texas with a rival vampire lord? Cyn didn't believe in coincidences. Especially not where vampires were concerned. They made Machiavelli look like a piker.

There were two other messages, one from Dean Eckhoff, her old training officer at the LAPD, and one from Lucia Shinn, her friend from college who ran the teenage shelter and whose name she'd given to both Ramona Hewitt and Liz's friend Kelli. She called Lucia first, hoping against hope that Elizabeth had gotten the number from Kelli and called in.

"Hello?" The teenager's voice held so much suspicion and resentment that Cyn wondered why the kid bothered to answer the phone at all. Not that she expected anything else. Luci gave "her" kids the run of the house as long as they observed some basic rules, which came down to no drugs, alcohol, or fighting. Other than that, they were encouraged to think of it as home—a concept which held few fond memories for most of them.

"Hey," Cyn said. "Is Lucia around?"

"Maybe. Who's calling?"

She rolled her eyes, but swallowed her impatience. "Tell her it's Cynthia."

"*Luci!*" The kid yelled so loudly that Cyn winced away from the phone. "*You got a call!*"

Cyn heard Luci's voice as she approached the phone, soft and unhurried, as always. If Luci ever raised her voice, Cyn had never heard it. The self-appointed receptionist passed on her name, saying, "Some chick, says her name is Cynthia."

"Cyn! Where've you been?" Luci exclaimed a moment later.

"Hey, Luce, you rhyme."

Luci groaned. "So what took you so long?"

"I picked up your message two minutes ago; I've been a little busy. When did you call?"

"Two days ago. Where are you?"

"Sitting in an airplane hangar waiting for sunset."

"Waiting for . . ." Luci sighed. "Vampires, again? I thought you were in Texas. Someone from Child Services there called, Ramona Hewitt, and she said—"

"Yeah, she told me. We talked. Thanks. You haven't heard from my missing girl, have you? Elizabeth Hawthorn? Blond, blue-eyed, on the tall side, probably with a bit of a twang?"

"No," Luci said slowly, as if running through a list in her head. "No." More confidently. "What makes you think she's here?"

"She's the reason I was in Texas. Her guardian hired me to find her, and I'm pretty sure she took off for L.A. I gave your number to a friend of hers, hoping she'd get in touch."

"Okay, I'm confused. Is this teenager a vampire or what?"

"Not if I can help it," Cyn said grimly. "It's a long story, but if the kid shows up, don't call anyone but me, okay? She does *not* want to end up back in Texas."

On the other end of the line, Lucia sighed. "If she says it's okay, you'll get a call, otherwise—"

"Yeah, yeah, I know the drill. Tell her Mirabelle's with me; she'll call."

"Who's Mirabelle?"

"Her older sister and the reason I'm sitting in an airplane hangar instead of on my way home. Like I said, long story. So you called, what's up?"

Lucia drew a deep breath and let it out slowly. "I need your help."

"Anything I can do, you know that."

"You might be the only one I can turn to for this. Listen . . ." Luci's voice became muffled, as if she was shielding the phone. "Can I come over there?" she asked. "I'd rather not discuss this on the phone."

Cyn drew back in surprise, but said, "Sure, if you don't mind baby-sitting a vamp. Hey, as long as you're coming, can you make a couple of stops for me? I'm kind of stuck here—"

WHILE SHE WAITED for Luci to show up with her requested supplies, Cyn called her friend Dean Eckhoff. Eckhoff had been assigned to Homicide not long after Cyn's rookie year, and they'd stayed in touch after she left the force. He'd help her track down a local Russian Mafia bigwig last month, when she'd first been hired by Raphael to find his kidnapped sister.

Eckhoff had also stuck by her in the aftermath when an undercover operative who'd been working the same crime organization turned up dead. There were plenty of people in the LAPD who were still convinced Cynthia was somehow responsible. The dead operative, Benita Carballo, had been a friend of Cyn's, or so she'd thought right up to the moment Benita betrayed her to one of Raphael's enemies—a vampire who'd intended to suck Cyn dry. Cyn had escaped, barely. Benita had not. Her bloodless body had been found two days later and Eckhoff was one of the very few who believed Cyn had nothing to do with it.

The phone finally picked up. "Eckhoff."

"It's Cynthia."

"Yeah. We gotta talk."

"I'm a popular girl today. Everyone wants to talk. Can you tell me what it's about?"

"Not right now." He paused. "You're on your cell, right?"

"Yes."

"I'll call you in ten minutes." He hung up.

Cyn flipped her phone closed with a frown. That was two weird calls too many. Something was definitely going on. She stood and stretched her legs, then walked around the empty hangar restlessly, waiting for her phone to ring. When it did, she answered immediately.

"Yes."

"We've got trouble and, like it or not, you're in the middle of it."

"I've told them everything I know about Benita."

"Not that. Or not only that, although it sure doesn't help. Someone's killing girls, teenage runaways most of them; we've got five vics so far. All done in by someone with sharp teeth and a taste for blood."

"Impossible. Raphael would never—"

"And that's your problem right there," he cut in. "You're too close to the bloodsuckers, Cyn. People around here are remembering Carballo and your name's coming up again."

"Oh Christ, what now? I'm helping some creep kill little girls? Get a grip, for God's sake."

"I didn't say I believed it," he said thinly, and Cyn could hear the anger under his words.

"You're right. I'm sorry. It's been a long couple of days. Listen, I haven't even been in L.A. the past week. I got back an hour ago."

"Well, that's something."

"I'm telling you, there's no way in hell Raphael would tolerate one of his own killing humans like that. Something's not right about this. How long's it been going on?"

"You know I'm not supposed to say anything. We've managed to keep it out of the papers because the vics have been all over the county and, for the most part, living on the street. But it's only a matter of time."

"You wouldn't have called me if you didn't have something to say, boss."

He sighed, remaining quiet as if thinking over his next move. "You're right. Okay. Five girls in under a month."

"Jesus! He's a busy little fucker. Luci Shinn's been trying to get a hold of me too. Is that why?"

"Probably. She's threatening to go to the press if we don't do something."

"Have you talked to her?"

"It's not my case, but I don't think anyone's talking to anyone so far."

"You know, if you'd take the few minutes to talk to her, she might actually help you out. And has anyone bothered to call Raphael? He'd know if—"

"Like I said, not my case, not my call."

"Well, shit, Eckhoff!" She thought for a minute. "Can I see the bodies?"

"What?"

"Can I see the bodies?"

"What the hell for?"

"Because I can tell you if a vamp really did them."

"The ME says—"

"The ME's in a hurry. Homeless girls don't make headlines. He sees a neck bite and blood and says vampire. Let me see the bodies, Eckhoff. I might be able to help, and you *know* I can talk to the vamps and Luci for you."

There was a long silence on Eckhoff's end. "Okay. But it'll have to be on the down low. I'll talk to my guy in the coroner's office and see what I can work out. You'll be reachable?"

"I'm pretty much stuck until sunset—"

"I don't *even* want to know why. Stick close to your cell. I'll call you when I've set something up." He hung up without saying good-bye.

Cyn stood and brooded for a few minutes, staring at nothing, pissed that she was trapped in this stupid hangar. *Damn it, damn it, damn it.* Now she felt guilty. What if all those calls from Raphael's number were because of this whole vampire murder thing? What if it wasn't even Raphael calling, but maybe Duncan or someone else wanting her help in dealing with the human police? Maybe Raphael wasn't pining away for her, after all. And didn't that just suck big time?

She was going to have to call. And not only about the murders. Mirabelle would need Raphael's blessing to stay in California, which probably meant petitioning for his protection or something. The vamps were big on ceremony and tradition. Mirabelle would probably have to swear some sort of archaic oath, something involving blood, she was sure. All terribly gothic and portentous, but whatever it was, it had to be better than living as Jabril's private kick toy. None of which changed the fact that Cyn had to call Raphael. Maybe she could reach Duncan instead. "Fat chance," she muttered out loud. Faint echoes mocked her from the heights of the empty hangar. She looked at her watch and nearly groaned. Hours yet to kill. She climbed the steps back into the plane and settled in to wait.

By the time Lucia called to say she was outside the hangar, Cyn couldn't get to the door fast enough. It had been nearly an hour since she'd spoken to Eckhoff. She had tried making lists of things to do, lists of clues to follow up, lists of people to talk to, lists of famous people she thought were dead. She'd even tried sleeping, for about two minutes. Finally, she'd pulled on her sweats and running shoes and had started doing laps around the interior of the stuffy building. When Luci arrived, she shifted her pattern and jogged over to the door to let her in, then stood there panting like a dog, one hand on her side which was beginning to ache.

Luci took in Cyn's sweat-soaked face and shook her head in amusement. "You couldn't find anything *else* to do with your time?"

"I couldn't sit still," Cyn panted. "Too much on my mind."

"That's one excuse. Okay, I think I got everything you wanted and I brought some food, but . . ." She gave Cyn a raking glance, somehow managing to look down her wrinkled nose, even though she stood several inches shorter. "You might want to clean up before you eat."

"What'd you bring?"

"Sandwiches from Bruno's. You'd never know it from looking at *you*, but it's cold outside and I thought something hot would be good. Is there a shower around here?"

Cyn grinned. "Are you suggesting I stink?"

"I would never be so crude." Luci stepped past, giving her shining black hair a quick toss. She looked around the empty hangar with a sigh, then shifted her glance from the jet back to Cyn, perfectly plucked eyebrows arching over dark, almond shaped eyes. "I guess we're eating in there?"

Cyn laughed and nodded. "It's pretty nice actually, and there's lots of cold drinks. Let me wash up." She started toward the women's restroom, turning around to walk backwards and say, "Dean Eckhoff called me."

"So you know why I'm here," Luci said grimly. "I can't get any of those bastards to talk to me. My kids don't mean shit to them."

"That's not true, Luce. Look, let me clean up and we'll talk."

Chapter Sixteen

CYN LICKED TOMATO sauce from her fingers and groaned with pleasure. "God, that's good. I swear I haven't had any real food in days. Between staying up all night with that asshole Jabril and chasing around a strange city trying to find someone with nothing to go on, I barely found time to grab a sandwich from room service. Although I did have some egg rolls or something in the hotel bar. Not what I expected from Houston, but . . ." She shrugged. "I guess I shouldn't expect a barbecue invite from a vamp, huh?"

"Hardly. Personally, I don't think I'd accept any dinner invitation from a vampire. I'd be too worried about what—or who—was on the menu. Especially me."

Cyn chuckled. "Don't believe the movies. Most vampires are pretty careful about consent these days." She popped the last of her sausage sandwich into her mouth and used a handful of napkins to wipe the leftover grease and sauce from her fingers as she chewed. "So," she said. "Eckhoff actually did call me because of your missing girls. Did you know the cops think a vampire's doing it?"

Luci frowned. "Why would they think that?"

"That's what I'm going to find out. Dean's going to get me into the morgue to see the bodies." Luci grimaced in distaste, but Cyn continued. "I should be able to tell if a vamp killed them. Although I really doubt it. The vampire lords ride their people pretty tightly. Something like this could cause a lot of problems and no one wants that."

"Maybe it's some sort of internal vampire thing. You know someone who *wants* to cause problems."

Cyn shook her head. "Not that they don't hate each other's guts sometimes. Believe me, they're exactly like the rest of us in that. But this looks bad for everyone, not just one or two guys."

"Well, if they're really like the rest of us, maybe someone's gone over the edge. You know, just plain crazy."

"Possible. Raphael's been calling me too; I don't know why.

Obviously, I haven't been able to call him back yet."

Luci frowned. "I thought you and he were—"

"We were, that is, we are," Cyn added quickly. "But this isn't personal; it's business. I know you don't like the guy, Luce—"

"Because he hurt you."

"It wasn't all—"

Luci gave her a reproving look. "He broke your heart."

Cyn sucked in a breath at the blunt reminder. She'd almost managed to forget it in the rush of events since she'd hatched the plot to rescue Mirabelle. Right. "Yeah," she said and continued quietly. "But Raphael's a businessman, Luci. And this is very bad for business. If he knows about it, then he's trying to stop it."

"I'm sorry, hon."

"No. No, you're right. I was getting carried away there for a minute. Look, Eckhoff's going to call when he has something set up. Probably much later tonight, when the morgue's quieter. I'll go over there and talk to him some more and I'll let you know what I find out. You've got to keep this to yourself, though, Luci. If Dean knows I'm talking to you, he'll be pissed as hell and I'll get nothing."

Luci made a zipping motion across her lips, then opened them and said, "I trust you. I don't trust Eckhoff or any of those guys, but I know you'll do what's right."

"Okay, thanks. So, what can you tell me about the dead girls? Were any of them yours?"

"I don't know much, not even their names, except for the latest one. She was pretty regular with us—Carlene. That's all I know, her first name, and that she was close to eighteen, maybe nineteen. You know how it is, Cyn, you're lucky if they tell you their real name. I've been trying to find out about the rest of the victims. You'd think the cops would be glad for someone who wants to help figure out who they are, but I can't even get that much cooperation."

"It's complicated, Luce. The murders were in different jurisdictions, different cities. It probably took the cops a while to connect them to each other, much less get any kind of coordination going. But believe me, they want to find the killer every bit as much as you do."

Luci gave her a skeptical look.

"Okay, well, maybe not as much as you, but you're one of a kind."

"Yes, I am," she sniffed.

Cyn smiled. "Go home, Luce. Go back to your little chickies and I'll call you."

Lucia stood, gathering up trash and shoving it into a grease-stained brown paper bag. "You're a bad influence. I don't know why I let you talk me into eating this junk," she groused, wiping her hands.

"Because it tastes good. Did you have a chance to—" She stopped when Luci held up a bag with the Gap logo across the side.

"Best I could do on short notice, but it's all there."

"It's perfect, Luce. Thanks. I'll take her shopping in the next couple of days, but you wouldn't believe what she's been wearing. She's twenty-three years old and dresses like someone's grandmother. Not my grandmother, of course, she'd never be caught dead in those things."

"Your grandmother has excellent taste. I saw her at a banquet last week."

"You see her more than I do."

"That's because I actually participate in my community's events."

"Uh huh." Cyn didn't rise to the bait. Luci was always after her to attend some fund-raising get-together. Cyn gave her friend a sweet smile.

Luci shook her head in disgust. "Okay. I'm off. Don't leave me hanging, Cyn. Call me. Even if you don't have anything new to tell me, you need to call, okay?"

"Don't count on anything tonight. It'll probably be pretty late by the time I meet Eckhoff, and it may take a while to follow up on what I find out." They walked together to the hangar door, and Cyn caught a troubled look on her friend's face. "Don't worry, Luce, I'll call you tomorrow night at the latest."

"That's not what I'm worrying about."

"Don't worry about that either. Raphael and I are history. This is strictly business."

"So you say." Luci beeped her car open, then threw her purse inside and slid onto the driver's seat. Starting the car, she gave a little wave through the open window and drove away.

Cyn returned the wave with a smile. She didn't make friends easily and rarely held onto them once she did. But the friends she kept were important to her. Benita had been important. Her death had been painful in part because she'd betrayed Cyn, but also because she was gone. Cyn missed her in spite of everything. Shielding her eyes against the sun, which had broken out of the cloud cover in time for a brilliant sunset, she watched until Luci's car made a turn that took it out of sight around the buildings. Then she pulled out her cell phone.

She waited through the automated greeting and said, "Duncan, it's Cynthia Leighton. You've got my number." It wouldn't be long now. The vampires would be waking up soon, and Cyn had some bodies to visit.

Chapter Seventeen

WHEN IT GOT dark inside the hangar, Cyn located the main light box and flipped the heavy switches until both long banks of industrial lights far overhead were fully lit. Back inside the airplane, she turned on several more cabin lights and opened the door to Mirabelle's sleeping compartment to admit as much light as possible.

After that there was nothing to do but wait some more, so she paced back and forth in front of the airplane, stopping every once in a while when she thought she heard a noise, then continuing to pace. She was so intent on listening for Mirabelle that the trill of her cell phone startled her badly. With one hand over her pounding heart, she checked the display and flipped it open.

"Hello, Duncan."

"Ms. Leighton."

"I'm sorry it took so long to get back to you," she said.

"You received my messages?" He managed to put a world of disapproval and disappointment into those four words.

"Um, yeah. Sort of. My cell's been acting weird."

"I see."

She signed loudly enough to be sure he'd hear. "I'm sorry, okay? I thought . . . Never mind what I thought. What can I do for you?" she said in her most chipper, businesslike voice.

"Where are you?"

"Santa Monica Airport, actually." Which reminded her. "Listen, I need to talk to you—"

"How long have you been back?" He sounded puzzled.

"Since this morning. I've been sitting here waiting for sunset."

"Sunset." He was silent for too long. "Is someone with you, Cynthia?"

"Yes."

"Mirabelle Hawthorn."

"Yes. Don't say it, Duncan. She's here and she's staying. I couldn't leave her there."

"Jabril will not be happy to have lost her, Cynthia."

"Tough. He can't keep her prisoner, can he? I mean you guys must have some sort of procedure for vampires moving around. They don't have to stay in one place forever."

"No, indeed."

"Christ on a crutch, Duncan. Enough of the inscrutable vampire shit. What do I do now?"

"Where is Mirabelle?"

"Still out of it. I chartered a plane and paid extra to have it sit in the hangar until after dark—" Cyn broke off, thinking she heard movement inside the plane. "Sorry, Duncan," she continued absently, still staring at the silent airplane. "I thought I heard Mirabelle moving around, but maybe not. Shouldn't she be awake by now? I mean you're—"

"Much older than she is," he interjected. "It is likely she does not wake until well after sunset, although not much longer now, I would expect. Have you made arrangements for her to feed?"

"Feed? Oh, shit. I didn't even think about that. What do I . . . Damn!" Cyn started pacing again, her mind racing through possibilities. "I suppose if it's desperate, I could—"

"Do not," Duncan interrupted forcefully, "give her your own blood. Do you understand me, Cynthia? Under no circumstances."

"Gross, Duncan. I was going to say I could call Lonnie." Lonnie worked for Raphael, running a circuit of party houses in various parts of L.A. where people eagerly lined up for the chance to mingle with the vampires, donating blood straight from the vein in order to enjoy the mind-blowing sex that was offered in exchange. Lonnie could usually be found at the Malibu house with the beautiful people. "But why—" Cyn was about to ask why Duncan had been so emphatic about sharing her own blood, then sucked in a breath. "Raphael."

"Lord Raphael," he agreed grimly. "He would not take kindly to another sharing—"

"What right does he—"

"The consequences would not be for you, but for Mirabelle, Cynthia. And it is not only feeding she will need, there is the matter of protection."

"Fine, fine. So what—" Cyn spun around as a dull thump echoed through the hangar. She stared at the small plane, watching it rock slightly, as if someone was moving around inside. "Duncan," she said softly. "I think she's awake."

MIRABELLE WOKE slowly, her body sluggish, her mind dull, with none of the clarity she usually experienced on waking. She lay still, as always, listening, scenting the air. She opened her eyes. Light. There was too much light. Had someone opened the closet door while she slept? Was someone waiting . . .

Her heart, barely beating after her long day's sleep, skipped in panic as her senses kicked in. She wasn't in her closet. This wasn't her blanket and—she brushed away the unfamiliar covering and looked at herself—she'd slept in her clothes, something she never did. Her lungs expanded, taking in the strange scents of metal and oil, and something spicy, food, but nothing she could remember smelling before.

She sat up, pushing the blanket away with trembling hands, struggling to climb off the bed. It was some sort of platform, tucked into a small room, surrounded by walls on three sides, and her long skirt made it awkward to move around. Her legs dropped over the mattress edge and her feet touched the carpeted floor. A narrow door stood open in front of her, bright artificial light beaming in from the hallway. She rose slowly, one hand sliding up the nearby wall for support. She was terrified of stepping out into the light, but equally terrified of staying in the dark. The hunger decided for her, striking without warning, painfully intense and coupled with fear. What if there was no blood? Would she die? She'd heard stories of vampires living for months, years even, with no sustenance. Horror stories.

She took a step toward the light, crying out as a sudden stab of pain drove her to her knees, curling her into a tight ball of agony in the narrow space. Jabril Karim. Only he could do this, but why? What had she done? The pain doubled, then tripled and she screamed over and over, unable to do anything but give voice to the torment wracking her body. Every nerve was on fire, every muscle bunching and stretching at random until she thought her skin would burst and her body would fly apart. With no warning, the pain was gone, stopping as quickly as it had started. In the silence, she heard whispering. She scrambled toward the light, but the whispers followed, growing louder, pursuing her, threatening her with more torture, more agony if she didn't . . . what? What did they want her to do? *"Listen."*

Mirabelle listened and shook her head in horror at what she heard. *"Listen,"* the voices demanded again. *"Look."* She glimpsed an image. A dark-haired woman, her body lying limp, beautiful face rended with great bloody gashes as Mirabelle . . . She gasped out loud and stared down at her own hands, at her diamond-hard nails, at her fingers curled into claws like an animal's. She tasted her own blood as her fangs split her gums, forcing their way between her lips. She drew a shuddering breath, then she stood up and lurched toward the open door.

Chapter Eighteen

THE SCREAMS POURED out of the small jet, filling the cavernous hangar and bouncing off the metal walls. Cyn raced for the stairs, stumbling through the narrow hatchway in time to see Mirabelle crouched on the floor outside the sleeping compartment, her eyes rolling white with terror. When she saw Cyn, she shrank back into the corner, teeth bared, fangs distended.

"Jesus, what—"

"Cynthia!" Duncan was shouting in her ear. "Don't—"

"Hurry, Duncan," she closed the phone and took a step forward, letting the cell drop from her shaking hand. Mirabelle was crouched against the bulkhead, hissing defiantly, her hands curled into claws in front of her.

"Mirabelle," Cyn said, holding out an empty hand. "Mirabelle, it's me. It's Cynthia. You're okay. You're safe."

Mirabelle froze. She stared silently at first and then closed her eyes and began rocking back and forth, whispering something, muttering to herself. Cyn took a step closer, trying to catch the words.

"Please, please. I'm sorry, I'm sorry . . ." The girl was repeating the same few words over and over, arms wrapped so tightly about her body that she was drawing blood with her own claws. Her body swayed in rhythm to her words, her head softly bumping the carpeted bulkhead behind her with every cycle.

Cyn didn't know what to do. Why hadn't she thought about this, arranged for someone to be here, someone who would know what to do? Jesus, how long before Duncan arrived?

The phone rang and she snatched it up. "Duncan?"

"Which airline did you use?"

"Lonnie?"

"One and the same, babe. Which airline?" She told him. "I know it." He said something aside, presumably to whoever was driving. "Hang in there, Cyn."

She wanted to scream at him to hurry, but one glance at Mirabelle told her screaming probably wasn't a good idea. She thought about the hangar door. Was it locked? She couldn't remember. But, what the hell, they were vampires. If they wanted the door open, they'd open it. And besides, Mirabelle had opened her eyes again and was looking at Cyn with a distinctly hungry gaze.

"Okay, let's stay calm here, Mirabelle. I know you're hungry, but that was Lonnie . . . Well, you don't know him, but he's bringing blood."

Mirabelle hissed angrily . . . and did she lean forward a little, like she was getting ready to attack? Christ, maybe it was better not to talk about food, after all. Cyn lapsed into silence and began calculating how long it would take for someone to get here—Duncan or Lonnie, she didn't care which one. Either one of them could handle this better than she could. She mentally traced Duncan's route from Malibu to the airport, maybe stopping to pick up Lonnie? Yeah, okay, but that wouldn't have taken long; he could have waited outside the house and hopped in on the fly.

Of course, there was traffic. But this time of day going south, it shouldn't be too bad, not on the highway anyway. Her legs were killing her, crouched there in the narrow aisle, but she was afraid to move. Mirabelle seemed to have settled into kind of a watchful waiting. Geez, waiting for what? Was this like those nature shows on television where the big cat sits and waits for the antelope to fall over in exhaustion before attacking?

She nearly dropped her phone when it rang; she'd forgotten she was even holding it, she was so focused on watching the vampire's every twitch. "Where are you?" she whispered. She heard the fear in her own voice and cursed.

"Five minutes, babe." It was Lonnie again. He spoke to someone on his end, and then said, "Are there any cars in front of your hangar?"

"Not the last time I looked. I've got all the lights on."

"Okay, I see it. We're almost there."

She heard the distant sound of car doors and then the crash of metal as the hangar door slammed open. A pounding of footsteps on the concrete floor, the heavy shift of the airplane as they hit the stairs. She turned toward Duncan as he came through the door . . . and Mirabelle attacked.

Chapter Nineteen

CYN HEARD THE rush of movement behind her and then she was falling as Duncan grabbed her shoulders and spun her into Lonnie's surprised arms. "Duncan," she cried, struggling against Lonnie's hold. "Don't hurt—" She broke free, stumbling around in time to see Mirabelle freeze in mid-step, her eyes caught as she stared up at Duncan. He held out a hand to her, low and nonthreatening.

"It's all right, little one," he said softly. "You're safe here."

MIRABELLE STARED warily at the strange vampire coming toward her. He had a kind face; his big, brown eyes were gentle with concern for her and his voice lilted with a Southern drawl that sounded so much like her daddy's used to. A warm feeling surrounded her, covering her, sealing her away from . . . the voices.

She started, suddenly realizing that the voices were gone, not even a whisper remained. She closed her eyes in relief, feeling the tears begin to roll down her cheeks.

The vampire had crouched in front of her and was saying something. She looked up. "Who are you?" she whispered.

"My name is Duncan, and I'll take care of you."

"He wants me back."

"I know."

"I won't go back. I can't."

He nodded. "I know. You don't need to worry about that. Are you hungry?"

"Yes," she admitted in a small voice.

"Of course you are. You've had a rough time, Mirabelle, but no more. Can you drink from a pack?"

"Yes. It's all I've ever done." She was ashamed to admit it.

"I see. Well, that's fine then." He twisted around without getting up and said something to the two people behind him. Mirabelle looked up, really seeing them for the first time. Another vampire with long hair and . . . "Cynthia," she said softly, wonderingly.

"Hey," the investigator responded with a smile. "You had me scared there. You okay?"

"I'm sorry."

"Don't you worry, hon. We'll take care of you."

Mirabelle ducked her head, both relieved and embarrassed. Duncan was still talking, saying something in a low voice to the other vampire, and then to Cynthia. Mirabelle was still too disoriented to hear the words, but the other vampire, the one with the long hair, was holding some sort of box. She caught the scent of blood and the hunger twisted fiercely inside her, as if it knew sustenance was close at hand. She watched avidly as the vampire put the box down and left the airplane cabin. Cynthia regarded Duncan with a stubborn expression. Finally, she reached across the seat and hauled up a big shopping bag which she shoved at Duncan with a muttered oath before exiting through the open hatch.

CYN STORMED down the stairs, frustrated that Duncan wouldn't let her stay. "What the hell was that?" she asked Lonnie.

"*That,*" he said, "was probably her Sire trying to force her to go back to him. Duncan closed him off for now."

She stared at him in amazement. "Duncan can do that?"

Lonnie gave her an amused glance. "You don't get to be Lord Raphael's lieutenant by being a sweetheart."

"Oh. I guess I never thought about it that way."

"No reason you should, babe." She gave him a halfhearted scowl at the hated endearment.

"What's he doing in there?" she said.

"The kid's feeding. I brought a few packs over, didn't know how hungry she'd be."

"Why wouldn't Duncan let me stay?"

"The girl's embarrassed. She's young, but a vamp her age should be taking from the vein by now. It's like a six year old still sucking on a bottle. It's not her fault, of course, but . . ." He shrugged.

"So what now?"

"We wait for Duncan to decide what happens next."

Cyn didn't like the sound of that. "I think Mirabelle will be deciding what's next, not Duncan. I didn't break her away from that creep so someone else—"

"Save it, Cyn. The kid needs help."

She had to admit that was true. And Duncan had certainly come through for her tonight, so she was willing to listen to what he had to say. That's not to say she'd do it, but she'd listen. "So you guys are back in Malibu? I thought you all headed for the mountains after that mess with Pushkin." The late, and definitely unlamented, Pushkin was the vampire who had tried to overthrow Raphael, kidnapping his sister Alexandra to use as bait.

"We did. It didn't last long. The big guy hates the cold weather."

"Raphael's here too?"

Lonnie gave her a sly look, then laughed, but sobered immediately when Duncan emerged at the top of the stairs, descended and strode toward them across the hangar.

"How is she?" Cyn asked him.

"As well as can be expected," he said briskly, his Southern drawl back to its usual distant memory. "She is weak and undernourished; her former master all but starved her in his efforts to keep her in thrall, and that was on top of abusing her physically for years. We had no idea." He shook his head. "We knew he had turned her too young; we suspected coercion, but this . . ."

"Have you ever met Jabril Karim?" Cyn asked.

"Not in so many words, no. I've seen him, of course, at meetings. The lords rarely socialize beyond the formalities, and Jabril Karim even less so than the others."

"Well, I have. The guy's a total sleaze ball. He keeps a harem of blood slaves in his basement, and I wouldn't be surprised if they've buried a body or two on that estate."

Duncan stared at her in alarm. "Did he, that is, were you—"

"No," Cyn said shortly. "It was close at one point, but no."

"Thank God for that at least. We were worried when we couldn't reach you. You didn't answer my messages, and Raphael . . ." He stopped abruptly and sighed, rubbing his face with one hand. "Did you listen to any of my messages, Cynthia?"

"I told you—"

"Yes, I know, but did you listen to the messages?"

Cyn frowned and looked away, unable to meet his honest gaze. "No."

"No," he repeated.

"I'm sorry, okay?"

He watched her for a few minutes, gave Lonnie a glance and said.

"Lonnie, could you give us a moment?"

"Sure," Lonnie said cheerfully. "I'll wait outside."

Cyn stared at her own feet, aware of Duncan's scrutiny while Lonnie strolled over to the door, closing it quietly behind him. She glanced up. "So?"

Duncan smiled in amusement, which only deepened her scowl. The smile grew to a grin. "I am glad to see you safe, Cynthia. Even if you do bring trouble with you."

"I couldn't leave her there, Duncan."

"I understand."

"What now?"

"She should return to the estate with me. She needs regular feedings—I didn't exaggerate her malnourishment. Jabril Karim should be staked for what he's done. Unfortunately, few of the lords are as enlightened as Lord Raphael."

"What does Mirabelle want to do? Did you even ask—"

"Cynthia, when will you learn we are not the monsters you think us?"

Cyn drew in a deep breath. She was getting tired of apologizing. "I don't, you know."

Duncan raised a quizzical brow.

"Think you're monsters," Cyn explained. "I don't trust humans either." She grinned.

"I am reassured," he said dryly.

"What's she doing in there now?"

"Changing clothes, I believe. She was quite excited when I showed her your purchases. It was kind of you."

"Yeah, well, I can be kind too, you know."

"Yes, actually, I do.

"Okay, now I'm worried. Why're you being so nice to me?" She was only half joking.

"He will want to see you."

Her good mood vanished. She didn't even have to ask who "he" was. "Why?"

Duncan sighed impatiently, rubbing thick fingers between his eyes, as if he had a headache . . . or maybe two of them. "Jabril Karim may indeed be a creep, as you put it, but he is also a powerful vampire lord. He surely knew of your connection to Lord Raphael—" He held up an impatient hand to forestall her protest that no connection existed. "You took blood from him; you had sex with him, more than once."

Cyn felt a rush of embarrassment heat her face, but couldn't deny the truth of what he said.

"For a powerful vampire, the exchange of blood is a way of marking those important to him, particularly human lovers. Jabril Karim almost certainly sensed that connection the moment he saw you. He may even have called you specifically because he knew you were Raphael's lover. The lords are fiercely competitive. The opportunity to take one of Raphael's . . ." He shook his head. "When we couldn't reach you, we feared the worst."

She didn't know what to say. A part of her felt a little thrill at the idea that Raphael cared enough to worry about her. The more sober part resisted the idea that she was "marked" as anyone's property and resented being nothing more than a game piece between the two vampire lords, valuable only because the other wanted her. Or once had, anyway. "Well, I'm back now," she said, letting some of her resentment show. "And I'm fine. You can tell him that. There's no need—"

"And then there's the matter of Mirabelle."

She looked at him, her mouth open in mid-sentence. "Mirabelle?"

"I have shielded her for now from Jabril Karim's attempts to draw her back to his side. She would go mad otherwise, but it will not last. This is Lord Raphael's territory, and Mirabelle is the child of another. She is, as you pointed out, over eighteen and free to make her own decisions, but far too young and inexperienced to actually survive on her own. She will need Lord Raphael's permission to remain, and, more importantly perhaps, his protection to survive."

"So?"

He gave her a flat look. "Mirabelle must appear before Lord Raphael and petition him for protection, and I can guarantee that he will refuse to see her unless you agree to stand at her side. You are, after all, responsible for her being here in the first place."

"If it's so important—" *And if he's so worried*, she thought privately. " —why isn't he here now?"

"Lord Raphael is otherwise occupied this evening."

"Occupied how?" she asked quickly, ignoring an unreasonable and unwanted flash of jealousy.

Duncan shook his head with a look that was half amusement, half exasperation. He drew a breath and frowned. "He received a call earlier from the human police."

"The murders," Cyn said almost breathlessly.

He cut her a quick glance. "You know of these murders?"

Cyn nodded. "I called Lucia Shinn when I got back to town. I need to find Elizabeth—Mirabelle's human sister. That's why Jabril hired me in the first place. Her eighteenth birthday's in a couple weeks and he planned to turn her the way he did Mirabelle."

"Thus giving him control over the entire Hawthorn fortune."

Cyn nodded. "Fortunately, Elizabeth isn't stupid; she figured out what he had planned and didn't stick around for the party. Which is where I come in. But once I got there, two things became obvious. First, Jabril only hired me out of curiosity and to piss off Raphael." She shook her head at his expression. "I'm not totally clueless, Duncan. And two," she continued, "while I will definitely find Elizabeth Hawthorn, I'll do my damnedest to see she never goes within a hundred miles of Jabril Karim ever again. Because monsters come in all shapes and sizes, Duncan, even vampires."

"Indeed," he murmured.

"Anyway, Luci told me about the murders here in L.A. She's pissed and thinks not enough is being done to find the killer. So I made a few calls for her and found out the cops think they've got a serial killer vampire on their hands."

"Not just any vampire, Cynthia. Lord Raphael."

Cyn stared. "Raphael? They think *Raphael's* the killer, but that's ridiculous."

"They claim to have a witness to one of the crimes."

"But, surely. I mean, Raphael . . . he's never alone, is he? His security—"

"Precisely, 'his security.' The police do not credit any of our witnesses because they are, every one of them, Vampire."

"Well, fuck. I told them it couldn't be a vamp doing this, that Raphael would never—"

"They are questioning him at this moment."

Cyn looked at him in alarm. "Why aren't you with him? Does he have a lawyer?"

"My master ordered me to assist you instead, and yes, both of his lawyers are with him. The police originally wanted to question him at the station, but our people prevailed in that much. Lord Raphael is not without influence."

"Okay. Okay." She began pacing, thinking hard. "Look, I've already started looking into this for Luci." She glanced up. "I'm supposed to see the bodies later tonight." Duncan's face showed his surprise. "I'm not without influence either," she snapped. "I don't know exactly when, but

I'll need to stash Mirabelle somewhere—"

"I've already said—"

"Yeah, yeah, but I've been thinking about it, and she'll be better off with Lucia Shinn. Luci's used to dealing with scared, lonely kids, and that's what Mirabelle is, vampire or not. I'll pick her up before dawn and take her back to my place. She'll be safe there, for now anyway." She stopping pacing. "You're right, though. She'll need something else in the long run, but I'm not sure Raphael's place is it. You didn't see the Texas testosterone palace. I did. She needs something . . . else. I'm not sure . . . Damn it. I need to move around if I'm going to follow up on this, and she can't go with me. She's not—"

"Alexandra."

"What?"

"Mirabelle can stay with Alexandra. She is quite a bit older, of course, but their initial experiences are not dissimilar and Alexandra is . . . lonely, I believe, since the kidnapping, since Matias died. They were together for a long time and very close. He was perhaps her only real friend. It might benefit her to care for someone else, someone she can identify with."

"But . . ." Cyn drew a breath, trying to figure out a way to say what she wanted to without offending anyone. "Mirabelle is a modern teenager. Or she was before that asshole raped her and stole her life. She needs to be free, to be young again, and Alexandra . . ." She sighed, remembering the female vampire's perfect French manor home in the middle of Malibu, with its antique furniture and candlelit drawing rooms, not to mention her elaborate dresses right out of a big budget costume drama. "She lives in the 18th century, Duncan."

"She did," he corrected. "I believe the recent events were a wake-up call of sorts for Alexandra. She has been experimenting lately with other ways. In fact, she has asked Raphael on numerous occasions if *you* could visit."

"Me?"

Duncan nodded. "She was quite impressed with your, shall we say, businesslike dispatch of Albin, when you rescued her."

Cyn gave a very unladylike snort, remembering the vampire Albin's death. It had been a contest between the vampire and an Uzi. The Uzi had won. Not that he didn't deserve it. Albin had not only betrayed Raphael and helped kidnap Alexandra, but he had nearly killed Cynthia as well. "Okay," she said thoughtfully. "Tell you what. For tonight, Mirabelle comes home with me—if that's what she wants, of course, and then—"

"That's what I want."

They both looked up in surprise to see Mirabelle standing in the plane's doorway, wearing the clothes Lucia had picked out for her. For the first time since Cyn met her, Mirabelle looked like what she'd been before Jabril made her Vampire, what she would now always seem to be. A teenager. The faded denims were a little too big and the t-shirt a little too bright for her vampire-pale coloring, but it was clear that with a few weeks of decent feeding, she'd be quite lovely. Her blond hair had been brushed and tied back in a neat ponytail, revealing startlingly large blue eyes and a full mouth.

Cyn smiled at her, delighted. "What say we have a bonfire and burn those old rags, Mirabelle? We can drink champagne and dance around the fire naked."

"Whoa, can I come?" Lonnie was standing in the open door, staring at the girl.

"No," Cyn said, giving him a dirty look. "Girls only. Come on, Mirabelle, time to blow this joint. I've got a friend I want you to meet and these guys have business to take care of."

Chapter Twenty

Houston, Texas

A DEFERENTIAL knock sounded on the door to Jabril's private suite. "Come," he said, his attention focused on the last of his cufflinks. He looked over his shoulder as the door opened.

"My lord, you wanted—" Asim stuttered to a halt, hunger warring with revulsion across his face as he surveyed the blood-soaked aftermath of his master's rage.

"Asim," Jabril said calmly, drawing his lieutenant's eyes away from the carnage and over to where he stood in the bathroom doorway. "I want the guards who were on gate duty at the sunrise shift change, both vampire and human, in my office . . . no," he said, changing his mind. "Better make it downstairs somewhere. There's likely to be a mess."

"The isolation chamber, my lord?" Asim said faintly.

"Excellent choice, Asim. Yes. The isolation chamber. See to it, will you?"

"Yes, my lord. Sire . . ."

Jabril cocked an eyebrow at him. "Asim?"

"About this." He gestured toward the enormous bed that took up most of the room.

Jabril glanced around, as if seeing it for the first time. Blood covered every surface, spattering the walls and furniture, drenching the sheets and pillows. The remains of what had been his favorite blood slave lay in the middle of the bed, her long, blond hair dyed red, her throat torn out and her eyes glassy and staring. Deep, clawing furrows had ripped across most of her torso, partially concealed by the body of a second blood slave, who hadn't been a particular favorite of his, but who'd had the misfortune to be chosen to serve him late last night. Which meant she'd been with him *this* night, when he'd woken to the realization that Mirabelle was gone. Stolen away by that cunt, Leighton.

A red haze covered his vision as raw fury threatened to overtake him once again, but he fought it down, bolstered by the life blood of the two slaves he'd recently feasted upon. *Well, at least their lives had been well spent, then,* he thought with satisfaction.

"Yes," he said absently, answering Asim's question. He was already thinking of other things, like how he was going to retrieve that ungrateful little bitch Mirabelle. She would pay for this little rebellion when he found her. It would be a very, very long time before she ever dared consider challenging his dominion again. "Have this cleaned up before morning," he told Asim. He turned to his closet—thankfully the doors had been closed, his entire wardrobe could have been ruined—pulled on a fine, tailored jacket and shot the cuffs of his shirt to precisely one half inch, before crossing the room toward the door. "See to the guards first, however, Asim. I want to know how this happened."

Asim nodded silently, leaving his head bowed and his eyes downcast as Jabril strolled past him and into the hallway. His lieutenant maintained his respectful posture until Jabril moved into the elevator and out of sight. Perhaps it was a good thing to demonstrate his power on occasion, Jabril considered thoughtfully. It reminded his minions of the price of failure—something the guards would be learning very soon.

Chapter Twenty-one

Los Angeles, California

CYNTHIA DOUBLE-CHECKED the address Eckhoff had given her, pulling to a stop in front of a two-story brick building. The street was quiet and dark as she climbed from her Land Rover; the only noise the sound of cars passing on Olympic Boulevard a couple of blocks away and there was little traffic this time of night. She looked up as she rounded the hood of her truck. At first glance, the building was indistinguishable from any other on the mostly commercial block, windowless and dark except for a few security lights around the perimeter. But the brick walls were new, and hidden among the security lights were discreet video cameras that tracked her progress as she made her way to the front door. There was no lock, just a keypad entry with an intercom.

Cyn wondered if she should announce her presence by pushing the buzzer. When Eckhoff had finally called her, he'd been adamant that this visit was off the record. She'd been at Luci's dropping off Mirabelle when the call came. At first Mirabelle had been nervous about staying at the runaway house, but the kids had greeted her with their usual friendly suspicion, neither knowing nor caring she was Vampire. To them, she was one more of life's casualties, damaged but not yet broken. The tip-over had been when Luci had emerged from her office, gone directly to Mirabelle and given her a motherly hug. It never ceased to amaze Cyn that Lucia could hug a kid who topped her by a full head or more and somehow make the child feel safe again. When Cyn had left to meet Eckhoff, Mirabelle was sitting in the living room with the other kids, watching television.

The door opened while she was still contemplating the intercom. "How long you gonna stand there, Leighton?" Dean Eckhoff was tall and skinny, with washed out blue eyes and hair that had once been red, but now showed mostly gray. To say it was thinning would be kind. He was dressed in his usual dark slacks and tweed sports coat, his button down shirt neatly pressed.

Cyn shrugged. "I've never been here before. Is it new?"

He nodded, his eyes scanning the street outside quickly before he hustled her inside and closed the door with a firm push. "Some bright light decided we needed a special holding facility for vamps. You know, no windows and all that. Then it was pointed out that maybe we should have a special morgue too. For their victims."

Cyn frowned. "Their victims?"

"Yeah, for when they rise from the dead after three days," he drawled.

She rolled her eyes. "Jesus, these guys need to stop watching *Buffy* reruns."

He snorted. "You're not suggesting someone should actually study the matter before making a decision, are you, grasshopper? You know better than that."

"Right. Sorry. What was I thinking? Okay, so you're telling me the powers-that-be have decided the latest vics should be stored here in case they rise from the dead."

"Got it in one. You always were my best student. Come on, it's downstairs."

"Of course, it is." In her experience, morgues were usually in the basement. She didn't know why that was. Maybe the practice dated back to when there was no refrigeration and bodies had to be kept underground to stay cool. Or maybe it was some sort of symbolic burying of the unwanted dead.

They walked past the elevator to a fire door. Eckhoff pushed through and headed down the stairs with Cyn right behind him. The basement door opened to that indefinable morgue smell of chemicals, cleaning fluids . . . and something else, the smell of death. It wasn't putrid, nothing like rotting flesh or visions of zombies. But it entered her lungs with the over processed air and lingered, taking up space and making her work twice as hard to catch a breath.

"Cyn?"

She looked up and realized she'd stopped walking. "Yeah, sorry. It's been a while."

Eckhoff grunted. "You're not gonna wuss out on me, are you? Not gonna faint or, God forbid, puke? It'd be embarrassing."

Cyn grinned at him. "Gee, Eckhoff, I didn't know you cared."

"Not for you, Leighton. For me. I'd never live it down if one of my own rookies tossed her lunch over a dead body."

She punched his arm lightly. "Don't you worry, old man. I'll be fine."

He led her through a set of double doors, slapping the flat, metal switch on the wall to open the doors well before they reached them. It was designed for gurneys, so the techs could get the doors open ahead of the corpse.

A wiry blond looked up as they entered, his eyes gliding over Eckhoff and settling on Cyn. He rose from behind his painfully neat desk and removed a pair of reading glasses with one hand while closing the folder he'd been looking through with the other. He seemed too young to need reading glasses, and Cyn wondered if it was an affectation.

"Detective Eckhoff," he said in a low, whispery voice.

Eckhoff swung his arm, making a quick introduction. "Ian Hartzler, Cynthia Leighton. Ian's the night tech here at the para facility. Used to be downtown, but when they opened this place up, he volunteered."

Cyn studied Hartzler. He was about average height, maybe five-foot-eight, with shoulders that were narrow but square and well-formed. He had wispy blond hair and eyes so pale they nearly blended into the white around them. Those eyes stared at her, almost unblinking. It kind of weirded her out.

"Why?" she asked him.

He raised his pale eyebrows in question.

"Why'd you volunteer? I don't imagine there was exactly a rush for the position."

He smiled, a thin stretching of his lips that bared no teeth. "I am intrigued by the unusual, and vampires are certainly unusual, don't you think?"

Hartzler shot up on the weird meter from *kind of* to *definitely*, but Cyn kept that opinion to herself. "Well, they're different; I'll give you that," she conceded.

Eckhoff made an impatient gesture. "Yeah, okay. Let's get this done before someone shows up."

"Certainly." Hartzler walked over to a bank of gleaming stainless steel doors, placing his hand on one of the handles before he looked over his shoulder to ask, "You'll want to see all five? In order of death?"

Cyn nodded. It didn't escape her notice that the tech knew exactly which drawer to go to without checking the file or even glancing at the tag on the door itself.

Hartzler gave a satisfied smile, then pulled the door open with a dull thunk of releasing seals. Stepping into the opening, he slid the body out, glanced up at Cyn, as if to make sure she was paying attention, then pulled the pale green sheet back with a flourish. "Patti Hammel," he said. "Age twenty-two; cause of death, blunt force trauma to the skull."

Cyn frowned. "Blunt force?" She looked at Eckhoff.

"Exsanguination was post mortem."

Cyn's eyebrows shot up in disbelief. "Post mortem? But that's almost impossible. He would have had to drain her within what?" She looked at Hartzler. "Ten minutes, maybe?"

He dipped his head slowly, like a small bow of respect, or maybe pleasure that she'd asked him the question. "The heart stops, the body dies and blood begins to clot within five minutes," he confirmed. "Exsanguination would almost certainly be impossible after fifteen."

Cyn gestured at the body. "May I?" she asked politely.

Hartzler gave her another toothless smile and a nod, before stepping back and making room for Cyn next to the pallid corpse. Hammel's skin, which had probably been pale in life, was all but translucent in death, already dry and paper delicate, collapsing onto the bones beneath. Death was death. Refrigeration could only do so much.

The morgue tech offered a pair of exam gloves which Cyn drew on quickly before tilting the dead girl's head to better expose her neck. Two small, round wounds were visible to the left center of the throat surrounded by a considerable amount of bruising. Cyn wasn't a medical expert of any kind, but even she could see that the attacker had exerted far more force than should have been necessary, which argued against it being a vampire. Dark, bruised fingerprints suggested Hammel had been held in place while the carotid was punctured. Cyn frowned. Something else about those wounds bothered her, but she couldn't quite figure out what it was. She filed it away for later consideration and glanced up to find Hartzler's pale eyes watching her avidly. She straightened and glanced at Eckhoff. "Can I see the file, the autopsy photos?"

Dean regarded her silently, and then nodded in Hartzler's direction. Cyn heard the tech's shuffling feet, and a folder appeared in front of her. She opened it quickly, skimming through vivid color photographs of the many traumas visited upon poor Patti Hammel. It took little imagination to conjure the brutality of her final, terror-filled moments of life.

Cyn closed the folder and said quietly. "Can I see the others now, please?"

Hartzler seemed surprised, but he responded with alacrity, covering Patti Hammel's body and sliding it back into the anonymity of the coroner's refrigerator. Again without referring to notes, he went directly to another door and pulled it open, repeating his actions of only moments earlier.

"Jane Doe number one," he said, with the air of a game show host.

"No ID?" Cyn asked Eckhoff abruptly.

He shrugged. "These are street kids mostly."

"Luci said she offered to help, but no one called her."

Eckhoff flipped through the new file. "This one carried no identification and no one on the scene admitted knowing her. Fingerprints came back negative." He picked up Hammel's folder again, a frown creasing his brow. "Hammel wasn't on the street. She was one of those traveling notaries, subcontracted to a bunch of different companies. That put her fingerprints on file for the ID. No next of kin, no one she worked with knew her socially. Most of her repeat contact was by phone. She kept to herself, rented an apartment in Culver City. Her landlord thought she was dating someone, said she was gone overnight a lot."

Cyn looked up. "Boyfriend? Did he report her missing?"

"Nope."

"Curious." She looked down at the body of Jane Doe number one. "This girl's a lot younger than Hammel."

"The ME estimates sixteen years old, maybe younger," Hartzler confirmed. "She was a heavy drug user." He slid a hand down her arm, almost in a caress, turning her elbow out to reveal a rash of needle tracks.

Cyn didn't comment but went directly to the girl's neck, finding two neat puncture wounds that matched Hammel's almost exactly. "Same MO on this one?"

"Not exactly," Eckhoff responded. "No blunt trauma. We figure the assailant learned from the first attack and did it cleaner this time. Death was exsanguination, pure and simple. Plus, this one was on a high, no need to subdue her before the attack."

"Uh, huh. Next."

They went down the list, one after the other, five young women including two Jane Does, beginning with Patti Hammel and ending with the girl Luci had known from the shelter, listed only as Carlene Doe. Hammel was the oldest, the only one who'd been struck first and the only one not living on the street. The others followed the same pattern as Jane Doe number one; they were all under the influence, either drugs or alcohol, and bled out through the neck. Cyn pulled the sheet over Carlene's face and nodded an okay for Hartzler to return the body.

He did so with smooth, practiced movements, closing the unit door with a reverential flourish, before fixing those pale eyes of his on her expectantly. Cyn avoided his stare uncomfortably, busying herself with making notes on a small spiral pad she'd rummaged out of her backpack, wanting to remember as much information as she could from her brief scan of the files.

She finished writing and was shoving the tablet back into her backpack when Eckhoff's phone went off. It was a discordant jangle in the otherwise silent morgue and she jumped slightly. Eckhoff gave her a skeptical look and then stepped into the hallway, his voice drifting back through the closed doors. Cyn shuffled uncertainly, unhappy that courtesy left her stuck in the morgue until Eckhoff finished his call.

"I know who you are." Hartzler's thin voice was fevered with emotion.

Cyn spun around, taking an automatic step back when she realized how close he'd come to her. "What?"

"I know who you are," he repeated, staring. "You're the investigator. The one they trust."

She didn't have to ask who *they* were. "I'm sorry, Mr. Hartzler—"

"It's okay. You can rely on me to be discreet." He shifted his glance meaningfully in Eckhoff's direction. "Are you working for them on this? Is there anything I can do to help?"

"Uh, thanks, but no. I'm not really—"

"Of course, of course. I understand. It's difficult for them, I'm sure. One of their own." He slipped a folded piece of paper into her pocket. "If—" His mouth snapped shut as the doors whooshed open, announcing Eckhoff's return.

"We about done here, Cyn?" Eckhoff asked.

"Yeah." She grabbed her backpack and pushed through the doors, hurrying down the hall to the stairs without bothering to see if Eckhoff followed. He caught up with her before the door closed, his long, skinny legs taking the stairs two at a time. He gave her a questioning glance, but didn't say anything until they were standing out on the street next to the driver's door of her SUV.

"What was that about?"

"Your buddy in there is a vampire groupie. They dress up in black, stick fake teeth in their mouths and jerk each other off with fantasies of becoming the real thing. This is his dream job; he's probably the envy of all his little friends." She threw her backpack across the front seat and rubbed her arms vigorously, feeling tainted somehow. "He offered to help me out in my investigation for *them*, anything he could do. He's a nut job."

Eckhoff glanced back at the building. "Maybe. But he's *my* nut job, and he's reliable. I've used him as a resource for years. He knows this stuff as well as the docs, and he's a lot more willing to talk about it."

"Yeah? Well, maybe you should be looking at your *resource* a little closer, because it wasn't any vampire that killed those girls."

"How do you know?"

Cyn inhaled sharply, frustrated with her own shortcomings. "There's something wrong about it. I can't quite . . . How much do you know about this case? Why would the ME specify a vampire attack? I mean, have we ever even had one of those before?"

He glared at her in disbelief. "You mean, except for Carballo? You remember her, don't you? The cop we found drained on the roadside?"

"Yeah, I remember her, Dean. But since it was supposed to be me lying in the dirt while Benita was busy spilling the department's secrets to her vampire boyfriend, I can't feel too bad about it, you know?"

He looked away, his jaw clenched so tightly she could see white bone jutting against the skin.

"Dean?"

He kept his gaze on the distant traffic. "The investigating officer suggested on the scene that it was a vamp bite. Everyone downtown is seeing vampires in the woodwork since Carballo died, and we've got this nice new facility all ready and waiting to be used." He hooked a thumb back over his shoulder. "The bodies were brought directly here and autopsied to confirm the COD, probably on the fly. They ordered the usual—tox screen, some tissue samples from around the wounds, but it's low priority, so no results yet. It's not like they don't have enough to do downtown. Hartzler was supposed to take care of everything else."

"Great," Cyn muttered under her breath.

"I told you this isn't my case. I had nothing to do with this clusterfuck, and I don't know much more than you do."

"Who's the witness?"

"What witness?"

"Don't be coy, Eckhoff. You guys are claiming to have a witness who ID'd Raphael."

"Hey, you're the one who said they needed to talk to him—"

"Not as a suspect! It's bad enough you guys think a vampire is doing this, but Raphael? You're out of your mind. The guy's alibied tighter than the fucking president; he's never alone!"

"Alibis can be faked, Cyn."

She laughed. "Dean, if Raphael wanted someone dead, you'd never find the body. Do you honestly believe a vampire lord is leaving dead girls on the street? Do you have any idea how much power he has?"

"No, I don't! None of us do and that's the problem. We've got a dead undercover cop who no one denies was killed by a vamp, and now we've got dead teenagers littering the streets. How do we know it's not the same guy?"

Cyn stared at him, debating how much to say. "I've told you what happened with Benita. She was dirty. She trusted the crooks more than the cops and it got her dead. As for the vamp that killed her . . . you don't need to worry about him anymore."

Eckhoff gave her a hard look. "And you know that how?"

"Like I said before, if Raphael wants someone dead, you'll never find the body."

"Great. That's fucking great, Cyn."

"What do you care? A vamp killed her, and that vamp paid the price. One less vamp is a point for the good guys, right?"

The look he gave her was disappointed, almost hurt, and she blushed. "Sorry, Dean, it's been a long few days with little sleep. But you know I'm right about some of the others."

He frowned and drew a deep breath through his nose. "This case stinks."

"Yeah, it does. Who's your witness?"

"I can't tell you, Cyn. You know that."

Cyn thought about arguing, but he was right. "Hammel doesn't fit, you know," she said instead.

"We think she was an accident, that the guy got a taste for the vein after her and started looking for easier prey."

"If a vampire in L.A. wants blood from the vein, he doesn't need to kill for it. People line up to volunteer. Hell, your friend Hartzler in there would probably give his left nut for the chance, him and all his buddies. You know about the blood houses. What do you think goes on there?"

"Maybe this one likes the hunt."

She shook her head. "It doesn't work that way. One murder and Raphael's enforcers would be on him like white on rice. He wouldn't last twenty-four hours. These guys don't play games, Eckhoff, and they don't give second chances."

He sighed. "This isn't my case," he said again, and she detected an obvious note of relief beneath his words. "I can have a conversation, but that's about it."

"I know." She checked her watch. "Listen, I really have to run. I've got one more stop to make before going home, and then I'm going to sleep for about ten hours in my own bed." She rubbed her face tiredly. "And *then* I've got to get back to my real job, which is finding a teenage runaway before she becomes the next victim."

"This related to the Texas business?"

"Yeah, I'm pretty sure she ran to L.A. I've got Luci on the lookout, and I gave my number to someone who might still be in contact, but . . ." She shrugged. "You know how that goes."

"Needle in a haystack."

"Something like that. Okay." She slid into the front seat.

Eckhoff rested one hand on top of the open door and leaned in. "You take care, grasshopper. Whoever's behind these killings wants us to think it's vamps, and he might not take kindly to someone calling his bluff."

"What else is new? No, no." She waved away his objection before he could voice it. "I'll be careful. Now let me go home."

He stood back, letting the door close before slapping the top of her truck and heading down the street toward his own American sedan. Cyn did a quick three point turn and waved through her open window as she drove past. She had to get back to Lucia's, pick up Mirabelle and get the girl settled into the condo before sunrise. Assuming no other vampires decided to make an unscheduled appearance.

Chapter Twenty-two

CYN WAS DEAD tired by the time she pulled into the garage beneath her Malibu condo. Next to her in the front seat, Mirabelle was fidgeting with nerves, worried about her first sunrise away from the safety of the only home she'd ever known—even if that home had been turned into a prison by Jabril Karim. Cyn tried to reassure her, saying she'd stay with her through the day, that the windows were all covered with blackout shades in deference to Cyn's own night owl habits, but the girl remained terrified. Cyn really couldn't blame her, but she was so exhausted herself that it was an effort to deal with a twitchy Mirabelle.

She unlocked the heavy door from the garage to the condo and held it open for the girl, waving her in the direction of the stairs. "Go on up," she said. "I'll be there in a sec."

Mirabelle gave the stairs an uncertain glance before heading up, while Cyn pushed the door securely shut and turned to disarm the security panel. She frowned, seeing the row of green lights indicating the system had already been disarmed. Cyn rarely forgot to arm her security, and never when she was traveling out of . . .

She looked up at the sound of a loud thud from upstairs, like someone had dropped a suitcase . . . or a body.

Cyn stood perfectly still, listening . . . and heard nothing at all. She slipped out of her jacket and unsnapped the safety strap on her weapon, moving quietly to the foot of the stairs. It was close to sunrise; maybe the girl had passed out already. Duncan had emphasized how young she was.

Cyn started up the stairs, one soft foot at a time. She rounded the first landing and paused. There was a dark huddle at the top of the stairs; it was Mirabelle curled into a ball and clutching herself, whimpering softly. Cyn hurried up the last few steps, going down on one knee and brushing a reassuring hand over the young woman's back, even as she searched the room and found nothing. She flashed on the memory of Mirabelle cringing under the lash of Jabril's cruelty and wondered if

Jabril trying to contact her again. If Duncan's shield hadn't been enough after all.

A half-seen blur of movement had her spinning around, her hand going automatically to her shoulder harness and the Glock 17 waiting there. The shadows in her living room shifted as her hand touched the butt of the weapon. The gun was halfway out of the holster when she realized who it was.

"No," Cyn snarled. She slammed the Glock back into the holster and stood completely. Three hard strides took her into the living room. "No, no, no. You don't get to do this, Raphael. You cannot come in here and . . ."

Raphael straightened to his full height, his powerful frame looming over her, black eyes glowing silver in the low light. Those sensuous lips were pulled back in a confident smile, and shadows caressed the perfect planes of his face, showcasing his beauty. Every moment of heartache from the past month came flooding back to punch her in the gut, choking back her words and stopping her cold.

"What do you want?" She kept her voice low, hoping he wouldn't hear the pain beneath it.

The vampire lord stared at her, his handsome face unreadable. But then, Cyn had never been able to read anything there unless he wanted her to. She wished she could say the same about herself.

"I wanted to know you are well."

He sounded so reasonable. "Fine," she said. "You see that I am, and now you can leave."

"Cyn—" he began, but she heard Mirabelle moan softly behind her and hurried back to her side.

"It's all right, Mirabelle," she said, crouching next to the girl.

"I'm sorry, I'm sorry," Mirabelle kept whispering through her tears.

"It's okay. Come on, honey, get up."

"She can't," Raphael observed coolly.

Cyn felt a rush of rage replace the hurt. She stood, spun around in a single movement and marched over to him, getting right up in his face. "Don't you do this to her," she hissed. "She came back here with me because I said you were better than this, better than that asshole in Texas. If you're pissed at me, fine, be pissed at me, but don't you dare use her like this."

He glared back at her, every bit as angry as she was, and Cyn's first thought was to wonder what the hell right he had to be angry at anyone.

They stared at each other for what seemed like an eternity, and then he stepped around her and went over to Mirabelle, going down on one knee.

Cyn watched as he put a gentle hand on the girl's trembling shoulder and leaned down to speak directly into her ear. His voice was too soft for Cyn to hear anything, but Mirabelle's thin body stopped its shuddering, and she began sobbing in relief, her sobs turning to laughter, as every muscle appeared to relax at once. Mirabelle raised her face at last, staring at Raphael with something close to worship, her blue eyes glowing with tears in the low light. Raphael reached out a tender hand and wiped them away, brushed a stray tendril of hair off her face. Cyn felt a sharp stab of jealousy, followed instantly by shame that she could be that small. And that stupid.

The vampire lord stood, bringing Mirabelle with him. He spoke to her again, and she nodded, giving him a shy smile which she then transferred to Cyn.

Cynthia walked over, careful to keep Mirabelle between her and Raphael. "Come on, Mirabelle, sunrise can't be far away. Let me show you your room, and you can get changed into something comfortable. You don't want to sleep the whole day in those clothes."

Without looking back, she shepherded the young vampire into the hallway beyond the kitchen and from there into the larger of the two guest bedrooms. It was a pleasant, albeit impersonal, room since Cyn rarely had guests to speak of. At one time her half-sister Holly had been a regular, if self-invited, visitor. But the last time Holly had come to stay, she'd tried to break into Cyn's private study to steal photographs and videos of Cyn's vampire clients. Holly figured the purloined items would be worth a lot of money to the various tabloids, both print and television. She was right.

Fortunately, Cyn had caught her before she and her incompetent burglar boyfriend had managed to get through the locked door. Which had probably saved their lives. Vampires didn't take you to court if you violated their privacy. Their solutions tended to be more permanent.

Of course, Holly didn't see it quite that way. Not that Cyn cared. Holly was no longer welcome under any circumstances.

Cyn walked over to the closet where some of her sister's clothes still hung. One thing she had to say about Holly; the woman had excellent taste. "Let's see what we have here," she said mostly to herself. She shuffled through the clothes and came up with a predictably lovely and expensive silk nightgown that looked as if it had never been worn. "How about this for tonight? Tomorrow we can go shopping and pick up some things of your own."

She turned around, holding the nightgown, but Mirabelle was by the window, pulling the drapes back and forth, checking their coverage. Cyn threw the nightgown onto the queen bed and walked over. Reaching past the girl, she stretched up and pulled down the blackout shade. "There, you see," she said reassuringly. "The shade covers the whole window, but to be absolutely sure, we can pull the drapes across as well." She suited action to words. "Believe me, Mirabelle, nothing gets through. This room is pitch-black in the daytime."

"He's nice," Mirabelle said abruptly.

Cyn frowned. "Who?"

"Lord Raphael. You said he'd be nice and he is."

"I don't think I ever used the word 'nice' to refer to Raphael," Cyn responded sourly.

Mirabelle blushed. "No, not exactly. But he is," she insisted. "Are you guys—"

"No!" Cyn said quickly. "Well, not anymore," she amended. "He may be nice, but he's also an asshole. Never forget that, Mirabelle. Men can be all nice and sweet when they want to, but underneath they're still a bunch of assholes."

Mirabelle stared at her with that carefulness one uses with the utterly mad.

"Never mind. You don't need to worry about that. Yeah, Raphael's a decent guy when he wants to be, and he *will* protect you. Let's leave it at that. Now. There's a bathroom right here." She walked over and pushed open the door, sticking her head inside to make sure there were towels and everything else a person might need for a night . . . or a day. "The bed's comfortable . . ." Her voice trailed off as she saw Mirabelle again looking around anxiously. "Listen, Mirabelle, that closet is plenty big enough. If you'll feel better, we can—"

"No," Mirabelle said quickly. "No. I'm done sleeping in closets." She drew a deep breath and pulled her shoulders back. "I'll be fine. This is wonderful, Cynthia. Thank you."

Cyn smiled, relieved to see the girl recovering her backbone. *Not a girl, Cyn. She's not that much younger than you are, no matter how she looks.* "All right. I'll leave you to it. If you need anything, I'll be right outside, or upstairs. My bedroom's one floor up, but if you call out I'll hear you, okay? And I promise I'll be here all day. I'm totally wiped; you'll probably wake up before I do."

"Okay. Thanks."

"No problem. Sleep tight." It was indicative of how weird her life had become that Cyn didn't even think it was odd to say those words to a vampire going down for the day.

Chapter Twenty-three

CYN THOUGHT Raphael was already gone when she walked back into the dimly-lit kitchen. She was both relieved and oddly disappointed. But then she saw him standing near the windows, his back to the room as he stared out at the ocean. He blended perfectly into the shadows, and she was reminded again of how powerful he was, that he could draw the darkness around himself like a cloak against normal human eyes.

"Why did you call Duncan?" he asked.

Cyn blinked, surprised out of her contemplation of his masculine perfection. "What?" she asked, confused.

He spun with an uncanny grace that made every movement seem like a dance. "Why Duncan? Did you think I wouldn't help her?"

"No," she protested. "No, I knew you would; that's why I brought her here."

"Then why call Duncan?"

She didn't want to answer that question. She didn't want to admit how much it hurt to talk to him, to see him standing there studying her with eyes as silver as the low moon on the ocean outside. "It's getting late, isn't it?" she said. "Don't you need to be back at the estate?"

He smiled, amused at her clumsy change of subject. He crossed the room, coming close enough that she could smell the light, spicy scent of his aftershave, could see the slight press of his fangs against lips that she knew for a fact were amazingly soft. "Worried about me, my Cyn?" he murmured.

She closed her eyes briefly against the urge to close those last few inches and bury herself in his arms. "I'm not yours," she whispered desperately. "I'm not anyone's."

Raphael reached out to tangle his fingers in a lock of her hair and tug her closer. His nostrils flared as he drew a breath. "He touched you."

"No," she objected, before remembering the clingy sensation of Jabril's casual touch. "Just my arm, I didn't want—"

"I should kill him for that alone." His mouth was against her skin, his breath warm against her temple, and she couldn't remember when he'd gotten so close. Soft lips nibbled down her cheek to her waiting mouth. She whimpered a weak protest when his mouth closed over hers, when his arm wrapped around her back and pulled her against the solid length of his big body.

There was nothing of romance or seduction in the kiss. It was hard and demanding, hunger and need. Fangs ran out, nicking her tongue, and Raphael hummed with pleasure as her blood flavored his mouth. She pressed herself against him, needing to feel his arousal, to know he wanted her as much as she wanted him. He lifted her off her feet, letting his fangs sink deeper into the softness of her lower lip, and growling when the warm blood began to flow. The feeling brought a rush of desire, and Cyn twined her arms around his neck, threading her fingers through his short hair. She bit him back, pressing her human teeth into his soft mouth, reveling in the taste of his blood in turn, feeling a surge of ecstasy as it slid down her throat.

Raphael cupped her ass in one hand and brought her leg around his hip, grinding his erection into the cleft between her thighs. She cried out, wanting him more than life at that moment, wanting to feel his weight pressing her down, spreading her legs and plunging his cock deep inside her, hard against soft, satin against silk.

And she remembered Duncan telling her how vampire lords marked their human lovers. Cold reality washed over her.

"No!" She forced the word out. Her body screamed in anger, eager to fuck him; her heart broke once again as she pushed him away. She chose the anger over the grief, gathering it up and shoving both hands against his heavy chest. She stumbled slightly when he let her go. "Why don't you just tattoo your name across my fucking forehead!" she snarled, wiping their mingled blood from her mouth with one hand.

Raphael reached out impossibly quick and snatched up her hand to lick the blood away with a sensuous glide of his tongue. He stepped back, licking his lips and staring at her, his eyes hot with desire, letting her know how good it tasted. "If I had known you were going to Texas," he said silkily. "I would have."

"Bastard."

He drew closer once again, his breath mingling with hers as he stroked a finger down her cheek to rest against the big vein her neck. "Tell me you don't want me, sweet Cyn," he murmured. "Tell me, and I'll leave you alone forever."

She sucked in a hard breath, shocked at the idea of never seeing him again. "Go away, Raphael. It hurts me even to look at you."

He dropped his hand and drew away from her. Something very like pain flashed in his eyes before it was quickly shuttered and replaced by his usual carefully blank face. Cyn felt a momentary regret for hurting him, chased by a surge of disgust that he could still manipulate her so easily.

"Your Mirabelle needs to present herself," he said flatly. "This is my territory, Cyn."

"How does she do that?"

He smiled, once again the image of confident arrogance. "Call for an appointment. How else?" He spun around and swept up his coat from the back of her sofa. "It's nearly dawn. I have to run." Before she could stop him, he'd grabbed the front of her shirt and pulled her against him for a hard, quick kiss. "Until later, my Cyn." And he was gone, no more than a blur of movement, out the front door and down the outside stairs before the door had even swung closed.

Cyn walked over and slid the deadbolt home, wondering why she bothered when the biggest threat to her could obviously walk in anytime he wanted. She glanced out the window where the sky remained dark over a black ocean, the moon finally set. Somewhere on the eastern horizon the sky was already beginning to pale in advance of sunrise, but her condo faced west. She pulled the drapes against the coming day and climbed the stairs to her master bedroom on the third floor, turning off the small kitchen light as she passed through.

It was completely dark in her bedroom; only the glow of various LEDs outlined the familiar shapes. She stripped out of her clothes, letting them drop to the floor, and slid beneath the baby softness of her thousand thread count sheets. Her eyes closed and long postponed exhaustion claimed her, releasing her to dream of the vampire lord's embrace.

Chapter Twenty-four

THE WOODEN DECK was cool beneath her bare feet, the piped railing wet in the misty night air. She rubbed her arms against the chill and Raphael stepped up behind her, pulling her against the firm muscles of his deep chest. It wasn't true what they said about vampires. They weren't icy cold, nor were they dead. Their hearts pumped, their blood pounded, their lungs bellowed. Their body temperature ran a little cooler than human norm, which was probably the reason for the old superstitions. But when Raphael's arms enfolded her, she felt warm and safe, sheltered against the damp night and any threats it might hide.

"I remember my first sight of the ocean." His voice was a deep murmur, his cheek nestled in her hair. "It was crowded and noisy, filthy with the stench of unwashed bodies and much worse. I could barely see the water for the ships moored three and four deep against the docks."

Cynthia listened, still and quiet. He never spoke of his past.

"St. Petersburg was the center of the world then. Or so we told ourselves. It was the center of the empire and that was enough."

Russia, Cyn knew. He was talking about Imperial Russia.

"The port city of Brest, in France, was equally bad when I finally left Europe to come here, and New York even worse. I never knew the beauty of an ocean until I moved west. I remember coming over the hill, drawn by the freshness of the air, the salt tang of the water. There was a full moon that night and I stared like an untutored boy at the vastness of the horizon, stretching as far as the eye could see and not a hint that man had ever been here with his noisome habits." He drew a breath, tightening his hold on her, letting his lips linger against her temple.

"I knew then that this would be my home. I have houses in other cities, beautiful places with spectacular views of their own. But I have only one home, sweet Cyn, and it is here."

His head dipped and his lips trailed along the line of her jugular and up the side of her neck to place a gentle kiss at the corner of her mouth. She entwined her fingers with his, letting her head fall back against his shoulder and closing her eyes, listening to the gentle murmur of the waves, feeling the beat of his heart match the pulse in her own veins.

CYN WOKE ABRUPTLY to the familiar darkness of her own bedroom, her fingers stroking thoughtfully along the path Raphael's mouth had taken in her dream. She sat up, checked the clock and discovered she'd slept through the day. It had been nearly light already when she'd finally fallen asleep, and this time of year the sun set early which meant the vampires would already be stirring with the night. Which was good, because she had a question only a vampire could answer. Reaching for her cell phone, she flipped it open and was scrolling through her numbers, trying to decide whom to call when the doorbell rang downstairs. A full minute passed while she thought about not answering, but then she decided it was at least worth taking a look. She stood, pulled on her wrinkled jeans from the day before, yanked an old sweatshirt over her head and edged onto the balcony to sneak a look down at the front porch.

The vampire at her front door looked up immediately, her stealthy movements no match for his acute hearing in the quiet night.

"Ms. Leighton?" The dim moonlight gleamed yellow in his eyes.

"Um. Yes."

Fangs flashed as he grinned and held up the small cooler in his arms. "Lonnie sent me. He says it's for Mirabelle."

"Oh! Okay. I'll be right down."

Cyn stepped back inside, leaving the sliding door open. It was cold, but the steady motion of the waves was a familiar sound and the fresh air a welcome intruder. The condo was quiet around her as she made her way downstairs, not a stir yet from Mirabelle.

It took a few minutes to slide all the locks back, but the vamp was waiting patiently when she finally pulled the door open. He gave her an expectant look, but Cyn had no intention of inviting him in. She'd learned the hard way that once invited, there was no uninviting. It was irritating enough to have Raphael lurking around her house at will, much less some vamp she didn't even know.

She reached out and took the cooler from his arms. "Thanks. Hey," she said, remembering the question that had been waiting for her when she woke up. "Is Lonnie around?"

He shrugged. "At the beach house."

"Do you have his cell number handy?"

He gave her a slightly suspicious glance, but pulled a phone from his pocket and read the number off quickly. With a flash of irritation, Cyn repeated it to herself as she hurried across the room and deposited the cooler on the island countertop. She grabbed a pen and wrote the number quickly, then turned back to the door, but the vamp was already gone. "Guess, he didn't expect a tip," she said to no one.

When the door was once again closed and all the locks secured, she frowned at the cooler, wondering what to do with it. She finally settled on shoving the whole thing into her refrigerator which, as usual, was almost empty, so there was plenty of room. If it turned out Mirabelle preferred her blood room temperature, they could always warm it up somehow. A somehow that didn't include the microwave. Cyn didn't relish the idea of a bag of blood bursting inside her favorite cooking device. Maybe they could use boiling water. She vaguely remembered some acquaintance or other heating a baby's bottle in a cup of hot water. She shrugged. They'd figure something out.

Coffee came next, a process so automatic she had no memory of even doing it until she was cradling the first cup in grateful hands. She took a few life-giving sips, topped off the cup and climbed back upstairs, going to her office. The door was locked as always, which is what had foiled her sister Holly's attempted thievery not long ago. Cyn had caught the two would-be burglars trying to pick the lock. They hadn't succeeded, but she'd changed the lock anyway. She took no chances when it came to her client's confidentiality.

Coffee cup in one hand, she tapped in a code on the newly installed keypad, listened as the heavy bolt disengaged, then pushed the door open and walked over to her desk, flicking on the low desk light and logging onto her computer.

A quick check of her e-mail produced a jam-packed spam folder and not much else. There was one e-mail from Duncan—Alexandra had agreed to meet Cyn and Mirabelle at midnight tonight. How quaint. He also noted that Mirabelle's appointment with Raphael was set for—she checked the date against her calendar—one week from today. She frowned and punched up Duncan's number.

"Good evening, Cynthia," Duncan answered in his usual calm voice.

"Why so long?"

"I'm well, thank you for asking."

"Yeah, yeah. Good evening, Duncan. I trust everything is well and blah, blah, blah. So how come so long?"

"Until?"

"Mirabelle's meeting with Raphael. Why wait until next Sunday? Won't she be safer if we do it sooner?"

"Indeed, but there are formalities which must be observed. Jabril must be informed, although I think we can assume that part, at least, truly is a formality by now. However, he is also entitled to have a witness present to verify that Mirabelle's decision is freely made and not under duress. Once properly informed of her intent, Jabril has one week in which to provide a witness acceptable to both parties. Which means she cannot pledge to Lord Raphael before that time."

"Wait, are you saying that *Mirabelle* has to call Jabril? I don't think—"

"Of course, not. This is a matter between the two vampire lords. Raphael will be calling Jabril this evening."

"What about this witness?"

"What about him?"

"Can Jabril himself—"

"Indeed not. Council members may travel within each other's territory only by express permission, which permission is rarely given except for the annual meeting of the full Vampire Council which rotates among the members."

"So who will the witness be?"

"I don't know."

"Not Asim."

"Ah, that's right, you've met Asim. Charming man. No, it will not be Asim. Raphael would never accept him. No, it will be someone minor, someone Jabril won't mind losing if he steps out of line."

"Yeesh."

Duncan laughed. "Don't worry, Cynthia. There will be no mayhem. At least not in your presence."

"Good to know. Okay. I'll put it on my calendar then."

"I look forward to seeing you."

"Mmmhmm. Wait," Cyn said. "Is Mirabelle in any danger until then? I mean, is Jabril likely to try and snatch her back?"

"It would be foolish on his part, but he might be desperate enough to try, yes. Mirabelle's fortune is considerable and Jabril has treated it as his own for many years now. She will be much safer once she is within the estate, whether with Alexandra or here at the main house. You will be bringing her by tonight?"

"We'd planned to do some shopping first. Your note said midnight."

"I'll send someone over to accompany you, then. Perhaps Mirabelle would enjoy meeting Elke. I don't believe Jabril has a single female among his minions."

"You really think there's any danger?"

"No. Not this soon, but why take the chance?"

"Okay. Elke it is. Should we pick her up?"

"No, she'll be at your door within the hour. Wait for her, Cynthia."

"Like I wouldn't."

He was still laughing when he hung up. Cyn smiled. She liked Duncan. Too bad his boss was such a bastard.

A whole week, she thought. She would have preferred to have everything settled sooner than that, but maybe it was better this way. Mirabelle could recover a little from her traumatic break with Jabril, plus she'd have time to find something beautiful to wear on the big day—nothing like a gorgeous outfit to make a person feel good about herself.

Cyn entered the date on her computer calendar, and then wrote it in big red letters on a sticky note for her refrigerator door.

She quickly scanned the rest of her e-mails, dashing off quick responses to two inquiries from potential new clients—vampires both of them. She attached a list of her standard fees and terms, and then switched over to Google and typed in the search she was really interested in.

As she paged through the results, she stroked the side of her neck, once again retracing the path Raphael's mouth had taken in her dream. The search finally produced the image she was looking for, and she studied it carefully before printing off a couple of pages. The Internet was a wonderful thing. As she waited on the printer, a loud growl from the vicinity of her stomach reminded her she hadn't eaten in awhile—sandwiches with Luci. Delicious, but long ago.

Grabbing up the pages as they came out of the printer, she picked up her now empty coffee cup and clambered back downstairs. After a quick perusal of the offerings in her freezer, she decided to reward herself with a muffin. And not just any muffin, but a giant pouf of calories and sugar specifically designed to fatten Cyn up and help her get a husband. They were the creation of her housekeeper Anna, who was distressed by Cyn's continued singlehood and determined to do something about it. Cyn didn't exactly endorse the woman's marital crusade, but she was happy to eat the muffins . . . sparingly. She'd never had one tested, but there was little doubt in her mind that each of the golden treasures was packed with tasty calories. She popped one in the microwave and flipped open her cell phone to call Lonnie.

"Cyn!" he answered. "This is a surprise. Did you get the blood I sent over?"

"Yeah, thanks, Lonnie, listen—"

"You saw my note about making sure she drinks all of it?"

"Note?"

"I left a note in the cooler. Make sure Mirabelle drinks both pints; she won't want to, you'll have to push her, and she can do one now and one later if it's too much all at once."

"Um, yuck, but okay. I've got a question for you."

"Shoot."

"You guys were talking yesterday about Mirabelle drinking from a bag, rather than from the vein. That's what you said, "from the vein.""

"Yeah." Lonnie dragged the word out as if wondering where she was going with it.

"Right, so, do you ever drink from an artery? You know like the ones in the neck that—"

"Yeah, Cyn," he interrupted. "I know what an artery is. The answer's no."

"No? Like in never?"

"No, like in never."

"Why? I mean, why veins, not arteries?"

"Human Circulation 101, babe. Veins go to the heart, arteries come out of it. Which means the blood in arteries is pumping, hence the human pulse, thump thump thump. When a hospital draws blood, they stick a needle in your vein. Same for a vamp, nice, smooth flow, no big deal. You pierce an artery and you've got a real mess on your hands, and a pulsing mess to boot. Not conducive to a quiet meal, if you get my drift."

"But wouldn't that make it easier? You know, faster?"

"So who wants fast? Think about a can of soda. You pop the top and drink it and it comes out at a nice easy pace. But if you stick a tiny hole in the side instead, there's too much pressure and it squirts all over the place. You can't control it and you can't drink it fast enough. Same thing with blood."

"Okay, so in the neck, you'd use the jugular vein, right?" she asked, remembering the feel of Raphael's lips against her neck. "Not the carotid artery?"

"You got it. Why you wanna know this stuff, Cyn?"

"Something I'm working on," she said vaguely, her attention focused on shuffling through the images she'd printed off upstairs. She found the two she was looking for, pictures that showed quite clearly the location of the major veins and arteries in the human neck. Pictures that told her no vampire had put those holes in the necks of five dead young women in the county's very special paranormal morgue.

"Cyn?"

Lonnie's voice called her back to the task at hand. "Yeah, I'm here. Listen, thanks, Lonnie. That's what I needed. Oh, and about Mirabelle. She'll probably be staying with Alexandra after tonight. She'll be safer there until this whole thing with Texas is worked out."

"Alexandra?" Lonnie's surprise was obvious.

"Yeah. Duncan suggested it. That won't be a problem, will it? I mean you send blood over to Alexandra anyway, right?"

"Yeah, yeah I do. Let me know when you make the move."

"Great. Thanks, Lonnie. Talk to you later." The microwave timer dinged as she was hanging up. By the time she had poured a fresh cup of coffee and sat down to enjoy her muffin, she was hearing the first sounds of life from the guest suite. Mirabelle was finally awake and no doubt starving.

While she waited for Mirabelle to finish her shower, Cyn pulled the cooler out of the fridge and quickly scanned Lonnie's note. In addition to his recommendation that Mirabelle drink both pints, he'd included instructions for bringing the blood to the preferred temperature. She was amazed that her life had reached a point where heating up a bag of blood for someone's breakfast seemed commonplace, but it was ready and waiting when Mirabelle walked into the kitchen.

"Thank you," Mirabelle said softly, refusing to meet Cyn's eyes.

Cyn frowned, remembering Lonnie telling her the young vamp was embarrassed that she had to drink from a bag. "I'm going to run upstairs real quick and shower while you have breakfast, Mirabelle."

"Sure." Her relief was evident.

"Good. So, here's the plan for tonight. First, you need some real clothes, so we're going shopping. Elke will be coming over from the estate to join us. She's one of Raphael's security team."

Mirabelle looked worried, so she added quickly, "Duncan doesn't think there's any danger, but he thought you might feel safer that way. And Elke's okay." She paused thoughtfully. "Although, I wouldn't take her advice when it comes to *clothes*, if you know what I mean," she said with a wink. "After shopping, we'll head over to the estate to visit

Raphael's sister, Alexandra. If you guys get along, you'll stay with her. If not, we'll figure out something else. By the way, your meeting with Raphael's set for a week from today." She tapped the sticky note she'd placed on the fridge. "I guess there's rules to this vampire thing. Who knew, right?"

She started up the stairs to her shower, but remembered Lonnie's instructions. "Oh," she said, turning to make sure Mirabelle was paying attention. "Lonnie said for you to drink both pints of blood, but if you don't feel like a second one right now, we can stop back by here after we go shopping and before we head over to Raphael's estate. I don't know about you, but shopping makes me hungry."

"We're going to Raphael's?" The girl's face lit up with excitement.

Good grief, a teenage crush, Cyn thought. And on Raphael, of all people. "We're going to the estate, but we probably—*hopefully,* she added silently—won't be seeing Raphael," she clarified. "Alexandra has her own house there."

"Oh," Mirabelle said, somewhat deflated. "Okay," she added hurriedly. "Thanks, Cynthia."

Cyn paused again, halfway up the stairs. "No problem, kid, and please, please call me Cyn. Enjoy your breakfast." She even managed to say it with a straight face.

BY THE TIME Cyn had showered and dressed in her usual working uniform of jeans, sweater and cowboy boots, Mirabelle had finished the first pint and was sitting in front of the television, flipping through channels. She looked up as Cyn entered the room, her eyes sparkling. "This is amazing, Cyn. You've got like every channel on Earth here!"

"Yeah. Five hundred channels and still nothing to watch." A loud buzzer sounded, indicating someone at her downstairs door. "That's probably Elke," she commented, but taking nothing for granted, she crossed the kitchen to the security monitor and brought up a visual of Raphael's buffed and blond security vamp, wearing the dark grey suit that was the uniform of Raphael's security team. "Hey, Elke! We'll be down in a sec."

Elke looked up at the camera with a scowl at Cyn's cheerful greeting. The two of them weren't exactly friends and they'd certainly never gone shopping together. But Cyn didn't want Mirabelle to feel anymore stressed than she already was.

"You ready to go?" she asked the girl.

"Sure!" Mirabelle flicked off the set and a few minutes later the three of them were cruising down Pacific Coast Highway, with Elke a silent presence in the back seat.

"We'll hit Third Street," Cyn told Mirabelle as they passed the Malibu Pier. "It's a little cold for outside shopping, but we won't take long this time. Just some stuff to get you by for a few days." She glanced sideways, appraising Mirabelle's figure, still pretty much concealed by the jeans and loose t-shirt which were all she had to wear. "You're a size eight or so, I think. Maybe a ten when you're properly nourished, but I bet you've lost some weight."

Mirabelle shrugged. "I haven't bought any clothes since my mother died. Jabril always insisted I wear what he picked out. Liz too, but she snuck around and bought stuff for herself. She'd figured out a way to get a hold of some of our money, but she never told me how. It didn't matter anyway. I never had the guts to go against him. My big rebellion was wearing an old silk nightgown of my mother's."

"Yeah, well, that's history. Off the rack will do for now, but once we find Liz, we're going to do some serious shopping."

"You think you'll find her?"

"Hell, yeah," Cyn said, hoping it was true.

Silence filled the car for a few minutes. "Is there something I can tell Liz when I find her, to let her know you're with me? Something only the two of you would know?" Cyn caught Elke's look of surprise in the rearview mirror and gave her a dirty look back. What? Did the vampire think Cyn didn't know her own business?

Unaware of the silent exchange, Mirabelle thought for a moment. "Tell her I said we cows have to stick together."

Cyn glanced over, eyebrows raised skeptically.

"It's a joke thing from when we were kids. Liz'll understand."

Cyn shrugged. "Whatever you say. Listen, like I said, after shopping, I'm taking you by the estate to meet Raphael's sister, Alexandra. She's a lot older than you are now, but she was even younger than you when she was vamped. I don't know all the details, but she had kind of a rough time of it before Raphael found her, and then last month someone kidnapped her, trying to blackmail him. We got her back, but another vampire, a guy named Matias, died trying to protect her and they were pretty close. Duncan thinks the two of you might have a lot in common, that you might be able to help each other get through all of this."

"Okay." Mirabelle was doubtful. "Are we staying there then? At her house?"

"Uh, no. Well, you are and, of course, Elke will stay too. But I need to look for Liz."

"Why can't I come with you?"

Cyn sighed. "Look, I know you want to help, but the places I need to go, the people I need to talk to . . . they'll be reluctant to talk to *me*, much less someone they don't know. Plus . . ." Cyn scowled, trying to think of a nice way to say it and coming up with nothing. "I work alone, Mirabelle," she said simply. "I'm sorry, but that's the way it is."

"But she's my sister."

"I know that, and I know you want me to find her as quickly as possible. So you need to let me do my job, okay?"

"Right." The young woman sighed and looked out the window. "What do you think Lord Raphael will do?" she said finally. "I mean, when I go see him?"

"I don't know. Something formal and pretentious, I suppose." She heard Elke snort a laugh from the back seat. "Those guys seem to love stuffy ceremonies," she continued. "Besides you're the one who said he was a nice guy."

"Yeah, but he's also really scary."

Cyn laughed. "Well, we agree on that much anyway." She slid into a lucky vacant spot on the first level of the parking structure and turned off the engine. "Let's go shopping."

Chapter Twenty-five

Houston, Texas

JABRIL STEPPED OUT of the isolation chamber, feeling the slight displacement of air as the heavy door swung closed and shut out the stench of death filling the room behind him. The interrogation of his guards had been quite satisfying. Not that he'd learned anything new. But they'd been more than eager to answer his questions, and he had questioned them thoroughly. Yes, he remembered, with a contented sigh, he'd been most thorough. It hadn't saved them, of course. Their failure had been unforgivable, its cost almost incalculable to him personally—just the thought of it had his rage swelling in a bid to overtake him once more. But he disciplined himself, tamping it down, storing it for use later, when it would serve his purposes to better effect.

That bitch of Raphael's was the one responsible for all of this, interfering where she didn't belong. He hadn't needed the guards to tell him that much. He might have suspected the Western vampire lord of conspiring against him, but he was forced to admit the mistake had been his own. He'd invited her here, like bringing a snake into his nest, thinking to toy with Raphael, to prick that bubble of confidence the bastard wore like a second skin.

Well. He drew a calming breath. This wasn't over yet. He didn't care about Mirabelle. She was but a means to an end. The Hawthorn money belonged to him and him alone, even if it did come with two useless females attached. But he was getting ahead of himself. He smoothed his tie, tucking it beneath his jacket as he started down the hall. The first order of business was retrieving his property.

JABRIL SETTLED himself behind his desk, taking a fortifying sip of red wine spiced with just enough blood to make it palatable. He considered his next move carefully. If he waited, Raphael would surely phone him directly. There was no doubt as to Mirabelle's whereabouts, or who was sheltering her. Raphael would know that as well as he did. And if the girl thought she was going to shift her allegiance permanently . . . he took a longer drink of wine, swallowing his anger at even the thought of such a thing. But if she did, there were formalities to be observed.

He lifted the delicate ivory and gold handset of his antique desk phone and dialed a very private number.

Raphael answered himself. "Jabril," he said.

"Raphael." He heard the other vampire lord chuckle softly and gritted his teeth. "I believe you have something of mine," he said finally, allowing none of his frustration to seep into his voice.

"It is my understanding she no longer wishes to be yours."

"I'm certain that is *your* understanding."

"You may, of course, send a witness."

Jabril stiffened in surprise, thankful that the vampire lord on the other end of the line couldn't see him. He hadn't expected Raphael to move this quickly, or Mirabelle to act so decisively. Raphael, at least, had to know the significance of the stupid girl to him. She was more than a simple minion. Far more.

"Did you have a date in mind?" he asked.

"Seven days, as is customary," Raphael said. "The ceremony will be next Sunday."

"Hmm," Jabril responded, leaning forward and flipping pages, as if checking a calendar, knowing the other vampire lord could hear every movement. "Yes, I can rearrange a few things and attend myself."

Jabril could feel Raphael's smug smile even before he said, "I think we both know that won't be happening."

"Really?" Jabril said, feigning surprise. "What happened to that vaunted confidence of yours?"

"I was thinking more of Mirabelle's comfort than my own. She was quite traumatized when she arrived."

"I'm sure that is so. It must have been quite a shock for her to wake and find that she'd been stolen away from her own home while she'd been helpless in sleep."

"Is that what happened?"

Jabril fought back his anger yet again. "Asim, then," he said with perfect calm.

"No."

"Really, Raphael. If you care for the girl's feelings so highly, I'd think you'd want someone she trusts standing with her for this momentous decision."

"Indeed. Do you have one such?"

Jabril wanted to spit. "Very well." He thought quickly, running through the list of his minions and finding no one of particular use to him in this matter. In truth, if he couldn't be there himself, whoever he selected would be nothing more than a witness anyway, so it hardly mattered. He picked a name almost at random. "Nasir, then."

"Have your people provide the details and my people will meet him at the airport."

"Done." Jabril hung up without bothering to exchange pleasantries. He'd never liked Raphael, but then he didn't like any of his fellow Council members. He sent a mental order to Asim, who was waiting in the hallway outside. *No doubt listening to every word*, Jabril thought with disdain.

The door opened and his lieutenant stepped inside, ducking his head respectfully. "My lord?"

"Make the arrangements, Asim," he said absently, thinking of his next move.

"Yes, my lord."

Asim turned to leave, but Jabril called him back. "Where's that investigator of yours, Asim? What's his name—Windle. Does he have anything useful to say about Elizabeth?" He didn't believe it would come to it, but if he lost Mirabelle, he would need to be certain of the younger one.

"He reported in this evening, my lord, while you were . . . otherwise engaged. He's confident he will have her in custody within days."

"Excellent. Where does he believe she's hiding?"

"Ah," Asim said, obviously reluctant to impart this bit of news. He swallowed hard. "In California, my lord."

Jabril rose from behind his desk, his rage breaking free at last. His power swept out in a torrent of fury, sweeping everything before it. Walls trembled, doors broke away from their moorings and flew down hallways, windows cracked and shattered, sending shards of glass flying to slice into every surface like slender, crystal stilettos. Vampires prostrated themselves on the floor, moaning in fear and begging for mercy. Across the compound, the servants' quarters rattled as if an earthquake had struck, but the humans there knew better. They dropped to their knees, trembling, and prayed to whatever gods they had that they would survive this night.

Jabril stood, eyes blazing, arms stretched out to either side, feeling the terror of his minions, the distant horror of the humans. He drank it in like the sweetest nectar, feeling it seep into his bones and blood, giving him strength, giving him *power*. He was more than Vampire, he was their lord and they would damn well bow before his majesty.

He closed his eyes at last, bringing his arms together over his chest and hugging himself tightly, relishing the sense of fullness, the overwhelming rush of invincibility. He bared his fangs and opened his eyes to find Asim lying against a wall near the door, one arm obviously broken and blood seeping from a gash on his forehead.

Jabril regarded him narrowly, knowing his eyes still shone with residual power. "I want Elizabeth found and I want her brought back under my control. Do you understand me, Asim? Hire whomever you require, spend whatever you require, but get her back here. Do not fail me in this."

"Yes, my lord," Asim whispered.

"Now, get up," Jabril ordered. "We have work to do."

"Yes, my lord." Asim staggered to his feet, pulling the shreds of his torn clothing into some order and sweeping his good hand over the bloody gash on his forehead, which had already begun to heal. He stared at the blood on his fingers for a moment and then raised them to his mouth and licked them clean.

Jabril watched all of this with growing impatience. As if sensing his master's displeasure, Asim looked up and paled further as he hurried across the room. "How may I serve you, Master?"

"I will require your assistance with the accountants. I doubt Mirabelle will find the courage to remain in California, but we must be prepared for the possibility. Raphael is no fool; he will see the advantage of keeping her for himself. Fortunately, I still have access to much of her wealth, which is only proper, but I want every penny we can get our hands on transferred out of the country as soon as possible.

"Your will be done, my lord."

"Indeed, Asim. Indeed."

Chapter Twenty-six

Malibu, California

IT WAS NEARING midnight when Cyn pulled her Land Rover up to the front gate of Raphael's Malibu estate. The guard, one of six in obvious attendance, nodded to Elke and recognized Cyn, but he gave the truck a careful once over anyway, frowning when he saw Mirabelle sitting in the passenger seat. Raphael's guards were hypervigilant after last month's attack on the estate, and Cyn approved of their caution.

"Alexandra's expecting us," Cyn assured him.

He glanced nervously at Elke who didn't say a word, just sat watching him with those pale gray eyes of hers looking almost white in the dim glow of the gate lights. The guard paused, then seemed to make a decision and waited until his partner got off the estate phone with Alexandra's guards before signaling the okay for the gate to open. Cyn heard Elke chuckling softly to herself as she drove onto the estate proper, and she realized the guard had been torn between following routine and giving them a pass because of Elke's presence. She took it as a good sign that the female vampire was amused. Although, come to think of it, if Elke had been offended, the guard probably would have been on his back and begging for his life. Elke wasn't a member of Raphael's inner security team for nothing.

She drove by the expansive main house with its clean Southwestern lines and infinity pool, passed beneath an overhanging canopy of eucalyptus trees and entered the small clearing where Alexandra maintained her own residence. It was a French manor right out of the 18th century, complete with ivy-covered walls and blue-tiled roof. The drive swung around the side of the house, delivering them to the kitchen door, which was the only one anybody ever used.

Cyn parked and one of Alexandra's security team approached the car as they got out. Elke walked over and conferred briefly with him before coming back to where Cyn and Mirabelle were waiting. "No more shopping tonight, right?" she asked. Cyn was taller than Elke by several inches and the female vampire was looking up at her with a forbidding scowl, as if daring her to suggest otherwise.

Cyn smiled. Elke had been a good sport, but she was in no danger of becoming a shopaholic. "Not tonight," she agreed. "Mirabelle's staying on the estate, either here or the main house."

"Great," Elke said, sighing in relief. "Mirabelle, we'll talk. Leighton . . ." She paused uncertainly, settling for, "Whatever." She gave Alexandra's guard some sort of signal, and then she was gone, racing down the driveway and disappearing into the shadows beneath the trees faster than Cyn's human eye could follow.

Cyn gave her own sigh. That was a neat trick. She could think of more than a few times it would really have come in handy. She turned to Mirabelle with a grin. "Come on, Mirabelle, it's this way."

They went through the kitchen and down a long hallway to find Alexandra waiting for them, standing at the bottom of a wide staircase and obviously posed for dramatic effect. Cyn saw her and stuttered to a halt.

When Alexandra had been kidnapped last month, she'd been wearing the very highest fashion of pre-Revolutionary Paris—an elaborate satin gown with lace trim and a skirt that stuck out alarmingly to either side of her tiny waist. Her long hair had been carefully coifed and curled, hanging in thick ringlets down her back. Everything about her had screamed 18th century. She had even eschewed electric lights in the house in favor of candles, with every room decorated—or overdecorated, in Cyn's opinion—in the style of Louis XVI and his doomed court.

But things had changed. The Alexandra waiting to greet her this evening wore loose black trousers with a silk blouse tucked into that impossibly tiny waist and buttoned almost to her neck. The blouse was the deep red of a fine Cabernet and showed off the rich, lustrous black of her hair, which was still long, but hanging loose behind a black velvet headband. Alexandra was petite, a little over five feet tall in heels, and could easily have passed for a well-kept Beverly Hills wife . . . extremely well-kept since her face was that of a sixteen-year-old girl. She smiled and held out both hands in greeting.

"Cynthia," she said warmly. "I'm so happy you decided to visit. I've been asking Raphael when you would come."

For her part, Cyn was somewhat taken aback. She didn't know Alexandra that well, had exchanged no more than ten words with her in their single previous meeting. But having been tutored in courtesy at the finest prep schools California had to offer, Cyn rose to the occasion and took Alexandra's proffered hands, giving them the requisite polite squeeze, before stepping back to draw Mirabelle to her side.

"Alexandra, this is Mirabelle. Duncan probably told you something of her situation."

Alexandra's black eyes, so like her brother Raphael's, shifted to regard the younger vampire, taking in the neat khaki slacks and tailored blouse which had replaced the ill-fitting jeans and t-shirt. "Mirabelle," she said graciously, if not with precisely the same warmth she had greeted Cyn. "Welcome to my home."

Mirabelle smiled shyly. "Thank you. I hope we're not intruding."

"Oh, no. I welcome the company. Now that I've rejoined the living, so to speak," she added with a meaningful look in Cyn's direction. "I don't know why I didn't do it sooner. The clothes alone would have been worth the effort." She stroked the soft fabric over her arm. "So much more comfortable … and no corsets! I can actually breathe." She drew a deep breath as if to prove the truth of her words.

"Come, let's go upstairs to the music room." Alexandra placed a tiny foot on the stairs, pausing to tell Cyn, "It's still my favorite, though I have redecorated a bit."

She'd redecorated more than a bit and more than the music room, Cyn thought as she and Mirabelle followed her up the stairs. The most obvious difference was the brilliant light dancing off a huge crystal chandelier and casting shards of color against the pale walls. Gone was the pervasive scent and smoky tang of old candle wax. Ornate satin wall coverings had been stripped away, the walls resurfaced and painted in a delicate color that was little more than a blush of warm gold.

In the music room, the Steinway grand piano still stood in the place of honor, but the fragile antique tables and the satin and brocade upholstered settees and chairs that had so crowded even this spacious room were gone. In their place, a few well-chosen pieces accented a comfortable, overstuffed sofa and chairs. Fresh flowers graced the mantle and design magazines littered the low coffee table. Apparently Alexandra was still remodeling.

Mirabelle gave a little exclamation of delight at seeing the piano and hurried over, pausing just before her fingers touched the glossy black finish. "May I?"

Alexandra nodded in very much the way of a fine lady granting favors, and Cyn turned away to conceal her reaction. Some things, it seemed, had not changed. She wandered over to the piano, watching as

Mirabelle ran her fingers somewhat stiffly along the keys. "My mother played," Mirabelle said softly. "I took lessons as a child, before . . ." Her voice broke off, and then hardened. "Jabril refused to have a piano in the house; he said he couldn't abide the noise. Those are his words. He gave it away. My mother's piano."

Cyn glanced over to see Alexandra watching.

"May I borrow Cynthia for a moment, Mirabelle?" Alexandra asked.

Mirabelle frowned, concentrating fiercely on her fingers as they picked out a series of notes.

Cyn touched her shoulder and met Mirabelle's questioning glance with a quick smile of reassurance. "We'll be right back," she said.

Cyn followed Alexandra down the hall and into a room that was set up as a kind of home office.

"My dayroom," Alexandra said with a wry quirk of her lips. "The sort of room a proper lady would have used for keeping her household books or handling her correspondence. Not that I'm burdened with such things, of course. Raphael's people take care of everything." She kept walking, leading Cyn all the way through the room and out onto a generous balcony overlooking the front of the manor.

"You've changed a few things," Cyn commented as they stepped outside.

"Yes." Alexandra smiled slightly. "A few things. I felt it was time. Past time, really."

"You look good."

Alexandra looked down at herself and back at Cyn, her mouth curving slightly with pleasure. "I do, don't I? I wasn't jesting about the clothes. I don't know why I struggled with those horrible dresses for so long." She paused, listening to Mirabelle's enthusiastic piano playing, and made a moue of distaste. "She is a child."

"She was fifteen when her parents died, when the courts turned her and her ten-year-old sister over to Jabril Karim. She was eighteen and a day when he raped her and made her Vampire."

"I see. And does she want to stay here?"

"I don't think she knows yet."

Alexandra turned to study Cyn. She was a lovely creature, but with a smile that was less than genuine and somehow calculated, as if it could be turned on and off at will. "I like you, Cynthia," she said. "You've no pretense about you, and my life has been nothing but pretense for too long."

She strolled over to the balcony's edge and leaned delicately against the stone balustrade to gaze at the courtyard below. It was paved in black and white checked marble, surrounded by a tall privet hedge that prevented anyone from mistaking it for a usable entrance. Alexandra glanced back at Cyn. "Tell me," she said, her gaze returning to the gaudy marble. "What do you think of this courtyard?"

Cyn rested a hip on the stone and stared at the marble, wondering what to say. But then, according to Alexandra, she was the "no pretense" girl, right? "I think it's truly awful," she said.

Alexandra laughed, the first genuine emotion Cyn had heard from her. "So do I," she confided. "Although, once it reminded me of a better time, but I think I only had it installed to see if Raphael would go along. I kept trying to find something he would refuse me."

"Why?" Cyn asked bluntly.

Alexandra thought about it. "Do you have siblings? A brother or a sister?"

"A half-sister. We're not close."

"Raphael and I were. Close that is. We had two other brothers, twins who were much older and gone before I was old enough to miss them. It was always Raphael who took care of me, indulged me, protected me from our father's anger, and from the men on the surrounding farms who were bargaining with my father for a marriage before I'd even had my first blood." She shrugged casually. "Our mother was beautiful; I resemble her, of course. So does Raphael, although he has our father's considerable stature."

She glanced again at Cyn, gauging her reaction. "That terrible night so long ago, the night our family was attacked and Raphael and I were made Vampire. I don't know now if I would change those events even if I could, but at the time I hated what had been done to me. Hated what I'd become. I blamed Raphael for not protecting me as he should have, for not saving me from those creatures. For everything. I knew he was still alive somewhere, my vampire master taunted me with the knowledge, saying Raphael had chosen to serve his new mistress rather than be saddled for centuries with a useless little sister. It was a lie, of course. I know now that Raphael thought me dead along with our parents. But I believed the lie. Or perhaps it was only that I wanted to believe it.

"Of course, Raphael did save me eventually, although it was quite by chance. He found me in a dungeon in Paris during the Revolution. There I was, little better than a whore, living on the streets, stealing, murdering, seducing men so my Sire and his other children could drain them, leaving me the dregs. And then Raphael appeared—powerful, elegant, a master in his own right. He had finally come to my rescue and I hated him for it, for never surrendering, for never falling as low as I had.

She turned, placing her back to the courtyard and giving an elegant, little shrug. "So I made him pay. It was as easy as if we'd never been apart. He was full of guilt that I'd been enslaved for so long, that I'd been living in the gutter while he'd dressed in fine clothes and slept on soft sheets. And he was desperate to make it up to me. There was nothing he wouldn't do; I had only to ask. Eventually, I began to test his devotion."

"Did you ever find it?" Cyn asked.

"What's that?"

"Something he wouldn't give you?"

"You know, Cynthia, I did. Very recently, in fact."

"What was it?"

"You."

"What?" Cyn stepped away from the tiny vampire woman, suddenly uncomfortable.

Alexandra laughed at her reaction. "I told my brother I was lonely. With Matias dead—he died trying to defend me, but you know that, of course—I had no one left. I admired you, your strength, your courage. I wanted you as my friend, my companion."

"You could have called me on the phone," Cyn commented.

Alexandra gave a tiny, very pleased smile. "Oh no, you don't understand. I wanted him to make you Vampire so you could be my friend forever."

Cyn froze, uncertain how to respond. But something must have shown on her face, because Alexandra laughed again, altogether pleased with her reaction. "Oh, don't worry, Cynthia," she said breezily. "He said no." She sobered then, gazing pensively over the marbled courtyard. "I don't think I've ever seen my brother as furious as he was that night, certainly never at me. He didn't speak to me for days, and then only to inform me that if any harm came to you because of me, he would personally stake me."

Cyn's face must have shown her doubt.

"He was quite serious, Cynthia. And he would be very unhappy if he knew you were here today; I don't think he quite trusts me yet." Again that private little smile before she said brightly, "I'm told the contractor will be here tomorrow to rip out this ridiculous marble."

Cyn forced a laugh, relieved at the change of subject. "Well, thank God for that."

"He missed you, you know." Alexandra said, giving Cyn a narrow look. "I've never known my brother to miss a woman, to miss anyone, as much as he did you when we were locked away up there in Colorado."

Cyn blew out a breath, frustrated. "You know, I'm getting kind of tired of everyone pretending this is my fault. Raphael's the one who walked away, not me."

"Men are fools, Cynthia. You surely know that by now."

"Tell me about it," she muttered. A fresh round of enthusiastic piano music erupted from the music room. Both women looked up.

"Perhaps Mirabelle would enjoy some piano lessons," Alexandra said grimly.

Cyn winced. "Good idea. Can I reach you through the estate operator?" When Alexandra nodded, Cyn said, "I'll keep in touch then. And Mirabelle has my cell number if she needs anything. Thank you for this, Alexandra."

"Yes, well. Perhaps we'll be friends then, after all."

Cyn doubted it, but hoped for Mirabelle's sake they could remain friendly. At least until they worked out something long term for the girl. She smiled at Alexandra. The vampire wasn't the only one who could fake a smile. "I'd like that," she lied.

Alexandra's eyes gleamed with a greedy sort of joy, like a child eyeing a favorite candy. Abruptly uncomfortable, Cyn stepped away from the railing. "I'll just say good-bye to Mirabelle and be on my way."

"What's the hurry?" Alexandra said, mirroring Cyn's movement and more, coming close enough that Cyn could see the tiny creases in her carefully applied makeup.

"Cynthia!" Mirabelle's frightened voice broke the sudden tension and had both women hurrying back into the manor house.

Chapter Twenty-seven

IT WAS A FALSE alarm—Mirabelle reacting to the sudden appearance of one of Alexandra's many security vamps. Used to the Neanderthals who populated Jabril's lair, Mirabelle had been huddled in a corner when Cyn reentered the music room. The vampire guard had been almost as stressed by the situation as Mirabelle. It had taken only a few moments to reassure all sides, but Cyn had begrudged even that. She couldn't get out of Alexandra's presence fast enough. The old Alexandra had been a pretty anachronism. This new Alexandra made the sharks of Beverly Hills look like childish poseurs.

A short time later, Cyn left Malibu and the west side of town behind, driving aimlessly up and down Hollywood Boulevard and its side streets, stopping occasionally to flash Liz's picture. She'd always thought it must be an unpleasant shock when visitors saw that the world-famous city of Hollywood was actually a seamy, rundown part of L.A., home to more hookers and homeless than movie stars. With the exception of a trendy hotel or two, Cyn couldn't think of anyone she knew, or knew of, that actually lived in Hollywood. Hollywood Hills, maybe, high up where the dirt and crime were nothing more than twinkling lights in the distance, but not down among the seedy denizens of Hollywood itself. She cruised the known hangouts of teenage runaways, the shooting dens, the busy streets where cars slowed and sometimes a young girl or boy would take a ride to earn a few bucks.

Depressed by the whole scene, Cyn turned west once more, sticking to the side streets and alleys where a young girl might hunker down and wait out the night. She punched up Luci's number as she drove, hoping against hope that Liz had checked in. Luci sounded uncharacteristically harassed and out of patience when she came to the phone, and Cyn could hear shouts in the background.

"You need backup there, Luce?"

"What I need is a cage and some sturdy handcuffs," Luci snapped, then drew a deep breath. "Never mind. It's been a rough night. Tomorrow will be better. Any sign of your missing girl?"

"Not a whisper, but I've barely started looking. I finally met with Eckhoff late last night and got a look at the uh . . . files. I'm pretty sure the cops are on the wrong track, but no one's going to listen to me. At least not until I find something to prove it. I'm working on that too." Cyn came to a stop sign and looked around; she was almost on top of one of the murder scenes. All the reasons for driving right on by zipped through her brain. It was late; she was tired; it wasn't her job. What the heck. "I'll get back to you, Luce."

She hung up and took a left turn, parking as close to the scene as she could get while remaining reasonably confident her truck would still be in one piece when she got back. She walked the rest of the way, very aware of the night around her, sliding a hand beneath her jacket and releasing the safety strap on her shoulder holster. She didn't expect any problems, but in this neighborhood, it was better to be sure.

She found the crime scene easily enough. It was a couple of blocks off the boulevard, a short alleyway used by low-end shops for deliveries and trash pickup. The alley was dark and smelled pretty much like alleys everywhere, *eau de garbage* with an undercurrent of desperation and urine. She pulled out a mini Maglite and crouched, studying the area.

"You don't look like a cop."

Cyn spun around as the disembodied voice came out of the shadows, right hand going reflexively to the butt of her weapon. A boy stepped into the meager light, maybe sixteen years old, thin and underfed like all the others. His eyes were bruised, his knuckles scraped. He'd obviously been in a fight recently. Probably not the first or the last.

"That's because I'm not," Cyn said calmly, her hand relaxing, her eyes going back to the weeks-old crime scene.

"Joni died here," the boy said.

Cyn looked up. "You knew her?"

"Sure. Everybody knew Joni. She hooked up a lot, always had money and was willing to share."

"Share what?" Cyn asked, thinking it was probably drugs, remembering which of the bodies had shown visible signs of drug use.

"Food, mostly," the boy said, surprising her. "Joni got drunk sometimes, but she didn't do drugs. She had a few regular customers, old guys who liked fucking a little girl and didn't mind paying a little extra for the repeat experience."

"Yeah." Cyn sighed, too familiar with the story. "You think maybe one of her clients killed her?"

"Maybe, but it was pretty late. Almost morning."

Cyn quickly reviewed what she remembered from the file. The vic from this scene had been reported on an anonymous 911. "How do you know what time it was?"

"I found her. Sat with her until the cops came."

Cyn's heart skipped a beat. There hadn't been any witness reports that she'd seen. "Did you see who did it?"

"Didn't see it. Heard it though. I think I scared the guy away."

"What'd you hear?"

The kid looked at her, suddenly suspicious. "Why you asking all these questions, if you're not a cop?"

"I'm a private investigator." She pulled out a card and handed it over. "A family member hired me to find out what's going on." It wasn't precisely a lie.

The boy squinted at the card and back at Cyn. "Kind of like that wizard guy Harry Dresden from the books?"

"Kind of, but without the magic. So, was she alive when you got here?"

"I don't think so." A tired sort of grief washed over his features and he looked away. "Not long, anyway."

"What'd you hear before you found her?"

"A car and a lot of noise, like something big being thrown into the trash. I went to see what it was because sometimes people throw away good stuff, you know? It was a nice car, so I figured maybe it was something good."

"You saw the car?"

"Nah, but I could tell. The engine sounded all smooth and low, and when the doors closed, you could hear that nice thunky noise, not all kinds of rattles and shit."

Observant, Cyn thought, *smart*. She felt a moment of despair and wondered for the thousandth time why society threw these kids away.

"So what happened then?"

"Like I said, I think the guy must've heard me coming. He drove off pretty fast, burned rubber all the way." He gestured at the ground and Cyn walked over, crouching to look closely at the thick lines of indistinguishable black.

"If you didn't see him, how do you know it was a guy?"

He thought about her question for a bit. "Just figured, I guess," he said finally. "I mean . . . aren't they always?"

"They?"

"You know, serial killers, the guys who bump off hookers."

Cyn considered. "Did you make the 911 call?"

"How?" he scoffed.

"So how'd the cops know to come?"

The boy shrugged. "Someone else called them, I guess."

"Did you talk to the police? Tell them what you saw?"

"Fuck no. I split when I heard the sirens. Didn't go far, in case they weren't coming here, but then they did, so . . ." He shrugged again.

Cyn stared at the ground, thinking hard. The killer had probably called it in. And why would he do that? Because he wanted it reported before the sun came up, because he wanted the cops to think vampire. She stood slowly, reaching into her backpack. "When's the last time you ate?" she asked casually.

Another shrug.

She pulled out several gift certificates for McDonalds, along with Liz's picture. She handed him the coupons. "Get yourself some food, share it if you want, but be sure you eat some of it yourself." She flipped the photo. "Have you seen this girl?"

The boy glanced at the photo, but didn't say anything.

"You won't believe this, but I'm trying to help her."

"How do I know that?"

"You don't. Listen, I understand if you don't want to talk to me, but . . ." She found one of Luci's cards and held it out. "If you see the girl in the picture, give her this number. Tell her to call. Tell her Mirabelle says it's time for the cows to come home. That's important. She'll know what it means."

He gave Cyn a look that said he doubted her sanity. "Cows?"

"Yeah, I know, but tell her anyway. If you see her, that is."

He studied Luci's card with its information on the runaway shelter. "I've heard of this place," he said, gesturing with the card.

"Yeah?"

"It's supposed to be all right."

"It is."

"Maybe I could call too?"

"Absolutely." Cyn handed over a few more cards. "There's always room."

"I'm not saying I will."

"Nope. But just in case."

"That's right. Just in case."

Cyn walked away, thinking he might go to the shelter, knowing he probably wouldn't. But hoping he'd at least use the food coupons and not trade them away for booze or drugs. *Can't save them all, Cyn.*

She walked back to her truck slowly, tired and discouraged. She hated the runaway cases. These kids never wanted to talk to anyone, and with good reason, but it made her job much more difficult when she really did want to help out. She reached the Land Rover and beeped the locks open, throwing her backpack across the seat. On the other hand, this kid had seemed to recognize Liz's picture. Maybe he'd pass on the message. Maybe Liz would know her sister was looking for her and get in touch. Maybe.

The rising sun glared in her rearview mirror all the way back to Malibu. She pulled into the cool darkness of her garage with relief and closed the door behind her, shutting out the daylight. Ten minutes later, she was in her own bed, with the quiet sounds of the ocean lulling her to sleep. She told herself she didn't care if she dreamed or not. But it was a lie.

Chapter Twenty-eight

SHE WOKE UP less than an hour later with the vague memory of a helicopter zooming down the beach. Irritated, she turned away from the open door and pulled the blanket up, determined to sink back into unconsciousness. After her third restless roll, she surrendered, throwing back the covers in disgust. She could never go back to sleep once she woke up and her mind started churning.

Sitting on the side of the bed, elbows on her knees, she rubbed her fingers back through her hair and stood with a curse. Might as well get something done. Maybe she could catch a nap later. Right now, she needed coffee. Lots and lots of coffee. Alone in the condo, she eschewed any clothing beyond the t-shirt she'd slept in and made her way down to the kitchen where it took two cups of coffee and the start of a third before her brain cleared enough to focus on any meaningful activity. A bleary glance around the kitchen brought a blinking light into focus, and she realized her phone was trying to tell her something. She hit speed dial for her voice mail.

The smooth bourbon of a Southern accent poured out. "Hey, Cyn, it's Nick. I'm getting a little worried here, darlin'. It's been a while. Call me."

Nick was an old friend. Actually, more, and less, than a friend. A friend with privileges. The two of them had a long-standing arrangement that was mutually very satisfying, both physically and emotionally. Nick lived on the other coast and called whenever he was in town. Over the years, they had both enjoyed great sex with no commitment, each free to move on if they met someone they wanted to spend time with. When the other relationships petered out, as they invariably did, the old convenience was always waiting. The affair with Raphael had come and gone so fast, Cyn had never even had a chance to tell Nick about it, and the wound was still too raw to even think about someone else. Nick, unknowing, had left a couple of his usual messages in the meantime, but she'd never called back. But now . . . *Now what, Cyn?*

She dialed. It rang twice before he picked up. "Well, it's about time,

Leighton. Where the hell have you been?"

"Nice to talk to you too, Nicky."

"Yeah, yeah. Come on, Cyn. I was worried."

"You're right. I'm sorry."

"Because we're friends, right?"

"Yeah. I said I was sorry."

"So what is it? Big case taking all your time? Met a new guy, madly in love? But then you'd be happy and call me. So I figure someone's broken your heart. You want me to kill him for you?"

Cyn laughed. "He might be hard to kill."

"Yeah? And I might surprise you. So what's going on? I'll be in town next week, if you want to get together."

Cyn was silent, thinking.

"Cyn, darlin', if you have to think that hard about it, you're not ready. The bastard. How about I just break a few of his bones?"

"I appreciate the offer, Nicky. Both of them. And you're right, I'm not ready. Not yet anyway. But I wanted to let you know everything was okay."

"Well, I do appreciate the call. So you keeping busy at least? You're not like hanging around the house and eating ice cream right from the carton, are you? 'Cuz it'd be a shame to ruin that fine ass of yours."

"Gee, Nicky. Here I thought you were worried about me and it turns out it's only my ass."

"Well, it is a very fine ass, darlin'."

"Maybe I'll take my ass for a run on the beach later. Might clear some cobwebs and help me figure out a way to get some answers."

"So you *are* working a new case."

"Missing girl, my favorite kind. Not. And to make it more interesting, we've got a serial killer loose in town, and he seems to favor runaway girls. No pressure."

"You've still got pretty good ties in the department, though, right? That should help some."

"The department's not too happy with me these days. Even my regular guy's being cagey. He let me in a little, but he's closed the door for now. It's frustrating."

"So talk to his secretary or clerk or whatever those guys have. That's what I do. Secretaries know everything that's going on, and if they like you, they'll talk."

"Since most secretaries are female, I'm sure that's not a problem for you."

"Hey, the ladies like me, what can I say?"

Cyn didn't respond right away. "You know, Nicky," she said thoughtfully. "You're not just a pretty face, after all. That's a great idea."

"Okaaay . . . I'm not sure if that was an insult or a compliment."

"A compliment all the way. I'm glad I called."

"Yeah, me too. I have no idea what you're talking about, but okay."

Cyn laughed. "Thanks, Nick. I'll stay in touch."

"You do that. And take care of that sweet ass."

Cyn disconnected, then raced upstairs to rummage through her closet. She found the paper Hartzler had shoved into her pocket and unfolded it. He'd written his name and a cell phone number in neat block letters. She checked her watch. It was too early to call a guy who worked nights. Maybe she'd take that run on the beach after all, get some daylight and fresh air for a change. By the time she got back, showered and dressed, Mr. Ian Hartzler should be getting ready for his shift at the County's very special para facility. Which was precisely where Cyn wanted him.

Chapter Twenty-nine

THE SUN WAS A smear of light in the fog shrouded sunset when Cyn parked again in front of the two-story brick building. The day had been cold and damp, the sun completely obscured by low hanging clouds. She'd taken a steaming shower after her run, staying extra long beneath the hot water, trying to warm up.

The security cameras swiveled as she made her way up the walk to the para facility. The cameras were much more obvious in daylight, their movements almost distracting as they tracked her progress. The door opened before she could push the buzzer.

"Ms. Leighton." Hartzler's voice held an excited tremble. He'd been more than eager when Cyn had called earlier, telling her in a hushed voice of his honor at this opportunity to help Lord Raphael. He was trying for cool now, with limited success. Cyn was still a little creeped out, but gave him a friendly smile. After all, he had volunteered to help her, knowing fully well it could cost him his job if anyone found out.

"Mr. Hartzler. Thank you for agreeing to meet me."

"Oh, of course." He closed the door carefully behind her. "As I said on the phone, I'm honored to be asked."

"Well. Thank you anyway. As I mentioned, what I'd really like is another chance to review the files you have on the victims. Of course, the case files would be ideal, but I understand you probably don't have access—"

"But I have those too," he said eagerly. "Well, not the latest ones, of course, and not the detective's murder book, but I've got all the initial reports, the crime scene photos, witness statements. I have a friend . . ." He paused, as if aware he was about to admit something that was definitely against procedure and possibly criminal. "Well, let's say I'm not the only one who wishes to serve."

Cyn blinked. *Wishes to serve?* "Great, that's great," she said, trying to conceal her discomfort. "Downstairs, then?"

Hartzler had been standing there staring at her, pale eyes glowing with excitement. He smiled. "Yes, of course. We'll take the stairs."

Downstairs, back in his own domain, the morgue tech became the efficient and knowledgeable professional once again. His eyes still watched her a little too closely and a smile kept playing around his lips, but for the most part, he was all business.

"Bodies or files first?" There was a hint of challenge in his words. As if Cyn had anything to prove to this guy.

"The files, I think."

He opened a desk drawer and withdrew several folders. "These are my own files, a combination of the ME's records and what I've been able to glean from other sources. They're confidential, you understand, and don't exist in any official sense."

"Of course," Cyn murmured. She took the folders, glancing around for a place to sit.

"Use my desk," Hartzler said, sweeping the chair out grandly. "Take all the time you need."

CYN WROTE A final note and closed the last file. She'd filled an entire yellow pad with notes and sketches and Hartzler had long since gotten bored and wandered away to his own duties. Apparently watching Cyn read the case files wasn't all that much of an honor after all.

He was nowhere to be found when she pushed through the double doors to the hallway, so she went on upstairs, figuring that's where he'd be. She might not like the guy much, but his files had been amazingly complete, so complete that she wondered exactly where he'd gotten some of it. Not that it mattered. The information had been tremendously helpful to her which was all she cared about.

The door at the top of the stairs swung shut behind her and she heard voices down the hall. Figuring it must be Hartzler, she headed in that direction, already digging her keys out of her backpack.

"What the fuck is *she* doing here?"

Cyn recognized the voice and spun around with a deceptive smile. "Lovely to see you too, Santillo."

"I say again," Detective Charlie Santillo said, ignoring her to glare at Hartzler. "What the *fuck* is she doing here?"

Cyn spoke up before Hartzler could get them both in trouble. "I'm a licensed Private Investigator, Santillo, looking for a missing girl. I requested and received through proper channels permission to view the bodies of the Jane Does in this facility in case one of them was my girl. I'm happy to say she's not here."

Santillo gave her an unfriendly look. "Next time you want to see a body on one of my cases, Leighton, you call me, understand? I don't give a shit what strings your daddy pulled to get you in here, I know who you work for and I don't want you mucking around my case."

"You have no idea who I work for, Santillo. But then you're pretty clueless about a lot of things, especially these murders." She turned away from him deliberately. "Thank you for your time, Mr. Hartzler. I'm sorry I wasn't able to help." She started down the hallway toward the door, but Santillo's meaty hand grabbed her arm, holding her back.

"What the fuck does that mean?"

Santillo was an inch or two shorter than she was, but his body was thick with muscle and fat. She looked down at his hand on her arm, and then rolled her eyes deliberately up to meet his with a cold stare. His hand dropped away.

"We've got your boy dead to rights, Leighton. He won't get away with it this time."

"You've got nothing, Santillo, and I can hardly wait to see the look on your face when you realize that." She started walking again, but was once again halted by his voice.

"What about Carballo, Leighton? Doesn't it bother you to work for the creatures who murdered your good *friend* Benita? Or maybe it was you helped 'em cover up the whole thing, huh? You know, I hear vampire sex is pretty damn fantastic. Is that all it takes to buy you, Leighton? A good fuck?"

Cyn spun on her heel. "Is *that* what this is about, Santillo? You got your feelings hurt? Did it make you feel all inadequate when you found out Benita was fucking a bloodsucker instead of you?" The deliberately crude words were delivered with a sweetly solicitous smile. And they had the desired effect.

"Bitch!" Santillo exploded, closing the distance until he was right in her face. His mouth smelled of the garlic he'd had for lunch, poorly masked by mint, and Cyn's nostrils pinched in protest as she held her ground.

"You got Benita killed, Leighton. They drained her dry and left her for road kill, and you're still defending those bastards."

"Benita got herself killed. She was dirty and you know it. Just like you know those girls weren't killed by any vampire." She stabbed her finger toward the floor and the basement below.

Muscles bunched as his hands curled into fists at his sides. "Don't you talk about Benita. Don't you dare."

He would have said more, but the door opened behind Cyn to admit another cop, someone she didn't know, but who obviously knew Santillo well. He took one look at the situation and stepped between the two of them. Cyn moved back a step rather than shoving against his bulk.

"Easy, Charlie," he said to Santillo. "You don't want to blow this now."

"You know who that is?" Santillo's arm swung out in her direction.

"Yeah, I do. And I know she's not worth it, so back off."

Cyn bristled at this dismissal from someone she didn't even know and was tempted to shove him out of the way after all. But she saw Hartzler's pale face watching from down the hall, eyes wide and panicky, and suddenly she remembered the real reason she was here. She took another voluntary step backward and reached out blindly for the door knob behind her.

"This isn't over, Leighton!" Santillo's tight voice followed her.

"Let it go," the other cop said. "Don't mess this up, man."

Cyn glanced over her shoulder, quickly pulled the door open and turned to leave. As she stepped outside, the door swung shut behind her, but slowly enough that she heard the unknown cop's voice again. "How much does she know?"

"Nothing," Santillo rasped. "Claims she was here on a runaway kid. Besides no one but you and—"

The door shut, cutting off his words. Cyn stopped at the foot of the stairs and scowled back up at the windowless building. Santillo was the lead investigator on this case. He was the one who'd gotten everyone else started down the vampire killer path, the one who'd pushed until it was the only trail anyone was following. If something was about to break on that, she'd really like to know what it was. Hartzler would probably tell her, but he'd already stuck his neck out far enough. Willingly, to be sure, but she didn't want to push him any further. Not now. She might need him more later, and besides, those girls hadn't been killed by any vampire. She was certain of that much. If Santillo tried to pin this on Raphael or any of his vamps, he was in for a big surprise. And definitely not the good kind.

Chapter Thirty

IT WAS LATE, BUT she stopped at an electronics store moments before they closed, earning dirty looks from everybody except the sales guy who wrote up her order for a laptop computer and prepaid cell phone. Later on, she'd arrange for Mirabelle to have the real thing, but the prepaid would do for now. Mirabelle wanted to help in the search for her sister, and Cyn had figured out a way she could do that without becoming even more lost than Liz was. She threw her purchases onto the back seat and turned toward Malibu.

Alexandra's manor was brightly lit when Cyn rounded the final curve of the driveway. Soft electric light filled every window, making the formal building seem warm and welcoming, the kind of house they always showed in those sappy holiday movies, except for the absence of a tree in the window. She wondered if Alexandra planned on getting a Christmas tree this year. Probably depended on which magazines she was reading at the time.

"Cyn!" Mirabelle came flying out of the house as Cyn was unloading her purchases. "I didn't know you were coming!" she said with a big grin on her face.

"I wanted to see how you're doing. Everything okay here?"

"Definitely! This is such a cool house and all the other vampires are so friendly. The guys even tease me about my piano playing. Oh, and Alexandra and I have been shopping! Did you know you can buy almost anything on the Internet if you have a credit card? If I'd known that I'd have spent a fortune. Of course, I would have had to get a hold of a credit card, but I bet Liz already figured that out and—"

Cyn held up her hand, out of breath just from listening. "Great. That's great, Mirabelle. In fact, I've got a new laptop for you here." She swung the large square box out of the truck, intending to carry it herself, but Mirabelle slid it easily from her arms. *Oh right. Vampire.* "I want you to start hanging around those message boards you and Liz use," Cyn said. "Get some messages out there that you're safe and looking for her. I bought you a cell phone too."

"Cool! Thanks, Cyn. I've been checking our usual boards; Alexandra let me use her computer. But there's been nothing since that first message." Mirabelle's forehead creased with worry.

"Yeah, that doesn't surprise me too much, though. Liz's computer might have been lost or even stolen, or maybe she put it in a locker somewhere for safekeeping. Either way, she could log on any day now, in an Internet café or on someone else's computer, and I want you out there waiting for her."

They started walking toward the house, passing the privet hedge that surrounded the marble courtyard. Cyn glanced over and saw that the shiny marble had been removed, leaving a dusty plot of dirt surrounded by the pristine hedge. "The workmen came, huh?" she said.

Mirabelle shrugged. "I guess. When I woke up tonight, it was like this. Alexandra says she's going to put in a maze. I always thought those were sort of creepy."

Cyn slanted a gaze at Mirabelle, but clearly the irony of a vampire calling a maze creepy was lost on her. "Come on," she said. "Let's get inside and get you set up. Hell, if they've got a wireless connection here, you'll soon be able to shop from any room in the house."

"Wait until Alexandra sees it. She'll want one too. We've already talked about how it would be better to be able to log on from any room. You know, because she's doing a lot of remodeling and that way we could actually be in the room we were working on."

"So you guys are getting along all right?"

"Oh, yeah. Absolutely." Mirabelle lowered her voice as they entered the house. "I feel kind of bad moving in on her, but she really doesn't seem to mind. She's kind of lonely I think. She's been telling me all about her life and about Matias. That's the guy who died defending her. He sounds really sweet. He was a dancer, you know—"

"No, I didn't—"

"—in Europe, I don't know like a hundred years ago or something, maybe longer. Anyway, it's so romantic."

Cyn nodded in agreement and tuned out, glad that Mirabelle was settling in, and that Cyn was free to continue her search for the missing Elizabeth,

Chapter Thirty-one

THREE NIGHTS WENT by. Nights spent driving up and down the dark streets of L.A., talking to runaway kids and shelter operators, visiting cafés and clubs, showing Liz's picture to anyone who would look. But Cyn was no closer to finding her. She stood in her closet on the fourth night, wearing nothing but her underwear and staring blankly at the racks of clothes while her brain struggled to think of a fresh approach, something new that would help her find Elizabeth. Several of the kids she'd spoken with had clearly recognized the picture, although not one of them would admit to it. It was frustrating, but it told her at least that Liz was alive and well somewhere on the streets of L.A. Now all she had to do was persuade the girl to come into the light.

Far more troubling though, was the growing evidence that Jabril's real investigator had finally followed the trail to California. More than one of the street kids had been questioned by someone before Cyn got there, someone the kids had described as looking an awful lot like the white-haired guy she'd run into outside Jabril's place. Which meant not only was he on the right track for finding Elizabeth, but he was far too close to Mirabelle for Cyn's comfort.

Of course, Raphael's security people understood the importance of keeping Mirabelle on the estate and out of sight, and Cyn had made a point of mentioning it to Alexandra. She'd also spoken privately to Duncan, who assured her the gate guards had been instructed not to permit Mirabelle off the estate without specific permission from either him or Raphael. She'd breathed a bit easier after that, buoyed by the knowledge that the danger to Mirabelle was temporary, only until the young vampire was formally under Raphael's protection. Once that happened, Jabril risked outright conflict with Raphael if he tried to force her back to Texas, something Duncan had told her even Jabril would not venture since the Vampire Council would surely side with Raphael in this matter. Her train of thought reminded her that Mirabelle's appointment with the vampire lord was three days away and Raphael expected Cyn to be there. She sighed.

As for Raphael and his involvement in the murders, there hadn't been a peep from anyone in the last few days about the investigation. Nothing from Eckhoff, which was expected given her run-in with Santillo, but Duncan had been silent as well. Did that mean the police had stopped looking at Raphael? Surely Duncan would have let her know if things were heating up. She sat down to tug on her Frye boots, telling herself she was a fool. What was she worrying about anyway? Raphael? The big bad vampire could take care of himself.

She shook her head, dismissing the thought. He was probably traveling or busy or who knew what else? So no one had called her. Wasn't that what she'd wanted all these weeks? To be left alone, to get over him?

Uh huh. She grabbed the first sweater she found and pulled it over her head. It was time to stop stressing over the vampire and get to work. She needed to find Liz and get her securely into the fold before someone else snatched her up.

Chapter Thirty-two

MIRABELLE DROPPED the empty blood bag into the plastic bin and wiped her mouth delicately with the fine linen napkin. There was a bit of blood on one finger and she licked it off quickly, savoring the rich flavor of the thick liquid. She'd never known blood could taste so good. Lonnie said Jabril had probably been watering her blood supply all these years, keeping her weak, keeping her biddable. Long-suppressed anger tightened her gut and she stood, stomping over to her small private bath to wash her hands and face.

It made her sick to think what her life had been all these years, how completely cowed she'd been by the Texas vampire lord. She wanted to believe it had been the malnutrition or simple ignorance. But honesty compelled her to admit she'd been afraid. Terrified, really. Not that Jabril Karim hadn't given her plenty of reason to fear him, but she should have fought back somehow. Hell, she should have left him. Should have walked out the door, gone to her parents' lawyer, to the cops, or even to Ramona Hewitt. Someone would have helped her, if only for the money. And gods knew there was enough of that. Cynthia had already talked to her about wresting control of the Hawthorn Trust back from Jabril. She'd put her in touch with some big-time lawyers here in L.A., and they'd already come by the house to meet with her. Cynthia had been there too, but only briefly. She'd been eager to get back to the streets, to the search for Liz. Cyn hadn't said anything, but Mirabelle knew she was worried about how long it was taking to find her sister.

Mirabelle was worried too. She'd left several messages in the chat room for Liz, each one essentially the same. *Everything's okay, I'm safe. Where are you?* Thoughts of Liz sent her over to the new desk which had been delivered yesterday. It was a beautiful piece, if not precisely what Mirabelle would have chosen. But, after all, this was Alexandra's house; Mirabelle was only a guest. Someday soon, after Cyn found Liz, the two sisters would find a place together and they'd decorate it any way they wanted. It made her a little sad to think about leaving the estate, though. All the vampires here were so nice, so seemingly ordinary. She'd even met several other female vamps, in addition to Elke who looked kind of scary, but who'd been really friendly, joking that Mirabelle needed some muscle and offering to help her work out in the gym.

For the first time, she felt part of a community. She'd put on ten pounds in the short time she'd been in L.A. and her skin was flushed with a pinkish color that was pale, but far healthier looking than she'd ever expected to be again. And ten pounds! Who'd have ever thought *that* would be a good thing. She laughed quietly. Maybe she'd take Elke up on that workout after all. She liked the female guard, even though Alexandra didn't approve. Alexandra had some pretty old ideas about how a woman should behave, and being a bodyguard wasn't one of them.

But Mirabelle thought it was great that Elke was part of Raphael's inner security. It was an honor, a mark of his trust. Of course, everyone here took security very seriously. And not only at the gates. Every vampire on the estate slept through the day in the safety of the basements. Not just Raphael or Alexandra, but all of the guards and Mirabelle, too. Each of them had a private chamber in the specially constructed vaults, one beneath the main house and another at Alexandra's manor. They were like giant bank vaults, but once closed for the day, the door could only be opened from the inside. Mirabelle had never known that kind of safety as a vampire.

She had yet to actually visit the main house, but she would soon. This weekend, she would present herself to Raphael and formally request his protection. Alexandra had drilled her in the proper words to say and how to act. She was afraid Mirabelle would embarrass herself, and by association, Alexandra, if she messed up. So they'd rehearsed the ritual nightly until Mirabelle was dreaming the words during her daytime rest. It wasn't complicated or anything, but it was important to Alexandra, so Mirabelle practiced because she definitely wanted to stay with Raphael.

Back at her computer, she went first to the familiar chat room and logged in. The message waiting icon popped up immediately. She was so surprised that she stared stupidly at it for several minutes. When it finally dawned on her what it might mean, her eyes widened and her heart began to race; her hand was shaking so badly she had to try twice before she managed to maneuver the cursor and click the message open.

Liz! It was from Liz! Tears of combined happiness and relief filled her eyes, and she grabbed a tissue before they could spill over onto the computer. She read through the message quickly, her elation quickly shifting to concern. Her sister was happy to hear from her, amazed that Mirabelle had escaped Jabril and was here in L.A. But all of Liz's belongings had been stolen on her second day in the city, leaving her with nothing except her small purse and, thankfully, the little bit of money she'd managed to put together before running. It had been rough for awhile, but she was safe now, she said. She'd met a guy, someone older, who was letting her crash in his spare bedroom until she figured out what to do. The guy had even offered to help her get a lawyer or something once she'd turned eighteen and could legally claim her inheritance.

Don't worry, she wrote, correctly anticipating Mirabelle's reaction. *He's not a pervert and he's not a creep. He's someone who knows what I'm going through, because he had to run away from home when he was sixteen. His stepfather was abusing him. Can you believe that? Disgusting. He doesn't like to talk about it, but I think it was pretty rough. Once I get Mom and Dad's money, I'm going to help him set up his own business. It's the least I can do.*

Mirabelle stared at her sister's message, the blood she'd so enjoyed a short time ago sitting heavily in a queasy stomach. God knew she certainly wasn't a woman of the world, not like Cynthia who was always so confident, so brave. She sighed. But even Mirabelle knew this guy was using Liz. It made her sick to think what games he might be playing with her little sister even now. She hit reply.

Cow baby! She stuck a big grinning smiley after the words. *I've got a place you can stay. Somewhere safe, with ME! Call me.* She inserted her temporary cell phone number. *Or meet me in chat. I'll be waiting for you.* She paused in her typing, trying to think of the best time, when she knew she'd be awake and already sitting at her computer. She shrugged and typed, *Every night. Tick tock, tick tock. I'm waaaaaaaaaaaaiiiting.* She finished with a vampire smiley, tiny fangs and a widow's peak hairline framed by a high-neck cape.

THE HUMAN GUARDS had begun to arrive for the day shift, and still Mirabelle hadn't gotten a response from her sister. She shouldn't have expected one right away, she supposed. That guy was letting Liz use his computer, but maybe not all the time. Still, Mirabelle been in and out of the chat room all night as she wandered through the manor house, laptop in tow, trying to avoid the latest group of craftsmen Alexandra had hired in her dogged search for remodeling perfection. Apparently, once the woman started something, she pursued it with a vengeance.

Mirabelle glanced at her watch. Before long, she'd have to start downstairs to her small room in the vault. The human workmen had begun to pack up, tools clattering, talking amongst themselves in loud voices. The vampire guards watched the visitors closely, aware of the coming sunrise, anxious for them to be gone.

Looking for a quiet place, Mirabelle hurried through the kitchen and outside, down the drive and across to the pathway between the two houses. It was peaceful out here, the noisy workmen and worried guards far behind her. After living as Jabril's prisoner for so many years, she relished the freedom to walk in the earthy silence beneath the thick trees and breathe the fresh air. The pale moon, low on the horizon, barely intruded, but her vampire sight easily followed the graveled path. Benches were dotted at regular intervals, small concrete constructions with fanciful gargoyles cavorting all around the backs and seats. Some sat boldly out in the open, others peered from behind or below. They'd made her laugh out loud the first time she'd seen them and now she thought of them as her own. She came out here almost every night before dawn and had never seen anyone other than the occasional guard patrol.

When she'd gone far enough that Alexandra's house was no longer visible through the trees, she sat on one of the concrete benches and logged on to do a quick survey of websites. Still nothing and there wasn't much more time tonight, less than an hour before she'd have to be downstairs and tucked into her bed, although the others would come later. She leaned back and tilted her head toward the manor, listening. Doors slammed amidst the sounds of engines, so the workers must finally be leaving. She stood, ready to head back, but a rush of noise drew her in the other direction, toward the elegant and expansive mansion where Raphael and his vampires lived and conducted the business known as Raphael Enterprises. She hesitated, torn between curiosity and the instinctive desire to get down to the safety of the vault beneath the manor.

Curiosity won, of course. She often sat in the evenings and watched the comings and goings at the main house. Most nights, there was a busy parade of vampires and humans. Some were there to do business with Raphael. Others, and Mirabelle recognized them easily, were there to offer themselves to the vampires as blood donors. Both men and women, they were ferried from blood houses maintained throughout the city, closely guarded by Raphael's vampires, escorted in for the evening and always gone before morning. Unlike Jabril, Raphael didn't keep any slaves, blood or otherwise.

She approached the final curve in the path. The main house wasn't quite visible yet. It sat several feet below the pathway here, right on the edge of the cliff. But she could see lights flashing against the dark sky. Red and blue in a rotating pattern. It seemed familiar for some reason, and she hurried forward only to duck quickly behind the trees.

Two police vehicles sat in the driveway below, one black and white, its light bar flashing silently, the other a late model American sedan with one of those portable red lights pulsing on the roof. Standing next to the cruiser were a couple of uniformed officers, their hands resting nervously on their weapons as they stared at the several large and very pissed off vampires surrounding them. The sedan stood with both doors open, the interior lights on, but no one inside.

As she watched, the double glass doors to the main house opened and Duncan emerged, followed by the two huge Asian vampires who seemed to go everywhere with Raphael. Duncan appeared to be furious. He was moving stiffly and she could see the tip of his fangs protruding below his upper lip. He jerked his head at the vampires surrounding the police vehicles and they backed away, forming a semicircle around the bodyguards and the two humans who followed them with . . . Mirabelle gasped. Raphael!

A low growl of anger rose from the assembled vampires as Raphael emerged, hands cuffed behind his back, held between two human men, probably the policemen from the unmarked car. They halted at the foot of the stairs and the blocky, dark-haired policeman next to Raphael said something.

The powerful vampire lord rotated his head slowly to stare down at the man. His black eyes were flashing silver with rage and he turned that lambent gaze on his vampires, scanning them slowly, touching every one of them, drawing them into a singular, focused entity, utterly under his control, awaiting his command.

Up on her little overlook, Mirabelle too felt the irresistible pull of his will. She trembled with the strength of it, knowing with absolute certainty that she would race down the hill to his rescue, even to her own death, if he desired it. She tensed, ready to launch herself at his command, but a wave of calm reassurance flooded her senses instead. She felt suddenly as if she stood shoulder-to-shoulder with the vampires gathered below as they stepped back in a single, unified movement to permit the humans to pass with their prisoner. Raphael spoke in a low voice to Duncan, who gave a sharp nod and stood aside, his face a mask of something close to despair, watching as his Sire slid gracefully into the back seat of the unmarked car.

With a chaotic flurry of slammed doors and spinning wheels, the police vehicles spun around the drive and gunned back toward the main gate. Almost immediately two heavy SUVs roared up and vampire bodyguards piled inside, Duncan among them. The big SUVs peeled away with a scream of rubber, hard on the heels of Raphael and his police captors.

The silence in their wake was deafening. Vampires stood frozen, staring down the drive after their master, unable or unwilling to leave. Finally, one of the vamps who had followed Raphael from the house gave an order and everyone moved at once. Mirabelle shook herself. She had to get back to the house, had to tell Alexandra and the others at the manor, if they didn't know already. She hurried back down the path, laptop tucked under her arm nearly forgotten. She had to . . . she had to call Cynthia!

Chapter Thirty-three

CYN SNAPPED HER cell phone closed with a curse, all but running from the homeless shelter where she'd been following a lead on Elizabeth. She hit the street and stormed down the two blocks to her Land Rover, popping the locks and sliding behind the wheel in a single motion. The blaring horns of outraged drivers were ignored as she sped away from the curb, flipping her phone open again to speed dial Eckhoff. It rang several times before his voice mail picked up.

"Thanks for the heads up, Eckhoff," she snarled. "You tell that piece of shit Santillo he can kiss his ass good-bye when this is over, because he's got the wrong fucking guy." She disconnected and immediately called Duncan.

The vampire's voice was little more than a growl.

"I'm on my way," she said.

"Do you know where?" The words were thick, forced past his anger.

"Olympic and Twentieth. I'll be there." She snapped the phone closed and made a squealing right hand turn onto the freeway. To hell with the speed limit. It was nearly daylight. Was the para facility equipped to handle a sleeping vampire? And what about Duncan and the others, their need to protect Raphael would outweigh even the instinct to retreat from the rising sun. She pounded the steering wheel angrily. Fucking Santillo. She could hardly wait to tell him how wrong he was. She just hoped the vampires didn't get to him first.

Chapter Thirty-four

DUNCAN WAS WAITING out front when she arrived, pacing up and down the narrow sidewalk. He looked up as she slammed her truck into park and all but threw herself from the driver's seat, his eyes glowing dimly in the glare of the security lights around the holding facility.

"Where is he?" she asked tersely.

He eyed her silently, his scrutiny unusually intense, even for Duncan. "Inside," he said finally. "They wouldn't let me stay with him, but his lawyers are there."

Cyn kept walking and Duncan fell into step next to her. "Where's everyone else?" she asked. "Mirabelle said there were a whole bunch of you that followed."

"It's nearly daylight. I sent the others home. There was no point in everyone standing out here." Duncan's cell phone rang. He glanced at the caller ID and took the call. "She's here," he said and disconnected almost immediately.

Cyn looked at him. "Who was that?"

"Lord Raphael's attorney. She's on her way out to talk to you."

"Me? Why?"

Duncan had the grace to look uncomfortable. "You've heard of Obaker?"

"Of course, I've heard of Obaker, but what—"

"Obaker vs. Oklahoma," a woman's voice intruded. "Any vampire taken into custody has the right to designate a custodial presence in order to ensure his, or her, safety if held outside the precincts of a specifically mandated federal facility. And, fortunately for us, this delightful structure is definitely *not* such a federal facility."

Cyn turned to see a willowy female vampire coming down the walkway. Long white hair shone in the faint light, contrasting sharply with golden skin and Asian features to give her an exotic look that fit perfectly with the delicate fangs bared in a vicious grin. As she approached, she held out a shapely hand. "Kimiko Lorick," she said. "Lord Raphael has entrusted me with his defense. Not that he'll need

158

much of one since these charges are patently absurd and completely without merit." She eyed Cyn critically. "Are you ready?"

"Ready for what?" Cyn asked, although she had a pretty good idea and didn't like it one bit.

"Duncan didn't explain?" Kimiko glanced at Raphael's lieutenant who shook his head.

"Ms. Leighton only just arrived, Kimiko. I was about to discuss the matter—"

"The sun is nearly risen, Duncan. There is no time for diplomacy." She swung her gaze back to Cyn. "Lord Raphael has asserted his Obaker rights and designated you, Cynthia Leighton. If you will not serve, I need to know now while I can still persuade him to accept someone else. I will not leave him unprotected. If necessary—"

"Why?" Cyn demanded, swinging on Duncan. "Why would he do that?"

"Because he trusts you, Cynthia."

"Why not his lawyers?" She turned back to Kimiko. "One of you must be human, right?"

Kimiko nodded. "My husband, Boyd. And he would be honored to remain, but he will be better used in court, securing Lord Raphael's release. He cannot be locked away here. Besides, my master has chosen you."

"And if I say no?"

Kimiko gave Cyn a baleful glare. "Then I will attempt to make other arrangements in time. If I fail, Lord Raphael will sleep unsecured, vulnerable to whatever the humans plan. And I do not doubt for one moment that this entire farce has been orchestrated toward that end. The timing of the arrest was too convenient for my taste."

Cyn glanced at Duncan. "Don't look at me like that," she snapped. "I'll do it. So what happens now?"

Kimiko gave her a very pleased grin, as if the whole thing had been her idea. "Are you carrying a gun?"

"Of course. Why?"

"Give it to me." Kimiko held up a hand to forestall Cyn's automatic protest. "They'll search you once you're inside." She paused, taking the proffered Glock from Cyn and tucking it inside her leather jacket. "But they won't search me. Make sure you stay close afterwards. They'll expect us to consult and, of course, we won't want to be overheard, so we'll huddle. I'll give the weapon back to you then. Can you handle that?"

"Yes," Cyn said, insulted at being asked.

Kimiko took her arm. "Duncan," she said over her shoulder. "It's going to be close. Boyd will drive back to the estate, but be ready to roll as soon as we're out of there."

As if to punctuate her warning, the security lights clicked off on their automatic timer and Cyn looked eastward to see the first watery light of sunrise. They hurried toward the door and she asked quickly, "Have you seen the bodies?" Next to her Kimiko did a double take.

"No," she said, somewhat puzzled. "I did request copies of—"

"The victims were drained with puncture wounds to the carotid artery."

"Shit. No wonder they've been holding back on those coroner's reports. Damn it." She jabbed the door buzzer so hard the button jammed and began emitting an anemic zapping noise.

Cyn handed Kimiko her backpack. "There's a file in here that Boyd needs to see. Be careful with it. Some of it, hell most of it, is stuff I shouldn't have."

Kimiko threw the backpack to Duncan and pounded her fist on the door impatiently. "Bastards know we're out here; they're jerking my chain. I'm gonna sue their asses off when—" The door finally gave a harsh buzz and inched open slightly. Kimiko shoved it the rest of the way, ignoring the rookie cop who was hurrying down the hall toward them. They headed down the hall, past the stairway, all the way to the back of the building. As she walked, she talked quickly.

"Okay, listen, these are the rules. No one enters the cell unless you specifically request it. Once you're inside, the door will be locked behind you. There is to be no surveillance of any kind inside the cell, another Obaker mandate, and boy did they hate—"

There was a flash of white and suddenly Ian Hartzler barreled out of one of the offices, holding a stack of files in front of his chest. He ran right into Cyn, hitting her hard enough to throw them both off balance, sending the files tumbling to the floor. "Ms. Leighton," he said. "I'm so sorry." He crouched to gather the scattered files, and Cyn automatically bent down to help, her face only inches away from the flustered technician. "Cameras," he whispered urgently. Cyn gave him a confused look. He met her gaze intently and hissed, "There are cameras in the cell!"

Cyn quickly handed back the folders she'd retrieved as Kimiko grabbed her by the elbow and began hustling her toward the back hallway. "Do you have any chewing gum?" Cyn asked. Kimiko gave her a distracted look. Cyn stopped abruptly, halting their forward progress. "Kimiko. I would really like some gum. They must have a vending machine here somewhere."

"Jesus, Cynthia, couldn't this wait? Do you have any idea—" Her eyes widened in sudden understanding. "Gum. Right." She looked around wildly, then urged Cyn forward again. "I'll take care of it. You've got to get back there."

The corridor outside the holding cell was three deep with blue uniforms who gave way grudgingly when Cyn and Kimiko pushed through. Santillo stood outside a closed door, yelling at a tall man with thick black hair hanging in a perfectly straight fall down the back of a nicely tailored blue suit. *Boyd Lorick,* Cyn assumed, and was proven correct when Kimiko stormed over and joined the argument. Cyn found a wall, planning to wait while the three of them had it out. She glanced at her watch and thought about Duncan waiting outside as the sun rose higher.

"Assume the position, Leighton."

Cyn looked up and found Santillo's unnamed partner glowering at her. A young woman in a blue uniform stood next to him, looking distinctly uncomfortable. Cyn acquiesced with a negligent shrug, standing away from the wall and holding her arms out to either side as the female cop did a quick but thorough pat-down.

"She's clean," the woman said and disappeared into the crowd. Cyn watched her go and spied a bank of vending machines at the end of the hallway. She nodded in that direction. "You mind? I didn't have dinner."

The partner gave her a skeptical look and followed when she strolled over to the two machines. One was cold drinks, but the other ... She dug a wrinkled five dollar bill out of her jeans pocket, smoothed it out and slid it into the reader. The machine mulled over the quality of her money for a while, decided it was okay and informed her in bright red numbers of her good fortune. Cyn bought a package of cookies she didn't want, waited while they dropped into the bin, and then added a light green package of Doublemint gum. Not exactly her favorite flavor, but then she wasn't buying it for the taste.

As she made her way back to the continuing argument, she unwrapped a couple sticks of the gum and shoved them into her mouth, idly smoothing the wrappers with her fingers.

Santillo's partner stared at the small pieces of tinfoil and Cyn grinned at him, chewing noisily. "You want my gum wrappers, Detective?"

He scowled and Cyn laughed out loud. She ducked behind a desk and deposited the wrappers in a trash receptacle. "You've been watching too many movies," she chided, then glanced over as the yelling finally stopped.

"She's unarmed," the partner confirmed, to the obvious disappointment of everyone but Cyn and the two lawyers.

"Way to go, Leighton," Santillo snarled. "Protecting *them* against your own. Didn't think even you'd sunk that low."

Cyn smiled sweetly, refusing to be baited. "Kimiko," she said, turning her gaze to the vampire lawyer. "A moment, please?"

"Of course. Give us some space, Santillo." Kimiko didn't even try to be polite, pinning the bulky detective with a slow, cold stare. Santillo swore beneath his breath, but stepped back several feet. Kimiko and her husband Boyd pulled Cyn over, turning their backs to the hallway and shielding her from prying eyes. Putting their heads together to confer, Boyd Lorick gave his wife a hard look. "You okay, Kimmi?"

Kimiko blinked several times and drew a deep breath. "Not for much longer." She slid the gun silently into Cyn's waistband. "You found some chewing gum," she breathed in relief. "Good." Boyd gave Kimiko a questioning look, but she shook her head, took a step back and glared at Santillo. "Let's do this," she snarled.

Chapter Thirty-five

RAPHAEL WAS standing in the middle of the room waiting for Cyn when she stepped through the doorway. They'd taken away his tie and belt—as if he would do them the favor of committing suicide over this, if that was even possible for a vampire—but he was still wearing his suit, a nearly black charcoal worsted wool, white shirt open at the collar. Cyn sighed. It took a lot more than the absence of a tie to make Raphael look anything but gorgeous. She looked up to find his flat black eyes staring at her. Unable to look away, she swallowed nervously to avoid choking on her gum and forced a weak smile. Raphael's gaze never wavered.

Kimiko came forward to assure him Boyd would take care of everything. "Go, Kimiko," Raphael said softly, his eyes never leaving Cyn. "It grows late and I would not give them the satisfaction." Kimiko nodded unhappily, but hurried out through the open doorway, passing Santillo who was pretending he had a reason to be there. Cyn jumped when Boyd laid a gentle touch on her shoulder and she turned to find him right next her. "I'll be back before sunset," he said softly.

Cyn nodded her understanding, intensely aware of Raphael's continued scrutiny. "See you then," she said.

Boyd hustled Santillo bodily out of the room, giving Cyn a final thumbs up before the door slammed shut. She stared at the door until the shuffling of footsteps faded down the hallway, and then turned back to Raphael, trying to think of something rational to say. He held up a hand for her to wait, his head tilted slightly as he listened with his far keener vampire senses.

Cyn took the time to look around. Knowing they were there, she found two of the camera lenses quickly. She drew the now tasteless wad of gum out of her mouth with a grimace—she hated chewing gum—and within a short period of time had disabled those two, plus one more over the door itself. She gave Raphael a questioning look.

He held out his hand. Cyn looked at it, shifted her gaze to his face and sighed in resignation. She took his hand and let him pull her into an embrace. His whole body relaxed as his arms came around her, and then stiffened again as he inhaled deeply through his nose. "You're carrying a gun, my Cyn." His voice was barely there, little more than a breath against her ear. She had blocked the visual on the cameras, but they might still be recording sound. "They didn't search you?"

Cyn nodded and whispered back, knowing he could hear. "But not Kimiko."

Raphael chuckled. "A formidable woman, Kimiko, even before—" He gave a choking kind of cough and seemed to lose balance for a moment, leaning heavily against her. Cyn drew back in alarm.

"Raphael?"

"My apologies, Cyn, it seems . . ." With a visible effort, he straightened and shook his head. In a bizarre flashback to Mirabelle and the airplane, Cyn tucked her shoulder under his arm and urged him in the direction of the bed before his vampire nature took away the option. They barely made it. Cyn managed to pull back the blanket and Raphael collapsed onto the narrow mattress, pulling her down with him. She gave him a skeptical look, wondering if he was as out of it as he appeared, but his eyelids never even fluttered. His head hit the pillow, he exhaled a last deep breath and then . . . nothing.

She panicked a little when he stopped breathing, her lungs seizing up in sympathy as she pressed her hand down over his heart. A wan beat pulsed under her palm, and she sighed in relief, only to jump in surprise when his chest expanded and he drew in another breath. She watched for several minutes, timing his vitals, finally relaxing when his body seemed to settle into a regular, if distinctly sluggish, rhythm.

Cyn had seen dead bodies, bodies in the morgue, bodies freshly dead from violence or even quietly dead at home or hospital. But despite the fiction of movies and television, the truth was that life fled the body fairly quickly. The personality that had once animated the flesh, the unique expressions that had sculpted the face their loved ones recognized . . . those were gone forever. She gazed down at Raphael and wondered how anyone could mistake this serene beauty for death. She brushed an imaginary hair off his forehead, running her fingers back along his scalp and caressing his cheek softly. Her heart squeezed in her chest, and she stood, feeling slightly perverted, as though she'd taken advantage of him in his helpless state.

She straightened and looked around the small cell—four square walls, painted a dull gray, with a single sleeping platform jutting from one side and a sink and toilet in the far corner. There were no windows—they got that much right anyway. She crossed to the vanity and used the toilet, after a very thorough scan for additional cameras. She washed her face and hands, wrinkling her nose at the harsh soap provided, and had no sooner dried her hands on a paper towel, than the lights clicked off with no warning. She listened to the fading fluorescent buzz and chuckled. Santillo and crew couldn't complain about her sabotaging cameras that weren't supposed to be there, so they'd clearly decided to punish her by turning off the lights in the windowless room instead. They'd be disappointed to learn she didn't care. She'd been up all night searching for Liz; this would actually make it easier for her to sleep.

Unfortunately, it was going to be the floor or the bed; there wasn't anywhere else to sit. Another intentional *oversight*, no doubt. She wondered again if Raphael was at all aware under that serene exterior, and figured he was probably laughing his ass off right about now. But she was too tired to fight it.

Grateful for the dark room, she slipped the gun out of her waistband and tucked it under the pillow, then stretched out on the bed next to the vampire lord, turning so she faced the door. She closed her eyes, grateful at least that it was nearly winter and the days were short, although she suspected this one would seem very, very long.

Chapter Thirty-six

CYN WOKE THE instant Raphael began to stir. It had been a restless day for her, with people coming and going almost constantly out in the hallway. The facility had been virtually abandoned only days before, but they'd probably brought in extra staff since they were holding an actual prisoner. Still, Cyn couldn't help wondering if all that noise in the hallway had been intentional. There were times when it had sounded more like a frat party than a police holding facility. She shifted on the narrow bed, ready to sit up, when a familiar arm curled around her waist to hold her in place.

"Is this my punishment or yours, sweet Cyn?" he murmured.

Cyn focused on breathing normally, intensely aware of his closeness . . . and the fact that the door could open at any minute.

Raphael's breath was warm on her neck. "Cameras?"

"The visual's still blocked." She too spoke in a bare whisper. "I don't know about sound."

He relaxed fractionally. "I have missed you, my Cyn."

"You left me, you bastard."

"I was a fool."

Cyn closed her eyes against the rush of emotion triggered by his words. She was thankful for the still dark room, even though she knew he could feel the sudden jolt in her pulse and probably smell the tears that were inexplicably filling her eyes. He gathered her close, sliding both arms around her with a regretful sigh.

"I am sorry, *lubimaya*."

Cyn let her head rest on the thickness of his arm. *Lubimaya*, he called her. It was Russian. My love. *You are* such *a fool, Cynthia.*

A door slammed somewhere outside the cell and Raphael tensed again. "Boyd," he said as the lights snapped on. "And others are with him."

WHEN THE DOOR opened, they were both standing, Cyn slightly

behind Raphael. He'd pushed her there at the first click of the lock. It was instinctive on his part, so Cyn tried to ignore the implication that she needed protecting. She scowled at his back, but couldn't help feeling a little pleased.

The first person into the room was Boyd. He slipped inside quickly and pulled the door nearly closed behind him, walking directly to Raphael with the vampire's confiscated belt and tie.

"My lord," he said, holding them out with a wry smile.

Raphael took the belt first, sliding it through the loops at his waist and buckling it on with rapid movements. The tie came next. He slipped it around his neck and turned to Cyn with a raised eyebrow. There were no mirrors in the room. She knotted the silk with the practiced moves of a woman who'd known a lot of men in suits, then straightened his collar and smoothed the tie down his broad chest. When she finished, he took her hand and raised it to his lips for a soft kiss, before turning back to Boyd.

The lawyer's expression was twinkling with poorly concealed glee as he reported.

"The District Attorney offers his profound regrets, my lord, and assures me that all charges have been dismissed. He would have been here himself to convey the same had I not convinced him otherwise, advising him you would most certainly prefer to maintain a low profile. By the way, Ms. Leighton's research was most helpful," he added with a nod in Cyn's direction.

His cell phone signaled an incoming text message and he paused, checking the display. "Duncan has arrived with an appropriate escort, my lord. We will exit through the rear of the building."

Raphael nodded formally, but clapped a hand on Boyd's slender shoulder in thanks before saying, "Cyn," without looking at her. She came up next to him. "Are you ready, *lubimaya?*" he asked her.

Cyn huffed out a laugh. "A thousand times ready," she agreed.

He pulled her into a quick one-armed embrace, kissing the top of her head. She caught a look of surprise on the lawyer's face, before Raphael let her go. "We're ready then," he said.

The hallway outside was once again packed with people, looking considerably less happy than they had earlier. Santillo lurked in the background, shooting daggers at the vampire, his gaze shifting to spear Cyn with no less hatred, as Boyd cleared a path through the crowd. Cyn ignored Santillo, but saw Hartzler standing in an open doorway staring at Raphael in awe. She caught his eye and nodded her thanks. She would do more later, in a less public venue. There was no point in getting the tech in trouble with Santillo and his buddies. She might not understand Hartzler's obsession, but he had clearly demonstrated his loyalties, and it wouldn't hurt to have him on their side in the future.

They turned left, away from the front of the building, heading for a narrow emergency exit. Boyd exchanged a look with someone in the crowd, apparently verifying that the alarm had been disengaged. He pulled the door open slowly. Duncan was waiting outside, the relief on his face short-lived as he snarled at the humans trailing behind Raphael. He made a curt gesture and the vampire bodyguards closed in, forming a protective circle around Raphael and Cyn as they made their way over to a big black SUV whose bulk all but blocked the narrow alley. There was enough room for the passenger doors to open on one side, but no more. Raphael stopped and gestured Cyn to go before him, but she shook her head.

"My truck's parked out front."

Raphael frowned. "One of the others—"

"No," she interrupted, then said softly. "I appreciate it, but no. I want to check on Mirabelle, see if she's heard from Liz yet. If not, I need to start looking again. It shouldn't be taking this long and . . ."

Her words wound down. Raphael looked . . . hurt? What had he thought, that she'd jump right into his bed, now that he'd made all nice to her, now that he'd apologized? Well, okay, that actually wasn't a bad idea, but . . . No. She wasn't going to be that easy. She had a life, a job, and a teenaged girl who was still out there on the street with a killer on the loose. But she wasn't going to say any of that right here with his vampires listening in.

"It's important, Raphael. I need to find her."

He regarded her steadily, his eyes glittering with emotion. "Very well," he said somewhat stiffly. "If you require—"

"I will." She stepped away, letting the protective circle close around him, forming a wall between them. He stared at her a moment longer, and then disappeared into the SUV. Duncan shut the door after him, but walked over to Cyn before climbing into the front seat.

"Mirabelle's appointment is—"

"I know, Duncan. Don't worry. We'll both be there."

He gave her a puzzled look, shrugged and said, "Then I will see you Sunday."

Cyn watched them drive away before walking slowly down the alley and out onto the street, to emerge more than a block away from the para facility. She crossed to the other side and went quietly over to her Land Rover. Her body protested as she climbed into the truck. She was stiff and sore after another day of little sleep, and that spent on a narrow ledge not even wide enough for Raphael alone, much less both of them.

She turned the ignition and picked up her cell phone, realizing as the call went through that it was probably too early, that as a young vampire, Mirabelle wouldn't be up yet. She left a message and turned for home, with nothing in mind but a hot shower and fresh clothes. She might have spent her first night in jail, but she didn't have to smell like it.

Chapter Thirty-seven

AFTER A SHOWER, Cyn drove into Malibu and had breakfast . . . or dinner. Whatever she called it, several days of odd hours and erratic meals had left her feeling drained of energy. So she sat at an actual table, with a bacon and cheese omelet, several pieces of wheat toast smeared with fresh peach preserves and a fresh carafe of hot coffee. Thus fortified, she was back on Pacific Coast Highway when her phone rang. A glance at the display told her it was Mirabelle returning her earlier message, so she let it go to voice mail and made a quick left turn onto the narrow entrance lane for Raphael's estate. Mature trees arched overhead, so thick and close they formed a living tunnel. Some nights, it was so dark beneath these trees that her headlights barely managed to light the way. Tonight, with some of the trees bare for the winter and the moon waxing toward full, bits of light filtered through the evergreens to glint silver on the naked, pale trunks of sycamore and birch.

Deep among the trees was the main gate, beyond which the grounds were nicely manicured and artfully lit, a graceful roll of verdant lawn to the main house, with the dark forest behind it concealing Alexandra's manor house.

The guards must have called ahead because Mirabelle was waiting when she arrived. She met Cyn halfway down the driveway, jittery with excitement. "Lord Raphael's home, Cyn, did you know? They kept him in jail all day! My God! Everyone here was totally upset, even Alexandra was jumpy tonight, and she's usually so cool. I thought for sure the vampires were going to go to war or something. You should have seen it!"

Cyn eyed the girl silently and heaved a deep sigh. She was thrilled Mirabelle had recovered so quickly. Really. She was. Her mouth curved in a fond smile. "But he's back now, right, Mirabelle?"

"Right. He got home hours ago. Everyone rushed over to the main house. They all wanted to be there to greet him. Kind of spooky, really. All these vampires standing there waiting for him, totally focused, not saying a word. And then suddenly this big black SUV pulls up and he gets out and . . . I swear, Cyn, it was like they all breathed at once, a big sucking air sound." She shook her head. "My heart was pounding like crazy, I was so happy to see him. You think that's what it's like?"

Cyn considered the question. "What what's like?" she asked finally.

"Having a master. You know, being pledged to someone like Raphael. Like you can't breathe if he's not around."

Since Cyn herself had trouble breathing when Raphael was around, she took the idea seriously. She thought about what Duncan had told her once, about his unswerving loyalty to Raphael, about the absolute power Raphael had over every single one of his sworn vampires. "You know, Mirabelle. I think that's probably exactly what it's like."

"Cool."

Cyn raised a skeptical eyebrow. "If you say so. I don't suppose you've heard from Liz?" she asked hopefully.

"But, I did! I was about to call you yesterday when this whole thing with Raphael blew up."

Cyn stared at Mirabelle. Forget about breathing, was this what happened between a master vampire and his children? All of Mirabelle's loyalty and affection, so utterly destroyed by Jabril's casual cruelty, was now being resurrected and channeled completely to Raphael. Was this the kind of undiluted allegiance that Raphael enjoyed from all his vampires? Good gods, there were thousands of them! No wonder he was such an arrogant bastard.

"Anyway, yeah," Mirabelle was continuing. "Liz left me a message. Some guy's letting her stay at his place, says he's going to help her get her money once she's eighteen." Mirabelle rolled her eyes. "As if. I told her that was a really bad idea and that we're here in California and Raphael's really cool, but she doesn't believe me. So I told her—"

"Wait. How are you having this conversation? Did she call you?"

"Oh, no. We met in a chat room earlier tonight. That guy's letting her use his computer. Hers was stolen, like you said. Anyway, so I told her to call that friend of yours, Luci. She said she would, but then we got kind of cut off, and word came up from the main house that Raphael was on his way and I didn't want to miss *that*, so . . ."

Cyn paused, trying to absorb the rush of information. "Okay. Let me call—"

Her phone trilled, interrupting. She checked the display and flipped it open.

"Hey, Luce."

"Hi, Cyn. Listen, I think I have your lost chickie here." Cyn looked over at Mirabelle and pointed at her meaningfully. "She's a bit twitchy," Luci continued softly, "but I'm trying to convince her you're one of the good guys."

"I appreciate that. Can I talk with her?"

"Not yet. In fact, why don't you drop by later? She's pretty stressed right now. The guy she was staying with kind of freaked out on her."

"Is she hurt?"

"Not physically, no. A couple of scratches, some bruises, but I don't think he gave them to her, not directly anyway. Not from what she'll tell me. Scared mostly."

"Let's hope she's telling the truth. When should I come by?"

"Give us an hour or two. I'll call, but I think she'll be okay meeting you."

"Can the sister come?"

"She's a vamp, right?'

"Right."

Luci was silent, thinking about it. Cyn could hear television in the background, punctuated by the occasional loud comment. "That's probably not a good idea," Luci said finally. "Let her see you first, nice human that you are, and then we'll see after that."

"Right. Talk to you then." Cyn never questioned Luci's instincts when it came to this sort of thing.

Mirabelle was on her as soon as the phone flipped closed. "Liz?"

"She's at Luci's place. I'm heading over there."

"All right! Let's go."

"Um, yeah, about that. Luci thinks, and I agree, it's better if I go alone first. She's safe at Luci's, so there's no reason to push right now. I'll meet with her later and we'll see where it goes from there. She's kind of jittery about the whole vampire thing."

"She knows I'd never hurt her," Mirabelle protested.

"Not on purpose, no. But come on, Mirabelle, she runs away to California and suddenly here you are. For all she knows, Jabril sent you to find her and take her back to him."

"Oh, right, like Raphael would ever—"

"Liz doesn't know anything about Raphael; she doesn't even know who he is," Cyn said with waning patience. "She only knows what you told her, and she can't trust that." She looked up as Alexandra appeared in the driveway. "Nice, Alexandra," she said, pointing at the topiary garden rapidly taking over the old courtyard.

"Yes, it's going well. I got the inspiration from a book I read while we were in Colorado. One of the other vampires recommended it. The author's name was King, I think."

Cyn blinked, a purely instinctive chill rippling her skin and raising goose bumps. She looked up to find Alexandra studying her with an amused expression and kept her own face carefully blank. Alexandra looked so demure that it was easy sometimes to forget she was old and deadly in her own way. But Cyn didn't appreciate being toyed with by anyone.

"Looks like we've found Liz," she said instead. "Or she found us. Mirabelle can give you the details." Her cell vibrated, indicating an incoming message, and she pulled it out, checking the display. "Right. That's Luci, so I'm out of here. I might see you later, depending. If not, then tomorrow." She looked at Mirabelle. "I'll call you, Mirabelle, after I talk with Liz, and tell you what's up. In the meantime, don't worry."

Chapter Thirty-eight

CYN HURRIED UP the steps of the house she and Luci had bought and renovated several years ago. It was a fifties-era structure, two-storied with a wide, old-fashioned front porch and wood siding. The half-acre lot was in a part of L.A. that had once been the neighborhood of choice for doctors and lawyers. But the city had changed, the doctors and lawyers had all moved south and west, and a lot of these old houses had been divided into apartments for nearby university students. She and Luci had gotten a good price on this one, mostly because it had been in such lousy shape. The elderly lady they bought it from had lived there over sixty years, and hadn't put a dime into upkeep for at least twenty.

She opened the door without knocking and went straight back, passing through a large living area. A wide-screen television was exploding with the color and sound of a movie Cyn didn't recognize. Couches, chairs and floor were filled with teenagers who gave her no notice as she walked by, although she suspected it was more a matter of choice than attention span.

Luci's office was at the back of the house near the kitchen, in a small room that had once been a butler's pantry or something. They'd ripped out the plumbing and put in windows for Luci's many plants which were threatening to overrun the tiny space.

Luci was sitting at her desk, her back to the door. A teenage girl sat in the chair next to her, and the resemblance to Mirabelle was undeniable. She looked up when Cyn entered the room, her eyes weary and suspicious. Cyn gave her a little nod, looked at her friend and said, "Luce."

Lucia spun around, concern dissolving into a welcome smile. "Cyn," she said warmly, standing and coming over for a hug. Luci was a very huggy kind of person. Cyn really wasn't, but she tried for Luci's sake. Liz watched the exchange closely.

"Liz, this is my very good friend Cynthia Leighton. She and I opened this house together, lo those many years ago."

Liz's big blue eyes studied Cyn carefully, checking her mouth, her hands, even her eyes. *Looking for vampire indicators*, Cyn thought. Not that she was offended by it. She'd have done the same thing.

"So, you're a friend of Luci's?" Liz asked doubtfully.

Cyn nodded. "From college."

"And you're working for my sister?"

"Not really working *for*, more like working with. I'm sure Luci told you . . ." She glanced at her friend for confirmation. Luci nodded, then sat, pulling over a scarred wooden chair for Cyn to do the same.

"Jabril actually hired me to find you," Cyn continued, reluctantly taking the uncomfortable seat. "But then I met Mirabelle and, well, hell, I met Jabril. I broke Mirabelle out of there and came looking for you. Lucky for me, you decided on L.A."

"There's some other guy looking for me too," Liz volunteered cautiously. A slight twang became more evident in her speech as she began to relax.

"Yeah. I met him. Beefy guy with short white hair?"

"I think so. I didn't see him myself, but some of my friends told me he was looking. That was before—" She looked away, uncomfortable, and Luci intervened, reaching out to take Liz's hand in both of hers.

"It's okay, sweetie. None of that matters now, and Cyn understands. Don't you, Cyn?"

"Sin?" Liz said. "They call you Sin?"

"Cyn with a C Y," Cyn said. "I always hated the name Cyndi and Cynthia sounds so . . . I don't know . . . proper." Luci snorted and rolled her eyes, surprising a little laugh out of Liz.

"My parents always called me Elsie," Liz volunteered. "I thought I hated it too," she added wistfully.

Cyn knew enough about the girl's parents and their untimely death to change the subject. "So tell me what happened, Liz. I've been looking for you all over the place."

"Yeah, I heard. You sounded okay, and you gave those food coupons to all the kids. But I didn't know who I could trust." She stared down at her hands, held tightly by Luci. "And all those girls were dying." She looked back up, meeting Cyn's eyes. "I was scared and Todd started coming around. He does a lot of stuff with the street kids, basketball games and shit like that. He started talking to me and he seemed really nice, although he's kind of old and out of shape for a guy who plays sports. He wears those big striped shirts all the time, you know, like those Australian guys do? But all the kids seemed to know him, so . . ." She shrugged.

"When he found out I was from Texas, he said he had family there too. Some cousins or something. And I told him about Mirabelle and Jabril and everything, and how if I could just hide out until my eighteenth birthday everything would be okay, because then I'd have my own money. So he said, why don't I come stay with him until then, you know, 'cuz it was only like two weeks away." She paused to give Cyn a forlorn look. "He seemed like a nice guy," she repeated.

"So what happened? What made you change your mind?"

"He never touched me. Not like that. I would have been out of there if he had, because he's . . . well, like forty or something. Anyway, he started getting really bossy. Like I had to tell him everywhere I went and what I was doing and everything. And then I got the message from Mirabelle saying she was here and we should meet. I'd lost my computer, but he was letting me use his to like check my message boards and stuff. He works at night somewhere, and I didn't want to go out after dark, plus it was a good time to try to reach Mirabelle and let her know I was safe. So anyway, I got this message saying she was here in California, and it seemed weird. I mean why would she be here? So I wrote back to her how I wasn't sure and how did I know it was safe? And she told me about that Raphael guy, that he's not like dickhead Jabril or anything, and she's living in a nice place and I can come stay with her."

Cyn nodded. She'd already heard most of this from Mirabelle.

"Anyway, so I'm online with Mirabelle, and he comes in and starts freaking out about vampires and especially Raphael, and he tells me Raphael's been arrested for killing those girls and he doesn't want me to have anything to do with him or with Mirabelle, because that fucking vampire—that's what he called him, that fucking vampire—he's using Mirabelle to get to me because I'm his type. And I said, what do you mean I'm his type? But then he says I don't have to worry because I'm not like all those other girls."

"Not like them how?" Cyn said quietly.

"He said all those girls hung out with vampires and that's why they died."

Cyn exchanged a look with Luci. "What'd you say his name was, Liz?"

"Todd. Todd Ryder. He lives down near the beach, but in that kind of scummy part where it's really crowded. Venice, I think they call it. Someone told me they have canals there like in Italy, but I never saw any."

"I'll show them to you sometime," Cyn said absently. "So what happened then?"

"The fucker tried to lock me in his house, that's what happened! After we argued, I like stormed into my room and fell asleep. And when I got up, he'd locked the bedroom door! And all the windows have those like jail bars on them, you know? So I'm pounding on the door, but he's gone to work and left me there without even a bathroom or anything!"

Luci looked over her shoulder at Cyn with a pleased grin. "My girl Liz here broke the door down," she said.

Liz blushed, embarrassed and proud at the same time. "Yeah, well, it was one of those cheap hollow doors. It didn't take much. He had this like old metal lamp on the table. Really ugly, but heavy. So, I pounded and pounded. Trashed my arm, but once I broke through it was pretty fast. I stuck my hand out and unlocked the door, and then I got the hell out of there. I didn't have anything but my purse anyway, so I grabbed it and ran." She looked up at Cyn and shrugged again. "And here I am."

"So here you are, and I'm very happy to see you," Cyn agreed. "What do you want to do now?"

"I don't know. I didn't really think past getting here."

Cyn nodded. "And you're probably okay here for now, but you need to be careful. Jabril's man won't think twice about breaking the law to grab you. I'd feel better if you stayed with me until we get everything cleared up."

"I don't want to live with vampires."

Cyn opened her mouth to point out that *she* didn't live with vampires, but Luci spoke up. "Maybe Liz could stay here for awhile," she suggested. "Everything will look different after you've had a couple days to think about it," she said to Liz.

"What about Mirabelle?" Liz asked, looking at Cyn. "Is she living with you?"

Cyn shook her head. "Mirabelle has nutritional needs I can't meet. She's staying on Raphael's estate, at his sister Alexandra's house, which is separate from everyone else. The two of them have discovered Internet shopping, God help us." She shivered dramatically. "If you don't want to stay with me right now, maybe you can at least go by for a visit with Mirabelle. I'd be happy to give you a ride, and I know she'd like to see you, to know you're really okay."

Liz twisted her mouth, biting the inside of her lower lip in thought. She glanced at Cyn, then back at Luci. "I think I'd like to stay here tonight at least. I trust Luci." Cyn ignored the implication that *she*, on the other hand, was not to be trusted. "And maybe tomorrow night," Liz continued, "I can see Mirabelle. Would that be okay?" She directed the question at Luci, not Cyn.

Luci leaned forward and hugged the girl, then stood. "Of course, whatever you want. Come on, we'll get you set up. You need a shower, and I think I've got some clothes that will fit you." The two of them pretty much ignored Cyn as they started out of the room, but Cyn touched Liz's arm, drawing her startled attention.

"Can you tell me where this Todd guy lives? If not the address, then how to get there?"

Liz gave her a worried look. She glanced at Luci for reassurance, and Luci patted her on the shoulder. "Why don't you go on up," she said to the girl. "It's the room at the top of the stairs, with the blue door. I'll be there in a minute." She gave Cyn a somber look as Liz took the stairs two at a time.

"I have Todd's address," Luci said quietly, going back into her office. "We've never had any problem with him. He does a lot of after-hours stuff with the kids, organizing games and so on, to keep them off the streets. He used to do some outreach, too, when he had a girlfriend, but they broke up and he sticks pretty much to the organized activities now."

Cyn played a hunch. "The girlfriend have a name?"

"Um, Patty something, I think," Luci replied, keying the search into her computer database. "She was younger than Todd, not beautiful, but pretty enough. Kind of a pointy face and small mouth. What?" she asked in alarm, seeing the distressed look on Cyn's face.

Chapter Thirty-nine

ON HER WAY TO Venice and Todd Ryder's house, Cyn gave Mirabelle a quick call, explained the situation and told her to count on a visit from Liz the next night.

"Why not tonight? She could stay here; Alexandra wouldn't mind."

"First of all, she's pretty wiped out, Mirabelle. It's been a rough couple of weeks for her in a strange city, all alone on the street. I mean, give her a break. And secondly, she's not exactly thrilled at the idea of living with more vampires, you know?"

"I guess. But doesn't she want to see me, at least?" The last bit was more of a plaintive wail.

"Sure she does. And she will. Tomorrow night. Besides, it's almost dawn already. By the time we got there, you'd be ready to go to sleep."

"I suppose you're right. But she's definitely okay, isn't she? You're not like protecting me from the truth or anything?"

"I wouldn't do that, Mirabelle. Liz is fine. Really tired, but that's it. You'll see for yourself tomorrow."

"Okay. Thanks, Cyn. You want to talk to anyone here?"

"No, thanks. I'm heading home too. Listen, I'll call you before we come over. Sleep tight."

Mirabelle gave a girlish laugh. "Right. You too. Bye."

Cyn dropped her phone onto the console as she pulled onto Ryder's darkened street. Contrary to Liz's dismissive observations, this was actually a pricey neighborhood, although at first glance it might not look like it. The homes were small and crowded together, and there was a bit of a crime problem from vagrants who made the beach their home. But it was only a few blocks to the sand, and Ryder had to be doing pretty well to afford to buy this place. Of course, it was always possible he rented. Cyn hadn't run a background check on him yet. She'd wait and see if a little felonious breaking and entering turned up anything worthwhile first.

She parked her truck a couple of houses down and across the street and sat studying Ryder's place. It was an older house, narrow with a single story and detached garage. The houses to either side had been remodeled to add a second story—the lots were small and people had to build up for extra footage—and Ryder's house seemed to huddle in on itself between its neighbors, cringing beneath the disdainful gaze of the two updated homes. Liz told her Ryder kept a regular schedule, leaving for work and coming home at pretty much the same time every day, which meant he shouldn't be back for a good couple of hours yet. It would have been better to wait and go in right after he left for work on another day, but it was Friday and Liz didn't think he worked Friday or Saturday nights. Which meant Cyn would have had to wait until Sunday night to catch him going to work, and patience had never been her strong point. Besides, Mirabelle's audience with Raphael was Sunday.

There were no lights on in Ryder's house, not even a porch light. His neighbors had both installed low-level outdoor lights and one showed the faint gleam of what was probably a night light upstairs. She tapped her fingers nervously on the steering wheel and decided to take the chance. Flicking off the overhead light, she switched her phone to vibrate, slipped it into her jacket pocket and cracked her door open silently. She made her way down the dark street, passing by Ryder's house only to cross and come up on his property from the garage side. The narrow driveway was unfinished except for two parallel lines of concrete pavers which Cyn followed as she made her way quietly to the back of the house.

It was a matter of a few minutes work for her to get inside. Pulling on thin latex gloves, she slipped the lock and went in through the back door. The front was too open to the street, and besides, like so many people, Ryder's back door had a much flimsier lock than the front. Why did people assume the bad guys would use the front door?

Once inside, she surveyed the small house in the glow of LEDs from various electronic devices—two bedrooms and a small living room, with wooden floors and not a single throw rug to soften the effect, not even a door mat. Cyn started across the front room, chuckling at the wreckage of the door Liz had left behind. She stopped laughing when she saw the mess inside the bedroom. Someone had torn it apart. Sheets and blankets had been ripped off the bed and thrown around the small room. The mattress, box spring and pillows had been savagely slashed with something sharp, and stuffing littered the floor. Tiny bits of it still floated through the air, backlit by a shaft of street light coming through a window now bare of the broken miniblind lying crookedly on the floor below. The lamp Liz had used to bludgeon the door was bent around the doorframe, its cheap metal split at the seam.

So Todd Ryder had a temper. Cyn scanned the trashed room quickly, but didn't expect to find anything here. Far more interesting was the main bedroom down the hall, which was perfectly neat and tidy. The bed was made, the pillows sitting one on top of the other, precisely aligned, the cases crisp and tucked in. No unsightly flapping linen for Todd. She did a quick open and look of each drawer, raising an eyebrow at the large, partially used box of condoms in the bedside drawer. Girlfriend or not, Todd apparently had plans. In the closet, shirts were grouped according to style, short-sleeved polo for summer, long-sleeved rugby for cooler weather. Several pairs of khakis were hanging, pressed and starched, still in the plastic bags from the laundry. Shoes were placed in neat pairs, side by side on the floor.

The tiny bathroom had even less to tell her. Todd Ryder was apparently the picture of good health. There wasn't even a bottle of aspirin to share space with his shaving cream and razor, and his aftershave was a scent too much like perfume for Cyn's taste.

Back in the living room, Cyn rubbed her hands together in glee at the sight of Ryder's desk and computer. A car door slammed outside and she froze, heart hammering, but the smooth purr of an engine moved away down the street. She went quickly over to the desk, reminded that her time was short. She sat and powered up the computer while going through the drawers one by one. There was a neat file for bills due and paid which she flipped through quickly, finding little of interest other than a bill for a storage unit in Culver City. She noted the location and locker number automatically, but kept searching. A separate blue folder was filled with paycheck stubs that told her Todd Ryder worked for a meat packing plant. Now *that* was interesting. A man who spent his nights butchering sides of beef wouldn't balk at a little, or even a lot, of blood. A final file contained flyers on the games Ryder ran for the street kids, a list of names and phone numbers—coaches, maybe?—a schedule of games, and some blank consent forms. Probably not much call for the latter, most of these kids didn't have anyone who cared enough to worry about consent.

By the time she was finished with the drawers, the computer had completed its startup. A quick check had her shaking her head. Tidy Todd didn't practice safe computing. Good for her, not so good for Todd. He knew enough not to store his e-mail password, which was disappointing, but not enough to install even a rudimentary sweep program. Cyn almost cackled as she began prying into a history of

Todd's computer use. He visited a lot of message boards dedicated to the discussion of vampires. Many of the sites were the kind Ian Hartzler would have frequented, boards populated by groupies who wanted to be vamps, and others who claimed to already have been brought over. Other sites were darker, conspiracy-oriented and filled with dire warnings of a vampire takeover, claiming everyone from the president down to the local tax collector was either in thrall to the vampires or a vampire himself. Cyn made note of the web addresses, using her cell phone to leave a voice mail for herself with the information and adding the storage company info for good measure.

Even more interesting, she discovered Todd had done several searches in the last few days, looking for stories on the dead girls, and specifically for deaths involving vampires. There had been little publicity about the murders and none at all about Santillo's pet theory. Raphael's arrest hadn't even made the news. It was partly because they'd taken him to the para facility which hardly anyone knew about, but also because the murders simply weren't news. Besides, Raphael lived well below the radar; it wasn't like his arrest would have made headlines anyway. Of course, working with street kids, Ryder might have heard about the murders, but why the vampire angle? Again, interesting, but not convincing.

Cyn continued her search of the computer, but learned nothing new. There was some accounting software and a few games, but it seemed Ryder used his computer primarily for Internet access. If he was keeping the diary of a serial killer somewhere, it wasn't on this computer. She shut the system down and pushed away from the desk, careful to tuck the chair under the way she'd found it.

The kitchen was next, more wood flooring with pretty blue and white tiled countertops and pine cabinets. The cupboards held an unremarkable assortment of food; underneath the sink were the usual cleaning supplies. The refrigerator was virtually empty, with a six pack of beer missing one bottle, and a quart of half and half. Pots and pans appeared virtually unused. Even the coffeemaker had been cleaned, the glass pot sitting upside down on a wooden rack to one side of the gleaming sink. Ryder would have made someone a great housewife. Or maybe that was the reason he was still single in his forties. He'd never met a woman who could match him in the housewife department. Unfortunately, being a neat freak was hardly a crime. The ambient light shifted as she stood in the doorway doing a final sweep. The street lights had switched off outside; time to go.

Safely in her truck and perversely disappointed that she'd found nothing really suspicious, Cyn watched as an older BMW sedan drove by and pulled into the driveway. Todd Ryder was younger than she expected from Liz's description. Probably closer to thirty-five than forty, five-foot-ten or so, with light brown hair and the slightly pudgy body of a former athlete gone soft. Probably played high school or even college sports. His chin, never strong, was made weaker by the softening effect of that extra weight. He was wearing one of his many pairs of neatly pressed khaki slacks, along with a blue and red rugby shirt. The shirt was about a size too large, which was probably an attempt to cover the extra fifteen pounds around his middle. He climbed out of the car and paused to buff a thumb over the door's trim, shaking his head in disgust before going on down the driveway and into the house. *BMW's were good, solid cars*, Cyn thought, remembering the kid in the alley who'd heard the killer's car. Definitely not full of *rattles and shit*.

She waited a few more minutes before driving home, cruising north along Pacific Coast Highway at freeway speeds and feeling sorry for the people stuck in the morning's southbound rush hour. She thought about what she knew. The only victim the cops had any information on was Patti Hammel, who happened to be Todd Ryder's old girlfriend and who, despite being the first victim, didn't fit the profile. Convenient that she didn't have any family or friends. No one to claim the body, no one to file a report except her old boyfriend Todd who hadn't so much as whispered a concern. Todd who was maybe wound a little too tight, and whose temper was violent when it blew. And then there was the witness who had fingered Raphael as the killer and who maybe hated vampires enough to make the whole thing up. She flipped her phone open and called Eckhoff's cell phone.

"Damn it, Leighton, do you know what time it is?"

"The city never sleeps, old man. Be nice to me; I'm about to do you a favor."

"You can start with a fucking apology for your last message."

"Who's your witness on the serial case? The one fingering a vampire as the killer?"

"You woke me up for this? It's not my damn case. Besides, I told you—"

"Yeah, yeah. But you checked into it when I asked about it earlier. I know you. So don't tell me. I'll tell you. His name's Todd Ryder."

"How . . . What the fuck, Leighton. Who the hell—"

"And what a coincidence . . . Do you know the name of Patti

Hammel's old boyfriend?" she asked with false enthusiasm. There was dead silence, followed by vicious swearing and the sound of movement from Eckhoff's end. Cyn smiled. "Gets around, doesn't he?"

"Where did you get this?" Eckhoff said in a low voice. "Not even Santillo would have overlooked something that obvious."

"You have to look for something to overlook it, Dean. Santillo heard what he wanted to hear. You want my info or not?"

"Shit. Yes, damn it. And don't *even* tell me where you got it."

"Okay," she said cheerfully, then passed on every detail she'd discovered, from her nameless lost-boy witness to Todd Ryder's vampire obsession, his nice car and his rental unit. "I've got the specifics on the web sites and his rental unit in my voice mail. I'll forward it on to you when we hang up, and I only want one thing in return for all of my effort on behalf of the LAPD."

"Yeah? What's that?" he asked sourly.

"Jeez, Dean. I think I'm owed something here!"

"Fine, fine. What?"

"I want to know why he did it. I want ten minutes in a room with him after the arrest."

Eckhoff was silent. "Just you, right, not—"

Cyn laughed. "I'm not going to kill your suspect, Eckhoff. Ten minutes, that's all I ask. Off the record, of course."

Eckhoff sighed deeply. "Why're you doing this, Cyn? You could cause some trouble here, if you wanted. Santillo and his friends hurt your boy, why not hurt them back?"

"Because, contrary to what all of you seem to think, I still believe in the law, boss. And all I really want is to stop this asshole before he kills someone else."

"I'm getting all teary eyed here, grasshopper."

"And that's my cue to hang up. Remember your promise."

Chapter Forty

Houston, Texas

JABRIL STEPPED OUT of his shower, toweling off quickly before donning the silken robe left hanging behind the door. He wrapped it around himself, enjoying the touch of it against his bare skin. No point in getting dressed. Not yet. He was trying out a new slave tonight—someone to replace his old favorite. She was proving more difficult to replace than he would have expected, which only told him it was past time he'd gotten rid of her. It was never good to become attached to a blood slave. They existed to serve him, nothing more.

He strolled back into the bedroom, admiring the new furniture. His staff had been admirably quick in refitting this room; he was quite pleased.

A knock sounded at the door. "Just in time," he murmured. "Come," he called out.

"My lord." Asim slipped inside the room in his usual sneaky way. The vampire never fully opened a door and walked through, but rather opened it just enough that he could slide through the gap.

Jabril frowned. "I wasn't expecting you, Asim."

"No, my lord, but I've news of Elizabeth that I thought you would want to hear."

Jabril felt a rush of avaricious pleasure. "She has been found then. She is secured?"

"Found, yes, my lord. Windle does not yet have her in custody, although he expects that to happen very soon."

"If he knows where she is, then what is the delay?"

"He has been following her trail closely for several days, my lord, and tracked her to a private home where she was staying. Unfortunately, she has now moved herself to some sort of home for runaways. There are several people staying in the house, and he has seen the Leighton woman come and go more than once."

Jabril swore viciously. "She cannot be allowed—"

"No, my lord," Asim dared to interrupt. "Windle has set a watch on the house and is quite confident he will have Elizabeth in his custody within days, if not hours."

Jabril studied his lieutenant, considering whether this news deserved punishment. Any competent investigator would have had the girl in custody already. Of course, he'd been forced to rely on human agents. He could push Raphael only so far, and sending vampire agents in to take the girl would cross a boundary he wasn't prepared to violate. Not yet.

A lighter knock sounded on the door and Asim stepped aside to permit it to open. A young woman stood there—naked, her long, black hair hanging to the curve of her shapely ass. Her skin was a lovely golden brown, and the pointed nipples on her small, high breasts were already pebbled with fear. Jabril blinked lazily and held out his hand.

"Very well, Asim," he said absently, pulling the girl closer and wrapping his fist in that abundance of silky hair. He jerked her head to one side, baring her neck. His fangs split his gums hungrily. "Keep me informed," he managed to say, before slicing his fangs into the soft skin of her neck, feeling the vibration of her screams echoing in his very bones.

He was vaguely aware of Asim backing out and closing the door as he drank deeply of the girl's blood, feeling it run warm and fresh down his throat. He growled with pleasure as his cock hardened, eager for a taste of its own. He lifted his head, picked her up and threw her on the bed, her soft cries of pain only making him harder. Yes, it had definitely been time for a change.

Chapter Forty-one

Los Angeles, California

THE PARA FACILITY was dark and quiet the night after Todd Ryder's arrest. It felt empty, a sharp contrast to the night Raphael had been brought in and the halls had been packed wall-to-wall with blue. Cyn strode quietly down the linoleum-covered hallway, making an effort to keep her boots from clacking, somehow unwilling to disturb the silence. Behind her, Duncan might as well have been a ghost for all the noise he made. If he hadn't come with her, she wouldn't have known he was there.

A door opened and Eckhoff stepped into the light. His gaze flashed from her to Duncan and he frowned. "Cyn." He opened the door fully and she saw his Lieutenant standing inside, with Santillo glowering behind him.

"Lieutenant Garzon," she acknowledged. She ignored Santillo.

"Leighton," Garzon said. "We appreciate your help on this." Santillo flashed his lieutenant a furious look.

"I'm always happy to help the department, sir," Cyn replied honestly. She stepped aside slightly and indicated Duncan. "This is Lord Raphael's Chief of Security, Duncan—" She realized she had no idea what Duncan's last name was, but he stepped easily into the breach.

"Duncan Milford," he said, his Southern accent once again making a blatant appearance. He reached out to shake hands and the lieutenant responded automatically, offering his hand in return. Eckhoff followed suit. For a minute, she thought Duncan was actually going to shake hands with Santillo as well, but he settled for a friendly nod in the detective's direction, which must have been an effort.

Cyn didn't know if it was the Southern accent or Duncan's human good looks, but everyone relaxed after that. It took all her self-control not to laugh out loud. Of course, one of the reasons it was Duncan standing there next to her and not someone else was precisely because he looked so very human.

"So what is it you'd like from us?" Garzon asked Duncan.

"Well, sir, it's a matter of security," Duncan drawled. "You understand. The suspect . . ." The way he said it invited all of them to join him in substituting the word "killer." There was no doubt in this room as to Ryder's guilt. "The suspect tried to frame my boss on some pretty serious charges and I can't figure out why. We don't know him; he's in none of our files. So I figured, since Ms. Leighton here was helpful in tracking this guy down, you might let us have a word with him, figure out what his beef is with Lord Raphael. We like to keep an eye on this sort of thing."

Cyn wanted to barf at the good ol' boy act, but it seemed to work. The Lieutenant was nodding before Duncan had even finished speaking. "Of course. Shouldn't be a problem. Leighton here knows the rules on interrogations, and you must have some experience yourself, Mr. Milford?"

"Duncan, sir. Just Duncan. And yes, I do. I did my time on the job."

Nearly two hundred years ago, Cyn wanted to add. Duncan glanced at her sidelong, as if he knew what she was thinking.

"Well, good, then," the Lieutenant was saying. "We'll be moving him out of here before too long. He belongs downtown, but we wanted to keep this little visit low profile. So, let's get to it. Ten minutes, right, Leighton?"

"Yes, sir."

"Good enough. Eckhoff—"

"How'd you know?" Santillo demanded, his glare making it clear he was talking to her.

Cyn looked at him, her eyebrows raised in question.

"How'd you connect Ryder?"

Cyn stared at him evenly, deciding whether to answer his question. *What the hell.* "The case paralleled one of my own," she said. "A teenage runaway from Texas. I talked to a lot of kids trying to find her and *they* all wanted to talk about the killer. Everything they said led back to Ryder. He worked with the street kids, had a habit of taking in a girl from time to time, he even had a job that would give him the knowledge to drain the bodies the way the killer did.

"But it was Lucia Shinn who ID'd him as Hammel's boyfriend. She's been trying to talk to you guys for weeks about this and no one would listen."

Santillo flushed an angry red, but he didn't say anything else. Eckhoff cleared his throat and made a move toward the door. "Let's get this done, Leighton."

ECKHOFF LED THEM down the hall and past the cell where Raphael had been held. "Through here," he said opening an unmarked door. "Standard set up, one way glass. We're equipped to record, but—"

"That won't be necessary," Cyn said quickly.

"Not this time," Eckhoff agreed. "You want me in there with you?"

"Duncan will be with me." Eckhoff opened his mouth to protest, but Cyn raised a hand. "He won't say anything, but I want Ryder to see him. A little intimidation never hurt, Dean, and if Ryder killed those girls—"

"He killed them all right. That storage unit turned out to be one of those RV places. Most rent a big parking space, but our boy had a full garage, complete with running water and a sink in case he wanted to wash down the old Winnebago. He'd created a personal abattoir in there."

"Evidence?"

"The whole place reeked of bleach, but it looks like Hammel was spending a lot of time at his place when he killed her, because he had a lot of her personal stuff—books, papers, that sort of thing. He should have incinerated the whole batch. Lucky for us, he filed it all away in storage, nice and neat."

"Yeah, Todd's a neat guy. Any murder weapon?"

"Most likely a plain old barbecue fork. There were a few in the unit, high end, heavy duty types. ME's running tests looking for metal fragments in the neck wounds."

"Which they should have done before now."

Eckhoff shrugged. "Ten minutes, Leighton."

RYDER LOOKED UP when they entered the room. He was sitting on a plain metal chair bolted to the floor. There was a matching table, but it had been pulled away and shoved against one wall so the prisoner sat exposed, hands cuffed behind his back, ankles manacled. He was still wearing a striped rugby shirt and khakis, but they didn't look quite as neatly pressed. "Who the fuck are you?" he snapped.

"Not important, Todd," Cyn said pleasantly. "But since you asked so nicely, I'll tell you. I'm the one who figured you out."

"Bullshit."

"Such a mouth." She tsked. "So tell me. I know it all comes back to Patti. I figure she was probably an accident, maybe an argument. She wants to leave, you're upset—"

"Fuck that! Do I look like the kind of guy who needs to beg a woman to stay around? Shit. Two hours after she'd left, I had someone younger sliding into my bed."

"Yes, but did she slide back *out* of your bed, Todd? Your girlfriends have rather short life spans lately."

"That's not my fault. They hang around with fucking bloodsuckers, stuff's gonna happen."

Cyn looked at him and gave a smile that would have made Raphael proud. Todd Ryder obviously saw it because he started to sweat. "I'm sorry, Todd," Cyn said sweetly. "I didn't introduce you to my associate." She stood aside so he could see Duncan clearly. "This is Duncan."

Ryder's eyes flashed over to where Duncan stood with his back to the observation window, arms crossed casually.

"Yeah? Big fucking deal. You gonna have your boyfriend there pound on me or something? I'm terrified. Hope you got a good lawyer, lady, 'cuz I'm not going down for something I didn't do. Fuck you."

Cyn shook her head in mock disappointment. "And here we've been nothing but friendly. But don't worry—"

"I'm *not* worried," he cut in quickly, but Cyn continued as if he'd never spoken.

". . . Duncan here's not going to hit you." She leaned forward and confided, "It's not really his style. Is it, Duncan?" She glanced over her shoulder.

Duncan never changed position; he just opened his mouth and smiled.

Ryder's eyes widened and beads of sweat popped out on his forehead as the room filled with the stink of fear. "What the fuck's he doing here?" he gasped. "You can't do this. I've got rights."

"*Patti* had rights too, Todd. So did all those other girls you killed to cover your own ass. Or wait . . . maybe you got off on it, huh? Are the cops going to find streaks of cum on those little souvenirs in your hideaway?"

He looked away from Duncan, his face twisted in disgust. "Jesus, you're a repulsive bitch—" His gaze snapped back, words cut off as Duncan took a step forward.

"You watch your mouth, human."

Ryder blinked furiously, his thigh muscles bunching beneath tan material as he struggled to push the bolted chair away from the vampire. "Look, look. I'd like to help but, I didn't—"

Duncan leaned a little closer and sniffed. "Nervous, little man?" he whispered, and blew a soft breath over Ryder's sweat-dampened skin.

Ryder jumped as if he'd been stabbed, his eyes rolling nearly white with fear as a high-pitched keening noise came from his throat. "You can't do this," Ryder said again, his voice a hoarse whisper.

"But, Todd, I was never here," Cyn said reasonably.

He stared at her, trying to make sense of her words. His face paled as realization struck. "No," he whispered. "You can't, I'm not . . ."

Cyn smiled.

"Okay," he croaked, his gaze shifting frantically between Cyn and Duncan as he strained to keep an eye on the vampire while talking to her. "Look. I'll tell you what you want to know, but don't let him . . ." He jerked his head toward Duncan.

"Confession is good for the soul," Duncan said softly. "Or so I've heard." He laughed and it was a terrifying sound.

"Please," Ryder whispered breathlessly. "I'll talk, but don't—"

"So talk," Cyn said in a bored voice. "Start at the beginning."

"Okay, okay," Ryder said, then swallowed noisily. "You've got to believe me, though. I didn't mean to kill her," he said quickly. "Patti. We had a fight, like you said." He nodded at Cyn. "She got invited to one of those parties with the vampires, those blood houses. She was so excited. It was sickening."

He obviously remembered his audience and looked up, eyes wide. "I didn't mean . . ." He swallowed again nervously and continued. "I loved her and I asked her not to go, but she didn't care. I got pissed and threw something. I don't even remember what it was, but I didn't mean to hit her. I loved her," he repeated in a pitiful whine, as if that excused everything.

"But I knew the cops wouldn't believe me, so I . . ." He sat up straight suddenly, sucking in a breath, as if aware for the first time what he was about to say. He frowned and gave Cyn a calculating look, but Duncan was suddenly there, right in front of him, blocking him from seeing anyone or anything. Ryder's eyes glazed over and he kept talking.

"I decided since it was the vampires that started it all, they should pay for it. But I had to do something fast. I took Patti to the tub and bled her so it would look like a vampire had done it, then I dumped the body somewhere the cops would find it. I only did the other girls to make it look like Patti was part of a killing spree. I mean those vampires kill people all the time, so what difference . . ."

Cyn tuned out Ryder's voice, disgusted by his pathetic attempts to justify everything he'd done. As if those girls deserved to die because Patti Hammel had fucked a vampire. She didn't need to listen to know the kind of shit he would shovel. And besides, no matter what Eckhoff said, she knew the conversation was being recorded. Not officially, and the cops wouldn't be able to use it as evidence, but it would tell them everything they needed to know to get Ryder for the murders. She sat in the chair, staring at her feet, until Duncan touched her shoulder gently.

"Cynthia."

She looked up, startled to realize Ryder had stopped talking. The whole room stank of sweat and fear and she wanted out. She stood. "Duncan? Are we finished?" She had enough presence of mind to keep her back to the window, but Duncan was studying her with concern, so she drew a deep breath and let it out slowly. "I'm okay. Let's just get the hell out of here."

WHEN SHE DROPPED off Duncan in front of the main house, it wasn't even midnight yet. She pulled up and left the engine running, and Duncan turned to her in surprise. "You're not coming in?"

"Not tonight. Listen, Duncan. Thanks. I couldn't have done it without you."

He shrugged. "None of what he said will stand up in court."

"No, but now they know what to ask and they'll get something out of him. Enough to convict anyway. Besides, you're one scary vampire. I don't think Todd's going to be in any hurry to get out of jail."

"I'll fill Raphael in on the details unless you . . ." He didn't finish, but looked at her expectantly.

"No, you go ahead. I need some sleep. There's always sort of a letdown after I close a case, you know?"

Duncan smiled knowingly which irritated her somehow, and so she grumbled, "What's with the accent? You had it at the airport, too, with Mirabelle. You don't normally talk like that."

His smiled broadened. "But I do, Cynthia," he said with a heavy drawl. "It's that northern speech that's not normal."

Cyn laughed. "You're a man of many surprises, Duncan Milford. Is that your real name?"

"It was once," he said somberly. "Now it's just Duncan."

"Well, just Duncan, thank you."

He tipped his head in a little bow and slid out of the car. "Enjoy your rest, Cynthia."

"Thanks. And I guess I'll see you on Sunday, right?"

"Oh, yes," he said with a satisfied expression. "I wouldn't miss it."

Chapter Forty-two

THE NEXT DAY, Liz was waiting when Cyn arrived at the house. Luci had found clothes for her somewhere, a pair of clean denims that hung low enough to show off the glint of silver in her bellybutton, along with a couple of tops layered over one another in a clash of color that was suitably defiant. Cyn smiled. She had a feeling she and Liz would have had a lot in common once upon a time.

"I talked to Mirabelle," Liz said without preamble. "She knows we're coming."

"So I hear. You ready?"

"Yeah. This your car?" she asked, eyeing the big SUV. "Nice. Can I drive?"

"You got a license?" Liz shook her head. "Then the answer's no. But we'll see about fixing that real soon. Come on, it's not far."

"Are we almost there?" Liz asked thirty minutes later. "I thought you said it wasn't that far?"

Cyn didn't answer immediately. She was concentrating on crossing four lanes of congested traffic in a last minute daredevil zip between freeways, earning more than one obscene gesture and a chorus of honking horns from her fellow drivers.

A few minutes later, they passed through McLaren Tunnel and were dumped onto Pacific Coast Highway in Malibu. "Anything less than an hour *isn't* far in this town. But it won't be long now," Cyn assured her.

Liz stared at the tight row of expensive houses sitting next to the highway, their front doors only feet away from the rushing traffic. Beyond them was nothing but the sand and the roiling black velvet of the Pacific Ocean beneath a nearly full moon. "L.A.'s bigger than I thought," she said in a small voice.

"It seems that way," Cyn agreed. "The problem is there's no real center. It's sort of spread out all over the place."

"I guess."

Cyn glanced over. "Mirabelle's really excited about seeing you."

"Mmm. Me too." She gave Cyn a sideways look. "You're sure it's okay, right? I mean, Luci said I should trust you and all, but you don't know what Jabril's like. He's really sneaky, and he gives the judges and everyone money, so they do whatever—"

"Liz."

"I love Mirabelle, and I know she tries, but he hurts her and—"

"Liz."

Elizabeth stared at her, eyes wide with trepidation.

"Elizabeth, honey, it's okay. Jabril doesn't have any power here, and you can trust Raphael. *I* trust him. He won't hurt Mirabelle and he won't hurt you. And even if someone tried to hurt you, I wouldn't let them, okay? I'll stay with you as long as you want, until you feel safe. And anytime you want to go back to Luci's, you say the word and we're gone."

Liz swallowed hard.

"Okay?" Cyn asked.

"Okay." It was weak, but definite.

"Good enough," Cyn said with a grin. "Because this is it." She gestured ahead and to the left where Raphael's estate was nothing more than a dark forest of tall trees on the side of the road. "It looks worse than it is," she confided. "Once we get through the gate, it's pretty nice." She made the turn but stopped before they reached the gate. "You're sure you're okay with this, right? If not, we'll turn around right now and forget the whole thing."

Liz bobbed her head, sucking in a deep breath. "No. No, I'm good. I want to see my sister."

"Don't worry about them," Cyn said, when they pulled up to the gate. Raphael's vampire guards closed on the Land Rover, looking it and them over very carefully. The one closest to her side acknowledged Cyn with a friendly nod, and she knew Alexandra had warned them about Elizabeth's visit, but they followed procedure anyway, which was the way it should be. She heard Liz's relieved exhale when the guards backed away and waved them through the opening gate.

"Scary," Liz said.

"Yeah, pretty much. Raphael's security seems a lot tighter to me than Jabril's."

"You mean Dickhead."

"Yep, that's who I mean. Here we are." She pulled the Land Rover to the side of the road near Alexandra's manor house and turned off the engine.

Liz stared out the front window. "What kind of house is that? It looks like something from an old movie."

"Uh huh. But don't say that to Alexandra, okay? She loves this house."

"Duh. Like I would. So what now?"

"Well, now, we get out of the car and . . ." Her peripheral vision picked up movement near the house. "Here comes Mirabelle."

Liz tensed as Mirabelle left the kitchen door open behind her and tore down the driveway toward them. "She almost looks normal," Liz whispered.

"She *is* almost normal," Cyn whispered back.

Liz laughed suddenly and threw open her door, nearly falling from the truck in her eagerness to meet Mirabelle halfway. Cyn watched the two sisters embrace, embarrassed to feel tears tugging at her eyes. "My work here is done."

CYN WANDERED AWAY from the manor house and in among the trees, pausing as she passed the newly planted garden maze. It was amazing what enough money could do in such a short period of time. You want a maze? No need to wait for the shrubs to grow. We'll bring in fully grown specimens and carve them into whatever shape you choose. No doubt Alexandra planned for these to grow even taller, especially if Stephen King's book *The Shining* was her model. She walked on past, having no desire to test the shadowy pathways among the shrubs. Maybe in full daylight, but not in darkness and not surrounded by vampires, no matter how friendly.

She heard someone start on the piano upstairs and smiled, wondering if Mirabelle was showing off her newly acquired playing skills. She couldn't imagine that enthusiastic rendering coming from Alexandra's fastidious hand.

Alexandra had invited her to stay, of course. Mirabelle and Liz had taken off almost immediately, their heads tucked together, exchanging conspiratorial whispers. But Cyn wasn't in the mood for Alexandra's games. It was too much like work and Cyn figured she'd earned a break. After all, she'd found Elizabeth and solved several murders, all in the space of twenty-four hours. The thought of Jabril's reaction to what his advance money had bought made Cyn smile.

She made her way around the perimeter of the maze and out onto the pathway between the two houses. The grounds were carefully groomed here, the thick undergrowth cleared away to create more of a forest than a barrier. The gravel beneath her feet shone white in the moonlight which was the path's only illumination. The vampires didn't need anything more, and no one else was ever invited to walk here. Except for Cynthia, of course. She'd come this way with Raphael the first night they'd met, when she'd agreed to help him recover Alexandra. The ground beneath her feet began to slope up gently and she knew the main house was beyond the rise. But she didn't want to go there. Not yet. So, she turned off the pathway and found her way through the trees, gliding her fingers over the rough bark as she passed until she reached a clearing of sorts, a private glen created by the gardener's art.

She dropped to the ground, enjoying the pretense of being alone in the woods. It was mild, not warm, but comfortable enough in her leather jacket. She leaned back against a wide tree trunk and closed her eyes, listening to the steady murmur of the ocean.

"You found your little bird." His voice came out of the night, honey smooth and hinting of dark things.

Chapter Forty-three

CYN HAD KNOWN he was there, had felt his approach through that indefinable connection they seemed to share. She opened her eyes, but he was no more than a deeper darkness beneath the trees. "I did," she said without moving.

Raphael shed the shadows that surrounded him and entered the clearing, selecting a tree of his own to lean against. He wore his usual elegant suit, and Cyn watched in amusement as he removed the jacket and threw it aside to slouch gracefully onto the ground. He sat opposite her, loosening his tie and stretching his long legs out, until their feet were nearly touching.

Neither of them spoke at first. Cyn could hear his slow, steady breathing and knew he could detect far more than that from her—the sudden racing of her heart at the sight of him, the blood that was rushing to flush her cheeks with nervousness and excitement, even the warmth of desire that was an almost instant reaction to his presence.

"Why?" she asked finally.

Raphael's black eyes were frosted with moonlight as his gaze found her in the night. He didn't insult her by pretending not to understand the question, but he looked away, staring into a past she couldn't see.

"My first decades as Vampire, I lived alone," he said. "I killed, but only when I was hungry—I give myself that at least. Some young vampires, flush with their newfound power, will kill indiscriminately until they are stopped one way or the other. I was never one of those. But even so, when I killed I gave no thought to the individual, to the life I was taking. It was food, nothing more, and I needed it to live, so I took it. I never consciously considered these things at the time, of course. I was little more than an animal, a creature of cunning and instinct, knowing only the drive to survive this day and the next and the one after that." He brushed an invisible speck off his trousers in a gesture she would have taken for nerves from anyone else.

"Time passed," he continued. "And I began to master my new life, to regain control over who and what I was. And what I found inside myself was power. True power for the first time in my life. No more of being my father's lackey or my prince's badly used tool. I was Vampire, and not *just* Vampire, but a master with power to spare. My Mistress, she who made me, sensed my awakening and my growing strength and called me to her at last, intending to use me for her own purposes, even as I had been used by others all through my life."

His voice hardened. "I had no intention of being used. Not by her, not by anyone, ever again. But there were things I needed to learn, things Vampire and human, of power and of life. I might despise the princes who used me, despise my father who kept me tied to the dirt of his farm, but they saw me for what I was—an ignorant farmer, nothing more."

An owl hooted far overhead, followed by a whoosh of sound as it flew through the treetops. Raphael flicked his gaze upward, tracking the bird's movement easily while Cyn strained to see even the barest flash of a pale wing. He lowered his eyes, glanced at her quickly and then away, as if it was too difficult for him to tell her these things while meeting her gaze.

"I stayed with my Mistress for many years," he continued. "I let her use my mind—and my body—to her own ends. And I learned. How to be a gentleman, how to rule others, or in her case, more how *not* to rule others, but still I learned, if only by her bad example. And I studied power. My power, which I quickly discovered was far greater than hers. I practiced in secret, testing my will on others, experimenting, expanding the bounds of what I could achieve with a simple thought. I was careful to conceal my growing strength from my Mistress. One on one, I could have taken her even then, but she would have rallied the others of her children against me, and I was not yet skilled enough to take them all.

"And then she died." He shook his head and laughed softly. "She was utterly self-indulgent, confident in her charm and in her beauty, which was considerable, I grant you. But in the end, her beauty was nothing, or perhaps everything. It was a jealous wife who destroyed her, stabbing her through the heart as she lay in her daytime rest next to her lover, who was also the woman's husband. It was a stupid mistake to leave herself vulnerable like that, and so completely predictable that she would end in such a shameful fashion."

He remained silent for the space of a breath, and when he spoke next there was an underlying sadness to his words. "Most of her children died along with her. They were inextricably tied to her will, and in her final moments, she sucked them dry in a vain effort to save herself. She must have known it was futile, must have known she was only dragging them into death with her, but she wouldn't have cared. No price would be too great if there was even the slimmest chance that her own long life could be saved.

"I and a very few others survived, those of us who had the power to resist her final call. Some of those died soon after, falling to the life of debauchery which was all she'd ever taught them. The rest wandered off in search of a new master, while I took my newfound freedom and carved out a territory of my own. By then, none of the old masters alone had the strength to challenge me. And when they would have united against me, I took my few people and came here to America, the new world."

He met her gaze directly, emphasizing his next words. "In over five hundred years as Vampire, I have acknowledged no master, no lord, no lady. Not since my Mistress's death has any creature, living or dead, claimed more of me than I was willing to give—the loyalty among companions, the fidelity between Sire and child."

"But Alexandra—" Cyn protested.

"Alexandra," he said almost wearily, "is a petty woman who was once a child I loved. I sometimes think she would have done better if I'd never found her in that Paris dungeon, or if I'd left her to make her own way or fail in trying."

He shook his head. "No, my Cyn, there has been no one in all these hundreds of years who mastered me. Until I met you. From the first, I wanted you, and your resistance to my advances only made me want you more. When at last I lay sheathed within you, felt you arching beneath me with passion, all I could think of was having you again and yet again. My hunger for you was as fresh as if we hadn't joined only moments before. I gazed down at your face, at your eyes filled with desire for me alone, and I knew I would give everything I owned to keep you safe at my side and in my bed.

"So, having at last met a foe I could not defeat, I fled," he said in disgust. "Rather than face you in my weakness, I thought to leave you behind, to forget about you, which I thought was surely possible. After all, how could one human overwhelm me with feelings in such a short period of time?" He smiled bitterly, shaking his head at his own foolishness.

"You told me once I haunted your dreams," he said softly. "With you gone, I have lived for those moments stolen from your sleep. I wanted you to remember me so that no other man could touch you the way I had. The very possibility drove me mad. When I learned you'd gone to Texas, my first thought was to destroy Jabril Karim before his eyes could so much as look upon you, lest he even *think* to take you for his own."

A cloud covered the moon high above, hiding his face until only the silver gleam of his eyes was visible as he met her gaze. "I have been mastered at last, sweet Cyn, helpless in the face of that most human of failings. I love you."

Cyn stared at him, her heart beating so hard, so fast, it crushed the breath from her lungs. A part of her wanted to remember every minute detail of this night, the deep shadows beneath the trees, the moon scattering light where it could, the scent of the Eucalyptus, sharp and acrid—the moment he bared his soul to her for the first time. She wanted to throw herself into his arms, to feel him wrap that big body around hers and tell her again that he loved her. And that he thought it a failing to love her this way? She understood perfectly. She'd fought against love most of her life—love for her father, her absent mother, the succession of nannies in and out of her world. Love let you down, made you vulnerable. No other emotion had the power to wipe away reason, to destroy carefully built walls and leave you bleeding in the wreckage.

But because she understood, because she remembered all too well the fresh pain of losing him, she remained still, sitting in the quiet dark beneath her tree.

Raphael smiled sadly, lifting his head suddenly in the direction of Alexandra's manor house, as if listening. "Your little bird is ready to fly," he commented. Almost immediately, he stood, sweeping up his jacket and offering Cyn a hand up.

She laid her hand in his, letting him pull her to her feet, feeling the effortless strength in every movement. He held onto her and tugged her close, sliding his hand around her lower back to hold her. "The choice is yours, sweet Cyn," he murmured in her ear. He lifted her face and kissed her then, a soft, slow kiss she couldn't help responding to. "Come to me when you're ready," he whispered, and then he let her go and stepped away.

"Raphael—" she began, but he interrupted.

"She doesn't belong here," he said, staring toward Alexandra's house. "The sister, Elizabeth." He looked back at Cyn. "She doesn't belong among my people. She should be out in the world."

"I know." Cyn nodded. "I'll find something for her, someplace."

"I don't want Mirabelle living with Alexandra either," he said in a thoughtful voice. "I understand Duncan's reasoning in bringing her here. In some ways, it was well done. But I have other plans for Mirabelle."

"What do you mean *plans?* What kind of plans?" Cyn demanded, suddenly feeling very protective of both sisters.

Raphael grinned at her, as if he'd expected the reaction. "Nothing without her consent, my Cyn. Have no worry for that. I was thinking of college actually. She's worth more than a life as Alexandra's plaything."

"Oh."

He met her eyes steadily. "But remember this, *lubimaya*, she is mine now, not yours."

Cyn sighed. "I know," she admitted grudgingly.

Raphael laughed. "Come to me, sweet Cyn. I will be waiting."

And he was gone, leaving no trace of his departure but whispering leaves and the lingering taste of soft lips against her mouth.

Chapter Forty-four

Houston, Texas

JABRIL SAT AT his desk, reading the latest reports from his accountants. He strove to remain calm, feeding his growing agitation into the tapping of an elegant fountain pen in his right hand as he scanned the long rows of numbers. His financial people were working feverishly, ransacking as much of Mirabelle's money as they could before the stupid girl figured out what he was doing and put a stop to it. It was the least she owed him for all the years he'd taken care of her when no one else would have bothered. Ungrateful bitch.

Of course, she'd already hired a slew of money-grubbing lawyers out there in California to challenge everything he'd done. No doubt Raphael had been more than happy to assist, which was why Jabril's people were moving the funds offshore as quickly as he could steal them. Not that it could be called stealing. He was only taking what was rightfully his, after all. If only he had more time. The delicate pen snapped and the ink reservoir cracked, spilling dark liquid over his fingers and the papers beneath. Jabril jumped out of the chair, swearing as he threw the broken pieces aside. He looked up with a furious snarl when the door opened and Asim hurried in.

Asim registered instant dismay when he saw the ink-stained mess. Jabril glared at him. He needed someone to bear the brunt of his anger and Asim would do as well as any. "Don't stand there, you pathetic idiot," he snapped. "Get me a towel."

Asim hustled to the adjoining bathroom, returning with a thick, white towel held out before him like an offering. "My lord," Asim said as Jabril snatched the towel and began wiping his hands. "You've a phone call."

Jabril hissed at him in disbelief. "Does it appear that I am eager to speak on the telephone, Asim? Who could possibly be calling that I would speak to right now?"

Asim's eyes swung nervously from one side of the room to the other, as if checking for unseen listeners. He stepped very close and whispered a name.

Jabril's eyes widened in surprise. "Well, that *is* interesting. What does she want?"

Asim coughed. "Friendship. I persuaded her to speak to you directly."

"Friends? How quaint." Jabril sat and reached for the phone, his mouth twisting with distaste at the sight of his blue-stained hands before he picked up the antique ivory and gold receiver.

"How delightful to hear from you, my dear," he said, his smooth voice modulated to reflect none of his earlier anger. He listened, leaning back idly and crossing his legs at the knee. "Mmm. And why would you do this for me?" He laughed lightly. "No, no, I *am* interested, I'm just surprised. You can hardly blame me for that." He listened to the soft, feminine voice. She was almost whispering, afraid of being overheard. And who could blame her? "And when would this be?" he asked. "So soon? Well, excellent. That might work out very nicely." He listened further as his caller made a request.

"I see. Suddenly, it all becomes clear." He laughed again, derisively this time. "Really, my dear. One learns a few things over the centuries. This changes nothing, however. Your purposes and mine happen to coincide. You are certain of the time?

"I will have someone waiting, then. Oh, and, my dear? It would not be wise to disappoint me." He hung up and met Asim's questioning gaze. "That incompetent investigator of yours, what was his name again?"

"Windle, my lord. Patrick Windle."

"And he is still out there in Los Angeles, searching blindly for Elizabeth?"

"Yes, my lord. He assures me he will have her in custody shortly."

"Does he? What an optimist. Well, we may have done his work for him, a chance to seize not only our sweet Elizabeth, but Raphael's treacherous bitch as well. I have dreamed of getting my hands on that one again, Asim, and she is about to fall into my grasp."

Chapter Forty-five

AFTER ALL THE anticipation and worry, Mirabelle's appearance before Raphael was relatively straightforward. As Cyn had told Mirabelle, she'd expected something pompous and formal, but she should have known better. Raphael was far more of a CEO than a king. Granted, a CEO with the power to kill anyone who displeased him, but then who said corporate America didn't do the same? Raphael's methods were simply more direct.

Cyn arrived at Alexandra's an hour before the appointed time of eight o'clock. The manor was quiet, all the remodeling done, for now at least. The sound of classical piano drifted down the stairs, letting Cyn know it was Alexandra in the music room and not Mirabelle. She thought about stopping in to say hello, for courtesy's sake, but continued on to Mirabelle's room instead.

Cyn appreciated everything Alexandra had done—that she'd taken Mirabelle into her home, given her a place to belong. But she wasn't quite comfortable with Raphael's sister. There was something about Alexandra that made Cyn think the vampire female's thoughts rarely matched her words.

Mirabelle's door stood open, but Cyn tapped on it lightly before stepping inside to find her wrapped in a long robe of sapphire blue silk and standing in front of the mirror. She was staring pensively at her reflection, her thoughts seeming far away from whatever she was seeing there.

"Mirabelle?" Cyn said softly.

The young vampire looked slowly over her shoulder, not at all startled, so she must have heard Cyn enter after all. "Hello, Cynthia," she said with a small smile.

"You ready for tonight?"

"Oh, yes," she said. She wandered over to the old-fashioned dressing table, picked up a brush and began running it through her hair with smooth, long strokes. Her blond hair, grown dark after years out of the sun, had been lightened by a stylist and now gleamed honey gold.

Cyn looked around. The room was all white lace and linen. The four poster bed was piled high with frothy pillows of all shapes and sizes, the down comforter thick and plump beneath its embroidered lace duvet. Cyn had a passing thought about why a vampire would bother to decorate a bedroom she never slept in. Why not design it as a sitting room instead? The vampires all slept in the vault downstairs anyway. Although, at some point, the bed might have another use, she supposed. She glanced at Mirabelle, who was once again sunk deep in contemplation, her arm lifting to brush her hair almost automatically.

"You redecorated," Cyn said.

Mirabelle looked around, as if surprised by the changes. "Alexandra did it."

Cyn cocked her head slightly, puzzled. "You don't like it?"

Mirabelle looked over her shoulder with a sad smile. "It's not really my taste, you know?"

"You okay, Mirabelle?" Cyn asked softly.

The girl's blue eyes focused on her, suddenly filled with tears. "I wanted to do the right thing, Cyn. Everything's been so messed up, and I . . ."

Cyn crossed the room and pulled the younger woman around, placing her hands on Mirabelle's shoulders. "You *are* doing the right thing, Mirabelle. You *did* do the right thing. It took guts to walk away from Jabril, to take your life back from him and make it your own. I'm proud of you. Your mom and dad would be proud of you. They would have hated what he did to you and to Elizabeth."

"Elizabeth," Mirabelle repeated, straightening out of the embrace and drawing in a breath. "Right."

She walked over to the closet where her outfit for the evening hung on a padded hanger. She and Alexandra had chosen it from among a selection sent over by one of Rodeo Drive's finest shops, along with the host of other clothes now filling Mirabelle's closet. No need to leave the safety of Raphael's Malibu estate—if you had enough money, anything was possible in this town, and Mirabelle had a lot of money. Cyn had been a bit miffed at being left out of the shopping frenzy, but she had to admit the choice was a good one. The fitted slacks were a fine, worsted wool, and the long, matching jacket would hit just below the knee. The entire outfit was black, but with a brilliant, almost iridescent blue lining on the jacket. The style was probably too old for Mirabelle, too somber, but the lining was beautiful, and the black would conceal any unfortunate blood stains. Mirabelle stepped into the pants and slipped the robe from her shoulders. Cyn walked over to help, taking the robe so the younger woman could don the sleeveless silk tank that went beneath the jacket.

"Have you talked with Elizabeth tonight?" Cyn asked.

"I called, but we didn't talk very long. She said good luck and to call her after. She doesn't really understand all of this, you know. This vampire stuff." Cyn watched silently as Mirabelle sat down to put on her shoes, black Ferragamo pumps with a sensible three inch heel. "Tomorrow is Liz's birthday. She'll be officially eighteen."

"I know. Luci's got a little party planned at the house. You going?"

Mirabelle ignored the invitation, saying instead. "Liz said you're taking her for her first driving lesson, too."

"Yep. It was either that or teach her myself," Cyn commented casually. "It'll be easier for her to get around after she gets her license. She can visit you on her own then."

"I guess."

Cyn walked over and sat on the bed, taking her down to the sitting girl's eye level. "What's going on here, kid?"

Mirabelle looked up, her eyes meeting Cyn's with a sudden, desperate intensity. "Liz is my baby sister. My *baby* sister! I never realized until I saw her the other day, that she's getting older, but I'm exactly the same. I will always be *exactly* the same. Pretty soon, she'll be older than I am and then . . ." She dropped her head and swallowed hard. "She'll die," she almost whispered. "And I'll be alone. Not like Alexandra. She has Raphael. She'll always have Raphael."

Cyn stared at Mirabelle's bowed head, deeply troubled and wondering where the hell *this* had come from. Mirabelle didn't have contact with that many people, other than Alexandra and the guards. She remembered Alexandra saying she'd wanted to turn Cyn, wanted to make her Vampire, to be her friend forever. Had she set her sights on Mirabelle instead? A nice little baby vamp, all alone in the world, for Alexandra to mold into a permanent friend and acolyte?

"You took a great risk in coming here," Cyn said softly. "In some ways, you made it possible for Liz to survive, to get away from Jabril and have a real life. And now you have to let her live it her way. But family is more than blood, Mirabelle. It's your friends, the people who care about you, the people you care about. You can make your own family." She stood, pulling Mirabelle with her.

"I *have* made some friends here," Mirabelle said suddenly. "Elke came by today. She showed me the gym, the one used by Raphael's guards."

"I've worked with Elke," Cyn said. Elke was, in fact, the only female vampire in Raphael's first line of security. There were other female vamps among his security personnel, but Elke was the only one Cyn knew about who was trusted to guard him personally. She and Elke weren't exactly friends, but they'd achieved an odd sort of respect for one another after Alexandra's kidnapping.

"She offered to help me do some physical training. You know, like weight lifting and martial arts stuff."

"Probably a good idea," Cyn commented.

"I thought so, but Alexandra said—"

"Let me tell you something, Mirabelle," Cyn interrupted, her voice low and intent. "Alexandra was kidnapped a couple of months ago. It doesn't matter why, but when they took her, do you know what she did?"

Mirabelle's eyes were wide open as she shook her head.

"She sat there in a dirty little cottage, right where they put her, and she waited for someone to come rescue her. You think that's what Elke would have done? What Liz *should* have done? Sit there and wait for someone else to save her? You take those lessons with Elke, you get as strong as you can, and you learn as much as you can. And if the time ever comes when you need to be rescued, you'll be ready to rescue your own damn self."

Mirabelle's eyes were suddenly glittering with tears. "I'm sorry, Cyn. I didn't—"

Cyn pulled back, surprised and dismayed by the reaction. "I'm not talking about you, Mirabelle. You were a child when Jabril took you, and all alone to boot, I meant—"

"Oh," Mirabelle interrupted. "No. I know that's not what you meant. Really, it's okay." She stopped and drew a deep breath, wiping away tears.

"You're not worried about Jabril's witness, are you? Because Raphael would never—"

"Oh, no," Mirabelle assured her quickly. "I'm not worried about that. It's just that everything's happening so fast. But you're right. I'm going to take Elke up on her offer and I'm going to be strong. Stronger than anyone thinks I am. Starting tonight."

ALEXANDRA WAS waiting for them outside the music room. She was wearing a caramel colored St. John knit suit, with almost military styling, over a black cashmere turtle neck. The body hugging skirt clung to her petite figure, the perfect picture of a St. John woman. She gave Cyn an odd look. A look that made Cyn think Alexandra had overheard every word she'd said to Mirabelle.

"Don't we look lovely tonight," Alexandra said as they came closer. "That's a wonderful color on you, Cynthia."

Cyn glanced down automatically at her own dress. It was a deep, rich emerald green sheath, shimmering in raw silk with a boat neck and long tapering sleeves. She'd chosen it intentionally, knowing the color brought out the green of her eyes, and the hemline showed off long legs made even longer by four inch stiletto heels. She might not know exactly what she wanted from her relationship with Raphael, but she for damn sure wanted to be certain he noticed her.

"Shall we take my car?" Cyn asked. "I don't think these heels were designed for a walk in the woods."

Alexandra laughed gaily and turned to lead the way downstairs. "Too bad you're not Vampire, Cynthia. Mirabelle and I wouldn't have any problem at all." She turned back with a private look for Mirabelle. "Would we, darling?"

Mirabelle flushed and gave Cyn a sideways glance. "The car's fine, Cyn. I don't want to get all sweaty before I even get there." She huffed a deprecating laugh. "I'm sure I'll sweat plenty once it starts."

"Don't be silly," Alexandra said breezily, waiting for Mirabelle to catch up to her and linking their arms. "You'll be fine. Won't she, Cynthia?" This last was cast over her shoulder as the two vampires proceeded down the stairs.

"Yes, Alexandra, she will," Cyn said. "Mirabelle will be just fine."

Chapter Forty-six

JURO WAS WAITING for them at the main house, his twin brother—who never seemed to talk and whose name Cyn still didn't know—stood next to him, as always. Two seven-foot, stolid trees guarding the gates of Raphael's inner sanctum. Juro eyed Cyn warily, clearly convinced she had a weapon concealed somewhere on her person, but having no idea where it might be hiding beneath her form fitting dress. He gave her a resigned look and Cyn patted his trunk-like arm in sympathy.

"My brother is expecting us, Juro," Alexandra said with a trace of impatience.

"He is, Alexandra," Juro agreed. Cyn saw Alexandra's ladylike mouth tighten slightly and wondered if there was some tension between Raphael's sister and his chief bodyguard. If there was, Juro was clearly unperturbed by it. He turned and led the way, his twin waiting until they'd gone past before taking up the rearguard position.

Up the stairs and down the long hall they walked in a little parade until reaching the huge pair of elaborately carved doors in front of Raphael's office. Juro paused to knock once, waiting as the doors swung wide, unaided by any visible hand. He stepped back and the three women entered, Alexandra foremost, Mirabelle and Cyn together behind her.

Raphael's was a working office, with bookcases reaching from the floor to a high ceiling. Rolling ladders were stationed at intervals to provide access to the uppermost shelves, which were filled with books of all shapes, sizes and ages. It was a room more suited to a researcher of some sort, a professor of history, perhaps, rather than a vampire lord. But when one has lived for centuries, history becomes a very personal affair, Cyn supposed.

Raphael sat behind a massive desk, Duncan standing to one side. Behind them was a wall of glass showing nothing but the moon-capped ocean. Juro had taken up a position to the right of the door, next to his twin brother, and sandwiched between them was a vampire Cyn didn't recognize. She took in his dark clothing and perpetual sneer and realized this was almost certainly Jabril's witness. No wonder Juro and his brother were guarding him so carefully.

She glanced at Mirabelle, but the young girl seemed not to have eyes for anyone but Raphael. Cyn met his black gaze and had to admit he was a sight well worth looking at.

Raphael stood as they approached, his gaze grazing over Cyn's bare legs and emerald-clad form before finally meeting her eyes with a heat that made her very glad she'd taken the time to choose carefully. His lips barely tilted in an appreciative smile before he donned a more somber expression and looked at Mirabelle expectantly.

"You requested to see me, Mirabelle?" he asked formally.

"Yes, my lord." Mirabelle's voice was raspy with nerves and it took her two tries to get the few words out. She paused, obviously irritated at herself, and then drew a long breath of courage and bowed deeply. "My lord Raphael," she said, coming upright. "It is my honor to request your permission to relocate from the territories and suzerainty of my Sire, Jabril Karim. I offer you my allegiance and my service if you would have me, my lord."

Alexandra nodded her approval and beamed proudly, her gaze switching between Mirabelle and Raphael.

"And does your Sire consent to this relocation, Mirabelle?" Raphael's smooth voice asked the necessary question, although everyone there knew the answer.

"No, my lord, he does not. I have come to you of my own free will and desire."

Cyn heard a stirring behind her at Mirabelle's words and saw Raphael's eyes flash over her shoulder to where Jabril's witness was standing. He held the vampire's gaze for only a second before turning his attention back to Mirabelle.

"You understand," he said to her. "That should I accept you, all prior allegiance to your Sire will be forfeit. You will be as my own."

"Yes, my lord."

"And is this what you truly desire?"

"With all my heart, my lord, it is my desire."

"Very well." Raphael slipped out of his suit jacket with a graceful shrug and draped it over his desk. Cyn felt a tug of desire low in her body as he unbuttoned his left shirt cuff and began to roll it up his forearm with economical movements. She had a weakness for beautiful hands on a man. Raphael's hands were strong, his fingers long and square, his forearms smoothly muscled. She swallowed dryly and squelched memories of what those hands could do.

Duncan had produced a small jeweled knife, no more than six inches long, its sharp edge gleaming against the age-blackened metal of the blade. Raphael glanced at the weapon and nodded as he walked around the desk. "Kneel before me, Mirabelle."

Mirabelle took a step forward and dropped to her knees, landing with a grace that would have done any courtier proud. All that practice was standing her in good stead tonight. Raphael placed both hands on Mirabelle's bowed head. Nothing seemed to happen for a few minutes, and then Mirabelle sighed in obvious pleasure and pink tears began to roll from beneath her closed eyelids.

Raphael lifted his hands, extending the right one toward Duncan who silently handed him the jeweled knife. Cyn swallowed a small gasp as, without warning, Raphael ran the sharp blade over the soft skin beneath his left wrist, opening a three inch vertical slice. Blood welled immediately, staining the rolled edge of his pristine white cuff before he lowered his hand and let it run into his cupped palm. Mirabelle's nose twitched and her eyes sprang open to gaze hungrily at the feast before her—the blood of a vampire lord, richer and more powerful than the blood of any creature on earth, far richer than anything Mirabelle would ever have tasted before, except perhaps for her nightmarish turning at the hands of Jabril. And Cyn had to believe Raphael's blood would be sweeter than anything Jabril could produce.

Raphael watched the young vampire silently, withholding his arm until the blood was a growing pool in his broad palm, until it filled the creases between his fingers and threatened to drip to the carpet, until Mirabelle was near to breaking from the temptation before her. And then he offered it with the most minuscule movement toward her waiting mouth. Mirabelle responded eagerly, reaching for his arm, her hands shaking with the effort to move slowly, deliberately. When Raphael made no move to deny her, to pull from her grasp, she closed her eyes in ecstasy and lowered her mouth to the rushing blood.

Mirabelle gave an orgasmic moan, her throat working steadily as she drank in Raphael's bounty. Cyn wanted to look away, feeling like an intruder, a voyeur witnessing something that should have been intensely private. Instead she watched, determined to witness Mirabelle's submission to her new lord, to acknowledge this part of Raphael's life. She watched him too, his dark head bent, eyes closed, the muscles of his forearm clenched to keep the blood flowing. How long could he keep this up?

No sooner had the thought occurred than Raphael was touching Mirabelle gently with his other hand. She pulled away instantly with a pleasurable sigh, her tongue sweeping out to lick her bloodied lips, to salvage every last drop of the precious fluid. She sat back on her heels and gazed up at her new master, a look of utter worship on her flushed face.

"Thank you, Master," she said in a low, sensuous purr, not at all like her regular voice.

Raphael looked down at her, his expression one of bemused patience. "You are most welcome, Mirabelle."

Duncan stepped forward almost immediately, reaching down to help Mirabelle to her feet. She stumbled slightly, giddy, drunk almost, from the potent blood. "Come, little one," he said. "We've planned a small celebration in your honor."

She gave him the delighted smile of a child. "A party? For me?"

"For you," Duncan agreed. He took her arm and guided her out of the room. Jabril's witness was gone, apparently escorted away at some point by Juro's twin who was also absent. Cyn could only hope the escort would take him all the way to the airport and a plane back to Texas.

Juro stood waiting outside the open door, his usually solemn face creasing in fond amusement when Mirabelle greeted him like a long lost friend. Alexandra started to follow, but paused, turning back to look at Cyn.

"Cynthia?"

Cyn was watching Raphael as he stemmed the flow of blood, bending his arm and putting pressure above the wound. His face was expressionless, as though this sort of thing happened all the time, as if the blood dripping from his fingers to soak into the elegant Persian rug was an inconvenience, nothing more. His black eyes came up suddenly to meet hers, and Cyn was struck by a need so strong it would have driven her to her knees had she not had a chair to hang onto.

"Go ahead, Alexandra," she said breathlessly. "I'll catch up."

Alexandra's burgeoning protest was aborted when Raphael's gaze shifted to her. There was nothing of brotherly warmth in that look. Alexandra sighed unhappily and spun around, her fashionable heels thudding softly against the carpet as she marched out the door which closed silently behind her.

Raphael let out a small relieved breath and leaned back to sit on the edge of his desk.

"Are you all right?" Cyn asked, indicating his wounded arm with a nod of her head.

Raphael gave her a crooked smile. "I love when you worry about me, my Cyn. No one else does."

She gave a little huff of disbelief. "Duncan worries about you," she disagreed. "He's worse than a mother hen."

"Yes, well," Raphael said softly. "That's not quite the same thing, is it?"

Cyn studied him from across the room, and then shook her head in disgust. "Who am I kidding?" she muttered. She walked over to the desk, taking advantage of the natural sway given to her hips by the high heels. Raphael remained motionless, but his careful gaze followed every movement.

When she was close enough to touch, he said, "Don't you want to join Mirabelle's celebration?"

Cyn's mouth curved upward. "I'd rather celebrate with her master." She reached out and took his injured arm in her hand, drawing it up to her mouth. Eyes never leaving his, she ran her tongue slowly up the full length of the wound, taking time to lick the soft skin of his wrist before closing her mouth over his pulse point with a gentle kiss.

A growl rumbled deep in Raphael's chest, and he reached out to pull her between his spread legs, his uninjured arm snaking around her back, fingers splayed over her butt to press her close. His lips danced along the bare skin of her neck and shoulders, following the line of her jaw before he took her mouth in a long, slow promise of a kiss. "This is a beautiful dress, my Cyn," he whispered against her lips. "How quickly can we get you out of it?"

She laughed in delight, fingers twisting through his thick hair, reveling in the feel of his lips against her skin, every nerve hyper-alive as the blood she'd licked off his arm sped through her system. She leaned fully against him and his arms came around to hold her.

He stood suddenly, taking her with him. "Come," he said.

She smiled against his soft lips. "Do you think it will be that easy, my lord?"

"Sweet Cyn," Raphael purred. "I have no intention of making it easy at all."

Cyn shivered at the promise beneath his dark voice as he picked her up and carried her across the room. The hard edges of a bookcase brushed her back before he reached out and flicked an unseen switch. The shelves next to her began to move, swiveling around to reveal a hidden door.

"A secret room," she teased. "How mysterious."

"An elevator," he corrected and backed her inside, slamming her against the wall and covering her body with his as the small box began to move downward.

Chapter Forty-seven

RAPHAEL'S OFFICE was on the second floor, but Cyn couldn't have said how far down the elevator traveled. She had no thought for anything but the need to touch and be touched by Raphael. His mouth devoured hers hungrily, their lips locked in a searing kiss that she never wanted to end as their bodies molded to one another, nothing separating them but a thin layer of clothing. And still it wasn't enough. She needed to feel him, bare skin against bare skin, the glide of muscles, the chiming of nerves stimulated to an almost painful intensity.

She was aware they'd left the elevator only because there was a deep-pile carpet beneath her feet when she kicked off her shoes. Raphael's cool fingers glided down her back as he unzipped the green dress, sliding the sleeves off her shoulders until it skimmed down her body and pooled around her feet. He hummed with pleasure at the sight of the lace containing her breasts before it too fell to the carpet, exposing full mounds heavy with desire, rosy nipples hard and aching for his touch. Cyn cried out as his mouth tasted first one pearled nub, then the other, his teeth grazing along the tender flesh to send bolts of desire charging through her entire body until she could barely remain standing.

While Raphael's mouth brought glorious torment to her breasts, his hands roamed down her back, dipping beneath the narrow band of her thong and snapping it effortlessly, one more bit of lace added to the pile at her feet. Cyn moaned with the need to have him now, hard and fast, pounding between her legs. She tore his shirt away, buttons flying in her urgency. His belt was no obstacle, his zipper merely the gateway to his smooth shaft within. She slipped her hand beneath the fabric of his trousers and found him hard and ready, her stroking fingers dipping lower to caress his heavy sac.

She laid a row of kisses down his chest, following the line of silky hair down across the smooth flat expanse of his belly. She sank to her knees, sliding her hands down his hips to push his pants away and free his erection. Raphael hissed in surprise as she took him in her mouth, swirling her tongue around the head and teasing the thickness of his cock, taking him deeper until he struck the back of her throat as her fingers continued to stroke his balls. He gripped her hair, holding her in place and groaning with pleasure, before reaching down to pull her to her feet and throw her onto what seemed like an endless expanse of bed.

Raphael's eyes glowed silver, his gaze never leaving her as he stepped out of the rest of his clothes and stretched out above her. His head dipped to her neck and lower, suckling her breasts with sweet pain, sucking mouthfuls of the tender flesh between his teeth, his fangs leaving trails of blood that dripped over the plump mounds until he licked them clean with a low growl of hunger.

Cyn writhed under his sensuous assault, every nerve singing on the sharp edge of ecstasy, her heart swelling with the simple joy of being with him once again. She arched her back, offering herself, wanting more, crying out when his fangs sank into her flesh and shuddering with pleasure when his soothing tongue followed. She protested when he took his mouth away from her breasts, only to gasp with delight as he slid down between her legs and began to lap up the slick juices of her arousal. His fangs sank into the tender nub of her clit, throwing her into a climax of such exquisite intensity she thought she'd lose consciousness.

She fisted both hands in his short hair and tugged him back up the length of her body. "Fuck me, Raphael. Fuck me na—" Her demand turned into a groan of satisfaction as he obliged, driving his huge, hard cock deep between her legs in a single powerful thrust. She was wet and ready for him, trembling with need, and still he stretched her gloriously, burying his full length within her and holding it there, barely moving, gasping as her heat surrounded him. Her vision fogged with desire, Cyn watched him above her, his eyes closed with the effort of remaining still. She could feel his cock pulsing inside her, could see his chest moving with the beat of his heart, the bellow of his lungs. She reached up and ran her fingers softly over his brow, across the beautiful arch of his chiseled cheek bones and down to the fullness of his lips.

His eyes opened and met her gaze, gleaming in the low light as he began to thrust. Slowly at first, a smooth slide in and out as her juices lubricated the movement, as her inner walls adjusted to his thickness and welcomed his invasion. Faster as the hunger grew, as she rose to meet him, wrapping her long legs around his back and pulling herself onto his shaft. Her climax started deep inside, a flexing of her womb that shuddered outward until it was caressing his cock, as he pumped even faster, driving them both to the point of delirium and beyond.

Cyn screamed as the wave swept over her, bowing her back, seizing her muscles. She clung to Raphael, wanting this feeling, this joining of their bodies, to go on forever, hearing him roar when her climax rippled along his cock and triggered his own, milking him, draining him as his hot release filled her body.

He collapsed against her, rolling over slightly to cradle her in his arms, taking his weight off her while keeping himself firmly sheathed inside. Cyn lay in his embrace, feeling his cock still flexing deep within her, trembling with the aftermath of their joining. Raphael tightened his arms, holding her as if she was something precious to him, something he'd feared lost and, now found, would never let go again.

Cyn turned her face against his chest as the tears began to flow. "I missed you, too," she whispered, not knowing if he'd hear.

Raphael kissed her forehead and then her cheeks, tasting the tears. He grew still. *"Lubimaya?"*

Cyn tried to control the terrible and foolish need to weep, embarrassed by her own naked emotion. "The dreams were nice, Raphael, but this was much better," she managed to say, forcing a light laugh.

He said nothing for a moment, while Cyn silently begged him to let it go. When he chuckled, she relaxed, hooking her leg around his hip and rolling over on top, with him still buried deep between her thighs. Meeting his gaze, she began to move slowly, rocking back and forth on his responsive shaft, tightening the muscles of her core, cupping her breasts in offering. His gaze grew heated and he hardened once again. He reached behind her to cup her ass in both hands, holding her against him as he began a steady in and out movement, taking control away from her. Cyn gasped as he went far deeper, filling her completely. Her eyes closed and she dropped onto his chest, relishing the feel of his hard muscle and silky hair against the softness of her breasts. She lifted enough to kiss him, caressing his distended fangs with her tongue, feeling the slight sting as she drew her own blood.

Raphael growled her name, a rumble of sound low in his chest, vibrating through her bones. As her blood continued to flow, he gripped her tightly and flipped them both over, pounding now between her thighs, lifting her legs higher to delve deeper, driving into her with powerful thrusts that lifted her from the bed. Cyn whimpered softly, lost in the rush of sensation. She wrapped her arms ever more tightly around him, trapping him inside her, never wanting to let go. Another orgasm

D.B. Reynolds

began a slow shudder through her body, and Raphael's mouth found the sweet vein in her neck. She trembled at the diamond hardness of his fangs against her skin, crying out when they pierced her vein, when she felt the pull of her blood as it slid down his throat. Every nerve in her body came alive at once, her soft cry of joy lost in the roar of Raphael's completion. His release shot deep inside her, and she convulsed in a searing orgasm, her nails opening bloody rows down his back, sending him into yet another climax, hard on the first.

CYN LAY IN Raphael's arms, panting for breath, stunned into stillness by the strength of her emotions, terrified she would wake up to discover it was nothing but another dream. Her heart sped even faster at the thought, and she tightened her hold on him, wishing never to wake up if it was a dream. As if sensing her fear, Raphael stroked a comforting hand down her back, kissing her sweat-dampened skin and licking the trails of blood from her neck.

Fresh shivers of pleasure shot through her and she groaned. "Stop that," she whispered, snugging closer to him. "I need at least a ten minute break here."

Raphael laughed and kissed her hard on the mouth. "Ten minutes, ten years, ten centuries, sweet Cyn," he murmured, suddenly serious. "I love you. Whatever time I have left is yours."

Cyn froze, her heart thumping from something more than just the terrific sex. "I love you too," she whispered, almost fearfully.

"Then stay, my Cyn. Stay with me forever."

CYN KNEW DAWN was coming when she heard the muffled thud of heavy doors slamming shut, closing them inside and everyone else out. Raphael stirred from a light doze as she sat up, the sheet falling away from her naked body.

"I promised Liz I'd take her to her first driving lesson today," she said.

Raphael pulled her back down and leaned forward to suckle lazily on breasts still swollen and tender from their night together. He lifted his head long enough to say, "You can leave whenever you want. Everything will lock behind you." Then he lowered his mouth to her breast once more, pushing her back to the pillows as his tongue wandered lower.

"Will you be back?" he asked, his breath warm against the damp skin of her belly.

"Try—" She gasped as his tongue rasped over her clit. She swallowed and started again. "Try to keep me away," she managed.

"No," Raphael murmured. "Nothing will keep me from you. Remember that, my Cyn. Nothing."

Cyn shivered in sudden foreboding and whispered a prayer to the winds that fate was occupied elsewhere this morning.

Chapter Forty-eight

CYN TOOK THE front steps to Lucia's at a cheerful run, even though she'd had little more than two hours sleep. Her body was sore and aching, but it was the good sort of ache, the kind that leaves you feeling energized . . . at least for a few hours. At some point, she was going to crash face first into a pillow, but not yet. Not even the wall-shaking noise level of the usual gang of teens watching television and playing games could faze her this morning.

Lucia was on the phone in her office. She gave Cyn a silent once over and raised her eyebrow knowingly before going back to whatever bureaucrat she was arguing with. Cyn backtracked down the hall to the foot of the stairs and yelled for Liz. Not her usual mode of communication, but when in Rome . . .

Down the hall, she heard Lucia slam the phone with a curse, and she reentered the office in time to see her friend writing furious notes, muttering under her breath about the mouth-breathing idiots who ran the government these days. Lucia spun around and glared at Cyn.

"And you!" she said, continuing her unrelated diatribe. "I know what you've been up to, you bitch. Look at you, all shiny and glowing with satisfaction while I'm down here in the trenches battling the morons over at social services. Tell me it wasn't the vampire."

Cyn gave her a wide grin.

"Oh, shit, Cyn, why would—" Luci stopped herself and looked closely at her friend. "You're happy," she said, then squinted even closer. "No, you're in fucking love." She sighed. "If you're happy, I'm happy. But, sweetie," she put a hand on Cyn's arm. "Be careful."

Cyn gave her a spontaneous hug, something she rarely did. Luci laughed and said, "Okay, now I *know* you're in love. But you tell that big bloodsucker if he breaks your heart again, I'm coming for him with a stake."

Footsteps thundered down the stairs and Liz appeared in the doorway. She stopped when she saw the two women embracing. "What's up?" she said, sounding a little worried.

"Not a thing," Luci said quickly, giving Cyn a warning glance before she could respond with the obvious tasteless rejoinder. Not that she would have. Honest.

"Hey, kid, Happy Birthday," Cyn said cheerily. "You ready for the big day?"

"Give me a break, like I've never driven before." Liz rolled her eyes in the timeless disgust of all teenagers. "I need these stupid lessons to get my license, but it's not like I don't already know how to drive."

"Right," Cyn said, with a private grin for Lucia. "Let's get this useless exercise over with then. We'll be back in a couple of hours," she added in Luci's direction. "You want anything while I'm out?"

"Yeah, how about some of what you had last night," Luci said dryly. "It's been awhile."

Cyn laughed. Liz looked confused, but unwilling to admit she cared what they were talking about, she danced impatiently. "So are we doing this, or what?"

"We're doing it and we're outta here. Call me if you think of anything, Luce. Anything I can bring you, anyway." Luci's laughter followed them down the hall and out the door.

THE DRIVING SCHOOL was in West L.A.'s business district, an area of warehouses and light industry, not too far from the new para facility where Raphael had been so recently incarcerated. Normally, the driving instructor would have driven to the student's location, but since Liz's only current residence was the runaway shelter, Cyn figured it would be better to go to them and use her Malibu condo as Liz's official address. Not that most of these places cared overmuch about such niceties as a permanent address, but they *were* supposed to, and it would be Cyn's luck to get the one employee who'd bother to check.

Liz had obtained a certified copy of her Texas birth certificate from Hewitt before she ran from Houston, knowing it would be necessary when the time came to safeguard her inheritance from Jabril. For now, it was her only proof of age and identification, and for backup, her "aunt" Cynthia was going along as a responsible adult. For her part, Aunt Cynthia wanted to stress that she was a *very* young aunt, more like a sister, really.

Parking on the street was always problematic in this neighborhood, especially during the business week, so they swung into a parking garage about a block away from the school. Liz was telling her about an ongoing disagreement in the house that broke down to boys versus girls and something to do with movie selection. Cyn was only half-listening, her attention on a dark blue sedan that seemed to have picked them up as they passed the school and was now following them into the parking structure. She couldn't see much detail in the dim interior of the garage, but the very blandness of the vehicle made her uneasy. She'd considered having one of Raphael's human guards tag along today, but had dismissed the idea almost immediately. Her Glock was tucked beneath her jacket, secure in its usual shoulder rig. And it was daylight. The worst she would have to contend with was some hired thug of Jabril's. She could handle that.

Nevertheless, when she turned off the ramp and saw the sedan drive by, continuing to the higher levels, she breathed a sigh of relief. Prowling up and down a couple of aisles, she finally slid the Land Rover into a slot not far from the open stairwell. Once out of the car, she paused for a careful look around the garage before opening the back passenger door to retrieve her backpack, telling herself she was worrying at shadows.

The sudden rush of movement spun her around, half inside the back seat, too late to avoid the Taser that was shoved against her chest. Her teeth clenched and she gave an involuntary groan as she hit the truck's running board before falling awkwardly to the cold cement floor. She had a confused glimpse of the flushed face and white hair of Jabril's PI before he delivered a second Taser burst, and then the sound of Liz screaming her name as she rushed around the car.

No, she thought as she fell into unconsciousness. *No, Liz, run!*

Chapter Forty-nine

"MY LORD."

Raphael sat at his desk, reviewing the proposal for a new compound in Seattle. The human population there had grown substantially over the last hundred years, and his vampires in Washington were feeling the need for greater security. What had once been a rural retreat with few neighbors was now a bustling suburb, and his people were suggesting a move even further beyond the city limits. He gave Duncan an absent smile, wondering where Cyn was and how soon she would return. She'd said something about a birthday celebration for the girl Liz, but he had spent too many nights without her and wanted her here. Now.

He glanced up casually and was abruptly aware of his lieutenant's solemn expression. "Duncan?"

"I just took a call from Cynthia's friend Lucia Shinn. She runs the shelter where Mirabelle's sister Elizabeth has been staying. It seems Cynthia and Elizabeth never returned from their excursion to the driving school this morning, and Ms. Shinn has been unable to reach them despite repeated attempts."

Raphael was on his feet. "Have you checked with Alexandra? Perhaps they're with Mirabelle." He didn't believe it. If Cyn was on the estate, he'd know it; he'd feel it in his blood.

"Ms. Shinn tells me she called Alexandra's manor immediately after sunset."

Raphael and Duncan shared a look. "And yet no one from the manor has contacted *me*."

"Ms. Shinn became worried enough that she called us directly, tracing the number through your commercial front."

The house phone rang and Duncan picked it up, listened for several minutes and issued a terse command. He hung up and turned to Raphael. "Our security hooked into the GPS on Cynthia's truck sometime ago. It was without her knowledge, but I thought it wise—"

Raphael cut him off. "Where is she?"

"Her *vehicle*," Duncan stressed, "followed the expected pattern this morning, going first to pick up Elizabeth, then to a location near the driving school, most likely a parking structure. It stayed there for a very brief time, a matter of minutes, not long enough to have conducted any sort of business. Since then it has been moving steadily in a southeasterly direction, allowing for multiple refueling stops. It is now slightly west of Tucson in Arizona."

"You called her cell phone?" Raphael asked as he strode for the door.

"No answer, but we've traced the phone's GPS to the assumed parking structure near the driving school, which suggests either the phone is not with her or—"

"Or she's not moving. Get someone on the ground."

"Already on the way, my lord. I should have a report momentarily." He hurried to keep up with Raphael, who was taking the stairs two at a time. Juro met them at the bottom and led the way through the big double doors and out to the driveway where two SUVs waited, engines idling.

Duncan's phone rang again as they sped down Pacific Coast Highway toward Santa Monica, the direction of both the airport and Cyn's last known location. Raphael was aware of the phone's ringing and of Duncan's low-voiced conversation, but his mind was filled with thoughts of Cyn. He had enemies. And Cyn was too human, too vulnerable. And too important to *him*, damn it.

Duncan finished his call. "The phone has been found in a parking garage, along with her backpack," he said grimly. "Her last call was to her own home number right after she left the estate this morning. Probably checking messages."

In the front seat, Juro looked over his shoulder and spoke without being asked. "We have filed a flight plan to Tucson, my lord," he said. "Your people in Phoenix will meet us on the ground."

Chapter Fifty

EVERYTHING ACHED. Cyn tried to move, to relieve the pressure on her right arm which was twisted somehow and beginning to fall asleep. Panic flared as memory returned, but she forced herself to remain still and quiet.

She was in a car, or a vehicle of some sort, and moving. There was tape across her mouth; she could feel the pull of the adhesive on her cheeks. Her hands and feet were bound, probably with the same tape as her mouth, and her hands were behind her back. She heard soft sobbing nearby. So she wasn't alone in her captivity. *Elizabeth*, she remembered, and knew immediately who had them, even before her brain produced the final image it had seen before her loss of consciousness. That damned thick-necked PI of Jabril's. Which meant they were on their way back to Texas. But how far had they gotten?

She rolled over and struggled to see something, anything, thankful the asshole hadn't blindfolded her at least. It was dark outside, utterly dark, made even more so by the tinted windows of the Land Rover. Land Rover. They were in the cargo compartment of her own truck, which was actually very good news. If she could get loose somehow, there were weapons hidden in here that would come in very handy, even against a vampire. *Especially* against a vampire.

She scooted around carefully, taking in more detail. Liz lay next to her, similarly bound. She was staring mutely at Cyn with eyes that were swollen and red from crying, so she'd probably been conscious for awhile. Hopefully that meant the younger woman hadn't been Tasered, or at least not as much. Cyn met the girl's gaze carefully, making certain she knew Cyn was awake and aware. The look of terror on her face said she understood as well as Cyn who had them and what the future might hold if they didn't manage to escape. Cyn felt a surge of angry frustration at their predicament, but fought it down, saving it for later. She would use that anger, but not yet.

Okay, so they were in her truck and the PI was probably driving. He'd been alone when he Tasered her—she felt a renewed surge of rage the memory and swore she'd pay him back in kind if she ever got the chance. But how to get that chance?

The ambient light brightened suddenly, and Cyn froze. They were pulling into some sort of a truck stop or gas station. She could hear voices nearby and the steady hum of diesel engines left idling while their drivers took care of whatever business brought them here. The Land Rover's front door snicked open and the interior lights flashed on briefly, before she heard a muttered curse and the lights went off. The car door slammed.

Silence, and then the clunk of a nozzle being inserted into the fuel tank right behind Cyn, where she lay against the side wall of the cargo compartment. She smelled the fumes and heard the gurgle of the gasoline as Jabril's PI filled the tank. It went on for long enough that she knew the tank had been almost empty. She'd topped off on the way to Luci's, but the V8 engine was hell on gas, so they'd traveled less than two hundred miles since the abduction. Unless this wasn't their first stop for fuel. Liz might know about that, but she was as mute as Cyn for the moment.

The gas cap ratcheted closed and then more silence until the car shifted with the weight of someone climbing back into the driver's seat. Cyn started making noise, kicking the side of the compartment, shouting wordlessly beneath the tape.

"Shut up back there or I'll give you another jolt," a man's voice growled.

Cyn responded by making more noise than ever, knowing he could not only hear her, but that it irritated him—hopefully enough to do something about it.

The engine started and the truck began to move. Cyn's heart sank and she thought she'd failed, but she didn't give up, screaming even louder, pounding her bound feet against the door and sides of the SUV. Liz joined in, either because she figured Cyn had a plan or just because she was scared and pissed off. Cyn cheered her silently, the more noise the better.

"God damn it!" the driver swore. The truck swerved, traveled a short distance and came to a halt with the engine running. It was darker here, and Cyn knew their captor had pulled away from whatever public area they'd been in before. The back hatch opened suddenly and the PI's flushed and angry face appeared. Cyn's gaze went immediately to the Taser in his right hand.

"You shut the fuck up, bitch," he said to Cyn, clearly seeing her as the instigator. "I only need you alive, not functioning, you got it? I'll give you a jolt that'll make a drooling idiot look like Einstein compared to you."

Cyn stared at him, but continued making noises, pleading now. The PI frowned, then turned to Liz and ripped the tape off her face. "What's the problem, missy?" he asked nastily.

Liz screamed as he tore skin along with the tape, and it took her several minutes as she struggled to control her crying enough to talk.

"Fuck this," the PI snarled and moved to close the hatch, but Liz rose up slightly and cried out, forestalling him.

"Please," she sobbed. "Please, sir. We have to—" She blushed furiously, swallowed hard and whispered. "We have to pee."

Good girl, Cyn thought. This was the Liz who had engineered her own escape from Texas.

"Shit. Fucking women got bladders like peas. Damn it. I should let you piss yourselves, but then I'd have to smell it all the way to New Mexico."

New Mexico. Cyn thought furiously. He was taking them to New Mexico which meant Jabril's territory. How much farther?

"All right. All right," he muttered to himself and glared at the two women. "I'm gonna' pull over to the head. You can go one at a time. And no funny business or the other one pays, you got it? The hands stay tied, so you better hope—"

"Please," Liz whined. "I won't be able to get my pants down." Her eyes widened and she stared at him in horror. "Oh God," she whispered and began to sob even harder.

"Fuck that, what do you think I am? Some kind of pervert? Look, shut the fuck up, the hands stay tied, but I'll switch 'em to the front and you count yourself lucky I can't stand the smell of piss. You too, tough girl," he sneered at Cyn. "You better think of little sweetie here before you try anything."

Cyn nodded.

He drove the truck another short distance, parked and came around to open the hatch again. He freed Liz first, cutting the tape from her hands while her feet were still bound, making no effort to be gentle as he rolled her over and quickly rebound her hands in front. Then he slit the tape on her feet with the same knife and yanked her from the back of the truck. "Go on. You got five minutes."

"Five minutes, but I don't—"

"Five minutes, missy. Take it or leave it."

Liz took it. The hatch came down and Cyn remained still, listening to the PI's gritty footsteps outside. He paused and the truck rocked slightly under his weight as he leaned against the side near the front. Cyn raised her head cautiously and took a quick look around. They were pulled up in front of a cinder block restroom, the kind one saw at public beaches and along highways all through the American west. In the near distance, she could still see the lights of the truck stop, could hear the whoosh of air brakes and the calls of the drivers—tantalizingly close, but too far away to do her any good.

She ducked back down below the windows and tried to come up with a plan. With her hands taped in front, she'd have a lot more options, but she didn't want to take the chance he'd either hurt Liz or, for that matter, kill Cyn and leave her by the side of the road. Liz had to be Jabril's first priority, but he'd want Cyn for payback, not only against her but against Raphael. She shivered at the thought of what the Texas vampire lord would do if he ever got his hands on her. Mirabelle had been quite eloquent in her descriptions of Jabril's abuse of his blood slaves.

Thinking of Mirabelle made her realize someone should have missed them by now. Luci would have called when they didn't come back for the birthday party. Would Raphael think she'd run away from him again? No. Even if he thought she'd run, it made no sense to take Liz with her. He'd know something was wrong and he'd know Jabril was involved. But would he find her in time? It had been hours since they'd been taken, hours filled with daylight and sunshine which gave their captor a considerable head start.

The hatch opened without warning to reveal Liz, tape once again silencing her mouth, binding her hands in front.

"Okay, bitch, your turn," the PI growled. He grabbed Cyn by the hair and yanked her out of the truck, letting her fall. She cracked her elbow hard on the asphalt and let him hear her cry of pain. The more scared and helpless he thought her, the better. He crouched next to her, one knee crushing her hip, holding her in place while he freed her hands from behind then roughly turned and bound them in front. Standing, he bent to cut the tape around her ankles and yanked her to her feet.

Cyn stumbled on legs gone numb and weak from the combination of the Taser shock and hours of immobility, but she was careful to keep her eyes downcast so he wouldn't see her rage.

"Go," he said, shoving her. "And don't forget I've got your little friend here."

Cyn started walking, slowly at first. She heard a ripping noise behind her, and turned to see the PI binding Liz's ankles again. Her mind racing, she headed for the public restroom hoping against hope there would be something inside she could use as a weapon.

The entrance was a dark, doorless hole, lit only by a single yellow bulb behind a cracked plastic cover. She tripped on the uneven walkway and stumbled heavily, falling into the entrance's block wall. She leaned there a moment, letting her captor see her weakness, using the time to think. When she thought she'd delayed as long as she could get away with, she straightened and went inside.

It was dark enough in the restroom that she'd have used a flashlight under normal conditions. Fortunately, she actually didn't need to use the facilities. Regardless of what any asshole PI thought, in her experience, women could hold it a lot better than men. They had more practice waiting in long lines.

She used her time to search the musty restroom, squinting into the dark, trying to find something to use as a weapon, or just a sharp edge. That's all she needed. Something to cut the tape. Windle had stripped off her shoulder rig, but she kept plenty of weapons in the truck, and she was assuming Mr. Super PI either hadn't had the time or hadn't thought to check for them, since the side compartment cover had been intact. If she was right, it was an oversight she intended to use against him. And if she was wrong? Well, she'd better be right.

Big words, Cyn. How you gonna do that? Think, think, think. She sank to the dank floor, her muscles still weak and twitching from her ordeal.

"Let's go, bitch!" her abductor yelled from outside, clearly not caring if anyone overheard.

Cyn rubbed her eyes wearily and twisted her feet beneath her to get up. Her boot heel caught on the hem of her jeans and she tugged it impatiently, swearing when the edge of the decorative metal heel caught on the denim. She froze, staring at her favorite boots, at their elaborate *metal* embellishments on heel and toe. One of which, she saw now, was loose enough to have ripped out a fair width of hem. It could work, but she'd need a lot of time . . . and her hands would have to remain taped in front of her.

Cyn shuffled back outside, doing her best to appear exhausted and beaten. She let herself fall twice on the way back to the Land Rover, lying on the ground the second time until the burly PI came over and dragged her to her feet. Even then, she let herself hang loose in his hands, making him all but carry her to the big SUV.

"Not so tough, after all, are you, bitch?" he gloated. When they reached the truck, he lifted her roughly and threw her into the back. She whimpered helplessly and began to cry, letting her shoulders shake visibly with sobs of despair as he bound her feet once again.

"Useless," the PI muttered in disgust. He slammed the hatch closed and was soon back in the driver's seat, accelerating out of the parking lot, tires spinning on the grimy asphalt.

Back in the cargo compartment, Cyn's sobs quieted and she smiled. "Got you, you bastard," she whispered fiercely.

Chapter Fifty-one

RAPHAEL STARED out the jet's window as the sleek Gulfstream dropped out of the night sky over Tucson. He was seething inside, wanting nothing more than an enemy at hand, someone's blood to quench his fury. He thought about Jabril Karim, about how carefully the Southern vampire lord manipulated the local politicians, plying them with money and gifts and playing the good citizen to the world. And all the while his private domain was like a scene out of some archaic play.

Jabril could easily have made for himself the money he sought to steal from Mirabelle and her sister. His family was well connected in his home country even now, with contacts and opportunities for investments enough to make him a wealthy man. But instead, he chose to play the idle prince, stealing what he wanted, letting his minions pay the price for his excesses.

Duncan's voice murmured behind him. His lieutenant had been on the phone almost constantly, staying in touch with their security people back in Malibu. They were still tracking Cyn's SUV, watching as it drove steadily toward Jabril's territory. Jabril had probably thought himself clever getting a human to kidnap the two women in daylight. It gave the abductor several hours lead while the vampires slept, and Jabril no doubt assumed Raphael would have no way of tracing their whereabouts, in any case.

Ironically, had the other vampire lord taken only Elizabeth, it might have worked. Raphael would have had no way to follow Jabril's human agent and even less motivation to attempt a rescue. But Jabril had taken Cyn. And Cyn belonged to Raphael. It was going to be the purest pleasure to educate Jabril in the wonders of modern technology.

Duncan leaned forward. "They continue on Interstate 10, my lord, but our people tell me the vehicle will enter a zone of questionable reception before too long."

"What does that mean, Duncan?"

"Our tracking program relies on the wireless network for

communication, like a cell phone. The satellite will continue to trace the vehicle, but it will have no way to update our system, to inform us of the current location, until it regains wireless coverage. It should be only a short time, and in any event, I believe the destination is clear. He is following a direct line into New Mexico, aiming for Jabril's territory."

"That will not save him," Raphael growled. Jabril clearly assumed Raphael would be reluctant to pursue him across the territorial bounds, which would involve the Vampire Council in the dispute. Jabril was a fool.

The private jet taxied to a halt and Raphael waited impatiently as one of his people opened the hatch. He would have exited the plane immediately, but Juro rose ahead of him and descended the short stairway alone while his brother effectively blocked the exit. Raphael scowled and was about to remove this obstacle to his departure when the bodyguard abruptly vacated the hatch, taking the stairs to the ground in a single leap.

There were three huge SUVs idling on the runway, their black finish and darkly tinted windows glinting in the plane's running lights. Six vampires from his Phoenix nest were waiting for him when he stepped onto the tarmac, including a driver who remained in each vehicle. A female vampire stepped forward, going to one knee.

"Master."

"Up, Winona," he said to the nest's leader. "We've no time for this. Duncan has briefed you?"

Winona rose gracefully, spinning to stride side by side with Raphael toward the waiting vehicles. "He has, my lord, and we've maintained direct contact with your security base as well. I know the area where the vehicle is headed. There is perhaps a fifty mile blind spot in the wireless coverage, no more, but it skims the state border."

"I understand. Get me close enough and it will not matter." Raphael was already feeling the faint hum in his blood that said Cyn was near. The closer he got the stronger it would be.

"As you say, my lord." Winona signaled her waiting people and everyone piled into the vehicles. Juro edged Raphael toward the second of the three SUVs, then shoved his bulk into the front seat while Duncan maneuvered into the third row, leaving the middle seat to Raphael and Winona.

In moments, they were speeding out of the airport, the rotating lights on the truck roofs marking them as official vehicles and easing their way through the late night traffic. It was all quite legitimate; Jabril wasn't the only vampire who maintained cordial relations with the local authorities. But eventually, the running lights were no longer necessary as they left the city far behind and headed into the impenetrable blackness of the Arizona desert.

Chapter Fifty-two

ELIZABETH HAD long since passed out from exhaustion, but Cyn continued to work doggedly on the tape binding her wrists together. Her arms were aching, her fingers numb and her wrists bleeding from numerous missed cuts as she struggled to slice through the tape using only the jagged edge of her boot heel. Even with her hands in front of her, it was difficult. The cargo compartment was crowded with both of them lying bound, and she had to be careful not to draw her captor's attention with too much movement. She paused to rest her trembling arm muscles and laid her head back on the carpet, wanting nothing more than to close her eyes and sleep, if only for a short time.

She jolted awake as a cell phone rang nearby. Her first thought was that it was her own phone, and she wondered where it was. Surely Luci or Raphael would have tried calling when they couldn't find her. The phone trilled again, but it wasn't hers. Jabril's PI swore, and then answered with a gruff, "Hello." Cyn strained to listen to the one-sided conversation.

"Yes, sir. I have them both.

"I'm not happy about this. That big bastard's gotta be coming after me. The sun went down hours ago. Yeah? Well, you try loading two unconscious women onto an airplane without anyone asking questions. Besides, I figure taking the bitch's car bought me a few hours.

"No one's following that I can tell, not that I'd know if—Yes sir, still on the interstate, maybe sixty miles from the New Mexico border. Yes, sir, whatever you want. The sooner I turn these two over to you, the happier I'll be."

Cyn could hear faint beeping noises as he entered something on her in-dash navigation system. "I've got it. Are you sure—Yes, sir. As you say, it's your money. I'll be there in less—Fucking cell phone." Cyn heard a thud as something hit the car seat, then, "Asshole vampire. If he was gonna meet me, why'd I have to drive way the hell out here in the first place?"

All thoughts of resting fled as Cyn realized her time had run out.

She scrunched over as far as she could and started rubbing her bound hands against the tiny metal plate, bloodied fingers and wrists forgotten. She had less than sixty miles to get herself free or she'd be worrying about a lot more than a few shallow cuts.

Chapter Fifty-three

IN THE DIM INTERIOR of the limo, Jabril gave Asim a questioning look.

"Windle will reach the border shortly before us, less than an hour now." Asim shifted nervously. "My lord, I am uncomfortable with the idea of crossing the border. It is unnecessary and provocative. You could let your guards go to the meeting instead and bring the captives to you here in your own territory." He gestured at the empty desert all around them.

"Who is it you fear, Asim? The human?" Jabril scoffed. "You are an old woman sometimes. Perhaps I should have brought Calixto instead of you, after all. He, at least, would not be fretting over unseen dangers. No, Asim. Soon, Raphael will be humiliated and Elizabeth will be mine. Permit me to enjoy the moment."

Having little choice in the matter, Asim acquiesced with a sharp nod. "Your will, my lord."

"Yes, Asim. Always."

Chapter Fifty-four

THE LAND ROVER had pulled off the highway some time ago, leaving the road behind and bumping across the hard desert. Their movement finally stopped, and Cyn heard the PI muttering as he climbed from the driver's seat. She dared a quick peek out the window. They were parked in the middle of nowhere, the lights of a small town in the far distance. Her truck's halogen headlights illuminated a cool rectangle of light close to the ground, making it harder to see anything beyond their glow. The white-haired PI was standing by the side of the truck, rubbing his back. Apparently the long drive had taken a toll on him physically.

"Try it from back here, you fuck," she snarled.

She ducked once again below the back of the seat. The tape on her hands and mouth was gone, but her feet were still bound, her fingers too slick with blood and clumsy with fatigue to get a grip on the multiple layers of tape. So the hell with her feet; she didn't need her feet to shoot a gun and Jabril could be here at any moment.

"Elizabeth," she said softly, shaking the younger woman. "Wake up, hon. I need you to move."

Elizabeth woke with a start, her eyes going wide with confusion. "What? Huh?" She struggled to sit up, and Cyn saw the knowledge of where they were flash across her face before she fell back to the floor with a moan.

Cyn agreed with the sentiment. "That about sums it up," she said briskly. With no time to waste, she took hold of Liz's arms with both hands and urged her to move away from the side compartment where her weapons were stored.

"Your hands!" Liz whispered in shock. "How . . . Can you undo me too?" She held her hands out eagerly, frowning when she saw the blood slicking Cyn's fingers. "What happened? Oh my God . . ."

"Don't worry about that; we've got bigger problems. Switch places with me."

Cyn glanced up again as they maneuvered around each other,

feeling the truck rock slightly with the movement, but their captor had walked away and was staring into the distance.

"I've got a bad feeling about this," she muttered, scrabbling at the edges of the side compartment. It came loose finally, and she shoved it aside, breathing a sigh of relief when she saw everything still there and reaching immediately for the Spyderco folding knife velcroed to the wall of the compartment. She cut the tape binding her own feet first, and then freed Liz's hands with a quick swipe and handed her the knife. "Do your feet," she said tersely.

She grabbed a black canvas case next, unzipping it to reveal two Sig Sauer handguns. She picked up one at a time, did a quick safety check on each and reached for a box of 147 grain Hydra-Shok ammo. This was her vampire killer load; it made a neat little hole going in, but a really big mess coming out. She figured even a vamp couldn't stand up to having his brains splattered into tiny pieces. If nothing else, it would put him on the ground long enough for her to stake him. She slammed the magazine into the first gun with practiced efficiency and picked up the second.

"Okay, we're in a world of shit here, Liz," she said, speaking fast and low. "But we're not down yet. Have you ever shot a gun?"

She looked up and saw total fear on the teenager's face. Cyn stopped what she was doing, put the gun down and drew a calming breath. Panic would kill them both. "Listen to me, Liz," she said slowly. "Raphael's on his way. I can feel him in my head, but I don't know how far away he is or how long it'll take him to get here. Either way, we can't afford to sit and wait, so I need your help." She took the girl's shaking hands in her blood-covered fingers. "Can you do this? You were strong enough to get away once, can you do it again?"

Big tears began to roll down Liz's face, and Cyn's mind was already running alternative plans when the girl suddenly returned Cyn's grip strongly. "I'd rather die than go back there," she whispered. "Tell me what I need to do."

"Good girl," Cyn breathed. "Okay. Have you ever shot a gun?" she repeated. Liz shook her head mutely. It might have been better if they could both shoot, but the truth was a straight 9mm shot wasn't going to do shit to a vampire, and Cyn had no intention of turning over a load of her "special" ammo to a novice. It would be too easy for the wrong people, like Cyn or Liz herself, to end up dead.

"All right. We can't beat them in a straight up fight anyway. They're too fast and too strong, so we need to be smarter. I want you to fight. Scream, kick, bite, I don't care what you do, but do *not* go easily. Jabril wants you alive, but he's a sick fuck, so he'll probably bite you for the hell of it." Cyn didn't honey-coat the possibilities. She wanted Liz angry and ready to fight, not hysterical because the big bad vampire had sucked a little blood, or even a lot of blood. "Remember this, Liz. It might hurt like hell, but it won't kill you and it *won't* make you a vampire. It takes a lot more than a single bite to do that."

Cyn ducked down as the darkness was suddenly drowned by a wash of light. Peering over the seat, she saw three cars drive past the truck and come to a dust-churning halt in a rough semicircle facing the rear of the vehicle. One of those cars was a nice long limo, and Cyn had a pretty good idea who was sitting in the back seat. The appearance of Jabril's bodyguards confirmed her guess, and she gave fate a nod of thanks that the giant Calixto wasn't among the vampire lord's traveling security detail. The vampires jumped from the still-moving sedans and took up positions around the limo as the white-haired PI went over to greet his employer.

Cyn watched long enough to see Asim emerge, carrying a black briefcase, then dropped back to the floor of their compartment and sent a silent plea to Raphael to hurry. "It's Jabril," she said to Liz, struggling to keep her voice steady. "Asim's with him and a whole lot of others. Are you ready for this?"

"No." Liz's voice was shaking and she gave despairing chuckle. "Do I have a choice?"

"Good point," Cyn whispered as she heard footsteps crunching closer.

The hatch swung upward. "Your carriage awaits, ladies," the PI said with a bluff good cheer that made Cyn's stomach turn. Jabril must be paying this asshole a whole lot of money.

The PI grabbed Liz first, jerking her out of the truck. His mouth fell open when he saw the cut tape and Cyn rolled to her knees, prepared to take advantage of his surprise. But Asim leapt forward and snared her with that uncanny vampire swiftness, taking the gun from her hand as easily as if she were a child. The PI grunted an embarrassed acknowledgment of Asim's help, and he glared at Cyn before manhandling Elizabeth upright to face the limo as Jabril emerged from its depths.

"Don't do this," Liz pleaded, twisting in the PI's arms. "Don't you know what he is, what he'll do to me?" She was doing her best to make it difficult for him to hold onto her. There was no need to fake the terror in her voice.

"The law says he owns you, missy."

"No! Not anymore. I'm eighteen. Today's my birthday. Please! Please, let me go. He'll kill me."

"Well, now, how do I know you're telling the truth, huh? Whereas Mr. Jabril Karim there has given me fifty thousand reasons to believe him."

"You bastard," Liz screamed. "Let me go!" She went ballistic then, flailing her arms, kicking him, even smashing her head forward in a failed head butt. The PI struggled to grab her and she bit him, sinking her teeth in hard enough to draw blood.

"Bitch!" he swore. He raised a meaty hand to hit her, but Jabril intercepted him with a casual gesture, locking the PI's thick fist in one delicate hand.

"That won't be necessary." He gripped Liz's chin in one hand, turning her gently to look at him. He smiled.

Cyn watched helplessly as Liz succumbed to Jabril's power, and wondered why she'd ever thought they'd be able to resist him. The vampire lord spoke softly, and Liz leaned into him, rubbing against him like a cat. Jabril embraced her in an obscene parody of affection and sank to the ground, holding her effortlessly across his lap as his fangs slid out and he lowered his mouth to her neck. Cyn turned away, unable to watch, but Asim forced her head around, holding her with a wiry strength unexpected in that skinny, sunken-chested body.

Her eyes closed against the sight, and Asim chuckled.

"Did you think to resist us, Cynthia?" he whispered in her ear. He tightened his grip, one hand gliding over her breasts and down her abdomen suggestively. Cyn didn't bother to conceal her shudder of revulsion, and Asim's voice hardened with anger. "Tell me," he said, shaking her slightly. "Did you think your puny weapon could harm my master?"

"With respect, sir," the PI spoke up from behind them, where he was rummaging through Cyn's hidden cache. "That weapon's packing a pretty heavy load. Bitch knows what she's doing."

"Really?" Asim purred. He jerked his head at the PI. "You there. Assist Lord Jabril Karim. When he's finished with the girl, you can put her in the limousine."

Cyn thought at first the PI would refuse, but then he dropped the box of ammo and took several steps closer to Jabril, muttering, ". . . not a fucking servant." Cyn stared at his back. She didn't need to see what Jabril was doing to Liz. She could hear the sounds of his feeding perfectly well.

"Is it true what he said?" Asim murmured at her ear. "Could you kill my master with that weapon?"

Cyn fought the instinctive urge to pull away from his hissing breath. "Probably. Long enough to stake him anyway. I was looking forward to it."

Asim was silent for the space of two breaths. "So do it," he said so softly that the words were little more than air.

Cyn froze, stunned and suspicious. Could she trust the vampire? Why would he do this? On the other hand, what choice did she have?

"Why don't you do it?" she breathed.

"I cannot," Asim said with simple honesty. "He is my Sire, my master of several centuries." His voice grew softer, more persuasive. "But you can, Cynthia." He gestured with a shoulder to where Liz lay unresponsive while Jabril lapped blood from her neck like a fastidious cat. "Is it not worth taking a chance? What do you have to lose?"

What indeed, Cyn thought. She opened her mouth to agree, but then remembered something Raphael had told her about his Mistress's death. "What happens when he dies? What about the others?" She nodded at Jabril's vampire minions who were focused with a singular hunger on what their master was doing.

"They are weak. I will handle them."

"Handle how?" Visions of Asim throwing her and Liz to the wolves flashed vividly through her mind.

Asim chuckled again. "So suspicious. Are we not allies?" He ran a thin finger down her cheek. "I would not waste such beauty on the likes of those. No, I had another sacrifice in mind." He glanced at the PI's back.

Cyn was repulsed by his casual cruelty, but if was a choice between her and Liz or the PI who had delivered them to the vamps . . .

"What happens to Liz?"

"She comes with me."

"No."

"Yes," his voice hardened. "Elizabeth remains with me and you walk away free. That is my offer. Rest assured, I will treat her far better than Jabril ever did Mirabelle."

"I want Liz safe."

"As do I. Time is running out, Cynthia. He will finish soon, and your only chance will be while he is distracted by the feeding. Do we have a deal?"

Cyn swallowed, choking on her next word. "Yes."

The gun nudged into her hand and she took it, running her fingers over its surface, verifying its readiness. Asim's hands dropped from her and she jerked quickly away from him, much to his amusement. She waited until Jabril's girlish mouth lifted away from Liz's pale skin, watched as he threw his head back to savor the blood rolling down his throat. In a single, smooth movement, she raised the gun, took careful aim and fired. Her finger squeezed the trigger twice in quick succession.

Jabril's eyes flashed open in the final seconds, more irritated than alarmed, but it was too late for even a vampire lord. Two perfectly round holes appeared above the bridge of his nose, quickly filling with blood as the rest of his head blew away. He fell backward, propelled by the force of the blast, Liz rolling from his lifeless arms.

Jabril's bodyguards froze long enough for Asim, in a burst of vampire speed, to sweep Liz up and throw her into the truck. Cyn made an aborted movement in the PI's direction, but Asim tumbled her on top of Liz and shoved the bewildered PI toward the dead Jabril with the same motion. Cyn tried to shout a warning but had to jerk away when Asim slammed the hatch shut.

She clambered back to the window in time to see several of Jabril's vamps collapse to their knees, their faces contorted in pain and grief. Others remained standing, but barely. Swaying from side-to-side, eyes blank and staring, their muscles tensing and veins bulging as if under some terrible strain. Suddenly one of them threw his head back and howled, his hands tearing at his own hair, ripping out great bloody chunks of scalp along with it. As if this was some sort of signal, the others responded by pounding on their own flesh, turning their faces to the night sky in a horrible cacophony of mourning.

The first one turned abruptly, his own blood running down his face and hands, his head swiveling slowly from left to right as he scanned the area, eyes flashing yellow with fury when he spied the terrified PI backing slowly out of the circle of cars. The vampire's mouth opened in a vicious grin, his fangs gleaming white and sharp. He howled again, but it was no longer in grief. The maddened vampires turned as one.

And Cyn screamed.

Chapter Fifty-five

THEY SPED THROUGH the night silently, the only noise the whistle of tires on asphalt. With no other cars on the road, the vampire drivers had turned off the headlights, seeing better with only the moonlight to guide them. Raphael's thoughts were on the road far ahead, where he could feel Cyn growing more frantic with every mile closer to the border. Surely she knew where she was being taken, and what awaited her there. His people had lost all contact with the outside world some miles back, entering the wireless dead zone. He found it odd that such a thing could still exist in a world where every person seemed to own a cell phone. He heard Duncan curse beneath his breath as he tried once again to establish contact.

"It doesn't matter, Duncan," he said softly. "She is very near."

"My lord—" Winona began, but Raphael cut her off with a sharp intake of breath. He stiffened abruptly, his gaze trained straight ahead, his eyes glowing molten silver as he reached out instinctively to shield his people against a sudden wash of unrestrained power.

"Jabril," he growled.

Winona's eyes were wide with confusion, but Duncan understood. "He is dead?" Duncan said in disbelief.

"He will be soon," Raphael said absently, straining to find Cyn through the storm of Jabril's death call. His head jerked up as Cyn's cry of terror suddenly pierced the tumult.

"Stop!" He said it with such force of will that all three drivers were hitting the brakes before their conscious minds were even aware that an order had been given. "Duncan," Raphael said sharply, and then he was gone, the door hanging open to the breeze of his passage.

"Bring the vehicles," Duncan ordered the surprised Winona as he shoved past her to follow Juro, who'd ripped the passenger door open with such fury that the metal was still groaning with strain.

In a matter of moments, the vehicles had emptied out, leaving only Winona and the drivers on the desolate road.

Chapter Fifty-six

CYN COVERED HER ears against the howls of the maddened vampires. She only wished she could tear her horrified gaze away from the sight of Windle being torn apart piece by piece, the vampires ripping off chunks of flesh, sucking on the meat and fighting with each other over the spoils.

Only Asim seemed unaffected, standing motionless with his back to the truck. One of the crazed vampires leapt for the truck, and Cyn tried to scream over the bile surging up her throat. She shoved herself away from the window and against the back of the seat, but Asim repelled the attacker easily. He threw the vampire into the arms of another, and watched calmly as the two began tearing at each other in a renewed frenzy.

Apparently, Asim's plan for dealing with Jabril's minions involved letting them destroy each other so he wouldn't have to.

Cyn stared in shock a few moments longer, and then jerked herself into motion. She had no illusions about Asim's willingness to keep their bargain, because she had no intention of keeping her part of it either. Did he really think she would turn over Liz to save herself? Of course, he did. This was the guy who, at this very moment, was letting his future subjects tear each other apart in order to make his life easier over the next few days. Nothing Asim did would surprise her.

Her glance fell on the gun he'd let her use to kill Jabril. *Well, almost nothing,* she thought. She searched the compartment until she found the second gun with its full magazine of Hydra-Shok, checked it quickly and tucked it against her back beneath her jacket, then turned to the unconscious Liz.

The neck wound had sealed over already, which was typical of a vampire bite. Nature was a wonderful thing. Sometimes. Cyn felt the girl's forehead, brushing away a lock of blond hair. It was cool, but dry, and when she checked her pulse, it was strong. Jabril had a lot of experience draining women; he knew how much he could take without damaging his victim. It was fortunate he'd needed Liz alive.

Cyn became aware it had grown silent outside the truck, and she looked up to see Asim laying his hands on a kneeling vampire. It reminded her of Raphael's ceremony with Mirabelle, and she realized he was probably doing very much the same thing. She wondered if Asim was strong enough to hold Jabril's territory, but didn't waste too much effort worrying about it. After all, if she had her way, Jabril's territory would still be very much in need of a new lord after tonight.

Asim lifted his hands from the head of his newest minion, his shoulders slumping briefly in exhaustion. The newly sworn vamp remained on his knees, swaying slightly, eyes closed. Only one other vampire knelt next to him, and he was in an even worse state, leaning back onto his heels, head lolling in semiconsciousness. Both were spattered with blood and bore the signs of a hard fight. As if aware of her scrutiny, Asim spun around and strode toward the truck, his eyes meeting hers across the distance.

Cyn steeled herself with a deep breath. Adrenaline had her heart pounding, her blood rushing and every nerve zinging. She fought the urge to touch the weapon hidden at the small of her back and instead clenched her fingers around the gun Asim knew about, the one she'd used to kill Jabril. She held it in plain sight, not even flinching when Asim reached for the truck and pulled the heavy cargo door upward. Faster than she could follow, he leaned over and took the gun from her hand, holding her wrist and squeezing it painfully. "We don't want any accidents now, do we, Cynthia?"

He gave her a quick grin, and then brought her hand to his mouth, licking away the blood still leaking from her torn fingers. "Jabril was right. Your blood is delicious."

Cyn swallowed her revulsion and glared at him instead. "Elizabeth needs medical help, a hospital."

He ignored her, dropping her hand and reaching in to lift Liz in his arms. "Do you know what happens when a vampire lord dies, Cynthia?" he asked. His eyes flicked up at her, then around the body-strewn desert. "I mean apart from this," he dismissed. "Do you know how his replacement is chosen? His assassin inherits everything. His power, his territory." He caressed the unconscious Liz with a dreamy smile. "Everything that was Jabril's is now mine."

"But you didn't kill him. I did."

Asim laughed. "Who would believe *that?* Jabril had Mirabelle, but I shall have Elizabeth." He shifted his gaze to her and it hardened. "And you too, my dear." He licked his lips as if savoring the taste of her blood. "My personal harem."

She wasn't even surprised. "That wasn't our deal," she reminded him gently.

"No, I suppose not," he agreed. "Perhaps I'll trade you back to Raphael eventually. In return for his support." He shifted Elizabeth in his arms and jerked his head toward Cyn. "Come along now. We'll leave these others for the sun." He turned and walked toward the waiting limo.

Cyn took two steps behind him, drew the second gun and fired. Three shots to the back of his head. Bam, bam, bam. She took care to angle the barrel up and away from where he was carrying Liz against his thin chest, but couldn't help the spray of blood and gore as the vampire's head blew apart. "Think again, asshole," she hissed.

The nascent vampire lord crumpled to the ground, dropping Elizabeth and falling on top of her. Cyn stood looking down at him, breathing hard, almost unable to believe it had worked. With a jolt of fear, she remembered the other vampires and spun around, gun raised to shoot. But the shock of losing a second master in one night was too much for the already weakened vampires. Both lay senseless in the dirt.

Cyn drew a tired breath and wondered where she'd find the strength to finish tonight's work. She leaned forward, resting her hands on her knees, knowing if she sat, she'd never get up again. Finally, too weak to carry Elizabeth to the Land Rover, she dragged Asim's body away and over to the others, got a blanket from the back of the SUV and covered the unconscious girl where she lay. And then she forced herself to keep moving, to walk around the clearing and systematically place a bullet through the brain of every vampire there.

Back again to the Land Rover's cargo compartment, she flipped open yet another weapons' case. This one was leather, butter soft and luxurious to the touch, with an elegant tooled design. Inside were four lightweight, machine-sanded wooden stakes, each tipped with a folded steel stabbing edge. They were beautiful and lethal, especially designed for her by a knife maker who'd taken pride in his product and etched intricate designs all around the band of each blade where it gripped the wood. It took strength to stab a wooden stake through a vampire's chest. The steel made it easier.

She stared at the stakes and then grabbed all four and went back to her gruesome task. A vampire wasn't dead if he still had a body. She wanted nothing but piles of dust on the desert floor.

A short time later, Cyn crouched next to what was left of her final victim, gun in one hand, stake in the other. All around her, piles of vampire dust began to shift softly as a cool wind blew in across the desert. As if danger followed the wind, the night turned suddenly darker and full of threat. She spun around. Beyond the narrow circle of light cast by the cars' headlights, the shadows moved, wrapping the night around them and drawing closer. Cyn gripped her weapons tighter, her lip curling in a feral snarl.

The wind blew harder, buffeting the cars with its ferocity. Cyn's hair blew across her face, and she brushed it away with an impatient gesture, staring as a sable whirlwind appeared from the storm, blacker than the night around it, moving faster, sucking up the darkness as it approached. She stood and moved closer to where Liz lay helpless, her heart pounding, her mouth dry with fear.

The midnight wind blew between the cars. Cyn raised her gun. And the shadows fell away.

Juro moved first, placing himself between Raphael and the gun Cyn held in a shaky, one-handed grip. Raphael raised a hand and Juro stood aside.

"*Lubimaya*," Raphael said sadly. "I'm sorry we're late."

Cyn blinked. Her arms fell to her sides, the weapons she'd wielded so effectively suddenly too heavy to hold. Her head drooped and she would have fallen, but Raphael caught her, cradling her in his arms as his vampires stared in disbelief at the damage one human woman had wrought.

Chapter Fifty-seven

CYN HEARD THE helicopter rotors winding down outside, as the doors closed and the elevator began to move. Raphael leaned against the wall, watching her silently. He hadn't said much since he'd found her amidst the piles of vampire dust in the desert. Not that there had been much opportunity. They'd driven back to Tucson, going directly to the airport. Raphael's personal physician was waiting for them there, and while he'd treated Liz, Cyn had time for a quick shower and a change of clothes. The clothes were Winona's and didn't fit her, but they were better than what she'd been wearing.

After a quick flight to Santa Monica and a helicopter ride out to Malibu, they'd arrived at the estate a little before dawn. Duncan and Juro had flown with them in the chopper, along with Dr. Saephan and Liz, but the rest of Raphael's team would be daylighting at the airport today. There wasn't time enough to see them all safely back to the Malibu estate. Some of Raphael's human guards were already on their way to secure the private hangar and watch over the sleeping vampires.

The elevator doors opened on Raphael's inner sanctum, and Cyn hurried out of the small box, shedding her borrowed jacket as she went. Candles scattered throughout the room flared to life as Raphael exerted his will, and she jumped, laughing at her own nervousness.

She couldn't seem to stand still and paced back and forth, her skin feeling too tight, her nerves jangling until she wanted to scream.

"Cyn," Raphael said.

She stopped and stared at him. "He was waiting for us," she said. "At the driving school. He knew we'd be there."

"Yes."

The single word was chock-full of information, but she was too tired to parse it all, and Raphael said nothing more.

She resumed her pacing and Raphael continued to watch silently. "Where's Liz?" she asked distractedly.

"Dr. Saephan is caring for her. His facilities here are quite modern and complete. She will wake and remember nothing."

Cyn paused to give him a hard look. "You'll wipe her memories?"

"Her memories will be wiped. Not by me personally, no. Cyn, it is important, vitally important, that no one know it was you who killed Jabril. The others don't matter, but Jabril . . ."

She crossed to stand in front of him. "Are you going to wipe my memories too?"

"No." He seemed slightly affronted that she would ask.

"What about Lucia? She'll know something happened; she's not stupid."

"I'll leave that to you," he said stiffly. "But Dr. Saephan has an excellent reputation in the local community, and she'll have no reason to doubt whatever he tells her. She's been informed that you and Elizabeth are both well and has been invited to visit later. If you wish, Duncan can . . . speak to her."

"Speak to her," Cyn repeated.

"Cyn." It was a demand for understanding.

"Stop that," she said.

"Stop what?"

"Stop looking at me as if you're waiting for the other shoe to drop."

"*Is* there another shoe?"

"No." She drew a long, tired breath and walked into his arms, finally letting him pull her to rest against his chest, where she listened to the slow beat of his heart. "They tore him apart," she whispered as her eyes filled with tears. "He was nothing but bloody pieces of meat. You couldn't even tell . . ." She swallowed hard. "They would have done the same to me." His arms tightened around her, and she let her arms circle his waist. He was wearing a long, silken robe and nothing else. She didn't remember him changing.

"You're not wearing any clothes."

"It is nearly dawn, *lubimaya*." The words were barely out of his mouth before she heard the solid sound of the vault closing around them. It was oddly comforting.

"I'm so tired," she breathed.

Raphael kissed her forehead and helped her remove the rest of her clothing, all but carrying her to the big bed and tucking her beneath the covers. She turned into him when he slid in next to her. "Hold me."

"Forever, my Cyn."

Chapter Fifty-eight

CYN LEANED AGAINST the window behind Raphael's desk, feeling it vibrate with every wave that rolled in on the beach below. Raphael sat in front of her, watching impassively as Juro escorted Mirabelle into the room. Duncan entered next, one hand on Alexandra's elbow, as if he were escorting her into an elegant salon. Raphael stood, lingering long enough to trail one hand along Cyn's arm before making his way around the desk to face them. He positioned himself slightly to one side so that Cyn could see his face clearly.

Mirabelle didn't wait for the vampire lord to speak to her. She broke away from Juro and threw herself at Raphael's feet, burying her face in her hands, her shoulders shaking with silent tears.

Raphael regarded her prostrate form somberly, before lifting his head to meet Alexandra's cool gaze from across the room. She raised her chin defiantly, black eyes flashing.

"Mirabelle," Raphael said.

"My lord," she cried, weeping so hard she could barely speak. "I would never betray you, Master! Never."

Raphael cocked his head quizzically. "Did I say you had, child?"

Mirabelle didn't look up from her submissive position, addressing her response to the carpet only inches from her face. "I heard the guards talking, my lord. I know someone called Jabril. But it wasn't me. I swear to you, my lord." She did look up then, her blue eyes full of pain. "I did not betray you, Master. I would not!"

Cyn studied Mirabelle's face. She saw despair there, and loss, but no guilt, no fear of discovery. *Mirabelle wasn't the traitor*, she thought, and knew it was true.

Raphael's gaze shifted to Alexandra where she stood proud and haughty, supremely confident.

"Did I not warn you, Alexandra?" he asked. "Did you think I could forgive this?"

"I have no idea—"

"Silence." It was a single word, spoken softly and without emotion.

But Raphael's anger was a physical presence in the room, weighting the air like a storm about to break. "You forget, Alexandra, that I am more than our mother's son. I am your master. You have no secrets from me."

Alexandra's eyes widened in surprise, and for the first time her face reflected an uneasy concern. "You have been bewitched by this human," she snarled. "I tried only to save you. You'll understand one day, and you'll thank me."

Raphael regarded her silently, waiting.

Alexandra jerked her hand in a nervous gesture, as if waving away his anger. "I am your sister, Raphael. Your blood. You cannot choose a human, even this one, over your own blood. You love me."

"Five hundred years ago," Raphael said gently, "I loved a child named Sasha." His voice hardened. "You I don't even know." He gestured and Juro stepped up to Alexandra, his massive paw closing around her arm like a manacle.

Alexandra struggled uselessly, trying to pull away. "Raphael!" she cried. "You can't do this! I'm your—" Raphael simply glanced at her. Her pleas were cut off mid-syllable as she struggled to speak against his compulsion, leaving her with nothing but wordless sobs of disbelief as Juro and his brother carried her away between them.

Mirabelle was still kneeling on the floor, her mouth hanging open in shock, her expression more than slightly touched by relief as Alexandra was *escorted* from the room.

"Mirabelle." Her head swiveled around when Raphael spoke her name and she cringed in fear.

"I would never—" she began again.

"I know that, child. I never suspected you. Go now. Elizabeth has been asking for you."

Mirabelle scrambled to her feet and bowed quickly. "Thank you, my lord," she said fervently. Her gaze skittered quickly over to Cyn and away before she hurried from the room. Duncan followed her, closing the door behind him and leaving them alone.

Cyn circled around the desk to Raphael, and he reached out automatically to pull her close. She burrowed against his broad chest and asked, "What will you do?"

"The Council has called a meeting to deal with Jabril's empty territory," Raphael responded wearily. "Most likely they'll throw it open to anyone who can hold it. None of Jabril's minions are strong enough to challenge for the right—no one who wants it, anyway. And besides, there are many young ones agitating for greater power in the territories.

This will release some of that pressure."

"That's not what I—" she started to say, but the look in his eyes told her he didn't intend to give her any other answer. She stared back at him, uncertain how she felt about that.

"I am Vampire, Cyn," he said, as if that explained everything.

"That's not good enough," she told him. "I won't let you hide behind that inscrutable vampire shit. I want to know what you're going to do with Alexandra."

Raphael regarded her out of flat black eyes. "You nearly died."

"I'm aware of that. And if I *had* died out there in the desert, my ghost would have haunted you mercilessly until you destroyed every one of the motherfuckers who did it." His soft lips crooked up in a slight smile. "But I didn't die, Raphael."

"She intended you to die. Or worse. Far worse."

Cyn frowned up at him. "Is this really about me? Or is it about you? She betrayed you too that night. More than me. Is this just some vampire bullshit?"

He gave an impatient sigh and pulled away. He would have walked away from her, but she put a hand on his arm, holding him in place. "Don't kill her, Raphael. You'll never forgive yourself. You'll never forgive *me*."

His eyes flashed to meet hers.

"This is the woman you moved heaven and earth for, catering to her every whim, for how many centuries, Raphael? You hired *me* to find her when your enemies took her from you, and destroyed every one of them in revenge. Don't tell me you have no love for her, even if it's only love for the child she used to be. Her death will hang over you, over *us*, like a cancer, eating away at everything we are until every time you look at me you'll see nothing but her death." She stepped closer to him, placing her palms flat against his chest. "I can't live that way, Raphael. I won't. I love you too much."

He looked away from her, but before his eyes left her face, she saw a brief flash of relief in their obsidian depths. She felt him sigh, felt his entire body relax beneath her hands.

"Very well, *lubimaya*. I will spare her. But she will know it was you she owes for her life."

Cyn shrugged. "I hope she chokes on it. Believe me, I have no love for Alexandra."

He smiled then, as if she'd once again said something he expected and it pleased him. He pulled her against his body, holding her firmly within the circle of his arms. "I'm thinking of chaining you to my bed from now on," he murmured against her hair. "I'm tired of waking up to find you gone."

She snorted. "You can try."

He swept her up and into his arms. "I can do better than try, *lubimaya*. There are many kinds of chains."

"Kinky," she commented. "Do your best, Lord Raphael."

"With you, my Cyn, always."

Epilogue

"BUFFALO?" CYN repeated in disbelief.

"I know," her friend Sarah agreed ruefully. "But it's a good university, and the job's tenure track. Plus, it's not in California, and you know I want out of here."

"Honey, Buffalo's about as far from California as you can get and still be in the United States. They have real winters there, you know. Watch the weather channel. They're always showing footage of Buffalo with people up to their asses in snow."

Sarah laughed. "You're so crude, Cyn."

"Yeah, well. It comes from being a cop."

"I think you just use that as an excuse."

Cyn smiled. "Busted."

"So," Sarah said, dragging the one syllable out. "You have something you want to share with me?"

Cyn took a sip of her martini, giving Sarah a wide-eyed look over the rim of the glass.

"Oh, come on, Cyn. Let me see the rock."

Cyn laughed. "Oh, you mean this little thing?" She held out her hand and Sarah took in the gorgeous *little thing*. There were at least five carats sitting on that slender finger, and that was only the pillow-cut diamond in the center. She'd bet on another few carats in the channel set band around it.

"It's beautiful, Cyn. But you know that. So, when's the wedding?"

"Wedding?" her friend scoffed. "You know how I feel about marriage. Besides, vampires don't get married, they have this whole mating thing they do."

"Mating? Like gorillas?"

Cyn laughed. "Very similar, yeah."

"So does this mean you're going to become a vampire? Should I start covering my neck when you're around?"

"Hardly. Vampires don't usually marry other vampires. I asked the same question once." She paused to take another sip of her drink. "You know how the sex is rumored to be—"

"Mind blowing," Sarah provided dryly.

"Well, yeah. Anyway, taking blood is linked to sex for them, so if I become a vampire, then Raphael would have to go somewhere else for his blood, and since it's tied in with sex . . ."

"Oh."

"Right. You know me. I don't share well."

Sarah chuckled. In truth Cyn was generous to a fault, but she'd never say that to her friend's face. It might dent that carefully cultivated tough girl image. "What about the age thing, though? I mean, he'll stay young and you'll—"

"That's the beauty of it. He takes my blood and I take his. Not much, but—"

"Gross! You're drinking his blood?" Sarah looked around quickly and lowered her voice. "Yuck, Cyn!"

"It's not that bad," Cyn chided her. "Besides it's just a little bit, and it keeps me young and gorgeous." She grinned and leaned forward conspiratorially. "And it makes the sex even better."

Sarah blew out a breath. "Okay. TMI. Let's change the subject. You still have your agency?"

"No," Cyn said regretfully. "That had to go. It's hard to do undercover work when you've got a bodyguard hanging around all the time."

"You've got a bodyguard?"

"Yeah. It was either that or a tattoo on my forehead. I took the bodyguard. As a matter of fact . . ." She gestured over Sarah's shoulder. "See that guy over there by the bar?"

Sarah twisted to look and found herself staring at a tall, well-muscled black man who seemed to be rather obsessively focused on their little corner of the room. Her eyes widened and she whipped back around to Cyn. "That's a vampire?" she whispered.

"Yeah. Hard to tell, huh? You get used to it. And speaking of vampires . . ."

There was a sudden stir in the crowded bar. Conversations died to whispers and people shuffled aside, clearing a path for someone entering through the street door. There were two men, one blond and one dark, but it was the dark-haired one who drew everyone's attention. Tall and broad-chested, with a face that could only be described as beautiful, he moved with the lethal sort grace she usually associated with something dangerous and wild. Women and men both straightened where they stood or sat, their faces rapt, eyes glassy as they sort of . . . *leaned* in his direction. She heard Cyn laugh gaily and looked over at her friend.

"Tell me that's not him," she said in disbelief.

"That's my honey," Cyn confirmed.

"Oh, man," Sarah said in admiration. "Where can I get me one of those?"

"Probably not in Buffalo," Cyn commented dryly. She took a final sip of her martini and stood. "My ride's here, hon. Good luck with the job. I hope they know how lucky *they* are to have you."

"I'll be sure and tell them," Sarah said. She reached out and they exchanged hugs.

"Send me your new address when you have it."

"I will. And good luck with . . . you know. Everything. I'm really happy for you, Cyn."

"I know." She kissed Sarah's cheek and whispered, "Yours will come too. You just wait."

Sarah watched as Cynthia walked over to meet her vampire lover. His arm went around her waist as soon as she reached him and they exchanged a kiss so tender it brought tears to Sarah's eyes. She shook her head. "Yeah," she muttered to herself. "But will he know he's supposed to look for me in Buffalo?"

To be continued . . .

Acknowledgments

As always, I want to thank Linda Kichline for her unflagging dedication and enthusiasm, and especially for getting this book out on schedule. Thanks and sincere appreciation to Patricia Lazarus for creating my gorgeous covers.

Special thanks go to all the readers who picked up Raphael, and especially to those who took the time to let me know they loved it. It means more to me than you can ever know.

Thanks again to Kelley Armstrong and everyone at the OWG, but especially those members of my own group who read most of this manuscript and gave me unstinting and always excellent advice – John G. (DoH), Lesley W., Michelle M. (Ghostwriter), SteveMc, and Mila (isdsm). To Adrian Phoenix who let me hijack her Yahoo group more than once, to Michael Moore for putting me on Squidoo, and to the many bloggers on both sides of the Atlantic who invited me to guest blog so that people could hear about my vampires.

Thank you to Dr. Heather M. who sat at a bridal shower with me and discussed the nature of human blood and why vampires might find it tasty. To Dr. D. P. Lyle for answering all of my questions about exsanguination without once reporting me to the local authorities. To Jessica B. who couldn't believe my vampires didn't have a Facebook page. They do now, thanks to her. And once again, I'm indebted to John G. for his expertise in guns and weapons of all kinds, and I'm sorry about the Sig, John.

To everyone at Gillette & Associates, especially Terry, Jamie and Josh, who helped me get moving again. Love and thanks to my family and friends who have been so amazingly supportive as I undertake this new journey, and to my wonderful husband who put up with a laptop in our bedroom on far too many late nights! And finally, to my beautiful Zarechka, who was there on the dark days to remind me there's always a tomorrow.